GW01164144

The Bell of the World

Also by Gregory Day

Melaleuca Perfumeries

The Black Tower: Songs from the Poetry of W.B. Yeats

Trace (with photographs by Robert Ashton)

The Patron Saint of Eels

The Flash Road: Scenes from the Building of the Great Ocean Road

Ron McCoy's Sea of Diamonds

The Grand Hotel

Visitors (engravings by Jiri Tibor Novak)

Archipelago of Souls

A Smile at Arm's Length (engravings by Jiri Tibor Novak)

A Sand Archive

Rejectamenta: From Real to Imagined Seaweed (soundtrack)

Words Are Eagles: Selected Writings on the Nature and Language of Place

The Bell of the World

Gregory Day

transit lounge

MELBOURNE, AUSTRALIA
www.transitlounge.com.au

Copyright © 2023 Gregory Day
First published 2023
Transit Lounge Publishing

This book is copyright. Apart from any fair dealing for the purpose of private study, research, criticism or review, as permitted under the Copyright Act, no part may be reproduced by any process without written permission. Inquiries should be made to the publisher.

Every effort has been made to contact all copyright holders. The publishers will be pleased to amend in future editions any omissions brought to their attention.

This is a work of fiction. It should not be read as history. The characters and events in the book are products of the author's imagination and any resemblance to real persons, living or dead, is purely coincidental.

Cover design: Sian Marlow/Peter Lo
Typeset in 12/17pt Adobe Garamond Pro by Cannon Typesetting
Printed in China by Everbest on wood-free paper

The writing of this project has been assisted by the Australian Government through the Australia Council, its arts funding and advisory body.

A cataloguing entry is available from the
National Library of Australia
ISBN: 978-0-6484140-8-7

for Sian Rachel Marlow

'The successor of the sublime is under construction.'

Bruno Latour

Big Cutting Hill

I

SHE RIDES THE train towards the trees, up front with the driver and the coal stoker, the window of the carriage smashed, the air cold as they cross the last paddock and the stringybarks loom towards them. It is daytime but it is somehow dark, and darker still as they enter the forest.

What had begun as a passenger train had become a gravel and firewood service. Hence her rough digs on the single passenger bench in the driver's car. The seat was cold, cold lacquered wood, and the wind was also cold; it seemed to come armed with the spikey shards of glass through which it entered.

Such spikes, such shards, were slowly sharpening themselves in her mind. This was a profuse place, a chaos, a chaos without autumn's falling leaves, and as they left the orderly residues vainly mimicking England – paddocks and open pasture, the chimney smoke scribbling itself onto the sky, the normally organised roads and fences – she felt her vision darkening to a marsupial light. As the train moved into it the bush seemed to be clambering all over the sun.

The driver, Mr Smith, and his coal stoker, whom he simply called, at all times, 'Guard', were both tall but portly men and thus they filled up the car. She narrowed herself on the bench therefore, not by natural disposition (for her spirit was wide) but simply by the command she'd been given 'not to get in the way'. Gravel was the priority passenger of the Saddle Line, Ferny had written to her, so try not to interfere with the workings, or they'll lay you out on the road as well! He liked a laugh, her Uncle Ferny, which had saved her in Rome, and then again when she was contemplating how her mind would possibly survive yet another shock, as she'd readied herself for the expulsion out of Melbourne by reading and re-reading his letter.

Now too, as the possum-dark sky began to whistle past, the branches of the trees slashing at the steady motion of the train at those spots on the line where the branches had not been trimmed, she fingered the stamp of the envelope in the deep pocket of her woollen coat. She felt the teeth of the stamp's edges on her skin, and saw its image in her mind – the Trevi Fountain – as well as the stamped postmark of her young uncle's letter. She carried that envelope with her as an item of faith, its thin blue paper and Ferny's racing lilac ink just enough, she thought, to stop her from combusting like the fire the Guard was stoking in the engine box.

On it ran then, this ochre-painted snake of choofing steel, along the narrow saddle which gave the line its name, on into the dank and sorrowful west and towards the isolated siding amongst the forest at Wensleydale.

How narrow could she make herself, folded small there as she was between Mr Smith and the Guard, who loomed and shovelled about, the buttons of his uniform flashing even as he was smeared in soot and bent by his superior's admonitions to

'Mind Miss Hutchinson there'. It was not as if she were a lovely piece of porcelain ware that needed to be cushioned, rather an unfortunately wedged-in superfluity amongst the essential roughage of the working reality of the train. Gravel weighs and marks, local gravel more so, with its vivid talciness. Firewood too, full of awakened grubs and umbrageous spiders, and bristling with sharp knots and splinters. Yet as a passenger she was a real residue, of the time not so many years before when there'd been great hopes for the line as a scenic route, a journey that might transcend utilities such as gravel and wood, and even the local seams of coal, for the sweet blue vision of the ocean that lay only a few miles (treacherous miles) south of the saddle. As it was, the line had only ever come as far as the misty highness of the bush, before the capital, or the will, ran out. The route south to the coast from Wensleydale had languished as a project of fantasy, unexplored but for some initial surveying. The passenger dreams of an antipodean Great Western Railway of unrivalled scenery were abandoned, but for that one single bench, that lacquered bench with its well-turned blackwood slats upon which she was now crammed into the operation, with her mind feeling every slash and clank and judder, and her soul trying to remain respectful of the men.

The seamy tint of the outside world through the smashed pane of window was beginning to fascinate her. Mr Smith asked over his shoulder if there would be anyone meeting her at Wensleydale. 'I believe so,' she shouted, over the wheels and the roaring fire. 'The woman there, who looks after the cottage. She is meant to greet me.'

'I see', hurled the driver, once again over his black serge shoulder. 'So why then, if you don't mind me asking, would a young lady like you be coming out here to the sticks?'

She smiled, and let the question die out in the continued rhythmic motion of the train. All she could see now through the jagged pane was winter-brown, winter-grey, and branches of leaves, leaves, leaves. It amazed her. She could have sworn it was night, or dusk, or even the onset of a solar eclipse, but in fact it was two in the afternoon of a normal autumn day.

From somewhere among the fragments of her dangerous mind she mustered the unity of humour. Why indeed?

She raised a pale face towards the heavy back of the driver. 'Oh,' she said then, as if blithely, 'it's merely a stopover before I go on to stay with my uncle at his Run.'

'I see, Miss,' he yelled. 'But what Run is that?'

'Ngangahook,' she replied. 'Down below, where all this bush meets the sea.'

'Ngangahook. Of course. By the lighthouse there.' He started nodding slowly, and she watched his flesh as it bunched up against his brisk collar.

Amid all the noise of the engine, the iron tracks, and the fire, Smith didn't manage to say anything else. She was left to observe therefore the intensely peculiar way the clanking of the train and the whipping of the trees punctuated her otherwise emptying mind.

Oblivious to local rhetoric, she could never have understood that Smith's question had already known its answer. It was an unpeopled district, and any passengers there were well known, and well talked about. He knew already, for instance, that she had returned from England, from school in England, followed by a brief sojourn in Italy. Smith knew her Uncle Ferny too, of course he did, insofar as he had met him on the train in his various comings and goings, and often chatted with him right there in the driver's car. Ferny's own volubility had furnished

Smith with details that he now drew upon in his appraisal of the niece. And they were a curious family anyway, the uncle friendly to all-comers, which was itself unconventional, and with scads and scads of money, and always going off on jaunts. Fernshaw Hutchinson would have been barely ten years older than the niece – another fact he could now confirm. Yet Smith wasn't exactly all bad; he did not credit inkling or intuition, nor silence (which gave him the shivers) and had shouted his question to Sarah as any host might, given that indeed he was her host for the gumclad duration of the five-stop Saddle line. Yes, he had made the effort, even above all that noise. And the gravel train rolled on.

❧

It was the woman Maisie at the Wensleydale station, in canvas trousers and a pilling farmer's jumper over her blouse, a rifle coat over that, but Sarah had not expected the way she blended with the masculine activity at the siding. As the train pulled in, Sarah could see a small group of men enthusiastically kicking a football to each other in the clearing between the siding and the trees. Then a woman walked out from amongst the players. 'I'm Maisie, Miss,' she said, in a wet gurgly voice, as Sarah stepped down.

The Guard helped Sarah with the luggage, and Smith stepped down too, to help one of the footballers, a fellow railwayman called Joe Busch, onload a wagon of brilliant red apples before the train was manoeuvred about and onto the turntable. The other footballers began milling about now too, the apple farmer included, also a man who looked, by the hat on his head and the satchel he carried, like a travelling agricultural salesman.

There were also two well-dressed young children and their mother, who were waiting to board the return journey to Geelong, and another local railwayman by the name of Rabbits, who, due to the sport that the arrival of the train had ended, wore no jacket, only a VR cap and braces on his hulking frame, and who seemed now to be governing the incoming goods.

Half a dozen people, she thought, but an ocean of trees. And soon just me and Maisie.

Fact was, the name was a little disconcerting to her. There had been a Maisie at the school in Ilfracombe who wasn't her worst enemy though they'd hardly got on. Maisie Cruik, pronounced *Crew-wick*. Like Sarah she was from 'a long way away', but in Maisie Cruik's case that was only as far as Norfolk, on England's north-east coast. In actual fact, despite it being a boarding school – Miss Hunt's Boarding School for Girls – all the girls, apart from Sarah, Maisie Cruik, and two sisters, Jane and Polly East from London, were Devon locals. This had kept Sarah on the outside from the beginning, and her accent hadn't helped, nor her complete disenchantment with being there. If any of the girls had asked, she could have told them that in fact it was nothing in particular about Miss Hunt's School, or Ilfracombe, or England for that matter, that repulsed her. It was quite simply that it felt to her like precisely nowhere, or at least nowhere that she wanted to be. Not there, not home with her mother in East Melbourne (if you could call that *home*), not on the farm with her father in New Zealand. No, *nowhere*.

The problem was that this idea of dislocation had gradually taken up residence in her mind. At the slightest trigger it would reinvade; now, for instance, at the mention of the name *Maisie*. As Maisie of the trousers and rifle coat showed her to the small spring cart, she could not even manage to be polite. She said little, but for a barely audible 'Thank you' when the woman cleared a space for her to sit beside her in the gig. They set off from the little hive of industry around the bush station.

II

It was a small weatherboard house which had been moved to the site by a bullock team from a farm near Birregurra. As such it had become something of an outpost in the forest, a watering point occasionally used by men travelling to the logging coupe, or even by swagmen, who all seemed to honour the comfort they were afforded by leaving something useful with the old brass key under the seastone by the back porch door. Sometimes it was a page torn out of a book, heavily underlined, other times a quail, or even a bundled-up quail snare.

The cottage was surrounded by bush that Maisie obviously knew well. In another driver's hand, the winding route down off the Wensleydale saddle may well have seemed treacherous, but Maisie's negotiation of the steep descents, the blind switchbacks and gluey culverts, was faultless. And all without uttering a single curse to her horse. Instead she spoke constantly to the twitch of his chestnut ears, chatting of the things she'd done and hadn't done around the cottage, and also giving her appraisal of the scene back at the station. This chatter may have all been for the benefit of Sarah, but you wouldn't have thought so.

As if lubricated by this gurgling monologue, the cart came down easily through the bush, across the brief plateaux and the tweedy thickets of heath, and along the wattle-lined rises. Yes, Maisie's talk was comfort to the horse, whose name was either Thataboy or Sugar and who seemed to live on stories.

Suffice to say that when they finally did arrive at the cottage, Sarah had been furnished already with a new set of ears. Cold ears full of new sounds, unlikely joins, of sense that jumped back and forth between known and unknown slang, while all the while, among those vertiginous hills, the cart stayed smooth.

'I been talkin like a crabby duck floating down the track but my paddles workin' the water under there, just to keep you aloft, Miss. You gotta paddle, chew the horse's ears orf well 'ave a look he's got enough of 'em pointing up at the sun like that, can listen like a wimba this horse, just got to keep him goin' so his eyes won't wander won't even see if he's entertained can't hear the parrots, the cockies, if I only keep talkin'. Some might think I lost the thread, but I been holding it by the tail all along. There's no spellin' out when you're too busy puttin' one word after the next hoof too. Just to keep ol' Sugar rollin'. That's right eh, Sugar, but didya know how wide the world is, she's come – hasn't ya, Miss – on the big ocean-horse, Sugar, all that way from the land of the King, her sky could keep you interested I'm sure, with the stories it must know and could tell, once she's settlin' in. Yair but for now her tongue's like a lake and no breeze to ruffle it, like old Modewarre in autumn sun, that old duck of a lake when the world goes still, that's her brain and no need for it to be otherwise, not out here for the first time, like somethin' gettin' ready – no, Thataboy, never is always unlike before, and that's where we're headin', yes, Sugar, to the garden, Thataboy… don't get twitchy… *Thataboy!*'

It was indeed the garden around the cottage that first filled up Sarah's vacant mind. She had always had something to war against, in Melbourne when her parents were on their round of social engagements and then conducting their own war as their lives fell apart; and then again at school in England, where every wet detail seemed overwhelming, sickly pale, except the sea. Even when she finally made it to Ferny's lodgings in Rome there was the looming prospect of being forced to leave for her to grind against. Such things kept her spirits awake, kept her electric, even if she felt so *left*, and the world so cruel and mad. And then, when she did get home to her mother in the new Melbourne house, she had precisely her – her own mother – to inflame things. But once she had been packed off again, put on the train and sent off to Uncle Ferny's in the hope that he might better understand her 'impossible nature', all that grinding, that warring and fighting and flaring-up had been doused. She was an empty glass vial through which Mr Smith, Maisie, and even the Saddle Line coal stoker, could peer in and see the low level of her fire. There was hardly a flame anymore, and, without so much as a course of laudanum, she had been neutralised. Having nothing particularly to like and nothing to hate, there was finally, after Miss Hunt's school, after her joy in Rome and her mother's traumatic drinking, just this. The winding downward track. Then the cottage. And Maisie. Her gurgling and gabbling on like a tea-creek. Just this. And that. And the horse. A transplanted cottage with its garden. The world. Or the end of it.

The rooms were dark, with figs leaning over all the eaves so that what dim light there was became solemn brocade. This was the case except for the kitchen at the back of the house, where northern light strode in brash like it owned the sink and benches, the dinner table, and the cooking stove. Maisie's little tour was cursory at best, but even so the sun on the kitchen boards hurt Sarah's eyes after the other rooms and the hallway. They would share this house, its darkness and light, but only Maisie would pick the herbs, the currants, and do the cooking and cleaning. 'Best you understand that first-up,' she told her. 'As that's the proviso of me being here and not shivering alone under the willows by the church on the Barwon. Until your young uncle shows up to take you down off the ridge to his Run, it's me that's the cook and you the little lady.'

Sarah managed to frown at this, a glimmer of old spirit returning. Always, always some implication of her not being fit or capable. Now this Maisie, then that Maisie, now one mother, then this mother, making no sense of her own predicament, only concerned with ameliorating their own. Briefly her spirit flared at the very thought of those Barwon church willows Maisie was trying to avoid, until, as they moved through to the bathroom, the back porch, and the toilet in the garden, she sputtered again, the flame in the grate of her tired young body. She endured the rest of the gurgling tour, then retired to lie on a shadowy bed as if her whole body was most narrowly embalmed in those self-same willow leaves.

A compress, the world was a compress. Clasping her, clamping her, in the cottage above the Big Cutting Hill.

III

ONE DAY WHEN she had only been at Miss Hunt's for a matter of weeks, the girls, all sixteen of them, were made to fit themselves out and taken to the Torrs Park sea cliffs in the middle of winter. It was to see a storm, Miss Hunt had told them, not from the comfort of the warm classroom or from beneath the blankets of their beds, not to observe it as a display of divine power such as was so often glossed in the Vicar's sermons, but as a meteorological phenomenon. They were to concentrate, even in the midst of discomfort, and to submit their written accounts, complete with the appropriate scientific terminology, by lunch on Saturday.

Sarah had walked beside Maisie Cruik and Emily Sash in the middle of the group, Maisie and Emily sharing an umbrella for the steady rain and sniggering at Sarah all exposed but for her Australian oilskin raincoat. She didn't mind, and she watched as Miss Hunt's terrier went ahead in reconnaissance every few minutes, returning with informative smiles, and not seeming to be smelling the sulphur of the coming specimen-storm at all. The rain was merely steady at this stage, and there was little wind, even as they left the roadside path and moved out into the heather proper.

They waited, becoming undramatically sodden, for over an hour. Miss Hunt talked of Nelson, of the vectoring of air currents where the sea met the land, and of something she called the 'elemental corpus'. The girls stood crouching in a huddle, not allowed now to stride out and keep warm but forced to watch these grand washes of scientific rain over the aesthetic sea surface. At the horizon Sarah spied contusions of dark cloud but knew it would never reach them. Such metaphors were passing them by, at a distance. Everything, everything that mattered, everything of interest, was at a vast distance, she thought. Everything was passing them by.

Three of the girls caught cold and Maisie Cruik got pneumonia. And because Maisie was in the next bed to Sarah, she caught it too. For days they lay there alone as Maisie moaned and abused her for being Australian. You bring the school down, Maisie told her, when actually she was elevating Miss Hunt's enterprise by dint of her far-off provenance. Everyone in the village, for instance, knew there was an 'Australian girl' at Miss Hunt's. It was the case, as Sarah learnt later on in Rome from Uncle Ferny's friend Martin of Mendips, that the Cruiks themselves had had the bottom fall out after a distastefully public scandal over embezzlements in their trade through the Levant. In such circumstances they would have been grateful for their daughter's admission to the respectable yet progressive school in Devon. But still Maisie Cruik had ranted and wheezed and harped on, even as she sensed all the while how oblivious Sarah was to the pecking order through which the Cruiks themselves were being so pecked.

Well, at the very least there seemed to be no such order to be oblivious of in the cottage above the Big Cutting Hill. She fell asleep there on the bed in the fig-bruised room, her body clad in its imaginary blanket-leaves, and was cooled thus, as a wound is by such compress. She did not know it yet, though it was as if something deeper inside her certainly did. She had come to the place of the drama of her healing.

When Maisie looked in on her with a tray of nettle soup at darkfall, she was as still as the sea had been that day in Devon. Even stiller, in fact, without the downward pressure of steady English rain.

IV

The next day she woke with a headache seemingly splintered by disorientation, and also to the news from Maisie, who had been out early riding along the telegraph route, that Uncle Ferny was still a long way off. Perhaps even a few weeks. Maisie had ridden out past dawn on Thataboy, heading up to the telegraph station at Wensleydale to receive the wire. He was on the ship, HMS *Paterson*, but exactly how far the journey had progressed it was difficult to say. The telegraph had been sent from Fiesole, on the hill above Florence in Italy, nowhere near the sea. Sarah knew then that Ferny would have been having a wonderful time with Martin of Mendips, who owned a villa there. The villa had a swimming pool, and an Alsatian that was looked after by the neighbour, who was also the housekeeper and cook. But it was hard to say how many stopovers and ports of call her uncle would avail himself of as he travelled south. Together Sarah and Maisie managed to compose a relatively direct reply, which Maisie rode back up to Wensleydale to deliver later in the day.

Miss Hutchinson has arrived. STOP. *Awaits your return to Ngangahook.* STOP. *She is already bored.* STOP

Though she had said it herself – something to put a fire under him, Maisie had suggested – strictly speaking Sarah was not 'bored'. Her condition was far more integral than that. The cottage was very still, as if somehow paused between heathered slopes of time, and in her mind she kept quarrying down through new layers of vacancy. So this was not boredom, rather it was a bright rainbow plunged into a dark and voiding sea. She was, in fact, not inert but in action, sundering down through the hidden vacancies, finding new, almost astonishing levels of emptiness under the desolate appearance of things.

Beside the nettle soup, Maisie cooked workaday stews with meat and potatoes as if she was cooking for timbermen. Every lunch and tea they would eat together at the kitchen table, but Maisie did not appear that interested in her. She did not pry or ask many questions, and so they sat and chewed for the most part in silence, feeling neither comfortable nor entirely uncomfortable, though from time to time Maisie would laugh to herself, as something in her thoughts became too amusing to withhold.

Once when she did this Sarah asked the question. 'What is it? What's funny?'

She genuinely wanted to know what it was that Maisie was enjoying so much, sucking her teeth as she did and letting her eyes close in delight like that.

Maisie seemed surprised by the question, but looked at Sarah kindly. 'Ah. You wouldn't know 'em and you'd have to know 'em to laugh,' she said. 'My old lot. I like to think of the good things from time to time. There's a whole lotta tears.'

'Why,' Sarah asked. 'Why do you bother taking orders from Uncle Ferny? Or from my father, when he called to ask you to look after me.'

Maisie seemed surprised by this question also, surprised by how suddenly all the entanglements of inheritance had been short-circuited, all the inferences immediately understood. There was a snake in the garden and Sarah knew it.

Maisie sniggered, lowering her brow, once she'd finished widening her eyes. 'I don't take orders from no one,' she said. 'Apart from those I respect and respect me.'

They sat in silence, as Sarah thought through the implications. Either Maisie didn't take orders from the Hutchinsons, or she respected her father and uncle sufficiently to do so. Or both.

Eventually Maisie said, 'Your men don't order me around anyway. I cook what I want and don't pay them no rent. It's our cookin' fire here, my love. They let me be and I tell them what I can do for 'em. Lookin out for you's no trouble. I knew it wouldn't be – and so did your dad.'

'What did he say about me?'

Maisie sighed wearily now, at how a poor young woman could be left wondering if she was loved, or even liked, by her own people. 'Nothin' much,' she told Sarah. 'Other than that you would be no trouble once you were free. So let her be free, he said to me.'

Sarah nodded, and they continued to eat, each of them alone with her thoughts.

Later that night, as she sat at the chair by the window in her room, Sarah felt a sudden sense of vertigo at the freedom of which her father had spoken. It opened out like a rocky gorge beneath her, a more vast implication, a too enormous expectation for her to bear. What if she would fall, fall, and fall right through that freedom, to the hard bottom. Unable to find her wings in all that contourless space, unable to feel the uplift. It was terrifying! It must also have been that way, she realised, for her mother. Her father and his bloody freedom. The structurelessness that came with the excess of money. The ability to change, to spontaneously change, to become who you are.

At the centre of dark vacancy, at the precise middle point of the volume of space she inhabited, she knew there was a footing, a place for her, a nub. But to think of it, and how impossible it might be to locate, like a grain in the universe, made her tremble and shiver. Right there on the chair.

How could the possibility of her own liberation be such a burdensome gift? And yet it was. It came with her father's characteristically insouciant insight, but without his love.

V

The vastness inside of her found a reflection in the bush beyond the garden. Up high there, on the southern slope of the Saddle, looking out on gully after ridge after gully full of wattle and prickly moses, of dusty miller, clad in moss and lichen, seamed with ochre dirt, quartz sand, cold-tinted stone, and towered over by gum trees that stretched in dark green and pale grey and milk-white profusion for as far as her eye could see.

Ridge after gully after gully after ridge. And her on top of the range. What went on out there, down there in the south, at Ngangahook? What could go on in all that silence, all that stillness, and with the ocean, at the bottom of it all, like a threat of violence? Power and violence. And her. Her and Maisie, and the cottage. The figs. The dreary hydrangea beds. The calendulas and cabbages. The wicker set under the verandah awning. The tank on its damp stand of bricks. The single tap. The garden path. So little. So awfully little amongst so awfully much.

You would never ever know of it in Melbourne, and in England there was never such a sense. What you were surrounded by.

You could put your fingers out and touch the sides. Always some gentleman out walking his dog, some boat rowing by, some not so distant industry, or the sense of the island. She would lie in her iron bed at Miss Hunt's and listen to the owls. Compose pictures in her mind of them. Their brindled coats, their tabby brows. The nightingales too. Could they be notated on a stave? And what about their shadows? She would hear their tunes and in her self's encasement she'd augment them with her own notes. That self-case was always there, a vast space installed by where she'd come from. It was the space where it all could go and be dissolved, the English owls, the Devonian piano melodies diminished, the sense of strict definition and confining contour within the school and around it. All the loveless structure, the haunted calendar, the tedium of hours and classes, the mindlessly repeating octaves, the dog-walking gentlemen, the grim soot and chimney smoke going into battle up on the salted slates and gables. It could all fit so easily inside her, and with vast amounts to spare.

But here now, as if inside-out, she was being asked to actually exist in the immense sense of space she'd drawn on: all that sky, gully after ridge and all the dusty grey trees between. Here she was. How would she ever make her way out again to the surface of the world?

*

She began to think, as she walked beyond the garden up onto the ridge and down into the sedgy gully, that Maisie might know. She of the rifle coat. She did not feel, after all, like a shut door, or a prim street. She didn't even wear an apron! There was something ajar; it could be kindness there or violence, Sarah was not sure. Honesty at least. There is nothing so rockily true, so factually vast and scientifically so close as honesty. It could open up the world.

VI

THAT MR RABBITS from the Railways came one day with a box of food: cauliflower, parsnips, oranges, a jar of chutney. It seemed that Maisie knew him as a friend, and they talked about the Saddle Line. They talked also about secret apple trees that, apparently, were somewhere out there in the bush. Maisie knew where they were. Delicious fruit planted near logging coupes long gone. She talked too – and Rabbits was very interested – about the taste of possum meat, the taste of plover, and the days when the pressures on the Saddle Line could not even be imagined. Two equidistant iron rails running on a piled-up earth embankment through the old bush? You must be kidding! There had never been a noise like a train, and if the line was to potentially close, as Rabbits came to tell her, then there would not be again. Just the *tick-tick* of living timber in dialogue with the sun. The embankment slowly sinking. That's what Sarah overheard.

She was sitting in shadow, behind shadow-glass, on the armchair in her room, as Maisie and Mr Rabbits spoke over a cup of Tuckfield's tea out on the verandah. Sarah was sure by now that Maisie was 360 degrees aware – she didn't miss a thing – so when she pulled her rifle coat tight around her and talked to Rabbits she was talking to Sarah too. Maisie knew she was listening. Rabbits, on the other hand, would have had no idea.

'There is a little patch of daffodils too,' she was telling Rabbits, 'that some homesick timber cutters planted to pretty up the spot. Like a living broidery they are, on a level place beside a creek. A peach tree too. But you gotta know your way in. Can't get there on your fucken iron train.'

Rabbits laughed, and then asked more questions, trying to construct a map to such treasure in his mind. But Sarah knew instinctively that Maisie was being confusing. Substituting one ridge for another as she detailed the way in, one gully for the next, so that Rabbits would never know.

'Well anyway,' he said at last, partially exhausted from trying to assemble such impossible routes in his mind, 'pretty soon I'll be lost to these parts anyhow. When they close the line. I'll be clipping tickets all day at South Geelong. I'll miss the gums arching over the track. Always a warm greeting we got at Wensleydale when we reached the end of the line.'

'Well,' Maisie said, 'you can always ride out here to have a talk. When you're missin' the place. Just ride the ol' embankment all the way. You won't get lost.'

'You're stayin' on then?' Rabbits asked. 'After Miss Hutchinson's gone down to Ngangahook?'

Maisie laughed. 'Aw you know me, Cedric, I come and go.'

There was a silence before the man from the Railways said, 'I might, you know. Bring you the odd comfort from town.'

'And I'll give you some secret apples to take back to your sister and old mother in Geelong,' Maisie said. 'Mushrooms too, if you're very good.'

They ate well from the box that Rabbits had brought, and when two days later a vase of daffodils appeared on the kitchen table Sarah had the quick sense that Maisie's conversation with the railwayman was completed. Was he married, she wondered? Perhaps not, given the talk of his mother and sister in Geelong. Was he free then to visit Maisie in the way he did, even despite his lumbering shape and conservative air?

Sarah was slowly learning to be in awe of her protector and host, and would not put anything past her. The way she found all she needed in her lonely thereabouts. Mr Rabbits would bring a box of food and would be paid in kind there with the secret tenderness of the cottage. Like apples deep in the bush and the hidden glade of daffodils, the whole arrangement was a marvel.

Somehow then, perhaps because of that atmosphere of secrecy and trust, Sarah began to loosen and to storm. The years as she'd known them began to intensify like clouds over the cottage garden, clouds charged with both mass and electricity, the electricity of the earth that could be seen gathering out over the ridgelines and gullies, coming closer to a bursting-out.

Her fear began to rise as the loosening frayed further and the unstudied storm that was her sky-case of self loomed in.

This was how Maisie would approach her, speaking from the doorway of Sarah's room: 'Sarah, girl, are you getting up? There's grub; porridge, and toast, with blewits. It's April, Sarah, the light's soft, the air's clear. Not quite chilly yet. Come on, girl, put your gown on and come into the kitchen.'

Just the two of them out there, Mr Rabbits having gone for the time being, and Uncle Ferny not yet anywhere close.

'C'mon, girl,' she would say, 'the day's begun.'

But then, despite the brief cajoling, Maisie would leave her lying there, a mass, a storm somehow bundled among the pale musty cotton of the bedclothes. Sarah was no sooner a girl who could rise for breakfast as she was some golden pastorale. The whole world, her body, made not of grassy clearings or uncluttered sightlines. Made instead of flammable horizons. And so she lay, increasingly, burning, her mind poised right at the edge of something. Her body was taut and sweating with anticipation of she knew not what.

It was an illness that was simultaneously a recovery, a fallen rotting limb becoming a fertile habitat. A new creature was remembering itself, for there had been an almighty forgetting, first in Melbourne then in England, an epic forgetting of everything that had held her in thrall, everything that held the sky up off the land. Where the paths were all clipped, and even as strong as she was, she had become absorbed in the forgetting in Ilfracombe, the whole sea-village a corset of gilded temperaments. And with this forgetting came an attendant lack of trust. No one could be sure of anyone, or at least that's how it seemed to Sarah. So this was a civilised climate, and it had worn her back. When finally school had ended and the telegram came from her father telling her to take the boat to Calais and then the train to her Uncle Ferny in Rome, there was but a wafer left of her. It was a wan wave she left as her final image at the school, before sleeping on the boat and then again on the train. As they pulled in to the Central Stazione she immediately saw-felt-heard-smelt the force of an unfettered energy. A relief. The activity around the station felt familiar, and when the carriage took her by the Vatican and over the river to Ferny's *appartamento* in the pink villa he shared with Martin of Mendips and the others, her uncle's ebullient embrace was like a shot of breath to her lungs. She cried a little right there and then on his bright blue velvet lapels and then she cried even more because she felt he knew why. Now it was pure relief. Ferny loved London but he well understood what Martin of Mendips said as they discussed things the next morning over French bowls of coffee and tough bread. 'Those schools can be beastly. All that floor polish! All that amateur *enthusiasm*. I've hardly got over it – even now!'

And still it was bearing down on Sarah in the cottage above the Big Cutting Hill. She would get up out of the sheets and sit on the verandah as Maisie went about the house chores, always keeping a oblique eye on the girl in the wicker chair. Sarah, wrapped in a blanket, as the weakening autumn sun eked her out, beginning to wring the change in her. And just as winter's prelude could be found in the lowering afternoons, she would heave herself up after lunch and stagger back in to bed. She would half-dream towards a dusk of delirium and preternatural phobias and fears, until Maisie's voice cut through true darkfall, calling her up for tea. She would emerge in a blur but offer no argument against tea, and so a bright kitchen, with its lemon table and a deck of cards alongside the bread and cutlery, would be waiting for her. A glary anchor of domesticity in a viscous open sea.

And there they would sit, both mumbling through their meal, Sarah from the inarticulacy of metamorphosis, Maisie often lost in her own gurgling recollections. Chops, bacon, cabbage and rabbit, sausages and potatoes, stewed pears and baked apples sprinkled with bush pepper would be their touchstones. And tea. Maisie's Tuckfield's tea from the dented old cottage pot. Sarah could drink that easily, and Maisie encouraged her to pile in more sugar. Something for energy. She'd seen enough now to know that the girl would need all she could find.

But the sugar — two, three, even four teaspoons in every cup — would just as often upset Sarah's stomach, and she would be up at night then, belching, swearing at herself, sweating, and vomiting into a wooden apple box on the floor beside the high bed of she-oak. Almost everything was heaving, and the forgetting was duly turning inside out, turning Sarah deciduously, mulching her into the bespattered carpet. She would swear and once or twice she would whisper confessional things, and occasionally cry out, and once even she got up and went into Maisie's room, only to find she wasn't there, in the middle of the night.

This terrified Sarah, and soon her vision was leering with owls, the local counterparts to those English owls she had been abandoned to. By the time she went back to her room the owls had been pushed aside by the sudden spectre of Roiseaux the old painter from Rome, forcing himself onto her. She cried out for all she did not comprehend in his sagging old body, but the cry only seemed to provoke the memory of English owls, their hooded eyes glowering into her, the tops of their skulls lifting off and going up and down as if on tiny malevolent hinges showing a hundred more tiny owls inside. Up and down they went, tormenting her in concert with the voices building from the various spotless rooms of Miss Hunt's. The other Maisie was suddenly there too, leaning back on Sarah's own boarding-school bed, her legs apart, touching herself, and with a pained diagonal expression on her face. She was groaning, and then Roiseaux was moving onto her too, and Maisie was panting like a train, brazen in the face of the 'Australian' who screamed as if to tear all meteorology out of the sky.

Then Sarah was in kind Maisie's possumy arms, in her own room in the cottage, and sobbing just as any metamorphic creature might when it dawns on them that they have to leave themselves behind. A husk, beer-coloured and ribbed, but empty and flung into a corner of the earth.

She cried a winter's worth, and hoarsely, as Maisie of the rifle coat gurgled and cursed the ghosts that were tormenting her. Maisie was warm, Sarah remembered later, warm and angry. But she smelt like the loose ground under the she-oaks on the shoulder above the garden. Solace and song came to Sarah's ear, in some language other than English, firm, plaintive, and gurgling all at the same time.

The next day was pouring with rain, and so she felt part of the weather – the following day too, as she cried and cried. In late April, Maisie wrote a letter from the cottage and sent it via the Saddle Line, through Moriac and Geelong. She was expressing her concern.

The girl is neither hear nor there, and she needs to setel. My world is lonely hear. She wood benefit from being near to others down in Nangahook. And from the oshun air.

VII

Sarah was seven years old when her father first left home. They'd been on the farm at Yea, north-east of Melbourne, but the rows just got worse and worse and then he left and Sarah was alone with her mother. One day not long after, and before they'd moved into the flat in East Melbourne, the little girl had been out wandering happily in the paddocks with her father's dog Richard, and then lying in the hayloft in the barn, while Richard stayed patiently below, and then finally she'd gone down to the river where she dared herself to cross the water on the slippery wide gumspar that had fallen over it at its broadest point. Eventually, she drifted back to the homestead to find all the curtains drawn. Below the bay windows the nasturtiums and calendulas hung as if in suspense, and but for the manager hoi-ing the plough horses in the front paddock up near the road to Murrindindi, a hush had settled over everything.

The collie Richard's tail dropped and the dog went quickly to the door of the kitchen entrance and sat down on the coil mat to wait. Sarah thought he looked worried. She stood herself for a time by the tankstand, with an uneasy feeling in her little guts.

All around the ground was drying fast, the hay nearly all cut and baled, the black cockatoos loping across the sky. She entered the house through the kitchen, to find the cooking stove roaring, its iron door wide open. The air was stifling. It was the middle of the day, in early December. Horse tails were whisking away the early summer flies, and on her wanderings she'd noticed a blue-tongue on the gravel near the stable, as well as skinks on the granite boulders in the upper paddocks bordering the bush.

Breakfast had been eaten a while ago, and lunch was still a way off. Her mother hated baking, so it wasn't that. All these things ran through her intelligent seven-year-old mind.

'Mother!' she called out, through the weirdness. *'Mother!'*

When she got no reply she lingered by the sink, looking out the window over to the milking sheds and the manager's house in the distance. There were white cockatoos now, filling the ground in between. The sky was blue. But she was scared.

After lingering at the window she made her way tentatively along the open glass-ceilinged hallway towards the main rooms of the house. Stepping back onto carpet she stopped at her mother's bedroom, where the door was shut. She thought of knocking but decided against it. Instead, she walked through to the sitting room, where she found the normally sunny bay windows all wrapped in gloom. Peering through, she made out their prized Howard & Sons sofas. The two Howard armchairs too, where her father used to sit and read, with whiskey, or tea, or lemonade sometimes with Sarah on his lap. The cushions, the lovely white cushions of the sofa and the floral cushions of the chairs had all been slashed open with Xs, their stuffing spilling out and down onto the floor.

Sarah immediately started to cry. She rushed out of the sitting room and, without hesitating this time, burst into her mother's bedroom.

Nancy Hutchinson was bundled up in bed in the darkened room. Sarah launched herself up off the floor and onto the bed crying, 'Mother, Mother, I'm scared. Mother!'

The drunken woman stirred. Groaning, she threw out her arm in confusion and annoyance, and the little girl fell to the floor. She groaned again and fell straight back to sleep. Her daughter sat on the floor, shivering despite the heat, not knowing what to do. Until she heard Richard's bark. She went back out through the kitchen then to be with him, pausing on her way to close the oven door.

※

On the Via di Panico in Rome she didn't say much, preferring to sit quietly and observe. Ferny's apartment was of bright terracotta brick, and his friends were colourful too, loud, flamboyant, and interesting, so there was a lot to take in. There were parties most nights, and outings most days, to museums, people's villas, artist's studios, to this or that trattoria, or to walk along the Tiber or on the slopes of the Vatican gardens. Once she'd arrived it was clear that Sarah would always be included in these forays, and despite her relative silence she was always treated as an equal. Both her uncle and his friend Martin of Mendips – as all the people of their coterie were want to call him – would make sure of the introductions, without placing any undue pressure on her by talk of her talents or the fact that she was more or less at a loose end. And Sarah's own beauty, the frank openness of her face combined with her sensuous lips and high cheekbones, not to mention the easy grace with which she carried herself, did her no harm. Amongst the kind of avant-garde aesthetes that Uncle Ferny had fallen in with – Russolo the noise artist, Saltarno the futurist – the girl was an earthy but pleasing addition, if not something of an ornament. She fitted in and was accepted, without having to do very much at all except smile intelligently and not be obvious.

Well there was no chance of that. She listened like a hawk, laughed at the best jokes on offer, and formed her own opinions. When Roiseaux, the older painter from Toulouse, spoke she found herself particularly engaged. On the face of it he was a moody old chap, and to Sarah at least he seemed nervous and shy about everything except his art. The rest of the coterie however, Ferny included, hung on his every word. As she herself listened to Roiseaux's comments and pronouncements, the idea began to form in her head that this was indeed the reality of what Miss Hunt might imperiously call an 'old master'. And yet Roiseaux did not have a sagacious or even a learned air. He was quite obviously vulnerable, excitable too, and dismissive, particularly it seemed of what the general population in Rome had come to understand as being 'fine art'. The problem, as Roiseaux saw it, was that words did not properly describe art, which was, as far as he was concerned, a language of its own. He was known as a radical painter, an identity no doubt confirmed by his very personal views on painting, which, when he did attempt to utter them in public, seemed almost uncomfortably raw. Often too he was downright confusing. He would say, for instance, that he preferred unfinished to finished paintings, declaring that most painters knew only how to ruin and strip the life out of their own creations. Roiseaux's paintings, which were typically very small canvases not all of which were entirely painted in, often included words as well as imagery. He once said that a painting of his was left in what one critic had called a 'naked state' because it could only ever be finished with a flourish not of colour but of music. He talked of 'le mélange des sens' in French, 'un impasto di sensi' in Italian. And he was always very respectful towards Sarah, often choosing to sit quietly with her amidst the festivities. 'Improving my English' was how he explained this preference when a sculptor from Cologne accused him of having an impossible penchant for the young girl. To Sarah however, Roiseaux seemed not in the least bit lecherous and in fact it was she, after having been in Rome for a number of weeks and having enjoyed Roiseaux's company whenever she saw him, who suggested, rather unconventionally, that they might go for a walk on their own by the Tiber.

Together then the old painter, who must have been over sixty years old, and the young girl, straight from school in England, took to walking and laughing, and touching, by the river in Rome. They would admire the reflections of the Castel Sant'Angelo in the water, also the ducks, cormorants and kingfishers as they intervened in these reflections, and, increasingly, they admired each other. Their conversation was seldom of art or any iconoclastic ideas but of what they saw before them. Thus they talked of rivers, food, and also the other people walking by. Countless times, during these *passeggiate di fiume* along the Lungotevere, they were mistaken for father and daughter by passers-by with whom they were obliged to stop and converse. More than once they were even mistaken for grandfather and granddaughter.

After a number of these strolls they began returning together to Roiseaux's studio, where they would lie side by side on his wide divan for hours. Roiseaux seemed proud of the way their affection had transcended the gulf of the decades that lay between them. They were, indeed, like father and daughter, grandfather and granddaughter, and they were also and equally too like mother and son, brother and sister, even like two teenagers, for their friendship was predicated on feelings a universe away from such categorisations. If, in Roiseaux's case, a painting could be finished not by another daub of paint, not by a final and deliberately oblique visual intimation, but by a flourish of music, then Sarah was exactly that, the flourish of music from the air outside the frame. And, as far as Sarah was concerned, Roiseaux exhibited the *life* of someone quite outside the printed templates of age and convention. At times, yes, *he* could make *her* feel old and jaded, rather than the other way around. He could be silly and naïve in the very breath after seeming so deliberate and wise. It was as she said to him one afternoon when they had dined with Ferny and Martin of Mendips near the Ponte Cavour. They were watching from the bridge as the river flowed under them and Sarah had said, in French: 'The river is like us, Paul. Old and young. It is everything at the same time, now and then and tomorrow, always the one river.'

Roiseaux had detected in Sarah an instinctive flair for freedom, and the bold logic that came with it. She perceived in the old painter a stubbornness she related to, and she drank in the spontaneity and the benefits of insight this quality bred in him. For both of them it was an unexpected relief just to be with each other, whether out by the river, up in Roiseaux's studio on Via Giovanni Vitelleschi, or in company with Ferny, Martin of Mendips, and the rest.

As far as the family was concerned Sarah was in the care of her Uncle Ferny whilst in Rome, and he had quickly made it clear that such care as he would give her would not be typical. She wouldn't have expected otherwise. Right back from the days when she was a small child and would visit the Hutchinson farm by the ocean at Ngangahook, this is how she'd found Ferny to be. Like her he was an only child and was therefore, at least when they were together, something of a proxy-sibling to her. As wild as Sarah's own parents could seem they were also in part made that way by always straining against convention's bit, tossing their heads about and making loud shrieks and dynamic outbursts and protestations. At Ngangahook however, where Ferny was already a teenager quite capable of running the farm, a balance of physicality and gentility existed which allowed for the youthful, the hardworking, the wild and the blithe. So that Sarah always felt welcome within earshot of the ocean roar, and entertained in the green glen of the Run by Ferny's various surprising jokes and alternative games. For Sarah, Rome had therefore a natural continuity with Ngangahook, and the double relief of being in Ferny's style of care and in Roiseaux's old but playful and passionate company was exactly what the girl needed.

The problem now though, as she lay in the gloom of her bedroom in the cottage above the Big Cutting Hill, was that everything seemed in jeopardy, even the benefits of influences such as Roiseaux and Uncle Ferny, who had only ever been kind and productive. Even Ferny's homosexuality, which she had discovered and accepted quite easily in Rome, caused yet another question mark in her mind now as she tossed about and sweated amongst the bedclothes. Indeed, it was as if life was a series of shocks she had undergone, shunted off as she was on HMS *Carisbrook* to Plymouth and school amongst the macabre sociality of Miss Hunt's at Ilfracombe, then pushed out across the channel to the relative moral anarchy of Ferny and his milieu in Rome. It was there that she had offered up her virginity to a man old enough to be her grandfather, a man with a purple rinse through his white hair, who attended to her body's satisfactions with all the attentiveness of a prisoner released from jail.

Briefly now this is how she saw it, felt it, was haunted by it, as doubts fuelled an instability which, in turn, fed her doubts, questioning everything and everyone, but most of all herself.

Nevertheless she dreamed of Roiseaux repeatedly, and in many different guises: as a personification of creative kindness but with a lolling tongue as long as a dog's; as a human bridge, his old grey body stretched across the Tiber's expanse so that she could walk over it in her Ravan heels. He groaned as she went, wincing and starting at every sharp touch of her youthful progress, but she did not cease to hurt him, nor did such waking daydreams cease to current through her mind.

Coming home of course had been the greatest shock of all. Home to her unwell mother, who had taken to Presbyterianism and cats as some cantilevered exoneration of her continuing nights on the bottle. In Sarah stepped, fresh from a pleasant voyage home on the *Carisbrook* where she had read Gissing and Verga in the morning sun on deck and where she played the white piano in the ship's cocktail bar in the afternoons. Rome was already a fondness in her mind until, like a guitar left out in the rain, it began to warp in the presence of her mother's madness. Sarah made her unhappiness felt, writing to her father to plead for a reprieve from the chaos. And so she had found herself in that windowless driver's cabin of the gravel & firewood train as it traversed the five stations of the Saddle Line from Moriac to Wensleydale. Heading into a density of eucalypts. Despite the obliquities of bush light it was another shock, and now amid its aftercurrents she trembled in solitary pain.

For as kind and encompassing as Maisie was in the cottage, the cottage was all shadow to her, a wild remorseless corner the world had painted her into. It was as if she had been cast out like a bundle of broken cords, to further rot and disassemble. With all hinges, joins and junctions come loose, all glue unstuck and nails unsprung, would there ever be a space — a space of air — into which the light of earth could fall?

    Her night sweats were at least one constant, and she grew to almost enjoy them. So it was that as a human wafer of porous skin over grey bone she sat one morning on the bricked verandah directly out from her room. Peering almost absentmindedly through the gossamer of the garden she saw the way the sunlight fell, picking out the glistening translucent threads that held the whole world together. And thus she caught a first glimpse of the radically innocent truth that would cause her to blossom in the months and years ahead.

    There were branches of Pomaderris and tea-tree reaching in from the bush at the perimeter. Reaching in from the sepia shadows of the taller trees. A thrush would creep from those shadows, the whole scene reflected in its large round rivertoned eye, the speckles and brindle of its plumage, so optically glossed among the slowly evolved and symbiotic forest, now risking its beauty in the clearing light. But Sarah did not notice the thrush nor its speckled coat and globe-like eye. It was the glimpse she caught of the gossamer threads that formed a glinting net at the edge of her doubting darkness. She would come to understand how such webs make a mockery of human self-absorption. She herself was a broken branch in shadow, a spar fallen too soon across the collapsed and eroded creek of being, a branch stripped of its close-up life, its esculent bark and its moss and lichen, and lying at an ungainly angle to her own soul. This was the same soul, the speckled soul-thrush of her deeper sight, which looked on as if at a troubled upper surface, while keeping down and hidden, waiting for the push and flush of rightmindedness that would allow for the wing-like flutter of breath that could usher her back out into the world.

It would come not as a shy opening though, not demurely or in politeness, but as a great instinctive clearing, a clearing commensurate with the power of the sun.

VIII

WHILE MAISIE WAITED for a response to her letter to Fernshaw Hutchinson, she suggested one day to Sarah that, after a full two weeks in which she hadn't bothered to dress in anything but her nightdress and dressing-gown, it was time that she made herself presentable, put on some shoes, and went for a walk beyond the garden.

At this the girl burst immediately into tears, leaving Maisie to wonder whether one more shock could be a shock too many. And yet she also knew that to let Sarah lower herself any deeper into the chasm she was in would, by the very gravity of its process, mean that that soul of hers, which watched on as if from underneath, that soul-thrush with its wings firmly tucked away at its sides, may never fly again. It would instead be crushed by the descending mass of the girl's malaise, the soul-thrush stripped of its light-given variegation, its round eye shut for all time against the webs, the glabrous reflections and glinting networks of the world.

And so Maisie, herself beginning to feel crushed in the girl's presence as if by the turgid freight of England, decided to risk it.

She would dress her herself if need be, strip her naked and reassemble her identity via Maisie's own choice of clothes. And, she swore, she wouldn't take 'no' for an answer.

But in fact Sarah did not say no. Instead she agreed to her keeper's terms, if only by way of a limp acquiescence. So the girl stood beside her bed, her arms straight up in the air as she had been taught as a child, when her mother, or the governess Esther, would pull her nightie over her head. Maisie paused to watch, amazed at the way those extended arms of the young woman reminded her of two long bands of kelp gone pale from their contact with the forest air. They were as limp as seaweed too, as seemingly helpless, and yet, she thought, perhaps if they could be returned to the right fold of earth, perhaps then they may reclaim their vigour, their muscle and structure, and become healthy again.

Over her fingers went the ivory cotton, the sleeves of the dress. Over her blank face went the embroidered neckline, and down over her wan breasts the garment fell to her knees. There would be no need yet for underwear, just socks, her woolly Fair Isle jumper and black cashmere cardigan and scarf.

It was like reassembling a doll, but with the doll watching on from deep inside, looking out now through the dark round eyes of the thrush, the vast spaces of the bush waiting silently amidst the even vaster continental space inside her being.

But the shoes, they may as well have been made of wood. In fact they were of Moroccan leather, flat-soled, with square gold buckles. She would go out into the garden in them, among the fruit trees, the budding lettuces and spinach. And standing firm on the leaf-strewn paths she would inhale the whole green world.

She chose to sit on the bedside chair to get the shoes on, with the help of the horn. Maisie applied a brush to her hair as she sat, admiring the tangled gloss, its hints of auburn earth. Nothing was said, not in words at least, and yet they both understood how she was being prepared. They also knew, as a seed contains the entire structure even before its life form issues from it – they somehow knew what she was being prepared for. Not for the first time Sarah Hutchinson was being born into life, and this time she would not be thwarted.

It was not as if Maisie was behaving as some kind of shaman, nor as if she was acting out the role of a mentor – she was merely seeking a better balance in her world. She herself had been young once; she knew well the skins that needed to be shed and how normal sun-fed days in the adult world could come in a rush, abruptly, as if by violence. She did not pity Sarah her troubles, nor especially care for her, but she had a mature feeling for what is right and natural, and thus she clothed her and brushed her hair. Enough was enough. The girl would have to tread the border between the inside and the outside, between the verandah and the grass, the garden and the bush. All the confusion and pain inside her would have to step out and dissolve itself in the more permeable distances of the world.

When the shoes were on, Sarah straightened her back. Maisie put down the brush. She held up the tortoiseshell clasp that Sarah had pinned her hair with when she arrived on the Saddle Line train and offered it to the girl. The clasp had sat brownly on the bedside table since the day after her arrival. Now Sarah took the clasp from Maisie and it glinted in what light there was as she fixed it into her hair.

That clasping of the hair, that act alone, was a sign. Maisie felt that things were about to turn. Her timing was good.

So now, a little buoyed by the glint of the clasp in the still dusty mass of the girl's hair, Maisie reached out and took her hand. It was an act of revivification, as if a new correspondence had appeared from behind the wispy edges of a green-tinged deepwinter cloud.

Together they walked across the boards, the older woman leading the younger out of danger to a place where she would no longer be pursued. A small act of common sense, but with an entire celestial drama thus entailed. A true salvation for the girl.

'Things are bigger than you, than me,' Maisie said quietly, as they stepped from the verandah bricks onto the garden path. 'Like all that out there, the scrub and the bush, is bigger than the garden. The wind blows in from the ocean and it's bigger still. And the rain falls from the sky, which goes on forever.'

Sarah's face tilted up into the watery light. She felt its weak warmth, as if it was coming to her through the mythological veils and narrative layers of the universe. She wriggled her toes in her shoes.

꙳

The next day she dressed herself, this time with underwear and the clasp again gathering her hair at the back. When it comes the velocity of the spirit is as sheer as any bird taking the updraughts out over blue waves; and so it was. And she also smelt like a bird as she knotted the scarf at her throat and stepped out into the air once more.

Standing there in the light Sarah felt a buzzing touch at the outer limits of her skin, as if it was thawing from the inside. Yes, something inside of her was pushing up against gravity and out of darkness. The eye of the thrush was rising, rising slowly, rising through her. It had begun its flight to marry up in oneness a living vision of the world. Her body's eye that could see ordinarily, materially, and the miracle of the soul's eye, would become one. The world would be magnified.

She walked among the lettuces and spinach. Slowly beginning to detect the green. The vital green. There was a rustling in the gums beyond, the leaves flashing their undersides; as she glanced up it was like a blush in the bush and it sounded like a river in the trees.

In what seemed like no time Maisie was there at the edge of the darkness of the house, calling her in for breakfast. Sarah felt her lack of appetite, a reorientation away from the inside. She had not felt this lack of appetite before; it simply did not exist. But now it was there, a neutrality in her stomach, a boredom more than a repulsion. And the wind once again made the tree leaves blush.

She walked back, drank tea, a compromise, out on the verandah. Maisie left her alone, going out to hang washing on the line that was threaded from the tankstand to the big manna gum standing hard and white in the garden's southern edge. Sarah watched the garments flick, the sheets, the tea towels unfurl. She detected a brightness in the washing like the green among the plants, squares and rectangles of light against the entangled bush backdrop. A sound came into her mind, then a word, the verb *crisping*. She placed the sound of this word in her teeth and registered the kinship of its sibilance with the river-wind in the trees.

Something smiled faintly inside her, a shy fungal sprout from under fallen bark. Was it in her mind, in her stomach, between her ribs, or perhaps on her ankle? Yes, a smile emerging lightly on her ankle. The wind among the leaves. She raised the cup and saucer and sipped Maisie's tea. On the Via Empedocles, she recalled, Uncle Ferny had one night read aloud from 'his book', not a book he had written but one that was almost as dear to him, and as synonymous, probably more so in fact, and he carried it with him always. An Australian book told in the voices of the old bullockies.

They were in the bar above the Trattoria Paradiso, where the voices of Uncle Ferny's book sounded stranger than Arabic, almost stranger than Russolo's noise. Ferny could not help but *perform* what he read but even so, she remembered thinking, it was not such a stretch. People at home *did* sound like that. Ferny stood with the green book held high in his hands, a mischievous smile at his lips, as he inserted this strangeness into the Roman atmosphere. Was the raw emphasis he placed on certain words, certain images, deliberate, or was he simply immersing in the pleasures he took in 'his book'? A book like no other. Sarah had noted the faces around the room, their confusion, amusement, their disdain, their curiosity, and also their rapture. She had felt how uncategorisable the whole situation was: Ferny and Martin of Mendips, Saltarno the Futurist, Luigi Russolo and his theories of noise, old Roiseaux, old Roiseaux and her, and Ferny's book, strining out in this musty yet elegant bar, with the terrifying columns of St Peters just a little way up the street.

'"Well, beggars ain't choosers," replied the apostle of brute force and ignorance. "Fact was, Arblaster, I bethought me what a lot o' work I'd done for Magomery, one time or another, on what good friends me an' him always was; an' I says to myself, 'Well I'll chance her – make a spoon, or spoil a horn.' That's the way I reasoned it out. See, if I got to turn roun', an' foller the main trunk back agen to the Cane-grass Swamp, an' take the Nalrookar track from there, I won't fetch the station much short o' fifty mile; an' there ain't a middlin' camp the whole road. Everythin' et right into the ground.

Starve a locust. 'Sides, I'm jubious about the Convincer Sand-hill, even with half a load. Bullocks too weak.'"

This wasn't some long-gone Etruscan shepherd come in on the Appian Way to tell a story – no, in this milieu this was starker, more various, vapid, astringent and *appalling* than that. An atonal glossolalia emitting itself in symmetrical Vatican shadows. And yet it was Ferny's Manifesto! At the very least his anchor and touchstone. 'His Book.' When Sarah asked him later on how he could be so brave, he told her he would perform from it whenever he could. In London, in Rome, in Cairo or Saint Petersburg, it was a shock to the system, and he knew it.

And now Sarah was back, back in the land where, despite the fact that the book went largely unread, its spirit-voices were not a shock but a Reality, a raw emanation of the tangy air. Soon Ferny would be back too. She so much looked forward to that. 'We can't ignore the sound in our soul,' she heard herself mouthing.

She sipped her tea, wondering at the emergence of such an idea in her mind. The book was the ballast in Uncle Ferny's ship, a talisman that would ground him no matter how hi-falutin or unlikely his passions, and no matter the avant-garde abstractions of his times. The truth that for old Roiseaux lay in the removal of line and the substitution of form with colour, for Uncle Ferny was all in that book. The magic that for Martin of Mendips could be found in the enigmas of geology around the site of the Colosseum, was for Ferny in the book. And soon he would return with it, securely in his luggage. His battered, bedevilled, torn and handled, and much travelled copy. A green binding of mad bullockies forever couched in the loquacity of their singing laughing creator. A case of cognac that had travelled halfway around the world only to return to the clime of origin where its sharp piquancy made most sense.

She replaced the cup on the saucer. For a moment she listened to the china ring. She stood up, and right there on the clinker-bricks of the verandah she felt a spike in her spirit, a seedling pushing through dark soil to the sun. Something was opening, and something was falling away.

※

In the days following she took to camouflaging herself amid the hazels and dusty millers that grew in such tangled profusion beyond the gums on the perimeters of the garden. The upper sun-gilded leaves and the lower sagey leaves captured the variegations of her mood. Always changing now in the light. She was dissolving, and liked to dress accordingly. No white, no red, but anything rust or green or bronze or sage, or even black. Her pale face became lost in those upper 'dusty' leaves, her form, subdued thus by the clothes, disappearing in the lower branches. This now was her relief. The way she could disappear like that, with no gaze upon her but for the round sun or round cloud or round moon. Not even Maisie, who was more than happy to discover that the string she had pulled was the right one.

One afternoon though, some three days hence, as Sarah was ranging in the ridge of bush on the high western side of the cottage, her eye caught an unusual movement in the direction of the kitchen window below. She also heard the cry, a simultaneous cry of a bird she didn't recognise. For a fearful moment she was sent back, divided away from the place, sent back into the mean enveloping darkness.

Scrambling breathless out of the dusty miller limbs she was quite suddenly all too aware of her reappearance from camouflage; she felt stark, exposed, without cover, almost naked, as Mr Rabbits, obviously himself sensing odd movement, flung a backyard look towards the window from where he was kissing Maisie, who was sitting on the kitchen table in front of him, her legs apart to either side of his railway-straight hips.

The eye of the seer and the eye of the railway man met in an instant that felt more like an eternity for them both. Until Sarah turned away, skipping back into the thick slabs of soft humus, the leaf litter and living plants, blending herself again into her surroundings.

For a moment, before Mr Rabbits had caught Sarah's eye, it was as if he and Maisie had been one shape, one thing, perhaps even the creature that had made the simultaneous cry. Through the reflections of the window glass Sarah saw a single form, the stooping plane of his back as he leant down and forward to kiss her, her legs like pinions, flanks, even full wings, to either side. But they were not wings, they were merely shapes she saw, and did not question. There were no resemblances, only life itself in its new energy. Until that stooping plane widened, grew straighter, then taller, and the curious eye, suddenly unmistakable in light, was matching hers. The spirit-eye, flashing quick, but seeing deep into and from the autumn.

With old Roiseaux, notwithstanding their harmonies and understandings, she had never felt as one. Well, no one could possibly see his old skin and hers as one. The way his chest and stomach were pouchy, and hers taut and firm. Fully clothed on their strolls by the Tiber they were perhaps like family, but fully naked on the divan in his studio above the river they were not so akin. Which was part of their strong energy. At last, after all the haphazardry of the careless shocks of her life, she needed a trusted guide, and he, with the onset of old age and with his famous optical acuity beginning to weaken, needed the glowing revivification that Sarah's body and intellectual youth brought him. Now though, there was no such healing via opposites. She had been shocked by what she had seen through the kitchen window, but as she wandered back into the dusty miller and hazel, stooping under their lumpy fronds and leaning branches, she grew only relieved and content. That Maisie was loved, and loving back. And abruptly, like another blush breathing through the high branches, a huge wave of gratitude rose inside her, for all she'd been given, for the place where she had landed, this far-off place where she could dissolve into something bigger than herself, bigger than her family's damage, a place where she could simply stop under an overhanging bush to find her soul blended with the hushed immensities of autumn.

Such was the gratitude brought to her by that private kitchen kiss, as she climbed higher through the bush beyond the cottage, coming out into a clearing, a rocky ledge of windstunted banksia and she-oak from where she could look west across the light to the Otways growing even taller in the sky, that her eyes began to moisten with the space and light ringing through her. She opened, her long clench releasing, as the vast continental space that had kept her balance amid the dank inhospitable confines of England became finally matched and made material. This was it. This was the mirror to the size and structure of her soul, stretching out now beyond the singleness of her single body, to all sides and in every direction.

The girl stood and cried with relief. The light cleaved her in half. Whatever load there had been seemed now mere furniture, objects arranged in the past, irrelevant, inconsequential things, and powerless to touch her. And with another breath she realised she was the very air, the moss and lichen on the ironstone at her feet, the stone horizon and high sky and every swale and valley in between. She was light, the light; she was the scent of the nectar moving through her veins; she was the sap, the sky in her brain. She was but one more tree, animated and fast, one more vertical blossom of a bee-loud heath; she was it, and it was her.

Soon then the correspondences had her eyes streaming. The sullen state, the torpor which she had barely survived, had not only run its course but had been categorically expelled. She was seized, gripped, *attacked* by a profound unification, not of different parts of her but of her being with the being all around her.

Finally then she pushed her cardigan with the sleeves of her dress up above her elbows, lifted her bare arms and hands high above her head and, with the tears running as if from the dark spring-cleft of all she had endured, she cried *thank you thank you* to the world, to the autumn morning, to everything and nothing, to everyone, and to no one and no time in particular.

Ngangahook

I

We gave the moorhens a story Ferny and I, even as we were coming down off the saddle in the spring cart. The happiness we felt at being reacquainted spilled out and into the world. And how the moorhens became our companions then! Not just black and Prussian-blue delights with gawky-flights and poultry-stars for feet but with tendencies and shoulder-hunch like relatives moving down a hallway. This hall of course was open air, with high-skied ceiling and tree-clad geologies on either side. I noted too from my perch in the cart, as we descended into the slushy valley-floor, the surfeit of common sheafy reeds, and by night in my first weeks on this Ngangahook Run I must recount how I dreamt the moorhens as family members, or at least as friends, gesturing with linen-white bobbing tufts or looks askance, dining on the crabs that perforate the muddy watery riversides, just as we might dine on chops, though the birds have more efficient cutlery.

But it was the playful story that inspirited them for us, the names we gave them – Alan or Caroline – and the sense that a fabulated story gives, just like the framework of a house or homestead, or the boards and bindings of a book, of them feeling deep, beyond any arrogant notion of existing in this life as merely one of god's enslaved machines. Which brings me thus to what was immediately preoccupying Ferny as we began this trip down from the Big Cutting Hill. On a visit to London on his way home from Rome, he had spent time with a philosophical coterie discussing Descartes and the mind/body dualism. So that as soon as my luggage was loaded and we were on top of the cart and moving he was straightaway full to brimming with stories of the famous pineal gland. This is the gland at the centre of the brain which Descartes claimed as the seat of the mind or soul that elevated us above the status of animals. As the track wound down from the Saddle towards the moorhens' lair so too did Ferny go on and on in his typically enthusiastic manner. Despite the notorious perils of the gluey and precipitous track, his mirth at Descartes' preposterously ridiculous idea made for an effortlessly buoyant way to travel down here to sea level. So that I knew immediately then, as I stepped down off the cart upon our arrival through the gate at Ngangahook, that this home in the glen was not a merely *productive* milieu, that it also thrived as a glen for a glen's own sake, without superfluous moral ledgers or hectoring audits. I hoped very much that we would live in companionship with that, as the wagtail lives within its three-rung song.

Often still, when I am stepping out over the grass and through the perfectly circular soaks which punctuate our paddocks in the wetter months, I have a sense of myself, in my bones and limbs, as stepping out just like the moorhens. My forefoot prods the ground, and the torso follows in an equally angular rhythm. And like that of the moorhens, my goal keeps shifting as I go along, down across the pasture from the house towards the river, things occur to me, feeding as I do on this or that vista, on this and that sound, shifting like the cloudshapes above the northern slope of trees, or like the trees themselves, which although firmly clutching the earth by root and trunk, are nevertheless always ticking with expansive life.

I realised even in Rome that Ferny sometimes speaks in his sleep, speaks in a hybrid tongue, with a lexicon crossing borders and traditions. But once I had become a hand in the glove of the Ngangahook Run I noted doubly, and most likely by contrast, that in Ferny's case this dream vernacular is not so much grunt and mumble but also rococo-cry, Italianate, Decembrist, blent as it is with the daily tasks here in the glen. He calls there in his sleep for a Mario, for an Alessandro, for a Sergei, or for Martin of Mendips, to meet him by the Cobb & Co coach bridge and help him with the post-and-rail. He cries out through his open door for a Paolo, a Nadia, to fetch the stock out of the ironbark swamp, to lead them back to grass through the drier messmates. The night-homestead becomes a music of dialect and dream, and I rise without lighting a lamp from my room in the second hallway, feel my way along the striated hall and, entering the vast room, seat myself at the piano. And as he calls, lovely Ferny, I transcribe, underscoring the inflections with chords of my own making, rhyming the words with sound until a song is born.

It is a native song but also a collage tune, just as tears are the dew of the eyes, and hair the flowing fronds of the tree. I call it 'she-oak canto', as if the oak comes as the original issue of the dream's spring and the flowing translation of this heart of music comes from its simultaneous and ongoing mate, the she-oak. The dreamspeak and the night's score of our Ngangahook Run.

And so before you would judge me, consider these airs I bring. Not uppity airs but excited encounters with a green corner of the world, the exhalations of the mosses and lichens, the undammed river's flow, the way all is made of kindred things, of wood or stone, of leather and linen and mind, and how the hollow flights of romance and the pernicious arrogance of 'god's servants' remain so indelible in us. What was sung here, the notes flowing out over the coastal pastures that helped prepare my piano, cannot be heard; but in what I write perhaps the afternotes, the echoes, remain. These printing words, appearing letter after letter, the residue of my performance, are husks of a flooding young body's song, its fingertrills and thumperchords. So listen well before adjudicating on my behalf.

Every second word to us here is made of soil, every fifth word is made of wood, every twenty-third from dew, every sixteenth from pollen, every thirty-eighth from the tang of the live but sepia creek. They say eel is oily but that damper can be dry. And so it is with poems. So seek, for my sake and yours, the right circuitry of mind and preparation of effects. Intervene by all means (and I do mean *all*) but don't desire for the gaps to be filled too quickly, allow the invisible frequencies their say.

II

IN THOSE FIRST days I would come in from walking, and in the large open room where the piano seemed an island Uncle Ferny would be gesturing with his arms, saying please, yes, play; and so I would, and I would listen to the effects of the things I played. I played and listened, letting the sounds ring out. I listened then played, and looked through the largest windows I had ever seen in an Australian house. They were exciting days, the surrounds so replete, and something in the music grew porous, or was yearning to be porous, as if through those windows the outside was wanting to come in. Eventually, after only weeks of being here, I found myself gathering things as I walked, then raising the grand piano lid and placing first sticks then bones between the strings, affixing fern-fronds too on the hammers that hit them, leaning over the keyboard as I depressed the notes to see the new hybrid thicknesses of felt advancing, and shards of worn old fence-wire loops between them. A kangaroo bone prevented one hammer from doing its work while a flint from a grey bullock shin sharpened the volume of another when it was propelled into action by the pressing of a key. Thus the piano gained new life as another creature, incorporating the glen into its fabricated design and its European – in this case German – circuitry, just as the moist mushroomy airs were acting upon my body, and still do, as I write and compose in the autumn.

Which brings me thus to a clipping I have preserved here amongst my things, from those early days when the world began to toll.

The Performance of 'My Autumn' by Sarah Hutchinson
At roughly 6 p.m. on Sunday, 15 May, as night was descending onto the paddocks of the Angahook Run, a small group of invited guests gathered in the homestead for an evening of music. After an hour of social conversation, complemented by cider and beer, soldiers of toast with paté, and Johnnycakes baked in the hot ashes of the fire, Mr Fernshaw Hutchinson, uncle of the poetess and proprietor of the Run, formally welcomed the guests.

He then introduced his young niece, who has only recently moved into the district.

Dressed strikingly in a brown & turquoise tea-gown, Sarah Hutchinson sat down at her grand piano and, without further ado, recited the following words even as she began to play.

Since arriving here I often wake in the morning and wonder if my autumn is like your autumn, is like The autumn, wherever that may be? A place perhaps where I can lie under the gills of mushrooms, where I can wash my soul in a bead of dew, where time prickles bright like emblematic heath, where a rainbow over the glen is an arc following the melody of a sonata in my mind.

It is a very big sonata this glen this rainbow this poem in the mind, so big in fact that it can't be in my mind alone but in My autumn.

> *Images. Like flowers of the ironbarks, which stand even where last November's flood broke the banks and sawed the ground now starred and creamy with those fallen flowers. They're in My autumn.*
>
> *Sounds. The ladder-song of kookaburras which I climb at dusk, rung by rung, to greet the storied stars. They're in My autumn.*
>
> *Ideas. Like the platypus which flips the riverskin into undone buckles of light. These are in My autumn.*
>
> *Nourishment. As in the truffles the wallabies dig for among the paths and leafy litter of the trees.*
>
> *Are they in your autumn, and are they in The autumn, whatever wherever whenever that may be?*

The editor of the district newspaper *The Echo* had come to Ferny after the evening was over, asking for a transcript of the words I had recited, explaining that he would like to use them in the article he was preparing for the paper's Social page. Uncle Ferny and I had sat then in his study and excitedly typed the lines out on his Underwood, as best I could remember them. Buoyed as we still were by the adventuresome coteries of Rome, we also furnished the editor with details of the way I had prepared the piano with items from the Run, details which, to Ferny's obvious delight, were duly printed in *The Echo* alongside the account of the evening's proceedings and the lines I had performed.

> *In a novel procedure Miss Hutchinson had adjusted the workings and thus the sound of the homestead's grand piano with the following items from the field: a bullock bone, a piece of ironbark, a banksia cob, a scrap of 8 gauge wire, a kangaroo rib, a train ticket, a fray of crinoline, a bandage, a letter, fern fronds, a bridle hasp and fox-fur.*

So it was that, encouraged by my darling uncle, I entered the coastal district with something of a splash, though of course I knew not the half of it. I had altered the piano with the world in which I now lived, a demesne which had immediately enthralled me, and we continued to hold these Sunday soirees with Ferny championing my musical and poetic offerings as something of a feature. I did not mind at all, caught up as I was in the joy of a new self and its possibilities.

But it is here in the more sustained echo of these pages that I would more properly release myself to you, removing the comportment of my brown tea-gown to describe things in a way I cannot when indecency is counterfeit, and fears the very thing it is. Were three brolgas shot from a neighbouring verandah, as I overheard someone say while they munched their johnnycake, or were they cousins in a costumed dance? To understand what has happened in this district you must leave the self like this gown on the hardwood floor, step into the naked air and dance. Is that indecency then? To slaughter the royal custodians and to claim they were but birds? All 'indecency' is counterfeit here, and formally clothed. Rather than pretending to be birds they pretend to be human.

That said, I myself am only an open book when you open me, like this, see, here we are, in the hush of the writing night, with the bush tapering away to orchid-folds, flutings and nubs, the hidden thing, the health of the river. The gown fallen away like bark, I am all strength sheer skin and moistened sap, and so grateful for your attention. All healing love lies in equidistance, what lies lush between us: not me here alone in this fraught glenned lineage nor you there alone listening to the echo of its future. Not in longwind and romantic ornament either, nor in the strains of synthetic acrimony that will come to surround you. Together though we amount to a compression of fresh airs. Between. In the time and space it takes for the thicknesses of felt advancing to strike the wound string. And if as the tonewright I set the key and you are the string the hammer strikes then together we create the time it takes, the stars through which time travels to make its song. It is a song of words that would not kill the dance, or the dancer, be it bird or man.

Which brings me to the bell, the story of the bell. We had not a village bell, for we have not a village. Only a lighthouse, the prismatic lens our lease from death between the rocks of birth and life's final headland. And all of it, these paddocks, the Hotel and Store and little school, as moths to the lanterns in November, clusters around the lighthouse, from whose heathy headland our Run is one league inland. The Light was built, with three keeper-cottages up there on the bite of cliff, and thus three families came to fill the deed, to watch-work and play and look across at the one crumb of land's biscuit broken off in the sea, the tufted roost for our monsignors the cormorants. The lighthouse children need their school; the schoolmaster needs his providore; the providore in turn, in such a remote inlet, needs his worship and belief, as does his wife, just as the monsignor needs to dive. And so the man of religion, be it in this case from Wales via New Zealand, needs his Hotel, whereas the Mine Host needs, rather than consecration of his wine, his bills to have no truck with time's strict deadlines. Though he needs his mail delivered.

Hence a school sprang up with weatherboards which Ferny's father helped to mill and plane, and due to how pretty the lighthouse was sitting out on that point, the suite of human fantasies began to coalesce. A guesthouse then, on the downslope of the ridge descending towards the eely stream; and with 'holidays by the sea' must come an occasional entertainment at Night. Johnny Briggs' Magic Lantern. Entirely daguerrotypical. But, as if that was frippery enough, no bell. Yes, a small church house, but as with the Protestant cross, no animation, pulse, or character. No peal, or repeal. Bass Strait unadorned. Thus nothing but surf resounding, and it seemed to some that the town having no auditory range thus had no formal boundary or barrier beyond which all was eerie squawk, godless and unleavened. Thus *all* was wild and there was no town. No *village*.

Some mornings in my first months here, while still emerging from the pupae of my weeks with Maisie in the cottage, I would lie as if in yearning for the dignity of chimes. I had hated them in Devon – *curséd things* – but such are the lying trysts of nostalgia. When I mentioned this yearning to Ferny he sarcastically agreed. 'Now wouldn't that be nice,' he said, sardonic. A niceness in the offing. Like a ship of taffeta, cloisonné and salted pork, instead of a bell unstruck, from a belltower barely imagined. Imagine then, imagine our days before the hour when a bell could simply be printed. I will write of the sound here at length not because I long for it anymore (understanding as I do how ocean consecrates all) but purely to describe this typical colonial ritual of 'a niceness in the offing'. Call it civilisation-on-its-way, even as it sets the very air we breathe alight with burning carbon.

As it happened a petition was being got up for exactly that. A village bell. To mark the satisfaction of what was always deeply sacred. The secrecies of the wallaby-mind, the ciborium of the shark. And as with all such local philanthropies, the Hutchinsons were the first, and traditionally the most generous, port of call.

Initially, and blithely, with no firm commitment, we signed, my uncle and I, in a lilac Naples ink. Turquoise actually, tipping towards the teal tint of the duck. Ferny still had a bottle from his travels. And so our brightness stood out on the list, amongst the moral-grey indignation. 'It isn't good enough' was a common cry of those in pursuit of a replica-settlement, while our brightness there on the ledger, I like to think, spoke only of our desire for *music*. And so, I am sure, it was interpreted. Ferny Hutchinson and his young flourish of a newly arrived niece. So be it. If I could be you I'd still shop for a wine-like ink such as that.

'It's a long way for a bell to travel,' was the reply from the Sydney diocese, via Melbourne, when the petition was sent. A long, long way, said the scholars. And yet, unlike the woolly Polwarth flocks the bell would not tamp the bulbine lily nor the yam daisy but only set their petals trembling – or so might come the educated (nee: native) counter claim. Trembling petals aside, my longing for the world to be described in sonic measure runs, it seems, deep beyond the topsoil of my apparent life. There is stone base under all this clover and paspalum, and perhaps it is of that that the tolling of a bell reminds us. We clear the air, tocsin quenching toxin; we clear the air of regret, of blame and guilt, sorrow and squeeze, thus each stroke voices those very dark presences it negates. Base iron bell and clapper, sounding deep from the earth element. A measure of what is, what has passed, and what is still to come.

This then could be the nature of the bell's blessing and why it was desired for the heart of the town. A sound to clear invisible arteries of the air, filaments of the cranesbill. But no, and as if everyone believed such sounds were a penumbra they did not want to dwell beneath, the word was no. No bell. But *surely*, you cry. And yes, you would be right. There was no true devastation at the Church refusal, just other things on the inlet's mind: shooting ducks, racing horses on the beach, keeping the paraffin up to the Fresnel lens, potting crayfish, skewering crabs, snaring quail, drinking muscat, whiskey, beer, wine, drinking the creek, playing poker, reading Boldrewood, and mushrooming, and more mushrooming. Each small earth-flower of the midwinter solstice was a bell of its own, with chocolate gills, lemony gills, these fish of the air that remind us, like no tocsin can, of how we are all bespoked to an earth that must turn on its wheel. Perpetually.

No schoolbell, no churchbell, no bell for service nor for storm. Just the silence that is so filled with sound. The reach of the pealing peal of the moonlured surf, beseeching no one at the rivermouth. That, I came to believe, through the pressure of engagement, is the only bell of auditory range that ever an inlet wanted to be heard.

But still: *a niceness in the offing*, something coming our way other than weather, that's what had caused the bitter unsuccessful petition to so deepen and endure.

III

Selwyn Atchison's spring cart announced itself as the bleached planks of the Coach Road bridge near our front gate paradiddled in the sunlight. The woody music of wood buckling and returning to its set. Wood wheels on wood, under its overhanging ironbark cousins. I heard the ripple from where I was picking foxgloves in the garden.

Atchison believed a bell was like the belt of his trousers; it would save him, save us all, from embarrassment. I have actually heard that many of the men in these parts see no need for conventional accoutrements such as underpants, but a bell was of a different order. It would keep us from being spiritually, civically, communally naked. Thus this mayorless ur-shire would be so dignified. Rung out and resonant rather than strung out and desperate. Selwyn Atchison, haughty barley and sheep farmer but barely above the ruminant, would not settle for less. Thus came his happy collie straight for me and my pocket of lozenges as Selwyn settled his horse and formally tap-tapped a bony knuckle on our russet hardwood door.

Uncle Ferny himself was hairy from reading. Absorbed he'd been, for three unshaven days and nights straight, in Furphy's *Such Is Life*, his favourite book. He had carried its voices through Egypt and Russia, read it aloud in Rome, Alexandria, Trieste, championed its inventions and pleasures all around the world, and now he was himself hearing it all again once more, as if for the first time, as he always did upon his return. For Selwyn Atchison however, reading was all about practicality. Music was too. The bell, as I said, would keep his trousers up. Save him from being the beast he was, that we all are. And so came Ferny's woody tread to Selwyn's ingratiating tap. And Ferny's smile, as always, was wide – as much, in this case, because a visitor would allow him a chance to convey the prodigiously detailed delights of his talisman book, as with seeing another member of a species of which he was so fond.

From the garden I heard them treading the boards back towards Uncle Ferny's study, deep in the bowels of the house. But not so deep that it didn't have a window, a handblown ripply square of glass that looked through crosspanes as if through gunsights onto where myself and the collie were laughing in the garden.

So it was I saw them settle down to begin to discuss the possibility that Ferny might finance the bell. Or at least that's what poor Mr Atchison thought they were going to discuss. But could he get a word in edgeways? It seemed to me not, with Ferny clapping his hands in rapture, slapping his big farmy thighs for emphasis, his reader's beard growing as if visibly upon the espalier of his renewed enthusiasm. Atchison looked as pinned to the wall as the butterflies I used to go to see in the Melbourne museum as a girl.

What interest had Atchison, after all, in literary invention, let alone *bullockies,* which were the unlikely protagonists of

Mr Furphy's book? But still the jugulating torrent of Ferny's words came, extolling the experiments of the novel, the life it had captured, the way the search for good grass at a day's end can inspire as well as shelter, and everything else that he had been reporting to me when, from time to time over the past three days and nights, he had emerged from his study to wee, or to eat, or to simply catch his breath between chuckling exultations.

At some point however it must have dawned on Selwyn Atchison that he needed to contrive a convergence. A convergence between the intensity of Ferny's admiration for Furphy's noisy art and his own Presbyterian need for a bell to civilise, indeed to *drown out* the pollinating salt airs of this small inlet into, and out of, the sea. Perhaps my uncle Fernshaw had actually mentioned the necessity of taking joy in a sounding culture; perhaps indeed, when I had seen him lean to his desk to take up the green boards of the Furphy volume, it had been to quote the following:

'Mrs Beaudesart possessed a vast store of Debrett-information touching those early gentlemen-colonists whose enterprise is hymned by loftier harps than mine, but whose *sordid greed* and *unspeakable arrogance* has yet to be said or sung.'

As they say in the gowned halls of learning, 'the italics are mine'. As were the gasps when Atchison's voice boomed out, 'But that's it, don't you see, Fernshaw!' Presaging a long interception of my uncle's monologue, as Mr Atchison strove to stake out their common ground of a civilising mission.

Whether Ferny was having any of it or not he did not need to say, either that day or the next. But knowing as I did his perspective on such a 'niceness in the offing', I grew to learn that he had not argued with Selwyn Atchison as such but rather told him a story of his own. Though Atchison was a grim type, a night-teethgrinder who I imagine ground his wife down likewise with an enormously hidden, compensatory and persistent physical impulse, Ferny was so good-natured, and also, I might add, so allergic to conflict, that without the clear realities of this family story he told he may have had trouble not becoming, as he had so many times since he was bequeathed sole custodianship of the farm and Hutchinson fortune, the chief philanthropist of local wishes, in this case the wish for the supposedly sacralising bell.

There was quiet for some time, just Ferny's low murmur as he imparted the seminal tale. Then I saw my uncle scrawling notes at his desk as Atchison spoke, and soon after that, turning again and waving Furphy in the air. Then, from what I could see, reflected in the glad eyes of the collie, they were taking whiskey. For although it was barely eleven in the morning, such was Ferny's *bon vivance* and Selwyn Atchison's *spirit-addiction* that the knob of the decanter was jostled out. The collie knew, as all collies know, the shadows of the master that she shared in life's walk-along. Atchison was a belligerent husband *and* a pent-up soak. Whereas Ferny was simply high as the Devil's Elbow on the harmonics of learning and friendship. Atchison was someone to talk Furphy's freakish achievement to, by god, and if that were to include an intimate narrative regarding the local import and significant voodoo of a bell, then so be it.

I, however, would like to linger for a moment on the bell that passes, the way a wave exhales as if with universal relief as it hits the shore. These are the deeper sighs, the passing bells we listen to every evening, untroubled by the fixative intent of humankind. My ears rejoice in a music nobody made, just as Selwyn Atchison himself regrets the same, and repeatedly bothers his wife as a consequence. He will not give up, yet the consolation I take is that neither will the waves. In the end it will be he who is drowned out, along with the rest of us. For such passing bells as that don't pass at all.

We live in the first league back from the mouth of the sea's song, this glen (this wicked glen, they sometimes say) where green is to the sky as is my face to the eyes of the gods. At times the paddocks are thick and close with seedy grass; at other times it's music hoarse and willed from the deep stone well of being which lies under all we feed upon: my poems, the piano, my Uncle Ferny's treasured book, our beef and barley, apples and mushrooms. All will be, as depth will be, yet for only as long as depth remains, until we tip into the thin immensities of space. I see the football kicked high in melody; I watch it land as the rainbows land, at a place never reached, a filmy tint so intact because it's never understood. I take these coloured rays, these games of elusiveness played by the air's painter, and pour them through my soul-case. My dew-of-the-eyes spills, glinting wet beads, astonishing my piano keys with the moistures of joy. Sun-joy met with sound and line. The glen my score, I trust, just as the ironbark stars do flower.

Truth is that though the perimeters of property seem to be king, there is another wealth such receivers must know. I wanted to shout stupidly to Atchison from the garden through the buckled glass. *Sight the glen! The winter sun on the gloss of green! Listen to that!*

I should say too that I sing this cursive song from a past that is not over but that fills me still, like nectar in the horn, the allowance of deep eternity.

       moss-clouds on the ledge-edge
       of the falls.
       the voice of wintertrickle hitting
       the stone bed below:
       inverse of summer's
       crackling fire

But I didn't shout out, for the pup lay on its back between the sunlit beds of silverbeet and hearting cabbage, in a way no self-respecting working dog would ever do. I took her cue and forgot the men inside, and rolled there too, my nose in her fur and my legs all asplay in mimicry of hers, donned in the pair of grey work trousers Ferny gave me when I first arrived on the farm. Perhaps it was the sight of that which propelled Atchison out of the house; I am not sure. But as the two of us rolled there amongst the silver-lit strings of winter's gossamer-work, I sensed a shift behind the sights of the window glass.

With the light from its eastern angle making the collie's inside-ear transparent to the sky, the paddock trees in the direction of our home gate and the coach road bridge filtered through a film of flesh-pink, she mock-growled as I grasped her snout and pulled her on to the top of me.

We were wrestling there when we heard the master's whistle and 'Hoy!' from the front side of the homestead. The collie and I paused, her warm torso snugly wedged between my legs, and we ever so briefly looked at each other as if to ask if it was true that our play must end. Did I see her grin at me then, before *whooosh*, she was up onto her paws and belting away beyond the vegetables to the call.

I had not even learnt her name but nor, I reasoned, had she known mine. We were just two bitches at play in a cul-de-sac of leafy greens, as the men discussed their strategies, not only in my uncle's study but the whole country over.

When the visit had receded sufficiently and Uncle Ferny was back in his study with Furphy's book, I slipped out of my boots and into my room to dig out the tiny dinner bell I had kept as one of the only treasures saved from my schooldays in England. This instrument – a handbell of brass with a sweet ring and a cameo of breaching whales to hold – was a darling to me. In my troubled days at Miss Hunt's of Ilfracombe I would sometimes ring it privately to give me bearing amidst the enclosures, which I felt I should be swallowed by. Now I took the handbell along the second hallway, at the end of which was Ferny's study. I knocked and heard him murmur his 'Come in'.

Expecting to find him at his desk, with finger on page and still absorbed in *Such Is Life*, I was surprised then to see him lying disgruntled on his divan with Mr Furphy closed up. He sprang though to a seated position as I entered, mischievously tinkling my little bell. 'Well, not you too!' he cried. 'You're winding me up!'

Pressing the dangling clapper hard against the bell-wall I gave my uncle a consolatory look.

'What?' Ferny expostulated. 'Well? What?'

'I sensed you'd need to discuss Mr Atchison's visit.'

Ferny sighed, like a beast, loudly, and through his nose. His three days of reveries among the diverse voices of the long paddocks of the Riverina had obviously come to an end. 'Well you can imagine, Sarah. I've nothing against a bell *per se*, and a campanile, or "tower" as he calls it, *if need be*, but he's just such a *Scot*. It's all just a stay on Death to him. Nothing lovely.

He'd knock up some blue prison-stone and have a bell-sound as cold as Ballaarat.'

He smiled then, relaxed, perhaps by looking at me standing there with the handbell. 'He's a fucking dullard, Sarah, but, even so, I had to tell him what's what.'

I sniggered, and gave my little whale-bell a tinkle.

Uncle Ferny smiled too then, and more fondly. 'See, that's nice,' he said, listening, as if to suggest that's all we would need. As if the town and its ambitions should be shrunk to that hand-held size. To that timbre. 'But no,' he went on. 'I'll have to deal with *clang-clang-clang*. Just thinking of it gives me the shivers. And Atchison knows of Furphy for his brother's water-carts and nothing more.'

At his wit's end now, in recollect, he lay back again on the divan. I noticed how beautiful his rose-leathered ankle boots were as he hoisted them up onto the scrolled rest at the divan's end.

'Well, he's got a lovely dog,' I ventured.

Ferny nodded. 'Yes, I noticed the two of you out there. That dog's a champion you know. I think it was more than Selwyn could handle seeing you both upturned like that.'

'I see. So you have me to thank for his leaving then.'

'Yes, but my time lost in Furphy has been cut. And the dreaded challenge now is to apply what I have gleaned, but outside the pages of a book. Hence my torpor. I can see by your clothes how his dog was moulting.'

It was true, I looked a little like a lamington. I gave the bell another ring.

'So I told him, Sarah, how when Grandfather Edward arrived on the ship at the beginning of all this, he was party to the erection of a bell on a hill outside Geelong that would, on the one hand, signal the mailboat coming up the bay, and on the other, warn the settlers of approaching natives. The bell was erected, and the gentlemen concerned, Grandfather included, would take it in shifts to keep the lookout from the vantage of the hill. And sure enough it was old Edward who was up with the bell when a group of the Wadawurrung came towards the spot, perhaps to stake their claim on what was rightfully theirs. Grandfather saw their approach, grasped the rope and rang the bell for all he was worth. The plan was that when his friends heard it they would converge and see off the trouble, most probably with musket and rifle. But that's not how it turned out. When the bell was rung it terrified the Blacks, who, seldom having heard such a sound before, took off into the bush in great haste and alarm. But, and here's the rub, so too did my grandfather's so-called settler friends! Rather than coming to help Edward, stranded up there alone on the hill, they flew the coop with even greater fear, leaving Grandfather ringing the bell louder and louder, and even louder still. *Clang-clang-clang. Clang, clang, clang.* Well, eventually he stopped, took the bell down off its post, and the story goes that he flung it into the Moorabool River. It was a bell that tolled nothing but cowardice, disloyalty, ineffectuality, and moral disgrace. And of course I would be ever reminded thus if the same sounds got up here. Imagine!'

He fell quiet then, slowly shaking his head. 'Indeed,' he said then, 'many years afterwards, a clan stopped here on the Run once, to camp and hunt the river, and play their football. Grandfather started to tell them the story, but they already knew it of course. He promised them they'd never hear a bell rung so round here. It was all he could do, as well as offering them the run of the place. But bell or no bell they never came back. And who could blame them? He'd had his Hutchinson hands on the rope after all. But Atchison wouldn't have known all that of course. So I spelt it out, yes, loud and clear. A bell rung in Edinburgh, I told him, is not the same as a bell ringing out right here.'

Ferny smiled at me then, taking pleasure at least in having made his point.

Emboldened by what he'd told me, I said, 'The thing is, uncle, a bell focalises an illusion. The oneness of the world when actually it's teeming.'

I paused to check whether he was feeling too sensitive to hear me out. But he nodded in agreement, and motioned for me to go on.

'So you have to weigh that against the charm of the ritual,' I continued. 'And against the chasm of sound. The idea of what we have in common – ears, for a start. This is not a village after all, and will never be. Even so, our souls should be close, and so we share in the intervals of the day. The range of the peal could help in this way. But it should not be a note of warning, nor of judgement, only of time and space.'

'Mmm, yes,' he said. 'Yet we have claimed those things already. Time and space.'

As if to befriend this idea, a surge of ocean landing in the rivermouth came penetrating and resonating on the air at that very moment. Then immediately receded.

'It's the weddings, Sarah, the funerals, the pious, the upright, and the *maudlin*. You know the sort of thing they have in mind.'

'The culture's hours,' I said. 'To lose all sense of time is as important as marking its passing.'

'I agree! But there'll be none of that with Atchison's *clang* every half-hour.'

'No.' I was thinking too of the world's ephemeral rhythms. Light on the stream. Then shadow. Afternote. Chill. Silence.

I gave the handbell another tinkle.

'Do we want our days parcelled out so?' Ferny asked the air in front of his nose.

'Would it be music?' I asked.

'If it could be,' he replied. 'But as Ruskin says: "There is hardly anything in the world that some man cannot make a little worse and sell a little cheaper."'

'Yet a dog will give away its coat for free.'

Another ring of the little bell.

'That's lovely, Sarah. You're cheering me up.'

'I love the flavour it gives to the air when the ringing ends.'

'Yes. I do agree.'

'There is nothing to accomplish, only to praise.'

'That's true. Furphy might have said it himself.'

'So we all need a model, don't we, Ferny. A book, or a mushroom, the balance of a standing kangaroo. I often think of that.'

'Or a negative example,' Ferny chimed in, 'to jemmy us up! Like the bell on the hill in Geelong. Or St Peters in *Roma*.' He pronounced it with a flourish of the rolling R.

'Atrocious powers.'

'They always give us new ideas though. Ideas for loveliness.'

'A sweet bell sound, rung irregularly, without reason or ambition.'

We listened out for a moment.

'I can hear it now,' Ferny said.

'In the silence,' I said.

'Yes. So I don't know where that leaves us?'

'It leaves us where the mushrooms grow.'

Ferny laughed now. 'Insignificant,' he said, with restored lightness of heart. 'Yet entirely indispensable.'

'To be a disciplined champion with time to cuddle and play,' I said.

'That's me!' he cried.

'Yes,' I said. 'That is you, uncle.'

And with a final ring of the bell I said, 'I'll make us a cup of tea, shall I.'

IV

I CANNOT PREDICT FIRST lines, no more than I can predict the precise location of a truffle. Though I know this much: a fence that Ferny builds keeps more than cattle in. It keeps the poems in their time and space and the wallabies out. And yet, athleticism is a wonderful thing. As the wallabies bound over the top rail, or bullet low beneath the splintering bottom, so too do my writings leak and sneak about.

But why should such movement need to be so discreet? Why so clandestine? It is their glen after all, from back when the limestone sides were roughed out by torrent shifts, the water sculpting the world even as it issued, and issues still, like a god's laughing tears: laughing at a notion of time beyond the pace and leap and run of emotional water.

Yes, the wallaby world, the world of these writings, insofar as the poems come filmed in the teardrops of the divine, which in turn keeps the wallabies fed on truffles every autumn.

Ancient fences were the contours of the ground, thus shaped. The shifting wet and dry and clicking language of the tongue. It is still so all along the north edge of the farm, which is defined by tone rather than line. Even so Uncle Ferny is known as a strong fencer, a quick fencer, a deep fencer, and his fences last – but only, I suspect, because he understands the passion for freedom. His holes are dug, the posts laid in; the original ties are cut. A healing poem will flourish in tool-disturbed ground. The underweb is pummelled, punched, and defensively. To keep things out. The bounding leaping life we want to rein in. The horse of the mind must submit to the harness of the word.

And so I became something of a stile here, between our small local gatherings and the others beyond, to whom I also speak. They ride through the air; they live in concatenation. We walk on the ground, amid the clods and pats, and I sniff for new clusters near the roots of trees.

This is my view of any potential dismantling of the farm. We might remove the stock before we remove the fences. Let the sounds escape between the keys. And therefore develop a taste for poetry as meat. Mmm. Welcome Poetivores!

❦

Deep in the moon-shaped pool I stay immersed as long as my lungs will allow. The intervals of the body, its meters and beats, determine my stay. There my face is flushed up again, I upmerge, forehead and cheekbones to the sky, my pale visage an open offer to the moon.

>   the moon-shaped pool
>   naked as the moonlight I
>   stretch and dip and
>   disappear under the tangy water
>   skin. What portal in the

>   paddock is this? Like a
>   little organ pipe down down
>   down below the weeping grass. When
>   I open my eyes there is only olive
>   and black, my own true eyes.
>   Everything in the world is close, my skin
>   folded into the land's skin, the way
>   I've slipped my note into the chord
>   of the earth, the base of all moon melody.

Like a tadpole the rest of me follows behind, until I'm fully out and I see Ferny standing aside, offering a white Christy towel from the lunar shadows.

'I heard you leaving the house,' he says. 'I promised your mother I'd look out for you, and sometimes, as hard as I try, I do worry.'

I smile at him, and take the comfort. My limbs are dripping, my breasts, hips, shoulders and feet, rhyming with the moon's lamp. All around us the green of the daytime glen is implied. This is that other country, where the body and its sources are merged.

'Beaut night,' says Ferny.

And I, now robed and with the grass tongues tickling my feet, can only agree.

'To enter the earth like that is to go to a chilly heaven,' I say. 'We leave the body behind.'

'We do,' he agrees. Then he stands to one side and peers for a sign of his Jerseys. The glossy black of their hides is ultimately blue in the moonlight. Like bowerbirds they are, but with four haunches. Ferny takes the opportunity to observe them in the night mode. Sempiternal the way they doze and graze, and browse in dew. Cattle of the moon. They are clustered down the swale a way, with the moon's pewter as a background. Cattle of heaven.

I dry myself, and sing as I do. The words come from what my lungs now know. The interchange with the fathoms of the portal where I've been.

I sing, while Ferny marvels at the cows. I sing the joys of a bigger, wider, fuller house. So much more than our homestead, I sing, so much more, and over and over again. I feel the possum eyes upon me; I sense the cow's heavy lids. The pool teaches, a perfect circle of reflection in the night.

This bigger, wider, fuller house. I sing, to stand here and know it like my own body. 'Can you hear me now?' I sing, 'Can you hear me?'

The moon, distributing messages through the light. The boobook hoots. As it did in the thirteenth, fourteenth, fifteenth centuries, here where there is no epoch or eternity, where we have never been modern, only a single wheel of perpetually revolving day and night.

'So swim,' Ferny, I sing now. 'Worry not for me, and swim.'

My uncle turns back to me with a sadness in his eyes. It is the night's black, a truth of his loneliness, a truth, the sadness of the cows. And I see, see the roles we play here on the stage of the glen, farmer and poet, scion and flourish, man and woman; I see our destiny clear, Ferny and I. O yes, we are quite a pair, the sun and moon, with the river winding there like a solder's thread between us.

'Bless the pair and bless the portal-pool,' I sing. 'The pool a ground-eye, a lens into which we have plunged.'

So yes, we all need a model don't we. A book or a mushroom, the balance of a standing kangaroo. Or a pale slim body stepping off the night paddock into the cone-shaped shaft of a winter water portal. Into that portal come follow me down, until I'm looking you in the eye. The lean stretch of my body is left behind. I am a stimulant dissolving into the future's blood, as time becomes the spokes of waves wheeling around a cliffed point.

This fearlessness, the way I step out of the tippet and lace, the way I step into the molten wedding dress of here, a body absorbing all light and becoming as if one with the rock. I am in fact a human-shaped insert into the soily strata, finicked by worms both before and beyond my time, and thus I'm able to resonate into the future. The knowledge that someone will be here and listening to my glen translation is compensation for the warnings, the obvious questions I must echo. Like, who's going to save our glen?

And that is just for instance!

I know too how you like to read, moving through the gates, one after another, each paddock a book, and closing them behind you, but please, come with me now, and come with this. This open field of letters and marks, of letters and spaces I welcome you into, so you're moving sinuously between the letters, like me, Sarah, in the soil. In the soil of your pleasure it gets even deeperricher if you leave the gates open behind you. You can't be sure, after that, what voice will come and seek you from the past. Yes, the gates, either open or shut, are all in your mind, and you can let the grass flow both ways.

Or, if I may correct myself, it matters not whether you let the grass do any such thing at all. These voices will seek you regardless, and louder is their shout if they think you want to shut them out. So the old farm-lore doesn't always wash.

Shut the gate! Not with me, and not with Ferny, and not with what I have brought to Ferny, and what he protects in me. Together we are changing the place. How I'd like to whisper, as quietly as the groundcovers, knowing all the gates are open. I could sing so softly that you might feel it rather than hear it, with Ferny on the side, supporting me, handing me the drying Christy towel, introducing me to the local gathering on a Sunday afternoon, his soirees, presenting me as no more or less radical than the creek, which is the most radical of them all. Of all the soft-singers.

When Ferny was in Rome with Martin of Mendips they were often attending soirees with their set, some of which were held at a house in Viale di Trastevere where Dante Alighieri was purported to have lived. So that when Ferny arrived back from Europe, and even as he was delighted to see me and to fetch me from the cottage above the Big Cutting Hill, he was restless. In actual fact he only stayed here in the glen for a few days at first, for the time that it took him to prepare his swag and gear for an inland jaunt, and then he was straight off on the train from Winchelsea and out into the low scrubs north of Mildura. And when he returned three weeks later – with a quintet of emu eggs for the mantelpiece – he was talking of the Murray River as our Appian Way.

Then one day not long afterwards I watched him go off into the trees near what we call the Faerie Pool. He came back with a blush. I wondered who he found in there, someone no doubt quite unlike anyone we know around here.

His trip along the Murray, he confided to me much later, was at least in part motivated by the influence of Martin of Mendips, who had counselled the antipodean Ferny on how a visit to the centre of things could forever after illuminate the margins.

But there's no getting round the fact, and I know this well, that it's often lonely when one returns home with such a new centre – like the seeded core of an apple that no one wants to eat. So to peer through the dark fluted jackets of the ironbarks to see the naked lamp-white skin of two males making love in the soft dusk and on the soft insectivorous ground by the pool was to see one awfully realistic tableau. Ferny himself after all is an ample thing, a big strong bag of a man, fleshy, and bullock-boned, and this look-alike of our Martin-of-Rome, whom Ferny had divined like a muscled sylph out of the very ground, was even bigger. Together, grappling there, they made percussive sport of their friendship, a moving *fantasia* of some intensity, to offset no doubt the way our paddocks immure us in the silence of these provincial days.

There are many long nights in the homestead after all, but to see that blush on my kind uncle's cheek, as he emerged resetting his flies, was to know that the imagination can always thrive once a stimulus is sown. He is a realist after all, Uncle Ferny (as any soul who relies on the weather for their productions must be), and common sense most especially could see how, despite the black cattle and the worn-out boots, he resides here as if in a magical fairy dell.

So sing with me, sing with me, of the well-travelled grazier, alone in his homestead with his library and beer…

And sing with me, sing with me, of the recollections he carries, of warm nights swimming drunk in the *Trevi* with friends…

No, no, we cannot erase what we have done simply by returning: the cold Italian stone we have quarried from our heart must be put to use; we must all build our kingdoms, our palaces with this very stone, for the self is always royal, and always requires its queen.

Beyond the solstice, when I see the wattles blowing in the wind, I myself imagine other personages, like the mulga and the wilga in Ferny's beloved talisman book. And these personages, these plant-characters, are as much of the future as you. And thus I sing in a bloodbuzzing still point which allows access. I know too how tender it is, how delicate the complete stilling of momentum is, and thus I call to you, even as I call to the wattles, even when the wattles are outside the windows and I'm here alone at night, with the moon in my mirror, or when I was reading to the soiree.

Will you hear her, my subself wonders, will you sense the proportions of which she sings? The proportions she had to break herself in two to understand. To overstand. To sidewaystand and hoveraboveandwithinstand. So that when you too see the commonest wattles bobbling in the old winter of these words you'll feel her too. Standing there as if suspended in the water of the paddock portal-pool. Past midnight, before midnight, beyond midnight, in the deep soil of the old slow time.

Out I come then, eventually, like the seventh sister, the beautiful baby of the Pleiades, with Ferny handing me the glowing towel. I see him looking at my red nipples, how they've gone grey-brown in the darkness. I reach across, my arm pale as the branch of a manna-gum sapling, and yes, I am a model, like the glittering sisters in the sky that girls have aspired to be for all galaxial time. See her then (the subself whispers). Listen to the sound of soft abrasion as she rubs her body dry with the terrycloth towel.

Time is nothing much more than a series of adjustments. Try a chord, add a note here, take one away there. Press two keys together, two keys side by side. Or use your whole forearm. Time is what we choose to describe as music, what we add or leave without. The whole we're in the residue of.

    Listen to me using the Christy towel.

V

So ferny's book was about as familiar as a skua. So many strange voices in it, mock-German, Hibernian, women dressed as boundary riders, and all that talk of adjusting fences so as to let the burdened creatures of its pages in for a night of free grass. Turning them in towards happiness. That, in fact, was really the only commonsense thing about the book, the delight it took in seeking free fuel for those dewlapped denizens of Bovinia on whom the haulage of this country so relies. At any rate the pages held much humorous companionship for Uncle Ferny and were a lively and enigmatic seedbank for me.

But the poor tome had been read and re-read, folded, creased, jonked, split, tea-stained, manhandled and silt-scented by the paddocks, and therefore needed to be rebound before Ferny carrying it about the whole wide world as a vade mecum saw it loosen and waggle and stretch to the point where it all might unbind and fly away, leaf by leaf. Yes, I could easily imagine those leaves transformed as if into the white cattle-egrets who usually, when Uncle Ferny comes by with his oilskins flaring and in mid-recitation from the book, alight from our pastures at a tilt towards rainbows. Off they flutter high over the greening Run, just as the pages themselves might, unless we make the effort to have them all brought back into line: restitched, retaped, safely bound back into their single and original codex. Hence our trip to the Bookbinder in Moolap. To keep the flock within the fences, the pages in sequence inside the boards.

Of course we didn't walk all that way to Moolap, and these were the years well before the Cessna, so we rode leg-rested in the undecorative gig, with only the book swaddled in muslin as if it, and not us, might be the one to cry. Yes, only it held the wisdom and the truth, and it was waxpaper-clad too, and finally sheathed in calico against the onsetting winter. Thence to Moolap we went. Some thirty mile. As if with the Christ-child.

Such a journey was for me a shawled and shuddery survey of the nearby but seldom-seen ground. Aspirational Uncle Ferny, or Fernshaw Hutchinson *Esq.*, to whom, as you may have already ascertained, a trip overseas from these deckle-edged shores is like devilled kidneys to a new mother (ie: a great stimulus to the new requirements of life), saw the miles as they were laid out in front of us as childhood-country, in a way that Rome could never genuinely be. Drooping she-oaks. Billowing moonah. Bass Strait clouds tinged with Antarctic ice-green. A landscape rarely ever travelled but still a recognisable-in-particulars family member. *Endotic* is the word, opposite of exotic.

Yes, the puffs of pollen, the striking ochres of the sea cliffs bleeding into the ungazetted track-sides, clayey cuttings handcut and weather-fluted as we passed on through them, and the same hue beneath us, blood-orange tamping itself to the wheel rims, caking the spokes and socking the horse with earth-brightness. We stopped for watering and tongue sandwiches on the creek which insinuates itself through Bells Brae and then, on the far side of that creek, pressed on diagonally towards the palette of backlands and reedy swamps around the swanned ponds of the plain, where we cusped from ocean littoral to embayed indent, and finally arrived slow into the thick soupy dampness of the Bookbinder's grounds at Moolap.

As he beheld the scene and adjusted the reins accordingly, Uncle Ferny wondered aloud, 'But how on earth does he keep his pages dry?'

The answer stood in front of us. A house quite demonstrably squat and bluestone-built, with hardly a window, and thus armoured like a bank against the gleamy saltwet airs. We found ourselves peering through and beyond an empty train line to where five, and five alone, rainstained Polwarth sheep stood as if frozen in the Bookbinder's house paddock. Even despite the solidity of his bluestone domicile, you would never have picked it as the home of a bibliophile.

By the time we had crossed the tracks, removed the horse from the traces and tethered it by some fair-looking spinach, there was still no movement from within the house. When Jones the Bookbinder of Moolap did eventually open the door to us and I mentioned the suspended motion of the sheep by way of an opening pleasantry, his face lit up and he confirmed that yes, they were often still, so often and so still in fact that he thought it because they were direct descendants of the small clutch of stubborn sheep who, coming off the ship at Port Henry in the early 1840s, had refused to be switch-driven inland like the rest of the flock to Tarndwarncoort, where the Polwarth breed had subsequently made their famous name. Instead this small recalcitrant gang, after a bilious trip from across the Strait in the hold of the ship, had decided that they never wanted to go anywhere ever again. They were in fact rather 'excessively ruminant', Jones told us in a jocular fashion, immediately betraying his literary bent with the double entendre. 'If they had heels you could say that they had dug them in,' he joked. 'Sometimes,' he continued, 'I've fancied that these ones here might be attempting an impersonation of the books on my shelves. Dead-still my books are, doing nothing for anyone, just like the sheep, until someone curious or hungry enough decides to open them up and discover the nourishment within.'

Whatever the case, it seemed that Moolap was quite enough for this peculiar stamp of creature. In Moolap they had stayed and developed as a meditative precursor to the champion breed, thus furnishing our own arrival with the first of the many narratives to come by way of the Bookbinder Jones.

※

The sky was silver mercurial and it seemed the Bookbinder was too. He stood short and squat, with a colonist's low centre of gravity, and with carpenter's hands. The light in his eyes held an interior glow which, in combination with the sea and swamp glare all about, betrayed nothing of the gluey look I've noticed in the eyes of librarians I have known. On the contrary, he was not at all gummed-up but full of chat as he welcomed us inside.

Ferny and he passed bravely under the lintel of his establishment and abode, with me, the ornament, travelling in behind. We swung to the right out of a hallway which was akin to the large intestine of the house, entering a square Georgian room, its walls lined with shelving of books. There was a crackling fire, a large table with books and papers all across it, and a sash window looking out onto the sheep and field. Below the window, where the light was best, stood a workbench with blackiron press and clamps, and tools such as I'd never seen before. And beside this workbench, positioned singularly on the wall above the wainscot, was a lithograph of a local football game, the players caught in mid-flight, their knickerbockered knees and hooped arms up, it seemed, both for attack and protection. The only other picture on the walls was above the handsome timber fireplace, a large framed double page of script which Jones informed us later on was the penultimate scene of the Mabinogion, in one of the earliest editions and written, inevitably it seems, in Welsh.

Everything about the room spoke of the tales Jones could tell and the knowledge he had, and nothing conveyed this more than the shipping rope slung over the exposed rafter, hanging from which was an almost transparent object that looked like a human skull. It hung in midair between the large table and the fireplace so that when I was welcomed to my seat beside Ferny on the warm side of the table, it hovered ominously above me and I didn't know where to look.

Jones the Bookbinder saw my discomfort and kindly assured me it was well secured. He took his own seat on the window side of the table.

He began: 'Though not a scholar as such, I have my pretensions.' And glancing up towards the skull where it hung, still in the air above us, he said: 'And Gellibrand there is one of them.' He laughed. 'Otherwise known as "your worship".'

Ferny looked momentarily pale but then began to grin. He got the joke, and proceeded to explain it rather suddenly to me. Joseph Tice Gellibrand was a lawyer from Hobart, the attorney-general of the early Port Phillip Colony, who, in 1837, during the first years of the European settlement, and together with his solicitor friend Hesse, had gone missing while riding west from Geelong in search of suitable property. The two lawyers had never returned, and multiple rumours as to what had happened to them had abounded ever since. It was said, for instance, that the two lawyers had died deep in the Otways, Hesse from starvation and Gellibrand in the care of a local clan from the Cape. His skull was purported to have hung from the rafters of a farmhouse in the deep south for years after the event. As a consequence, Ferny explained, a local joke had developed whereby farmers, or even townsfolk in Geelong or Warrnambool, would hang an animal skull from a rafter in the house and call it 'Gellibrand'. Jones' 'Your Worship', was of course a further jocular reference to Gellibrand's profession. Indeed, it is said that before his disappearance he had a hankering to become a judge.

This was all very well, but the 'Gellibrand' hanging from the Bookbinder's rafters was nevertheless, and most unmistakably, a *human* skull. This fact alone gave our meeting a certain added gravitas, which Jones himself seemed well aware of, going so far as to inform us of the subtleties of this 'pretension' to wisdom whereby his own Gellibrand's lineage sat, as he saw it, in the philosophical and mythological appurtenances of the memento mori of yore, as depicted in literature and by the great painters.

Indeed, once he saw Ferny's grinning glance at 'Gellibrand', Jones began to outline the genealogy: Aristotle through to Holbein and Shakespeare's Hamlet, via the talking head of Bram in his old favourite the Mabinogion; there seemed no end to the memento mori that dwelt in the background of the skull hovering above my head. Thus it became clear, as Jones held forth, that he was indeed a scholar of sorts, and of some idiosyncrasy too, as well as being a tailoring craftsman of paper and leather bindings. And, as clear as that was, what was equally as unclear, and as unnerving, was the literal provenance of this skull which served as the rather bracing introduction and initial conversational lubricant of our little consultation.

With the history of the colony and the mortality of us all decidedly foregrounded, indeed dangling, in this workshop amongst the reeds and saltmarshes, Jones moved on to the second topic of interest, in no seeming hurry at all to want to talk about Ferny's book, ie: the job in hand.

No, firstly, and without so much as a mention of tea, coffee, whiskey, or even water to slake our thirst and restore our travelling bones, he wanted a full report on the 'state of play', as he put it, among those with sporting interests in our part of 'the Western world', as he also put it.

As I began to reflect upon the eclecticism of the Bookbinder's interests, Ferny, whose sporting interests were perhaps not quite as diverse as those of other men in the landscape, recounted the enthusiasm around our inlet for horseracing at low tide, for gameshooting, for the impromptu 'cross-country' round of golf, and for the sporadic fixturing of local football matches which rely so heavily on the transient labouring force of the shearing sheds, the haycutting, and the fishing calendar. 'That said,' opined Ferny, 'there are nevertheless a quotient of champions in our midst: treeclimbers, woodcutters, and, of course, strong surf and river swimmers.'

Jones of Moolap beamed at this last descriptive picture, and immediately cast his gaze in my direction.

'Oh the ocean, Miss Hutchinson,' he declared. 'Do you swim yourself, or row, or get out amongst it?'

'I love the river,' I replied. 'Particularly some of the freshwater pools on our Run. At least for swimming. The ocean is... well, it is pure music to me. I'm always leaning towards it.'

'Sarah is a composer, Mr Jones,' Ferny interrupted. 'And a poetess.'

'And what about whales then?' asked Jones, seeming to ignore the information Ferny had furnished him with. 'And the ambergris? Do you ever find it washed up on your shore?'

Ferny pushed both his lips and brow in thought. 'Ambergris, no. But whales, yes. Just the other day a humpback was breaching out from our rivermouth.'

'Ah, Miss Hutchinson,' Jones exclaimed. 'Now there's something to write about! You being the poetess and all. The symphonic leviathan! Anyhow, my guess is that you would never be short of subjects out there in the west.'

I nodded. 'Indeed, Mr Jones. And leviathans aside, ordinary life itself is such a rich stimulus, don't you think? I daresay it would be no different here in Moolap.'

The mention of the place – *Moolap* – seemed to tighten a synaptic screw in the Bookbinder's brain, as if suddenly he had perceived his ordinary cast and type of daily life and was brought back from general to local matters. He looked down at the tabletop and, without further prevarication, said, 'Right you are then. And so, the book. Let's have a look shall we?'

Ferny had been holding his Italian satchel in his lap all this time. Now he sprang up straight in his chair and flipped it open. He produced the book, wrapped as it was in the folds of muslin.

Clearing a space in the middle of his table, Jones created a plain of scuffed blackwood timber from his side of the room to ours. Ferny placed the book on the timber grain and unwrapped the coverings.

Sprung from its coddlings the book when revealed seemed green, greener than ever, virulently green. It appeared obvious, to me at least, as I looked at it in this new context, that it had itself accrued hues of the glen. It was clearly *loved*, and *used*, and thus misshapen to the oblong, but its boards were obviously of quality and its title of course had its own, somewhat republican, renown.

It was to Uncle Ferny's great surprise then that Jones of Moolap did not know the book at all. With eyebrows raised, and after a perfunctory 'May I?' the Bookbinder took this local Christ child of our flight to Moolap in his hands and inspected it with an intrigued curiosity.

'Mmm,' he said, gripping the tome and waggling its loose bindings in his hands. 'It talks and walks. And generates wildernesses we are yet to understand.'

The fact that the cover and boards were detached from the spine was straightaway exposed in its undergarments by the expertise of the Bookbinder. He inspected the still linen-white tapes and the discoloured joins where the glue had failed, and briefly snorted through his large nose. 'A wanderer,' he said, as if to himself. 'Remarkably loose for something still intact, and barely hanging on.'

'It may not appear to be the case,' Ferny ventured. 'But I cherish the book.'

Jones of Moolap ignored him. Instead he went diving amongst the frontispiece for the publishing, or should I say, the *printing* details. Finding these, he raised his eyebrows, expressing still further surprise that he didn't know the title, given the reputation of its nationally famous publisher. Flicking carefully through its pages then, he took in some of the quality of the prose. We waited in silence, as still on our chairs as the sheep outside the window, which I could spy with their jowls pointed across a blotch of bracken towards the worty baywaters. The Bookbinder read on, and on, until eventually, after what must have been five whole minutes or more, I could feel Ferny's incredulity, or amusement, becoming palpable, as he gazed sideways in my direction. I dared not look up however, in case Gellibrand was grinning at me too.

Strictly speaking a bookbinder need not be a reader, but it seemed, by the long pause we now endured, that Jones of Moolap was exactly that. Further minutes went by as he appeared to immerse himself in the narrative, the cadence, the vernacular humour, the historical detail, the bucolic autodidacticism, or whatever else my Uncle Ferny had no doubt enjoyed before him. He had begun at a point roughly midway through the extent of the book, but his ignorance of whatever action or characterisation had occurred in the pages previous did not seem to hinder his undivided immersion. Perhaps twenty minutes, perhaps half an hour went by in that manner. Quite obviously he had reading-lungs more capacious than a cormorant, and the Gellibrand skull itself was also as quiet and still as the closed books on the shelves. Indeed, it was just as Jones had suggested when we first arrived: despite the marine winds and the changeable light of the slushy surroundings, his establishment was somewhat of an inglenook in the marshes, a site of time-transcendence inhabited by obstinate sheep, raw-cut bluestone, and a solitary scholarly craftsman.

Finally Jones emerged from his amusement, not with a bounce but with a slow raising of his head.

'Aye, this book needs fixing,' he said. 'But it will take me some time. You can leave it with me of course?'

'Yes, of course,' Ferny replied. 'As expected, given its condition. How long do you think?'

I could feel the anxiety underlying Ferny's question, knowing as I did how much he depended on the book for company and amusement during the long nights on the Run. And during the days also for that matter. My own creative expressions, experiments and emanations were all well and good, and he enjoyed them, but it was precisely the continuity of the companionable solitude of his time with the book that could not be replaced. I daresay though that Jones picked up no trace whatsoever of Ferny's worry.

'Hard to say exactly,' the Bookbinder replied. 'Depending on the materials I may need. What say I place a call through to your Post Office when I'm ready. Angahook, isn't it. Without the velar nasal.'

'I'm sorry,' said Ferny. 'Without the what?'

'The *velar nasal*. Yes, the phonetic veil, at the beginning of the word, the way these things begin,' the Bookbinder said.

He opened his lips into a strange formation, his cheeks taut and his teeth exposed. '*Ng*angahook,' he said, drawing out the initial sound. 'You know. The *ng*. The colonial ear typically only hears what it wants to, and your place name is seldom spelt with its initial sound. Of course, this is predictable enough, given that our Australian alphabet starts with an A.'

'Ah, I see,' said Ferny, still a jot perplexed. 'The velar nasal. How interesting.'

'The sounds of the world are often crudely interpolated,' I added.

Jones of Moolap smiled. 'Yes, Miss Hutchinson. And the skeleton of English will always struggle to support the flesh and blood of a new land. Just ask my friend "Gellibrand" here. We are thus entrained. But I find my interest in Welsh does help.'

'To understand the place?'

He stared at me. 'That's it exactly. To understand the place. But never mind. Things get written down don't they? The printed page, when it is bound in boards, is akin to stone. But I often think of the things that don't get written down. What happens to them?'

'It can be as if they never existed,' I offered.

'Quite so,' the Bookbinder said. 'But this book,' he said, patting his palm on the virulent green of the jonkable boards in front of him, 'this book has, shall we say, a somewhat wider palette. From the briefest of looks I'd say there are things in here – sounds, voices – that may otherwise have stayed dropped in the grasses.' He paused, and smiled. 'So yes,' he said then. 'I enthusiastically consent to accept the commission.'

I turned to Uncle Ferny. The truth was that neither of us had for one moment considered that we may have undertaken the long voyage for nothing. We'd not thought it possible that the Bookbinder would turn down the job on the grounds that he didn't approve of the book. But such a possibility did seem implied by his last remark. Ferny, feeling my gaze, turned in my direction, and the two of us nodded at nothing in particular.

'That's settled then,' said Ferny, turning back again to our curious craftsman. 'I'm so glad you find merit in the book, and we'll await your call in *Ng*angahook. We're all for the wider view. Aren't we, Sarah?'

'Oh yes,' I said, 'and we are all for the music, the grace notes, the *velar nasal*.'

Jones of Moolap stood up and shook our hands across the eclectic ingredients of his table. 'Good then. And rest assured, Mr Hutchinson, I won't charge you like a wounded bull. Mr Gellibrand here will see to that.'

꧁

That night we stayed at a hotel in Geelong. The Velar Nasal Inn. Or so in mirth we nicknamed it over a dinner of corned beef and mashed swede, washed back with a sauterne. Jones of Moolap, with his sheep, his fortress of a house, his solicitor's skull and his passion for what would normally be 'dropped in the grasses', amused Uncle Ferny no end.

Over dinner Ferny was ruddy with laughter as he recollected our visit.

'And his nose, Sarah, his nose,' he exclaimed. 'The way he had it buried in the book like he was sniffing for his ambergris. Surely, I thought, he's going to say something soon. I was as fidgety as fleas. But I'm sure it slipped his mind that we were even there. I'd say old "Gellibrand" was more conscious of our presence than he was. And then, finally he lifts his head, only to regale us with his velar nasal! Excuse the French, but I was wondering what the fuck he was going on about!'

'Yes, but he had a point.'

Ferny waved his napkin. 'Oh no doubt, no doubt, and on our return visit I'll be sure to reassure him that back at the farm we've always spelt it different to the town; we've always spelt it well. As anyone can see by the sign at our gate. This I am certain would be thanks to old Grandfather Edward, who knew, after the fiasco of the bell on the hill, how to listen out for what is already there. But what a way for Jones to make the point! Just in the run of things like that, as if a bloody velar nasal was as common as a wool cheque. I tell you, the bush is a lonely place and lonelier still for anyone with any erudition or intellectual interest. It's like pork left out in the sun. It soon goes off.'

'Still, he approved of your book.'

'Yes, yes, I'm not saying he was *dumb*, far from it. But what a *character*. Binding his fascicles out there with the swans. And such a long way from Grub Street!'

We had taken two upstairs rooms overlooking the junction where the road west from Inverleigh meets the town. After dinner, having no gramophone, and no radio in those days, we returned to our respective domains, to write up our diaries, to read, and to reflect on a long and eventful day.

I pulled a chair up by the window overlooking the junction and gazed out into the starry moonless night over the square blocks and wide streets. My limbs were tired, and just as I sat down my monthly blood began to move as well. I went to my travelling case, and then to the bathroom, and when I returned to the chair at the window I looked out at the south-western sky in a different way.

No longer did the sky seem a veritable proscenium spanning the Geelong town blocks; no longer did it hit the pit of my stomach with the immensity of its silence. No, now over the rawly surveyed matrix of the town, over the settled dust of the front garden roses, over the blurry calligraphy of chimney smoke rising, and the silent printed facades of the commercial establishments, came a pattern of sounds, of syllables uttered as if from the soft palate of the sky.

With the hilled junction the hotel was perched upon serving as an arched tongue pressing up against the roof of things, the sounds were squeezed out thus. From every one of the many stars I could see came its own utterance, a subsound, a drone, a click, a trebley *thsk* in light. So that gradually as I sat there the sky began to fill with all the sounds that in the normal run of things I cannot hear. It was as if the world itself, its planetary bodies, were proving themselves to be in fact fundamentally fashioned from sound, and all the space between the stars was merely *resonance*. Time for the sound to travel in.

I listened in thrall to this unforeseen celestial music until I was distracted by moisture beginning to form in my eyes. Before long my cheeks were as if damp with dew. As the sky went on sounding its essential character into the south-west, from the high vantage point of the hotel's upper floor I felt as if I was borne out amongst it. This I slowly, and simultaneously, grew to realise, was an experience of an inner sight, or *site*, a novel version of the colony I had had to travel to see. Oiled by the excitement of the day, and even as my own blood drained, I understood that I was filling up as if with the ur-tones to which all languages aspire. The sky itself had been revealed as a melodic progenitor constantly playing us into existence.

As these sky sounds amplified until I almost had to block my ears for the cosmic din, I recalled how the Bookbinder of Moolap had spoken on such a theme that very afternoon, and that we were, my uncle and I, some thirty gluey miles from our glen, indeed accommodated in the Velar Nasal Inn. It was as if, by our jovial rechristening of the pub, every such sound we neglect to include, every phonetic veil, *ng*, ur-note or other unwriteable thing, had suddenly become available to me there.

Suddenly though, from down on the street below, a neighing horse and then the creaking tread of a wide bullock dray overburdened with bales broke the sonic reverie. The notes of the stars immediately vanished, as if into Himalayan cloud, and I was returned to the knocked-up town of wood and iron, of tightened harness and fastening grip, of things pushing against and issuing from the motherlodes of gravity.

Below me the dray passed on. I stood up to watch it crossing the junction. It had multiplied from one dray into a whole team now, a vernacular caravanserai, on its way no doubt to unload at the mills by the docks. The sight of this activity below, from my recently cosmic position at the high window, resembled nothing other than the industry of ants. And so the world cried out within me, and not for the first time, to be properly scaled sounding its essential character into the south-west, from the high vantage point of the hotel's upper floor I felt as if I was borne out amongst it. This I slowly, and simultaneously, grew to realise, was an experience of an inner sight, or *site*, a novel version of the colony I had had to travel to see. Oiled by the excitement of the day, and even as my own blood drained, I understood that I was filling up as if with the ur-tones to which all languages aspire. The sky itself had been revealed as a melodic progenitor constantly playing us into existence.

As these sky sounds amplified until I almost had to block my ears for the cosmic din, I recalled how the Bookbinder of Moolap had spoken on such a theme that very afternoon, and that we were, my uncle and I, some thirty gluey miles from our glen, indeed accommodated in the Velar Nasal Inn. It was as if, by our jovial rechristening of the pub, every such sound we neglect to include, every phonetic veil, *ng*, ur-note or other unwriteable thing, had suddenly become available to me there.

Suddenly though, from down on the street below, a neighing horse and then the creaking tread of a wide bullock dray overburdened with bales broke the sonic reverie. The notes of the stars immediately vanished, as if into Himalayan cloud, and I was returned to the knocked-up town of wood and iron, of tightened harness and fastening grip, of things pushing against and issuing from the motherlodes of gravity.

Below me the dray passed on. I stood up to watch it crossing the junction. It had multiplied from one dray into a whole team now, a vernacular caravanserai, on its way no doubt to unload at the mills by the docks. The sight of this activity below, from my recently cosmic position at the high window, resembled nothing other than the industry of ants. And so the world cried out within me, and not for the first time, to be properly scaled dinner, having no gramophone, and no radio in those days, we returned to our respective domains, to write up our diaries, to read, and to reflect on a long and eventful day.

I pulled a chair up by the window overlooking the junction and gazed out into the starry moonless night over the square blocks and wide streets. My limbs were tired, and just as I sat down my monthly blood began to move as well. I went to my travelling case, and then to the bathroom, and when I returned to the chair at the window I looked out at the south-western sky in a different way.

No longer did the sky seem a veritable proscenium spanning the Geelong town blocks; no longer did it hit the pit of my stomach with the immensity of its silence. No, now over the rawly surveyed matrix of the town, over the settled dust of the front garden roses, over the blurry calligraphy of chimney smoke rising, and the silent printed facades of the commercial establishments, came a pattern of sounds, of syllables uttered as if from the soft palate of the sky.

With the hilled junction the hotel was perched upon serving as an arched tongue pressing up against the roof of things, the sounds were squeezed out thus. From every one of the many stars I could see came its own utterance, a subsound, a drone, a click, a trebley *thsk* in light. So that gradually as I sat there the sky began to fill with all the sounds that in the normal run of things I cannot hear. It was as if the world itself, its planetary bodies, were proving themselves to be in fact fundamentally fashioned from sound, and all the space between the stars was merely *resonance*. Time for the sound to travel in.

I listened in thrall to this unforeseen celestial music until I was distracted by moisture beginning to form in my eyes. Before long my cheeks were as if damp with dew. As the sky went on and done, to be heard and sung, in its true interchangeability. And then, as if in reply, came the curse of a drover below. 'Woah, Bonty,' he cried, in the vowels of the long paddock. 'Agin, an' on there, Butt'n an' Joe!'

I closed my eyes and opened them again in a slow blink, hoping to be somehow returned to what I'd heard. And sure enough, as my eyes opened, there they were: the groaning beasts, the rustling bales, the grinding wheels, the clanging axles, and the men, all come in through the night of the western road. But it was as if they'd come in along their own sweary track through the stars.

That music I heard when looking out the high hotel window on the evening of our visit to Jones of Moolap is forever with me now, as a correspondence perhaps of my own urge to music, my urge also towards the undulant poetic line, the thread of creek running across the glen of the page. And thus I never feel entirely quiet until I am at the very centre of sound, of my own sound, a concert sung as if in unison with those celestial stars, the way they drop to the ground in the daylight, as trees, bushes, grasses, rocks, animals, and *us*. Pure notes ring out of this sound-made matter, and such is my joy that I long to *match* them, to meet such inborn music with my own sonic kiss, my own inner bell forged from the materials all around me.

VI

Upon our return home to Ngangahook, while out walking on the road by the creek one late afternoon, I saw through the low western glare two baggy spaniels approaching, with wagging tails and broad gummy smiles for all the winter wetness about. Duck dogs, I thought, spaniels in their element. And then behind them came the wife of Selwyn Atchison sitting high on her chestnut, and just as happy-seeming in the scene as her dogs.

'What a lovely evening, Sarah,' she said as we grew closer together, and I agreed, saying something like, 'Yes, well the dogs seem happy. But where is the collie?'

Although it's fair to say I couldn't imagine Sara Atchison letting her tongue loll out the side of her mouth like her dogs did – she was far too collected for that to be the expression of her joy – nevertheless her tone of voice did betray a touch of exhilaration at the gleaming evening. There was too that moment when the two of us were undecided as to whether we should prop there for a chat or keep moving on, letting our friendly greetings suffice.

But, just as I sensed she was about to tap her heel into the flank of her horse, I had the urge to canvas her opinions about the bell. 'Sara, has your husband made any further enquiries about the town acquiring a bell? I know he's spoken to Ferny about it.'

'Sarah,' she replied, tightening up the reins, 'I believe he's obsessed! He's forever on about it. Any time there's a little drop in the wind, any time the birds stop singing, any time you can hear a pin drop, any quiet moment I get of stillness and peace is soon ruined by Selwyn rabbiting on about the bell. "Listen, Sara," he says, "listen to that. What do you hear? Nothing. That's right, *nothing*. And right on the hour. Can you imagine how wonderful it would be to hear the bell in a moment like this? Imagine the charm! The way it would bring us all together. And imagine how useful it would be!"' She shook her head with chagrin.

I had not expected such a willing outburst against her husband and was quite taken aback. I realised though what the state of her present affairs must be. Obviously a large part of her exhilaration at the evening had to do with the distance she'd managed to put between herself and her perseverant husband. It was the bronzing emanation of the light through the glen to be sure, the firm feeling of her legs astride the horse yes, but it was more than that. It was freedom she sought from her frowning man, and this freedom would be with her for the length of the ride. Just as he was no doubt commanding his collie to calibrate their stock down to the most precise moment and area, she was taking the pleasure in allowing the loose and slobbering smiles of her duck dogs to spill over. They were out for a stroll, a gambol, a run and splash, in the lomandra, the common reed and other slushy rushes. And although Sara Atchison had her rifle slung across her back, I felt sure she had not used it. For it was in the preternatural quiet of a shot unfired that we had encountered each other, though as much as this was to my liking I cannot take the praise. It was Sara Atchison after all, on glad leave from her husband, who had not fired the shot.

'Well Ferny and I were discussing the issue after your husband's visit, and we see benefits either way.'

'Is that so?' She grinned. 'What do you see as the advantages of not having a bell?' She laughed. 'I only ask so I have a little more ammo to fire at him when next he is harping on about it.'

I smiled fondly at her humour. I felt rather honoured too by her forthrightness. It was almost as if I'd found a new friend, though I couldn't say why or how this had occurred. I remembered that Sara Atchison had attended our last Sunday soiree with her sister Ada, and Ada's German husband Ted Smautf. That's of course where I had met her, but my audience that day were polite. As in *silent*. I would never have thought our relations would evolve any further. Well anyway, she must have liked what she heard. Either that or Sara simply felt a sense of the potentially liberating horizon underscoring it all. Had I then become a motif of freedom for her, I wondered, as no doubt to others I most definitely appeared as 'mad as a cut snake'. Whatever the case, the pair of gang-gangs I noticed twirling in the ironbark by the creek bridge would have heard two rather similarly named women having a friendly and even mildly conspiratorial chat, before eventually saying a fond farewell to each other and carrying on into a bell-less world.

What, indeed, you might ask, does a bird hear when a bell is sounded? Some double-bird, extraterrestrial, or inconceivably bold? A monster song, too firm, too perfect in its unseasonable consistency? For even the varying bells, the bell-rituals, the bell cadences of particular occasions and calendared combinations, surely lack the personality of timbre one hears from a bird. Perhaps to introduce a bell into the inlet would be to introduce a head-bird, or a shadow-bird, in the chill of which all the other birds would then be forced to dwell. Or perhaps it would be as electric light is to the candle, lacking the permeable qualities which respond to temperature and wind, ever reliable yes, but unfeeling, unassailably and constantly so. It would be a human marker, that's for sure, but would it be *for all*? Indeed even back then, in those years before the Great War, this new and already suspicious federation of a nation had laid its demarcations white and strong. Most demonstrably so. But it has always been worth remembering that the fences that make good neighbours are no more than shitting posts to birds. Indeed my brief meeting with Sara had confirmed how bells could be a torture, a preparation for a world more like a nightmare than a dream. For the birds would not be silenced of course, so worse, they may become confused.

Such then were my fears as I walked across the bridge and into the rose-gold gloaming. And I daresay it is enough perhaps for you to consider such ideas at least; you who, in reading these pages, also might risk the impossible relief of the gang-gang's smile, twirling there among the tear-shaped leaves, its creaking whiskey cork in dialogue with the late-light river's trill.

❧

I can't so much as take a prayer in church, a homily or psalm, but when it comes in other ways I'm all ears. John Ferguson had a knack for technology and also for the way a little bugling can bind us all. He began to roneo a sheet, just one each season, summarising some notable events of the area and signalling some dates worth remembering in the future. In one sheet (which as yet he had still not titled, though some clear soul suggested 'The Angahook Cry') he had taken it upon himself to commission a reflection from the intrepid coastal Catholic priest, who passes through and gives a mass once every six weeks or so. So here is what Father Farrell offered up:

Jesus began a journey, which is our journey. We walk on his way. He is the road we walk on, our companion on that road, and he is also the destination to which the road leads us.

I was seated at our big oval dining table, in front of the even bigger windows which look across paddocks to the trees along the creek, and further on to the northern upslopes of the bush, when I noticed Ferguson's sheet beside the candle. Among the other notices, my eye was immediately drawn to the priest's contribution.

Prayer, companionship, study and willingness to go beyond our self-imposed boundaries will always be the stuff of Christian life, for the simple reason that Christ leads us on the road. If we could see this journey of the Christian, it would seem strangely chaotic. We walk off the road, get lost, yet somehow by God's grace and mercy we find our way back. Sometimes we refuse to move at all, we discourage other travellers on the way. We forget the basic rule of any journey, which is to put one foot in front of the other. We look back at the places we have been, we fear the places that God may call us to pass through.

Whether it was because I had just come in from the garden, where I had been washing mucky grey aphids off broccoli and clipping dead strands from herbs while noticing, and not for the first time, how passing island-clouds resembled white mosses of the sky and thus how all things, even the aphids and the herbs, rely not only on sun but also on moisture to survive, and how we, like the gum trees, store up the moisture we are given, the spiritual moisture of analogy, parable, metaphor and all other such connectors and likenesses; yes whether it was because of that very set of likenesses I had just experienced in the garden of the house-paddock and the garden of my mind, I do not know. Whatever the case, I fixed on the words of the priest in a way I would not have had I been cajoled, if only for some social reason, into the church service.

Here I am then, at the service of the glen instead, the way its pasture is in dialogue with the bush and heath around, the clear sight of its valley the pluming breath and pause in the otherwise laden poetic line of the place. It makes it easier for us here to digest the world and also to receive its nourishment into every cell of our being.

Thus was I open and receiving on the quiet midweek morning, alone in the house with my pot of tea at the oval table, my own face being reflected in its sheen, as I was also reflected in the priest's words.

It was his understanding of Jesus, that barefoot man from the dry dust of Palestine, that did it. And then how all of us, in our most naked selves, are always more than one thing, always capable of being the traveller, the destination, and the very road our travelling self journeys along, at one and the same time. Normally, of course, the constraint of moral religion has no traction for either me or my buoyant uncle, but here, in the season's newsletter, was the grace that is otherwise peddled, repurposed, diluted. There it was in its purest form.

Yes, I said internally, as I held the sheet in my hands and read. I am the soil, the blade of grass, the air it exhales, the drop of dew that is poised upon its tip. My body is a limit, the sharp edge of the blade; my spirit was born to worship and transcend.

And yet that drop of dew in which my whole world is reflected must fall.

To understand this, this effortless kinship between the road, the travelling, and the destination, is to understand why I write as I do in these pages, across mortal bounds and Time's dreary decades. It is to know why I must access our kinship as in a waking dream, to talk to you from the springs of a shared predicament.

The ocean is prayer, the river is companionship, and the 'study and willingness to go beyond our self-imposed boundaries' is the only way to understand how we come to be kin. It is, on the one hand, a connectedness, and on the other not at all, for we are hardly separate. The companionship washes into the prayer and in turn its vastness, the endlessness of ocean prayer, renews our river. And here we are, dear reader, supposedly divided by time, *insipid time*, time and space that is meant to make our friendship impossible, yet here we are, still pulsing in the process.

According to Father Farrell – his words wedged as if miraculously between an account of the April supply boat's mysterious non-showing, and an announcement placed by the Bell Committee about a meeting in July – the Holy Trinity involved three things. But not the three you would expect. Not the Father, Son and Holy Spirit, rather the road, the companionship to be had upon it, and the destination to which it leads.

I sipped my tea and read the piece again, and couldn't help but wonder how it would be interpreted in the town. Just as from time to time I fall to pondering how, or if, I myself am being interpreted. It made me giggle then, the way the circuits of the mind can so easily place us on an equal footing with one that others would describe as god. Audacious me! Allowing nature to run on in its natural way like that!

THE BELL OF THE WORLD

※

While his talisman tome was with the Bookbinder in Moolap, Uncle Ferny had been reading Ruskin and I noticed he'd been a touch lacklustre around the farm. 'Do you know,' he said one morning, as I was preparing my breakfast in the kitchen, 'for much of his writing life Ruskin shared his own local two miles square with at least 200 furnace chimneys surrounding him on every side?'

It was barely seven o'clock, but for the farmer in Ferny this of course was a late hour to rise. He was usually up even before the magpie begins its nesting tune in late winter, well before the kookaburra announces the rising ladder of the light. He would be washed and fed and out on the pasture before either bird had left off their song in favour of the hunt. But not this morning. Still in his claret dressing-gown, he asked me what I knew.

'No, I didn't know that, Ferny. Did you get some sleep?'

He grumbled something in reply and waited by the stove for the kettle to boil.

'Were you right with the wood?' he asked, after a pause. He had had a woodbox built on the outer wall of the kitchen so that you could easily open an especially large cupboard to access the supply.

'Yes,' I said. 'The cupboard is so much more convenient.'

'Good,' he said. 'There's no need for you to be out there in your slippers in the dew.'

I looked down at my feet and the thick grey woollen socks that housed them. 'But I don't have slippers,' I said, in an amused voice.

'Well no,' he said. 'And that's my point. Can't have you going out there in the cold in your socks.'

'But Ferny, I would put on my boots. I always did. Before you built the wood cupboard.'

'Over 200 furnace chimneys in two square miles,' he repeated. 'A man with such an eye as he had, with his *senses*, must have been driven half mad. And this was years ago I might add, in the early '70s. They were still panning for gold up in Bendigo back then!'

'You do know though, Ferny, that I've never worn slippers. Nevertheless, I know that feeling when you put your feet in cold gumboots of a morning. They've such thin soles, and all cold rubber. The cupboard really is a masterstroke.'

He looked at me, first confusedly then fondly, as he realised I was trying to ameliorate his obvious despair.

He took the kettle off the stovetop and for a few minutes nothing needed to be said. The logs shifted in the firebox, and Ferny poured his preferred morning cup of chicory.

Just then the world seemed birdless outside, almost as if the sun was about to be eclipsed, casting the glen into a premature darkness. But would it have been premature, I ask you? In the mood Uncle Ferny was in such a cataclysm may have seemed right, just, and even good.

As a wattlebird squawked, Ferny looked up from his cup and said, 'You know, Sarah, sometimes I feel so far away out here. So cut off.'

I nodded. 'A long way from those 200 furnace chimneys.'

'Well yes,' he said, 'now that you make a point of it. Yes.'

'Yes, and so cut off from the discussion of what it may all mean.'

At this he pushed his chin forward on the stalk of his neck. In pure eagerness. 'Well yes. That's right! Sometimes I'm sure we live here as if in an illusion.'

'But there are some furnace chimneys in Melbourne. Even one or two in Geelong.'

'Yes, but one or two. Surely you can comprehend the juxtaposition, Sarah? A man of Ruskin's sensibility, the man who wrote *The Stones of Venice*, who declared there is no wealth but life, who pored over the finest human productions as if his eyes were microscopes – there he sat, surrounded on all sides by the polluted motifs of the era. Over 200 bayonets thrusting their filth into his cherished skies. This was not a case of a few dribbles of smoke floating out over Port Phillip. This was a catastrophe! And it has only worsened since.'

'I see. And so here we are.'

He sat back on his chair, hard against the orchid that he'd had Old Ben Hetherly carve into each item of the dining furniture. 'Yes,' he said. 'Here we are.'

Although Ferny had his back to the large windows, I had sat down at the table such that I could look out onto the pastures. Shrouding the green of the glen the blood-black fluted jackets of the ironbarks seemed almost somnolent now. Yes, like a sorrowful framing of the green.

'Tom Browning writes to me from Paris, Ed Greeves from Saint Petersburg, Severin Crawley from Washington. They are all modern men. And they all say the same. Where is it all heading?'

Affected at two removes by Ruskin's sensibilities I could see, suddenly and quite starkly now, how the scene I was looking at through the window was, at least in relative terms, somewhat antique. A plush pasture that had never known the fumes of anything but its own timber burning in the bush or fires like ours to warm the hearth. And this green field framed in a fringe of fluted blood-black, the ironbarks, the ngangahooks, with their lemony star-flowers brightening the winter ground. A few healthy cattle mooning about, their hides shining in a dark bowerbird blue. The solder thread of the clear running creek just glimpseable through the background trees.

Visioned through the homestead glass like this, as if in a painting, and especially in contrast to Ferny's lamentations, the scene did indeed have something of a storybook air, that might in fact deem it an irrelevancy to all that seemed pertinent to our cultural time. But it struck me too how such a critique simply vanished like the heat from the kitchen stove once you stepped out into it. The glen I mean. Even despite Grandfather Edward's disillusion when it came to the treatment of the Wadawurrung, we were surely at one remove the way we'd settled there, in colonial comfort. We were split into two creatures, each of us, and thus my Uncle Ferny and I were four. Cultivated, yes, *and* driven mad by our lust. Educated, yes, but nevertheless knowing nothing more edifying than a crush of blue-gum leaves brought to the nose by our own muddy hands. And not for the first time, as I gazed out onto this view so sadly inflected with the *fabrications* of our culture, this woodcut vista through the window that had, via Ruskin's visionary gloom, recoloured the health of our situation, I understood that the work I had to do, perhaps the very reason for my life, was somehow to consider a uniting of the two ways of being. To make the *four* of my Uncle Ferny and I return to *two*. To remove the screen between home, place, and us or, better put, to allow the natural exchange between perceiver and perceived to move in both directions, to dissolve the relativist antique view and bring the intervention of the kangaroo, the wallaby, its sound of thuds, the openness of a possum's eye, *inside* the homestead. Hence the riverstones I had recently placed in my piano, the pigments I had brushed onto its soundboard, the creekslung vertebrae fixed to its hammers and strings. We had, I firmly felt, to get out of the western book, to rub its text with salted light, allow the pinkness of the heath, the wild and ferny worlds upstream, to *intervene*.

'You've been in your study too long, Ferny. And you're no doubt missing the Furphy while it's in Moolap. You've replaced it with another, but our library here's the world. Read *it*, while your book's away, not Ruskin. For isn't that what he did? He absorbed just what he saw.'

Ferny looked at me as if he was quite stunned. Had I misunderstood something essential in what he'd said? Could he not comprehend my wilful ignorance, this embrace of a backwater, the delight in being a backwoods woman? Or was it just that his lack of sleep and his stupor of obsessive study had worn him down to the point that his mind had emptied like a bowel?

It seemed not. 'When you were with Maisie, in the cottage beyond the Big Cutting Hill,' he said to me then, 'what did you see, in your mind, in the world, that gives you such *unlikely* modernity?'

He was looking grave now as the question hung. He sought my response in the same way we want to hear, from above a waterfall, the multimotioned water resolve into the firm splash of the pool below. He understood this was a privacy he had not pried into before, but surely too he knew that, as was the case with the waterfall, the answer he was waiting for had already arrived. It was in fact *always* arriving, in everything I did and said, as surely as the waterfall is never divisible via analysis of Time or Sound but is continually making music in the pool.

And yet, it was early in the morning, and he was tired. So I did not dismiss him. I thought for a while, dipping a pannikin into the music of memory's pool, and told him this:

'I felt a great scream go through nature.'

I paused.

'And then I found a great light was breaking in my mind.'

VII

The Subtle Track Of The Wallaby Mind
or When The Naturalists Came To The Glen

Four times wallaby is twelve
Yet you're interested or compelled
to delve beyond a pattern put upon
Such a free but ruly thing
The reach of their bound if measured
Brings incidental pungent treasure
to the noses of visiting naturalists
Otherwise bedded down.
Even the soft thud of paws
In the night-heath behind our guestrooms
The starlight whisk of bracken
As they close their journals to sleep
Lets them in on the secret. They dream
As the wallabies inspire, leap
As they transect their precise demesnes
Where now it is we who take dictation.
Thus the mythologies at breakfast.

Spawning formulae over teapot & sausages
Only discrepancies remain as residue
Of the moon's sepulchral lore.

⁂

Not long after that morning when Ferny asked his first question of me about my time in the cottage beyond the Big Cutting Hill, I decided to ameliorate his situation somewhat by enabling a group from the Victorian Field Naturalists to come to the glen to undertake some research, ie: to observe and annotate the flora and fauna of the very illusion which Ferny and I had been at pains to discuss. I made initial enquiries through Uncle Ferny's farm manager, Jem Morgan, whose wife Georgina I knew was an enthusiastic botanist and had been a paid-up member of the 'Field Nats' for some years. The intellectual stimulus a visit of that sort would involve might, I thought, act like a tonic on Ferny, who could discuss his joys and fears with people whose interests in the nuances and nomenclatures of natural beauty would inevitably mean they shared at least some of his fears, given the obviously fumey progress of Western civilisation within which their enthusiasms were set. Of course I made no mention of this ulterior motive to Georgina, who could do without worrying that Ferny was about to up and leave once again to England or Russia, and this time to get his hands dirty, so to speak. No, all I told her was that there would be rooms in our guest wing for some half a dozen naturalists who could spend a weekend, or even a week if they had the leisure, investigating the animal and plant life of the Run. I did however make mention of a notion, at the back of my mind, suggesting that perhaps the Field Nats could themselves suggest ways in which we could enshrine the property as some form of Sanctuary, as opposed to an 'illusion', for the benefit of its creatures and its plants, and ultimately, for us as their apex cousins.

And so it was that through Georgina Morgan's connections and correspondence a group of four of the more inveterate Field Nats arrived by Cobb & Co coach one Friday afternoon, having caught the train from Melbourne to Winchelsea.

Such was their enthusiasm for Georgina's invitation that, between my making the initial suggestion to the Morgans and the arrival of the coach, there had elapsed only three short weeks. I soon learnt that this small coterie of the Field Nats, a group who all hailed from the banks of the Yarra River in the Melbourne suburb of Ivanhoe, were without exception supported by private incomes, which at least in part explained their surprising readiness to make the trip. Nor was there either any question that they would stay only a weekend. It was clear from the start of their brief correspondence with Georgina that a whole week it would be, and as the news came through, the prospect did indeed seem to cheer Ferny up no end on at least two counts: one, that he might be able to get some extra labour on board to help him prune the orchard; and two, that the Field Nats' visit would allow him some scope for the organisation of one or two social events, the visitors providing enough exotic curiosity to bring the locals out of their winter burrows for a good look, ie: a freshly sceptical assessment of city folk, the likes of whom seldom visit our region. 'We'll have a booze-up, Sarah,' Ferny declared. 'What do you think? Maybe we'll even drag out ol' Johnny Briggs and his Magic Lantern.'

Thenceforth Ferny seemed to have no trouble in putting Mr Ruskin aside. Instead he got about the glen with added scientific enthusiasm, noting its topographic dimensions, scrawling observations in his notebook on the velocity of the creek, as well as the estimated age of its oldest of old trees, the variety of grasses, and a current approximation of the line where the saltwater of the ocean met the freshwater coming down from the hills. Such was his anticipation of the mentality of Science, with a capital S, that was about to descend upon us, that he even donned a decidedly Scientific-looking wide-brimmed white hat as he ventured out each morning, in exchange for his typical battered driving cap, which despite its short peak, its mottling and fungal perforations, he had long said suited him in all weathers. This new hat however was a safari-style addition he had picked up not on safari but in a marketplace on a visit to the Moorish city of Palermo. As there is not much pure white at all in the palette of our winter landscape, the hat made Ferny as conspicuous in his own field of work as he had ever been.

I, on the other hand, as soon as the telegram confirming the date of the visit had arrived, was forced to retire to my room with a terrible Bass Strait cold. And in my heavy-boned, infirm, snivelling state, I had not Ruskin nor Furphy but old Gellibrand's skull come to greet me in my dreams, talking to me there of his burial place and of his own ol' beaver hat which, along with his folded trousers, provided a soft pillow for his head in the grave his kind local caretakers had provided.

The emergence of such ingredients is, of course, typical of the weave of dreams. That association of hats, first Ferny's then Gellibrand's (of which I'd learnt over dinner at the hotel in Geelong) had come in the course of my cold to show me a pattern of my own making. For surely you can see, from your vantage point, how both pastoral development such as that with which Gellibrand had been quite hellbent, and Science, which allows the acquisitive Child in Man to abstract from despairing truth in favour of an orderly statistical ordinance and diagnostic of the land, are as sisters stitching the same quilt. Gellibrand's skull had come to tell me so, of that I could be sure, and as I woke from the dream he hung from the rafters of my mind like a metronome, squaring the normal undulance and variation of Time's passage, and squaring also my body's music. I began to worry that in my attempt to help Ferny from his fume-fed doldrum I had *engendered* the most inane and distracting of enterprises. Why, I asked myself, sitting glumly now at my own desk just as my uncle had sat glumly at his own, why was I not content, indeed courageous enough, to leave Ferny's notion of our glen as an irrelevant idyll to its own evolution, so that we could more deeply understand its eternal relevance by indwelling there, so far from the furnace chimneys, and inside the incontrovertible truth that it is our own consciousness that makes the world. Always. But no, I had to entertain him so, like some fretting aunt, as if, yes, the male is a child and the female always shielding him from what he should know best. I will now wait for the naturalists, I told myself, coming out of the dream, like a river waits for a dam! I had a headache too due to the rapacious colonist keeping Time in my head. And the skull swung on, back and forth, back and forth, so I could hardly even bear to look out, as if with its eyes, through the window onto the weeping grass of the Run.

Still, the naturalists were coming, it was all arranged, and I would not risk interfering for a second time with Ferny's moods. And anyway, as I've written before, we can't go back with respect to *History*. Lunge all you like but you'd be better served by *listening*. Indeed, the essence of *Herstory* is to know that all things are cyclical and that the Western God made Time in order to shield us from the potent way in which everything is connected, everything happening all at once, and everywhere.

This, can I add, is for me where the piano-poems come in. There is no statistical record after all of the incidence of colonists' skulls acting as metronomes in the thoughts of a young lady's head. And yet, a genuinely multimotioned creation can acknowledge it with ease. Our imaginations are as fluent as the creek, as nimble as the wagtail, as dark as any space between the stars. And thus I sat, with the universe in my pen, and with my Bass Strait cold, day upon day, until the Field Nats arrived.

※

Joe Badger, who drove the coach each week from Winchelsea, has been the only person on this earth who ever deigned to call me 'Hutch'. I was out by the gate on the day of the Naturalists' arrival – with a handkerchief still in the pocket of my dress, but feeling much more worldly – when I heard the jingling of his horses' traces, the bumping of his spokes, and his unpretentious cry. Looking up from the fading of the crimson heath under the creekbank trees I saw his coach of the same reddish colour, with the luggage and equipment of its passengers strapped on top of the roof as well as on the ledges provided at the coach's rear. I swear there were more poles and nets and boxes and traps, as well as suitcases, than the Goncourt brothers took to Egypt!

My first thought was that Ferny would love all the gear. Though he is not exactly a slave to the modish he nevertheless enjoys almost everything up-to-date, and the equipment spilling out all over Joe Badger's vehicle had certainly an air of that.

'Perhaps I should come through the gate and up to the house, Hutch, whaddya think?' Joe called out. 'I mean, given the extent of the cargo and all.'

'Certainly, Joe,' I agreed. 'And good day to you all, by the way.'

A young man with red side whiskers had stuck his head out the side of the cabin to take in the surrounds of the Run. I could see at least two more people, who, surprisingly, seemed to be women, looking out demurely from within.

'Hello,' said the young red-whiskered man to me, as Joe Badger jumped down from the coach to help me place the walking-boards over our hardwood cattle grid. I smiled in reply, ignoring Joe's request that I desist helping him. Together we lifted the boards from where they were permanently stored in the gate-shed nearby, and placed them over the grid.

'I'm Joe too,' said the young man from the coach. 'And you must be Sarah.'

'That she is,' said the older Joe. 'And don't you bother yourself, young fella, I'm sure the two of us can manage.'

Suddenly awoken then to what may have been expected of him, the younger Joe made to step down from the coach. His driver bade him stay. In a trice Joe Badger was back up in the forebench and, with a ripple of the reins and a click in his cud, had steered the Cobb & Co across.

At the house it emerged that young Joe's companions were not the females I'd imagined after all. As the coach came to a stop under the gums by the garden, down stepped three other gentlemen, all a little older than young Joe, all fine-boned and delicate looking, which may have explained my prior misapprehension. From the house Ferny emerged too, obviously having heard the horses and the voices. He greeted Joe Badger, tipped him as well, prompting the Cobb & Co man to take the voluminous scientific luggage to the entrance of the guest wing.

'Good trip, Joe?' Ferny asked. 'No rain at least, but how was the road?'

'Bad.' Joe Badger smiled. 'But nothing to stop us. In July that's pretty good.'

Ferny turned then to the four naturalists, three of whom who were busily brushing themselves off after the up-and-down ride. Apart from young Joe they all looked a little shaken up by the trip. And I could see by the mud on their trouser cuffs and jackets perhaps why. Joe Badger was, as usual, casting a rosy glow on recent events. And sure enough, after brief and rather clipped introductions, the Cobb & Co man, whose disposition to view the world in dry terms no matter the extent of the quagmire, admitted to having to enlist his passengers' help with 'shovel and muscle' on four separate occasions between Wensleydale and the descent to the coastal inlet. Ferny couldn't help laughing at this – which, I suspect, didn't initially enamour him to the newly arrived guests.

'Still,' Joe Badger said phlegmatically, 'you know how gluey it can get. And you know last week we didn't even bother to try getting through. But I've never missed more than one week in a row. The show must go on eh, Ferny. Even in July.'

Ferny nodded enthusiastically. Then, turning to the naturalists, whose frowns were deepening with every passing moment, said, 'Please, fellas, all of you, please come inside.'

Before I draw a picture of these three slim characters and their red-whiskered mascot I should first make you aware of how different they were, in stature and temperament, to what Georgina Morgan had led us to expect. According to Georgina, the Field Nats were typically spirited and tirelessly intrepid types, for whom providing physical assistance to the coach as it traversed the ridge of the Otways would have been merely part of life's adventuresome texture. They would be an intelligent lot, to be sure, but they would also be, according to the picture she drew, hale, hardy, wide-hipped, and as capable of extra-urban extemporisation as any coterie you'd be likely to meet.

To say then that my initial impressions of the group that had arrived in the glen were varied, would be to put it rather mildly. The way young Joe had not seen himself clear to assist with the cattle-grid boards was understandable due to his innocent thrall with the nature of his new surrounds, and he did, in both his countenance and effusive energy, seem personable enough; but the fact that his companions were so slight, so prim, and, how shall I put it, so seemingly *terrorised* by simply coming over the ridge and down off the Saddle, was a shock rather than a mere surprise. My heart sank somewhat, as any hopes for pulling Ferny out of his malaise with open-eyed and robust company were rather doused by my instantaneous fear that this anaemic lot would send him straight back into it. Poor Ferny would become as bogged as the coach, and these naturalists would certainly not be the ones to dig him out. They seemed uptight, and, what's worse, as they alighted at the house they seemed entirely disinterested in the natural surroundings. I stood a few paces off, having walked up the long drive in the rear of Joe Badger's coach, and noted with some surprise how the eyes of the three senior members of the party did not so much as take in a gumleaf at their feet or a passing cloud above the scene. Instead they were all about the mud and dust on their garments, and although I was careful not to betray any scepticism to Ferny, I could not have entirely disguised my assessment.

If he noticed though he did not give me even a sideways look, but rather followed the naturalists up the front steps to the verandah with a decidedly hospitable spring in his step.

Not for one second has Ferny ever expected of me the usual duties a woman would perform with superiority around the house. This is due of course to the fact that I came at first to the Run precisely because I was apparently not minted from any typical or customary behavioural template, but also in part because after my crisis up beyond the Big Cutting Hill, the place was designated to be an untitled sanatorium of sorts rather than a bachelor uncle's farm where a woman's touch was needed. Upon my arrival however, we struck a workaday balance that turned out to be rather more traditional than we might have expected. For it was the happy case that by the time I reached the glen the great light had indeed broken over the mantle of my mind, dissolving my distress as if by metamorphosis, so that my ability to *receive* the place was not only unencumbered but also well prepared in a freshly fashioned self. Nor either did I need to adopt any suffragettish stance, Uncle Ferny being so progressive and artistically curious, and so futuristic when it came to my specific potential. And so I found I could blend my meditations and sonic experiments with the comfort of achieving daily tasks, at the sink and mangle, by the clothesrope strung between northfacing trees, with the broom and mop, the hot iron and the stove. When the naturalists arrived it seemed perfectly natural therefore that I would mask my unconventionality and, by implication, Ferny's, by arranging flowers in their rooms, lavender and bluegum water, their bedlinen, stiff towels, and other daily needs. This, Ferny and I agreed, would, initially at least, make them feel welcome in the ocean wilds, and when we discovered too that all four guests were male, it seemed to confirm this as the most effortless way to proceed.

But how was I to know how abstemious these amateur scientists would turn out to be? They took two of the guestrooms off the second hall, Red Whiskered Joe, whose surname we learnt was Sullivan, sharing with Simon Parslow – a balding and bespectacled man, Sydney born, and perhaps the most accommodating of the chaps aside from Joe – while James Selleck and Ivan Kantica shared the room beside them. At barely five feet high, Mr Selleck was the smallest of a very small group, with only Joe Sullivan clearing five and a half feet and even then by not much more than the thickness of a pardalote's wing. But James Selleck was genuinely tiny, and slender too, though his baby-face had at least a blush of health that Mr Parslow's and Mr Kantica's did not. Mr Kantica, who seemed to be the Captain of their ship, was ash-grey, with hawkish brows and hair bushing out of his nostrils and ears in a quite noticeable way. If he was Captain of the expeditionary party it was no doubt because of his intellect rather than his physical stature, and so it seemed almost polite to imagine privately that the sprouting hair was issuing from the over-fertilisation of his botanical brain.

They disappeared into their rooms, taking their scientific gear with them. After seeing them to their digs in an ebullient fashion, Ferny continued down the second hallway, at the end of which was his study. Darling Ferny, I'm sure just the presence of the naturalists, no matter their demeanour, was enough to inspire in him a studious mimicry.

As all this was going on I said farewell to Joe Badger and his coach, following him out to the gate and helping him again with the duckboards. Joe waved goodbye to 'Hutch', and as the heath-toned coach drove off over the fox-coloured road a kookaburra struck up his song from a nearby bough. I stood still, arrested afresh, with brow knitting at the thought of what the bird's voicings were suddenly resemblant of. Yes, a new slant upon the bird's ascension-song was trying to find a clearing in my brain.

How strange. But ah! Finally, there it was. Whether it was due to the new ethnographically tinted perspective brought to the glen with our Scientific guests I could not say. Whatever the case, for the first time in my life I noted how the kookaburra song sounded not like the rungs of a ladder ascending to the heights of living but uncannily like a chortling Darwinian monkey.

꙳

When I returned to the homestead there was not a sound from the rooms, no coursing of water through the pipes to the basin taps, no knocks or bumps, no voices through the walls, nothing. I stood in the kitchen as if alone in the heath, but with a grin on my lips for the absurdity of such unexpected feelings of solitude. When I really had been alone in the cottage up beyond the Big Cutting Hill, if Maisie was off on some errand or another, I had, at times, never felt so crowded. Crowded by the spiders in the house, yes, crowded by the old fig among the gum trees that overshadowed the house, certainly, but crowded mostly by the ligatures of my mind, which contorted and strained like the roots of the messmate into every which direction, causing hauntings and terrors, and visions of abomination that had me pushing and shouting as if trying to make my way through a throng. And yet to all 'enlightened' eyes I was alone. Even with the pin-drop stillness of the forest out there I was surrounded by crosscurrents arguing, as if a battle was being staged within my very soul. And now, when I felt that so much of what had beleaguered me had grown soluble to the world, dissolved by a light, and a *lightness*, such as I had never known before, so that I could properly be with my own self-revolving and with other people, instead I found my world a prim, unneighbourly, indeed silent enclosure.

As if repressed. I was surrounded by men as recalcitrant as snakes in the gloaming.

Soon however, there was a knock on the door. It was Georgina Morgan, come to see how things were getting on and to greet the party. I told her immediately of the situation: that, in a sense, there was no party; that the Field Nats were huddling like hermit crabs in their rockpool rooms.

As I fixed us a pot of tea, Georgina wondered, 'What can they be doing in there? Perhaps I'll go and see. Do you mind, Sarah?'

But now instead of answering Georgina's question, I became distracted by something quite outside these trivialities of the human house. Immediately then, and without so much as a transition, I found myself *listening out for*, and *picturing*, two waterfalls which run in the winter months down the high rocky clefts just to the north-east of the glen. These waterfalls descend, as if through glands of the country, on either side of a prominent rising headland. But they seldom run at the same velocity. The more eastern and lower one can be rumbling like twelve carriages while at the same time the higher and more classical cataract, whose ledge is distinct and falls away into yards and yards of open air, is issuing only a trickle. Conversely, and always with what appears to be the same amount of rain, the higher falls can be crashing down as loud as the ocean at the mouth whilst the rockier and more gradual gush remains hardly that, no, hardly a falls at all.

In my mind then, and even as I stood on the sprung hardwood floor in front of the picture-frame paddock windows, with Georgina first waiting for my reply and then, undoubtedly perplexed, heading off to the Field Nats and Uncle Ferny, for some good reason I began tracing each winding route in my mind, following each chain of water back up its respective hillside, and noting in my mind's eye the way they pooled or stalled at particular points, how they were temporarily weired by quartzy barriers, or how they would sluice a field through a gulch of sedge; or how indeed the shapes of these soily glands would turn the narrows of the water-chain momentarily back on itself as if flowing uphill, and all this in its search, its eternal, universal, and nevertheless always local search, for the bottom of things. I listened out for the music of each of these waterfall stories, knowing it was the ground they travelled through that had the chief influence on their sound, as much indeed as the rain of which they were born. And I *pictured in* so that I could *see into*, beyond the large architectural living space about me, what effect in turn they were having on the shapely ground.

Thus it was that the fact there was not one but two hallways in the homestead: the one which held my own bright room, the seldom used dining room and Ferny's bedroom, the storage room and a room with Norwegian bunks for children; and the other hall where the Field Nats were, and Ferny in his study at the end, and now Georgina Morgan presumably tapping on the doors as she went along the runner in search of a connection, became for me a simulation of the very waterfalls I was meditating on. It was as if the logical integrity of quiet in one of them was being matched only by the swallet of the other. Suffice to say there was water in both, absent water in one, and buried water in the other. But I was reassured by this idea, having seen for myself while out walking the rocky bush how a creek that shines in thread under the sky can *go under*, yes can disappear into a swallet of the ground and run underground, unseen, unheard, unlistened to, *unpictured in*, for a good half a mile until it reappears between two ferns or where the rusty Pomaderris has grown to lean and beckon. And so, as I traced with a surveying inner-eye the match between these inner and outer worlds, I knew the naturalists had been swalleted too. They'd run underground to where the space seemed best and would only re-emerge with the right conditions. Georgina had – this by now seemed evocatively true to me – gone to *dig them out*, taking the spade-a-spade of country manners to a disappeared creek. And suddenly, as such imagery affected me, this seemed an awful and a violent thing. I felt sure that the hallway watercourses must be left unbroken but by their own cousinly momentum. And so it came to me, and perhaps all this only took a second or two of the objective day, that I should step over to the piano, prop up its carapace, lift the lid of the keyboard and let its glen-altered innards ring and say. Say: *Welcome*, to a place where the inside is out and the outside is in, to a place where the natural phenomena you are passionate about – the ferns and the blanketleaf, the orchid and the mountain ash, the white tip of the wallaby's tail, the spinebill and the bandicoot, the black shoulders of the kite, the cretaceous lineations of the overhangs, the common reed and the platypus – these things which have led you out on the long journey by train and the Cobb & Co, and had you suffer the kind but bald humour of Joe Badger even as you helped shovel aside the obstacles of his gluey track, can ring out and influence, indeed help make and inflect our own expressive art even as we create it.

And so I moved silently above the hardwood boards in the silent homestead. I went around to the keyboard of the piano and sat down to play.

How long it took for them all to emerge I cannot say, for I had gone away then, off into the music of shining threads above the two waterfalls. Only the previous day I had fastened a braid of twelve she-oak needles to the wound bass string of my middle C, and also affixed with glue a banksia leaf to the same said soft hammer; and now, as I played, each time I returned to that *thisky* note from cadences running to bass and treble on either side, I was not returned to ground but thrust with the music as if up into the levitation of the black-shouldered kite. From that height I could see the northerly windings of each tendril creek behind each cataract. I could also sense the strength of the very gravity I defied while hovering there, and thus by my imaginative harmonics gained a deeper inkling of the natural depths of the newly swalleted inhabitants of our second hallway. They were a long way from home after all, even further from the far-off home counties where most likely their families had only recently issued from by some slow ship, and thus it was that in all eventual sincerity I played for them an impromptu sonata sourced in the local repertoire of our gently mysterious Ngangahook surroundings.

I did not hear the first footfall as it came out for it was red-whiskered young Joe, and as he told me later he crept quietly into the room, timidly even, entranced by the intensely familiar yet strange sounds in the air. The ground of chords would sound, arpeggios running like the moorhens across them, the fourths and fifths, the sevenths and augmented thirds, the ladders of bass, the figurative melodies of my right hand arranged like petals around a stamen, and ringing out high up in the eaves of the house. Yet amongst it all came the woody *thsk* of the she-oak, the leafy *clack* of the banksia, and down in the very bottom octave the resonating *thwack* of the roo-rib I'd fixed between the deepest D and D-sharp string. The piano, formerly a Mühlbach, now a bush-machine, was played as it was understood. I pictured in the chords the solid hill and in the melodic figures the seeking creeks, *thsk*-ing and *clack*-ing their way to the ledge when, with a C-sharp minor surrounding the roo-rib note, the water found its sudden drop, its glistening air, and then its landing zone. In this I played as if with a trembling forked stick in my hand, as first Joe, then his room-mate Simon Parslow, and after an interlude where I played only the altered notes and left the others alone, James Selleck and Ivan Kantica also came out from their rooms like the shyest trickles from underground springs.

By this stage, even with my eyes closed for inner sight, I could sense an audience on the walls, so I leant further back into the charm of mixtures. You must understand how any abrasion in the sound came fully forth with fascination because of what surrounded it. The rainbowed soundboard of the instrument projected the music from a traditionally reverberant base, meaning that the undoubted *oddness, unforeseeness,* even *eeriness* of the improvised strings and hammers were always housed in a resonance rich and familiar, which therefore made sure that what I was *picturing* was, at the very least, implied in the sound itself.

When Uncle Ferny finally entered the room he came with Georgina, and I took my cue from his recognisably enthusiastic footfall to resolve the performance with a Romantic chord in which I envisaged the she-oak *thsk* as me walking. Yes, me walking. Sarah Hutchinson, indoors and out. There I was; I had emerged in the music, just as now our visitors had come out of their rooms.

What followed was an excited discussion in which, before even formally introducing themselves, the three older gentlemen of the party, Mr Selleck, Simon Parslow and Ivan Kantica, demanded that I show them how it was done; how I, with the help of my avant-garde champion Uncle Ferny, had *doctored the instrument*, as Mr Selleck described it. This extemporised seminar – not my term but, once again, Mr Selleck's, who turned out to be an associate of the painter Mr Streeton – bemused

Georgina Morgan no end, but for me it was really like a dream. I could not articulate to the naturalist the *necessity* of what I'd done, how I lived as if only to somehow match and measure up to the gifts of local light that had saved me in the cottage beyond the Big Cutting Hill, how in fact I could now live no other way and in no other mode. Still, with Ferny's technical enthusiasm for describing the mechanics of how we'd augmented the erstwhile family Mühlbach, and with the naturalists' own fumbling but willing attempts at comprehending the *meaning* of the music it produced, I felt nevertheless as if suddenly, and after unpromising beginnings, I was in a milieu of my own making.

To those of you who live in a time beyond nations, where technological capacities seed beliefs in the supersession of geographies, or at least of political states, this hybrid instrument may not surprise. But in the era I am recounting the precise opposite was true. Only nine years into the new Australian Federation the tendency to place the Nationalist transect over any piece of ground, thus rendering it symbolic to the cause, was very strong. So that the augmentation of the piano I found when I arrived in the glen, the Mühlbach grand that had appeared hearse-black even in the window light but which now seemed to take on hues of char and ironbark, casuarina root, and the satin of the male bowerbird, was viewed by these progressive nation-founders through that excited Nationalist lens. What had been a bush-bashed sea-cold party of visitors, only one of whom appeared at all friendly, was now an inquisitive audience gathering around the hearth of a new idea. Only the sociable one, young Joe Sullivan, said nothing, offered nothing, but stood away still by the wall, as if a little dumbstruck by events. Georgina meanwhile, as the rest of us clustered around the instrument, went to the stove, gingered up the coals, threw in some cut black wattle boughs from the wood-cupboard, and put the heavy kettle back on. Despite the uncommunicative beginnings to this first day of the visit, it seemed we would all be having a chat over a pot of tea after all.

❦

As the days of our week with the Naturalists passed it became easy to forget how, without the music on that first afternoon, they may have continued to remain aloof to the point of estrangement. But no, their initial withdrawal, or arrogance, or turn of urbane superiority, or whatever it had been, was disarmed by my piano-work. They now felt as comfortable as if they were back on their Edwardian boulevard in Ivanhoe. The erudition flowed, and it turned out that their knowledge of the Australian biome, at least in its constituent parts, was profound. Orchids, Greenhood, Striped Greenhood, Fringed Midge, Brown Tipped, etc, were key elements of Ivan Kantica's interests, while Simon Parslow had ambition with respect to what he considered the unfinished classification of Casuarinas. Mr Selleck's main endeavours were to do with birds. Joe Sullivan, on the other hand, had an abiding interest in the very high, the very low and the very dark, that being tall trees on the one hand, and funghi on the other. He was also a swimmer of note and thus had a curiosity about the life of the river. It was clear from the outset that this Joe Sullivan was quite unlike the other three; he enjoyed a game of cards, could talk with Ferny about farming, and funghi, in which Ferny also shared an interest, as well as the general landscape the farm had been laid upon. It seemed that Red Whiskered Joe had not quite as many peccadillos as his compatriots, especially when it came to the judgement of others.

The first two days of the Field Nats visit were spent in assiduous fieldwork, and I traipsed out with them as well, augmenting as best I could, amid the constant volley of gunshots, the guidance Ferny and also Georgina gave on the animals, plants and any likely bowers or sanctuaries in the thereabouts. I watched them all closely as we went about, first upstream beyond the northern reaches of the pastures and beyond the cumbungi swamp, then into the lichened land-thigh of trees above the lower valley, and then downstream by canoe to the saltwater and dunes. I waited for their expression of anxiety about the venomous aspects of the landscape, the copperheads and tiger snakes, the scorpions and bull ants, but they did not come. The naturalists were sedulous, studious, urbane, indefatigably opinionated, but not at all afraid. They were, in fact, decidedly hard cases.

On the second evening, as they were compiling statistics of the specimens they had taken during the day, and while Mr Kantica was painstakingly dissecting a freshly dead tawny frogmouth on the benches of the kitchen (it was almost as if he were preparing it as a delicacy of French cuisine), I once again went to the piano and began to play, and this time to sing, about what had been preoccupying me as we went about the field, namely, the chilled affection at the heart of Science. Were they listening as I parroted their spoken inventories of the day's activities, singing back to them, for their own philosophical inspection, the extent of their abstraction?

4 willie wagtails Rhipidura leucophrys
one with winter-browning of the wing
1 white-throated treecreeper Cormobates leucophaea
whose cloudwhite throat can no longer sing

6 yellow-tailed cockatoos Calyptorhynchus funereus
for whom the night will never be so black
3 spiny anteaters Tachyglossus aculeatus
you'll travel to the museum in an ice-cold potato sack
7 short-finned eels Anguilla australis
their slime is drying even as I sing
1 white-tipped wallaby Wallabia bicolor
cut off the tail to throw into the ring
1 flame-breasted robin Petroica phoenicea
its cheering note all peppered now with shot
2 platypuses Ornithorhynchus anatinus
the most darling thus the deadest of the lot

Were they listening? I have no doubt. How could they not have comprehended the echoes of their endeavours, sung back to them as if from the future in that way? Truth was, I had been confronted with this owl-soup passed off as intellectual endeavour all day long, and while I am not particularly squeamish I had nevertheless been aghast, not so much at the numbers of the kill but by the countenance with which it was performed. We know of course that life is gyre-like, perpetual rather than linear, but even so, in this case it was easy to see what would follow from such scant regard for nature's individual spirits. The shot was fired, the specimen bagged, the next one sought, and not for the belly but for the mind! What mind, I had to ask? What mind can it be but a cold circuitry of brain if it is divorced so from the heart and the wider deeper heart that forms the temperament of the place?

Still, unlike their first expressions of interest in my glen-inflected piano, an interest which, once they'd comprehended the fundamental set of juxtapositions involved – chiefly the fact that all is sound, and all sounds can be music – had left them restlessly curious about still other things, this time they left me stranded as a somewhat crated specimen, my self an undiscovered species now discovered, if not quite adequately *classified*, in their eyes. No, this inventory-song I played did not outwardly seem to interest them in the least.

Uncle Ferny through all this was too-awake, though still not to exactly why their visit had been arranged in the first place. Nevertheless he sat with the Naturalists and helped sort the species even as I sang, and in his devoted openness never cast even a frown my way. He had indeed been distracted from his prior depression by all the earnest activity, and was growing friendly in the most delightfully easy way with Joe Sullivan, with whom he'd agreed to swim the river to the sea in the morning.

Ferny had also arranged, as he promised, a night of entertainment, with Johnny Briggs and his Magic Lantern in the large dining room at Mr Hastie's Guest House. This event was to take place the following evening after another day's collecting (nee: *slaughter*), provided that neither Ferny nor Joe Sullivan had caught pneumonia in the stream. It was still wintry after all, but never as inclement, from my view at least, as the cold snap of Scientific Fervour.

As I retired to my room that evening, to remove my shoes and unsheath my legs from their woollen stockings, to sit at my table with my hair untied, and to gaze across the quarter-mooned grass outside, my heart continued to go out for that poor owl. For I knew, as you will come to know with the certainty of the demise you have inherited, that the owl was not in fact an owl, nor a 'nightjar' as Mr Selleck had enthusiastically pronounced, but in fact a *God*. God of the low bough, God of the chilly stars, the Zeus of the slug and worm, the *oom oom oom* God of the Ngangahook sonata. If the alterations of my piano were as interesting or intellectual as the naturalists thought, then this sub-bass, this *oom oom oom* song would have found its place like a heartbeat among the hammers and strings. But it was not for me to play. Some things can never be housed thus in human culture, just as the workings of such a God can seldom be seen in our midst. They are out there regardless.

At my desk I sat and had the owl in me, the owl that is not an owl, the God whose sound expresses the night, all its spheres, its stars and glitter-leaves, its deep deep ground, as if through the clear glass jar of its outside knowing. It knows because it does not know; it sees with its song. And yet, I cried, my knuckles wet now as I held them to my chin, there it lies, dead as a musicologist upon the kitchen bench.

'What then?' the night seemed to ask through the window. 'What then?'

※

The next day Uncle Ferny and young Red Whiskered Joe did not return from their swim until lunch, having drifted downstream in a conversation as meandering as the river itself, through the ironbark shade then the open sky above the green clouds of boobiallas and waving whisking reeds of the riverflat, and finally in the tea-hued estuary on the leeside of the dune hummock. Once delivered there, they stomped over the sandbar to the sea, laughing easily now, with Ferny managing impersonations not only of Mr Kantica's ardent factual tones but also of Mr Selleck's habit of hitching his pants up high so that the physiognomy of his private parts became too clearly delineated. As they had swum along, any pretence either of them had to the solemn superiority of Joe's companions slowly unstitched its strictures in the loosening stream. By the time they'd got deep into the river's course all worries were off. The two men confirmed that, despite their difference in age, Ferny being in his late thirties and Joe more than ten years younger, they were mentally, temperamentally, physically, kindred. At first Joe's youth saw him wary of expressing himself but finally, under the warmth of Ferny's navigation, his franker perspectives came out. How rude his travelling companions had been in old Joe Badger's coach, how miffed they were about having to help with the bogged wheels, how embarrassing their ungrateful behaviour had been when they'd first arrived and retired to their rooms. Eventually, bend by whiskered bend as they swam, with the landrails and the moorhens no doubt listening in, Joe Sullivan's confessions had freed up Ferny's talent for mimicry and thus the whooping laughter with which they finally hit the beach. They leapt into the waves as if into friendship itself, and by the time they'd surfed and walked the league back to the house they were close in that manner that only men in the freedom of spontaneity can be. Mateship, this was it, as natural as the wagtail wags, and just as insouciant. A firm reminder, as they came through the gate and on up to the homestead, to reject all inane phraseology, indeed all substitutes for the grace and fun of true intimacy.

And thus it was that the balance of the visit of the naturalists did change, its initial and grim formality jettisoned by Uncle Ferny and Joe Sullivan's compact. It was two hours before nightfall when the others returned from their day's activities, their drinking flasks dry, their capture-bags once again full to overflowing, though this time of botanical specimens. It was also then another two hours before we were due at the Magic Lantern Show.

❦

There was in hindsight something about the atmosphere in the large dining room of Mr Hastie's that evening that spoke of what would ensue in the coming weeks. I had never myself had occasion to set foot in Hastie's Guest House before, my predilection being for my writing table, my preparations of the Mühlbach, and the somewhat more ancient hospitality I found in the froth and sud of the winter creek and the way such accumulations were modified with the seasons. The sound and sense of the glen were magic show enough for me, the way they put me in mind of an eternal thread and its component yet comparably trivial parts. You in 'the future', me in 'the past'. By this stage my enjoyment of my new home was such that the peopled world which Uncle Ferny needed so much was not exactly anathema to me as much as it was a digression from the traction afforded my inspirited mind by the things of this world that no human has made. Thus my participation in events such as that which Ferny organised for the naturalists had been limited since coming to the glen to our own occasional soirees, and thus I found my sensitivity to the 'meteorology' of the room at Mr Hastie's was consequently acute.

For locals however it was a time to play, and to make a rare appraisal of the non-provincial mind. As everyone arrived, and before the Magic Lantern Show was begun, the Field Nats mingled with the schoolmistress Miss Emma Donovan, with Jack and Dorothy Bilborough of the General Store, with the three lighthouse families (excepting Mr Lanyon himself who was up with the prismatic lens of the light), and with two or three farmers who happened to come along. I was observant of these conversations and exchanges, and aware therefore of considerable tensions in the room. A barometer might have said the air was *Changeable*, as Selwyn Atchison and others related to his interests and the Bell Committee received rather short shrift from Mr Selleck, Ivan Kantica and Mr Parslow, who once again seemed remarkably disinclined to foster friendly relations. When Selwyn, for instance, began to recount his ambitions for the campanile and bell, Ivan Kantica wasted neither time nor nicety in assuring him of his own atheistic view. 'A bell perhaps to measure the day, I can see perhaps some merit in that,' he said sternly. 'But the sun provides a sufficient record of Time already, as do the Stars, if you'd only take the time to observe them.'

I excused myself from the company at this remark, thinking not only of all the other ways of measuring the Circadia of life beyond a sun or bell but also of all the other and kinder ways there might be to speak to our fellow man of our passions. A bell was indeed rung in my mind, an alarm bell of the City versus Country divide, for which Ferny, typically, had no regard. He could not abide an air of superiority from either side, but that's exactly now what we had managed to place ourselves in the midst of. After less than an hour of this increasingly taut mingling the social barometer had plummeted and, in my mind at least, a Weather Warning was in place. The empty centre of the room vibrated as if to allow the brewing storm to resonate in space, while the local residents and the Field Nats clung to the shadows on either side. Even Joe Sullivan seemed rather hamstrung and awkward so that rather than talking with the locals or the naturalists, he sat on his own near the doorway with a cigarette, reading the Visitors Book, as if merely biding his time.

With Ferny helping Johnny Briggs attend to a technical difficulty in setting up the acetylene source of the Magic Lantern, it was suddenly left to me therefore to ameliorate the situation, which I did by going across to Red Whiskered Joe and asking if by chance he recognised any of the names in the book. He looked up at me calmly from his chair and said, 'No, not a one.'

'I suppose that's hardly surprising,' I offered.

'No, I suppose not,' he said. 'And I daresay I'm not about to get any more familiar any time soon.'

The two of us looked out with private amusement across the room, where the two estranged camps, all with glasses of claret or lemonade in hand, were resembling two opposing families on the difficult day of a shotgun marriage. Interestingly it was the Field Nats who fitted the archetype of the groom's party, the locals who seemed to carry the aggrieved air of connections of a jilted bride. Even despite the fact that the Lantern Show had as yet not even begun, Joe Sullivan and I were in tacit agreement that the sooner the 'ceremony' was over the better. In lieu of that happening however, I gratefully accepted his offer of a cigarette followed by an impromptu tutorial in his expertise of blowing rings from the blue smoke.

Eventually the technology was righted and Uncle Ferny walked back into the stormy-space to announce that proceedings would begin. And so they did. With everyone relieved to take their seats the room was further darkened, Emma Donovan began to play on her Hohner harmonica, and the images proceeded to emerge.

We saw over a hundred views of the local area that night, each one of them a fascination and also a 'poor cousin' of its source. The first picture was of the grand old King Cormorant Rock.

Then came the Lighthouse, taken from three different points. Crayfishing among the rocks, Bassian Falls in summer and winter, a greenhood orchid trembling in the previous spring's wind, the Atchisons rowing behind the dunes, a wagonette making its way along the Scotchman's track, boxes of local fruit being readied for the long trip to market. To my great surprise three of the views were of skulls displayed around the home, one hanging from a verandah rail, one from a hook on the back of a laundry door, and one sitting atop a plinth in a study. The study skull had the word GELLIBRAND displayed on a brass plate beneath it. Such images incited a noticeable mirth from the local half of the room, although it was unclear to me if the humour was intended or not by Johnny Briggs. Some of the other productions however were highly amusing, especially the one called 'Stealing Apples' where the culprit (Ray Stephenson, whose small dairy sits on the eastern ridge) was stooping to pick up an apple as a farmer appeared (Jem Morgan our farm manager) coming around a tree brandishing a fair-sized paling. This tableau brought loud laughter from the local side of the room, though not a murmur from the three older naturalists. Beside me however I could sense that Joe Sullivan enjoyed it very much, as, it seemed, did Ferny.

As the images appeared one after the other, I became fascinated with the singular power the Magic Lantern had, not to render but to dilute the reality of our thereabouts. Even Jem Morgan, whose thespian abilities were admittedly not very honed, looked different in his new manifestation of projected light. The man so familiar to myself and the glen now appeared quite another creature. Though external resemblances could certainly be made out, this new Jem nevertheless appeared speckled and wan, and was also jerky in his movements, so that it occurred to me that he was indeed a separate person altogether when displayed via the 'magic' light. Indeed I got it into my head that Jem looked peculiarly Russian in the way the lens paled his skin and seemed to imbue it with a chiaroscuro of imaginary quasi-Asiatic shadows. There were fuscy stripes of gloom across his face, and the air around his hat was flecked and seemed to granulate and swirl as if with ocean whitecaps. All this struck me with a surprising force, and when I should perhaps have been laughing along with Joe at the common humour of the pantomime I could only focus on the idea that Johnny Briggs' Magic Lantern was actually the conduit of another world altogether, a world unto itself, a reality with its own atmosphere, temper, and light. Soon I was concluding that rather than being hailed as the miraculous capturer of the world in which we live, the Magic Lantern could be better described as an equally miraculous, or *magical*, projector of quite another world to our own, a world which uses reality's materials as only the base metals critical to a remarkable alchemical process. Thus the miracle was achieved via a collaboration of elements: the source of artificial light – in this case acetylene gas – the glass slides, and whatever raw material was being metamorphosed by being placed upon those slides.

Excited by the directness of this realisation my mind's eye flew off and away, a bit like the turkey bustard I used to sight from the cottage beyond the Big Cutting Hill. Leaping away from the sound of the schoolmistress's harmonica, away from a room so divided between amusement and stony-faced superiority, my thoughts filled instead with such viscous optical textures as I had never previously imagined. Soon I saw no functional forms at all, no recognisable shapes of orchard, homestead, lighthouse or headland, but an atmosphere multimotioned and dreamlike, the equivalent perhaps of a transfigured meteorological pressure system projected onto the screen of my imagination. It involved a mixing of the senses and a blending of ambiences that was itself akin to a wash of optical music.

I was aware that beside me Red Whiskered Joe was shaking with laughter, but he was only a dim rhythmic sense at the edges of my vision. I can reflect now that what I was seeing was resemblant not only of weather, not only of music, but also perhaps of the fluent yet fragmented texture and shape of thought itself, before the demands of our social intervolvement transforms it into agreed-upon units of language. Any actual scenes coming through Johnny Briggs' Magic Lantern were thus obscured by the interior realities they had engendered. At least in me! I was captivated by looking into an active seam, as if I was seeing the seed before the flower, or rather the soil in which the seed is sown. This was something the painter Roiseaux had talked to me about in Rome, the way such an achievement as the photographic lens could ultimately create another version of the world by projecting a reality beyond the outward appearance of the Tiber or the Colosseum, and now indeed beyond the glen and the course of its creek to the sea. This was a new world indeed, with new oceans glimmering behind my closed eyes. Neither city nor country, countrymen nor scientists, were bickering there. All was texture, tone, ambience. Background had become foreground, the sound of flowing atmosphere in space. Away and away I went, deeply enthralled, until finally I sensed a new external warmth falling upon my face. I opened my eyes to see the ordinary lamps in the room were back on and the Magic Lantern Show was over. I gasped, for the pure shock of my transition. Beside me Joe Sullivan was looking at me with concern.

THE BELL OF THE WORLD

❦

The Field Naturalists were due to leave the very next day, but that night when we had got back to the house after the Magic Lantern Show, and long after everyone had taken quietly to their rooms, the naturalists no doubt writing up their field notes from the day, there was a knock on my bedroom door.

I had been preoccupied at my writing table – but not with writing. I had been listening to the ocean. It had occurred to me as we walked home from Mr Hastie's Guest House under starlight that the far-off sound of the waves roaring in towards the rivermouth was some kind of acoustic equivalent to the flecky, fluxing, scratched and stippled ambience engendered in me by the Magic Lantern Show. And so, alone in my room, I had been listening to the wild sound as if indeed I was *looking* at something. The ocean sonics were forming new pictures in my mind too, pictures which in turn resembled the wash of atmosphere that I often describe privately to myself as *world music*. On this occasion, as I sat there, my eyes wide open but unseeing of the room, seeing instead the moving image of the sound of the ocean playing itself out upon my soul's emulsion, I thought I could detect a central key in which the sound was being played. The teeming harmonics of the far-off sound, as it travelled towards me over the league of the meandering valley, appeared to consist of an infinite number of notes, filaments of sonic pollen really, that nevertheless issued forth an initiatory note and coalesced within the boundaries of a single unifying key. Amazed that such a deep singularity could exist in something so various and of the airs, I was sitting in a state of awesome fascination when the knock on my door came. So that just as I felt that I was myself climbing the night sky along with the sound, and reaching high in the assurance of a commonality of all things as evidenced by this ocean-key, the sound of knuckle on wood came as if from the imperative of Gravity itself. My vision collapsed in less than an instant and I felt suddenly pinned to the earth.

The knock came again. But paralysed by the instant, I could neither speak in reply nor move to answer the door. As I say, I felt quite *pinned*.

I did not so much wait then as hover in my chair, a planet between two very different moons. And thus I was both pinned and in suspension, and only dimly aware of my semi-undressed state, and of the fire of she-oaks still flickering in my grate.

The knock came a third time and with this third knock I may have heard the faintest mention of my name. Whatever this additional sound was it managed to completely dissolve the oceanic dimensions of my room. And when the fourth knock came its foregrounding erased all sonic expanse, so that you wouldn't even have known an ocean was ever there. In front of me my writing paper, as suddenly I noticed it, was bare in its sheaf. The whiteness of the paper was alarming to me, the way it extruded all other colours. The world indeed had become a blank page.

I looked down at my nightgown, as pale too as the page. But the skin of my small bosom was itself all blotchy red, undoubtedly from the excitement and now the tension of what I was experiencing. Apart from Ferny no one had ever knocked on my door, ever. But now they had, and were waiting, as persistently as a hawk of sorts, on the other side of the door.

It was then I imagined, for the first time, opening the door onto a rufously featured thing with piercing eye, a primary creature, and full with intent. I made as if to move, but did not budge an inch I'm sure. But soon after, I was standing upright beside the writing table, my body pulsing as stars do above the ridgelines. And I was stepping, across the floor, the way a heron steps precariously across an exposed reef while knowing all the time what she is seeking.

The cold touch of the brass doorknob matched the glint it reflected from the wavering light of the she-oak fire. The fire came and went with the wind. She-oak timber when cleaved open can be quite heath-pink, and now such colours of our surrounds, colours of the salt and sylvan place, were fuelling the glow of the room. And it was into that cleaved timber and candle glow that the hawk then entered, a creature with narrowed focus, and outspread wings. Could I shelter there beneath those wings, I momentarily wondered, or will I be torn to pieces in my flesh? Or could I, a woman of my species, and no mere maiden, somehow summon that ocean key and the fusing of a truly unforeseen moment into deep equivalence?

In truth such thoughts are as rapid in their vanishing as in their emergence. Yet though they are fleeting the world is too dangerous without them. And with them we are prepared for a great receiving, as when a physical touch silences the mind.

Suffice to say that before long the ocean was roaring once again at the mouth. The night's moonlured water went climbing into the sky, the stars falling into unrecordable depths. The sound suffused the room, indeed it was as if the room *was* the sound, and this unexpected visitor and I went transporting there, among it, and of it, by wing and gill, on the smoke of centuries and the truth of blank pages, towards the dawn.

The next day, the day of the naturalists' departure, came with an unexpected proposal. Joe Sullivan it seemed had no appetite for getting back on Joe Badger's coach to endure his fellow nature-lovers' superior air as they surmounted the gluey mucky track of the ridge on their way to meet the Melbourne train at Winchelsea. He didn't say as much, but he extolled the beauties of the Run with great enthusiasm and expressed a wistful desire to stay a while longer. Uncle Ferny of course was more than happy to oblige, having befriended Joe Sullivan on their great swim to the sea. Plus, we needed another hand in the winter orchard, for even though the wattle was beginning to bloom there was perhaps still time enough to conduct the planned pruning of the trees which, before he became acquainted with the Field Naturalists' airs of self-importance, Ferny had hoped they would assist us with as a well-meaning exchange for their food and accommodation.

It was arranged then for Red Whiskered Joe to stay on with us for a time, and breakfast that morning was largely spent with Joe explaining his decision, sotto voce, to his companions, while Ferny and I, and Jem Morgan, who had come by for breakfast as he occasionally did, sat out on the verandah with our porridge and tea.

It must be said that this was not how you would prefer to imagine the last morning of such an auspicious visit. Rather you would have hoped for conviviality to be flowing, the exchange of ideas and addresses reaching its crescendo, and promises of future visits in the offing being made. But no, instead the naturalists – Messrs Kantica, Selleck and Parslow – were in one room with their young defector Joe, while we, their hosts, sat outside almost as if in exile amongst the birdsong.

'So be it,' Jem Morgan remarked, with a shrug of his broad middle-aged shoulders.

'Such is life,' seemed to be the attitude of both Ferny and the birds.

VIII

Soon enough then the second hallway of the homestead became emptied again, but for one room. With the farewelling of Joe Badger's Cobb & Co coach full of Field Naturalists the air of tension, and the whiff of unaccounted-for opprobrium, had left the Run. On grew the lichens and mosses, as well as the bell-shaped funghi hanging pendulant from the ironbark trunks fringing the pastures to the north. These indeed were bells that seemed to toll the season well, and among the many vistas and vantage points we had access to around the Run it could well have been a stereotypic scene of plenitude and running burns were it not for the bark weeping everywhere in the bush, the pale unsheathed columns of the gum tree spars, and the rasping uncharismatic *raark* of the cockatoos flying up into their roosts in the rocky gorge.

Some nights I was content to wait for the creature to come again, for him to brush his semiplumes against my door – there was no need to actually knock anymore – but on other nights my spirit spilled out beyond my name, beyond any *Sarah* the world had filed me as, and I took him with me to the trees and peeled him like a fruit. Which was ever the Me he was seeking in the first place. So take pause before you name the world, and listen first to the music that's already playing there. In the hearts of those raucous cockatoos there is a loving song, a family song, and they would be shocked I'm sure to hear what is to them the sweetest cries sound so violently in our human ears. The more I stand among the weeping licheny winterbarks and listen to them the more I understand that this is so. We live in a world of misunderstanding directly attributable to the limitations of our perceiving instrument. My 'Sarah' thus can only ever be a convenient appellation, for like the cockatoo I am more an inner than an outer being, more a set of sudden urge and instinct than any *alias* would allow. In this respect all language is but a sobriquet. Our true names have no alphabet, and the self, be it in cockatoo or man, in jeopardy or security, is always real. Before and after its name.

Those barky lichens too have a voice in my ear, as real as night. And so on nights when the creature did not come I dreamed of an apparatus I could take outside, to the source, as it were, and play. A piano made of limestone perhaps, but with melaleuca keys, and hammers of hardy sphagnum moss, and strings of seaweed. I felt blessed that Ferny understood such horizons as I was gazing at, and though he could not fly there with me I also knew he had his own independently bright geography of concordance, of which his everyday personality was both an expression and a residue. Birds flew over and we noted them but as time went by we had learnt never to mistake our notation for the bird. I think Joe Sullivan sensed this; it was part of the reason he could not bear to leave. He had sensed perhaps that he could not access the textures of Ngangahook merely by reading a transcript at the end of a day collecting specimens. And it was so strong, the feeling that he wanted to stay. And yes, it was also somewhat of a larrikin's lark for sure, the way his staying allowed him to snub his nose at the Naturalists, and laugh about them with Ferny, but it was more than that, in his body and his soul.

A few days hence we were in the orchard, Red Whiskered Joe and I, Ferny, Jem and Georgina Morgan, and their little girl Caroline, when Selwyn Atchison rode by to inform Uncle Ferny of the progress of his plans for the bell.

My old darling friend, Selwyn's champion collie, with tongue lolling from running alongside the horse, came straight for me. The blessed thing. Among the furry limbs of pear and apple trees, which we had laid in pruned piles around us as we'd worked among the rows, I rolled straight down on the ground with the dog, renewing her acquaintance, until Keel, Jem Morgan's mutt, came barking in among us. The collie and Keel then had a decent set-to, all exposed pink and oyster black gums and clashing teeth and gyrating necks as each of them tried to gain true purchase.

Meanwhile Selwyn, taking no notice of the animals, was wasting no time in mounting his case to Uncle Ferny, in the manner which around these parts is commonly called *earbashing*. The fact that he was divulging so much of the progress of his Bell Committee's plans within easy earshot of me and the Morgans, and Joe Sullivan for that matter, bespoke perhaps of his confidence that he would not be brooked. He spoke of how the Bell Committee had now had approval from the Bishop, who, unbeknown to Mr Atchison, was a fourth, or maybe fifth, cousin of ours. And the fundraising efforts had apparently received a boost from this said relative, who had promised to help campaign on the committee's behalf in Melbourne. 'The civilised impulse of a dry roof against the weather collects its own pure water,' was how Selwyn described this success to Ferny.

Selwyn Atchison's visit of course was all in lieu of procuring Ferny's philanthropy. And Ferny knew, astute in these things as he is, that Atchison would not have ventured out to the glen unless there was still some absolute necessity for Ferny's involvement. So that, despite the unsolicited account of the Bell Committee's successes, and the reported support of our cousin the Bishop, it seemed certain that Selwyn Atchison's own collection of pure water still amounted to not much more than a dram of mizzling rain.

Ferny was, as always, perfectly pleasant throughout Selwyn's visit and, once he'd fended off the disingenuous gambit with expressions of encouragement, he strolled the guest through our orchard rows, reacquainting him with Red Whiskered Joe, whom Selwyn had met briefly at the Magic Lantern Show. This was all very well, and Atchison was polite enough, but you could see he knew that Ferny was attempting to lead him down the garden path. His face was tensed in the jaw, his blue eyes full of undertones, and his smiles and pleasantries to Joe, myself and the Morgans were squeezed out like bitter juice from the press. Ferny had him, didn't he, Atchison being on our place, and therefore, in an interlocutory sense, on our terms. The apparent informality of the situation precluded him from coming out and asking for funds directly, or even from enquiring as to what reflections Ferny might have had on his previous reconnaissance call. They would have to retire again to Ferny's study for that, and that would only be achieved if he was invited. But I knew well enough already that Ferny, who was by both temperament and inclination the most democratically minded of men, felt himself rather superior around Atchison, even *snobbish*. That he considered Atchison a dolt and his desire for a bell a ruse for his own self-aggrandisement was self-evident enough to me.

And so it was that, as Georgina Morgan chimed in innocently about how pleasant it would be to hear a bell ringing through the gum trees, and as Joe Sullivan seemed to agree, and as I devoted all my attentions to collie-cuddling now that Keel had been whistled off, and as Jem Morgan went on with pruning, Selwyn Atchison was indeed *brooked* by Uncle Ferny.

It was as Atchison had managed to return the conversation back from a debate of the various usages of must, to the way in which the peal of a bell would provide a symbolic canopy for us all to worship and shelter under in what had, until only recently, been a den of iniquitous neanderthals, that Ferny, quietly enough, began to champion a different *tone*.

'But, Selwyn,' he said, 'given the account I have previously shared with you about the events my Grandfather was involved with on what is now known commonly as the Bell Post Hill near Geelong, I am surprised that you do not consider more fully, as I do, the hardships the aboriginals have been subjected to by our arrival, the blood that has been spilt, the strychnine that has been unofficially dosed into the damper, the "blue pills" dished out, and that it is a possibility therefore that the bell you would ring would sound out something else entirely? Not the stable peace of our days here in Ngangahook but our moral, not to mention *legal* illegitimacy as the scions of settlers, yes, and our brutality as a Christian culture so deaf to our own guiding precepts, the precepts of the Nazarene?'

At that a currawong let out a tri-gargled cry, each note of which seemed to grow further away from us as if the bird was retreating from the conflict and warning others not to come. I swallowed once, and buried my face into rich collie fur. Jem, Georgina and Joe Sullivan were silent, as was Selwyn Atchison.

It was Ferny himself who spoke next. 'It's most certainly

something that I think about,' he said. 'And to be honest, I'm not sure I want an hourly reminder of our local Christian hypocrisy penetrating deep into the redemptive rustling of my trees.'

At this Selwyn Atchison grew strong-faced, and for some reason or another turned to stare directly at Joe Sullivan. Sensing the shift in his focus I raised my nose from the fur.

'And what would you have to say, young Joe, about such a perspective as that?' Selwyn demanded to know. 'I daresay your trip out here to the south-west is certainly affording you some new perspectives. Unless of course it is a view you yourself share, and that's why you are here?'

This of course was the height of rudeness from Selwyn Atchison, to inveigle our guest into the local situation in this way. It was a malicious move by him, and Jem Morgan seemed to be having none of it. 'Aw, come off it, Selwyn,' he said, looking across from a pear tree with a bowsaw in his hand. 'Leave the young fella out of it. Why don't you look Ferny in the eye? He's the one pickin' a fight when he should be pickin' fruit.'

But Ferny took umbrage to this. 'I'm hardly picking a fight, thanks, Jem. It was Mr Atchison here who brought the subject up in the first place. And I might add, if you want to talk history, it's best to face facts.'

'Oh well,' said Jem, with a disinterested air, and turning back to continue his work on the tree, 'maybe you'd be better off then with a bell. That way you could face your facts every day, on the hour in fact, or even the half-hour.'

Selwyn Atchison, with hands on hips, turned then to look back fiercely at Ferny. They considered each other closely.

'Well in that case,' Ferny said gently, almost as if to himself, 'it would be a penitential bell. And I'm not sure that's what Selwyn here has in mind.'

From the pear tree now Georgina Morgan laughed. 'You can say that again, Fern!' she said, before getting back to sawing the tree.

'In actual fact,' Ferny continued, 'and to be quite clear with you, Selwyn, I'm just not sure how I feel about the bell and whether I want to contribute to the cause. But can we not discuss the matter in a realistic way? I would have thought that as things currently stand it should not just be treated as a formality, a fait accompli.'

Selwyn Atchison pursed his lips and blinked rapidly. It was becoming quite obvious he did not like to be brooked. 'Yes well,' he huffed, 'I did not ride out here today to be lectured on British history.'

'No, I wouldn't have thought you did,' Ferny replied. 'So let's leave it at that, shall we? I'll continue to think about the bell and I'm sure you will think about what I've said. Meanwhile, we have an orchard to prune.'

It was clear to everyone present. Selwyn Atchison had just been given short shrift by Uncle Ferny. He whistled his dog, and I was left cuddling the air, while beside me Joe Sullivan was looking shocked and confused. We watched in silence as Atchison remounted his horse and made for our gate, his noble champion running beside.

From that moment on, for the rest of the day and into the evening, all that any of us thought about was the bell. When Atchison had left, it was Joe Sullivan who first piped up. 'Can I ask,' he said, 'what that was all about?'

To which Georgina replied, 'Your guess is as good as mine, Joe.'

But it wasn't. In fact Joe Sullivan's guess was a lot better than Georgina's. For at the dinner table that night he speculated as to why a bell would be deemed necessary at all. 'We have a bell in a tower on High Street, back in Ivanhoe,' he told us. 'It drives me spare, to be truthful. Sometimes I walk for miles down along the river, just so I can get away from it.'

Being himself quite a lover of bells, Ferny was greatly amused by this anecdote. He tucked into his chops with even greater relish than he already had been, nodding all the while and smiling. There was certainly something strangely bemusing about Joe, which Ferny liked an enormous amount. Joe's perspective on the bell only confirmed his affection. It seemed indeed to clarify something in Uncle Ferny's mind. 'Well, Joe. Only once before have I ever heard of anyone actively escaping the sound, but yes, if I want bells I'll go to London,' he said. 'Or up to Fiesole above Florence. Or even to Melbourne. Here in the Ngangahook Run, though, I'm really not too sure…'

After dinner, with Uncle Ferny and Red Whiskered Joe playing cards by the fire, I sat at the writing table in my room, my journal open in front of me. Red Whiskered Joe had gone on to further garnish the voluntary expression of his attitude by describing how the very miles of the river which he walked in order to escape the High Street bell in Ivanhoe were themselves proliferate with the sound of bell-*birds*. 'The most remarkable ratio of body mass to vocal projection is exhibited in those birds,' he told us. 'They ring and ping, and when you're just beneath a branch from which they call it is quite deafening. Fascinatingly so. Then when you catch sight of their humble stature and compact dimensions you really can only wonder at how they do it. These bells ring constantly along the Yarra there, and I've never once had the impulse to run away from *them*. Rather, I prefer, whenever I can, to get out amongst them. Exchanging one bell for another, eh.'

I was thinking of those words of Joe's as I sat there before the open page. Thinking of how iron clangs, how certain rocks resound, while others, such as those which frame the pools and caves under the lighthouse, have little sound at all. Although they are the receivers of the ocean's blows, they do not in themselves transmit. Not like Joe's bellbirds, or Selwyn Atchison's intended bell, which he imagined would transmit sanctity and safety to all in the thereabouts. But what of the dumber rocks, the quieter birds, and the birds whose bell can grate the eardrum yet still enrich the soul – what of their safety? Are they in need of the Bell Committee's protection? Or do they in fact, as Joe Sullivan implied, need protection themselves from precisely such an intervention?

Before long I found myself writing. But not out of certitude. No, I wondered still as the pen went whispering over the page. Was there a difference between my preparations of the piano and the Bell Committee's intended 'preparation' of the land? Were they to insert a bell into the place just as I might insert a banksia cob amongst the strings? *And so*, I wrote, (and I have the page in front of me right here), *perhaps the entire glen and its surrounds, the inlet and the cliffs, the heights of the ridges, be they cleared or originally timbered, the river and its reedy banks and every animate singer, or drummer within it, constitutes one whole instrument of sound and sense? Thus the clopping horse, the barking dog, the lowing steer, the baaing lamb, the knocking coach, the splitting axe, and the gunshot, are all the preparations of our being here. But the bell, if it comes, surely it will not be so incidental? Surely it will leave nothing to chance and will in fact symbolise the dominance of such preparations as we make? So that, every time we hear it, every hour, every half-hour, of every day, we will hear nothing else, nothing else but the bell of ourselves, ringing a sonic virus out over the land. For this place is not our audience after all, nor our piano. No, it is the Symphony of Long Before We Came, and Well After We're Gone, and everything I borrow from that Symphony for my piano or my poems is exactly that: a gift from the music that has been here playing all along.*

I put my pen down and closed my book. I was more aware than ever at that moment, of the unconventional nature of my perspective. And yet, in Ferny's house, and with Joe as our guest, I felt supported. My mind, buttressed and invigorated by love, was not at risk.

And so I listened. I listened again to the night, the bright sound of wind in the trees, the *oom oom oom* of the frogmouth. And to everything in between. I listened, to the bell of the world.

IX

AND SO MY story keeps descending from the ridge down to the sea. From the ridge beyond the Big Cutting Hill to the ocean roar beyond the river's glen.

One day in the early spring, as Ferny, myself, and Red Whiskered Joe were having our lunch together on the verandah, Ferny recounted a strange event.

'A rather odd thing happened this morning at the General Store,' he said, while picking seeds from his teeth just as a gang-gang might do high in a melaleuca. 'In these parts this is the season for rainbows, and I remarked upon that fact to old Jack Wattletree, as I walked in. "Bloody rainbow's so strong, nearly took my eyes out," I joked to Jack. But no. He was having none of it. Usually such a personable old chap. I remember the time when I lent him the seine nets. He was so grateful. Had holes all through his. Reckons the cockies had got into them eating something they particularly liked in the sea lettuce and weed that was tangled in the netting. But no, today he hardly gave me a grunt.

'Then, when I asked Jack Bilborough behind the counter for the paper he said they were all out. "But I've one reserved, Bill.

You know that." "Sorry, Mr Hutchinson," he said. "We were short on the order."

'Well, that was a first – on two fronts. First, he's never called me anything but Ferny, or occasionally, and just jesting, "Squire"; and secondly, I've never heard of him being short on his newspaper order before. No, I tell you it was peculiar. Something wasn't right.'

Uncle Ferny's confusion at these encounters with Jack Wattletree and Jack Bilborough at the General Store sent me off into my own thoughts. What was it exactly, I found myself asking, that disturbed me so much about the tale he recounted? Was it simply that it had cracked open the seedpod of my loyalty to my young uncle, my hackles rising like an echidna's tines in defence of his character and situation? Or was it that I knew already something of the future of which it spoke, a future of domestic comfort, and gradual disintegration, as opposed to the improvisatory utopia of ironbark and sable stream which Ferny and I actively pursued. History has its junctures no doubt (whereas *Herstory* has truer turns and rills of sidereal time), and I felt all the ingredients converging at this particular one. What I may see and what I may predict of all the revolving days and nights ahead has all ensued from moments such as these. Not newsworthy moments, nor moments you would find in the annals of Hansard, but local moments from life's General Store. The General Store too of our betrayals, our failures to imagine and accommodate the genial, the kind, and the quiet music of each day and each winding river in spate. This is the General Store of our discomfort with variance, our disregard for the provenance of a nature-to-human covenant, which would protect as much as survive, with song and image as much as by tooth and claw. For the soul needs its light as the child needs milk.

It is perhaps true that in another man's hands the desire for a bell could be as sweet as that milk, the very *colostrum*, as it is in the worshipping sites of Greece and of China, but for us I daresay it seemed something else was to be smuggled in along with the sound, so that the air would become as if inappropriately dyed, or at least would resemble an unvaried quilt. It would be a tonal regimentation, in its way, of the mosses and leaves. The very airs which they inhale and exhale would cease to synthesise, and would thus dry and wilt, particularly the mosses, until an imbalance would be laid bare.

Such were my fears, based as much on what I felt around me as on what I suspect I have the gift to foresee. That is: you looking back through the glass of your own time, and through the remaining available apertures of a eustatic atmosphere, wondering how we could not have realised.

Red Whiskered Joe however, who had been with us now for over a month and who had, more than once, expressed the sensation of his hand finally finding its glove here in the glen, was keen to know more. What, he asked, could either Jack Wattletree (whose own father had grown up with Ferny's in the days of Governor La Trobe), or the Store proprietor Jack Bilborough (an innocuous man whose passions previously only came to the fore in the Christmas horserace on the beach), possibly have against Ferny if it wasn't to do with his resistance to the ambitions for the bell?

'I simply don't know,' Ferny told Joe. 'Jack Wattletree himself has made great gains with his plough in recent times, and especially on the ground that he leases from me. As his father did. Old Turnip Tom was his name, and he was as close to my own father as anyone either side of our rivermouth. They even used to knit stockings together. I remember them, when I was a child, sitting by the fire like too old wood ducks, talking of their forebears in Devon, where their families had in fact also been neighbours, or of barn-work, or whatever was going on. Their friendship was plain, uncomplicated as an exchange of lemons. Type for type. And so it's continued between myself and Jack. Though we've never been so great together as Dad and old Tom. But still. We've been friends, mates. And he's admired your performances hasn't he, Sarah? Also the poems you put up on the corkboard in the Store.'

I nodded. 'Yes, he told me as much.'

'Well, it sounds like he's been got at then,' declared Joe. 'That Selwyn Atchison bloke's involved for sure. He went pale as paper when you said what you said to him in the orchard. I think "illegitimacy" was the word you used. Quite a loaded gun a word like that, to a god-fearing man.'

Uncle Ferny laughed. 'I s'pose you're right, Joe. Though I never thought of it like that. The new Nation as a bastard! That would have landed a blow.'

'I daresay,' Joe agreed.

'But how he could get any purchase with fellas like Jack Wattletree and Jack Bilborough is what beats me,' Ferny said. 'Everyone knows old Selwyn's a wowser, an earbasher and a bore. Sarah, any thoughts?'

Thoughts. I had enough to fill the Bass Strait!

Firstly, that layers of acrimony are like the layers of memory. One leads to another which in turn needs the next one to survive. In a small community it only takes the smallest ripple to bother the reeds. And that's what we had here. There was no escaping it.

I chose however to placate rather than fan the flame. Uncle Ferny's confidence was in question it seemed.

'Surely,' I said, 'you've no need to worry. Lovely Jack Wattletree is not capable of carrying Selwyn Atchison's dark burden for long. I wouldn't worry. Let the river flow. I think you're just missing your book.'

'Ah!' Ferny exclaimed. 'How funny you should bring it up! There was a letter from Jones of Moolap at the Post Office this morning. I picked it up directly after my encounter with the two Jacks.'

I smiled with satisfaction, realising my diversion had gone even better than I had expected.

'And what did he say?' I asked, eagerly. 'Is it ready and done?'

'Well, it was the most curious letter. He spoke of a figurative "bullocky path" he'd been led down by the book, or, as he put it, "a long paddock of wit and imagery, an inland seaway of our struggle with existence". In fixing the binding he's apparently got to reading the book, and become captivated. Hence, he apologised for the delay. But he needn't have bothered. By looking at his half dozen sheep, the way they stood in front of his house as still as wood, and ruminating so slowly, I already figured he would be a while.

'Anyway, the upshot is that not only is the book indeed ready, but he says he has other items of interest to discuss with us as well. Whatever could that mean? He has suggested we pick up the book at our earliest convenience and that we do him the honour of being his guests to lunch.'

Well, I could tell by Ferny's tone that another sojourn to Moolap had definite appeal, especially as it would release him from the matter of the bell for at least a brief time. And, of course, he was eager, if not desperate, to take possession once more of his talisman and teacher: the very book. Would I accompany him again, he wanted to know, as Jones the Bookbinder had made a point of extending the lunch invitation to Ferny's 'companionable niece'. I said that I would. Taking in the coast from the box seat of the gig, and a night at the Velar Nasal Inn, could be a tonic. And, I suggested, even more so given Red Whiskered Joe was on hand to help the Morgans mind the fort while we were away. That was if he was amenable to a day or two of solitude in the homestead.

In fact I detected a shade of disappointment in Joe Sullivan's countenance when I made this suggestion. Either he had fancied a trip to Moolap himself, or he expected that a day or two alone with him on the Run would appeal to me to such an extent that I would refuse the Bookbinder's offer. Did he expect me to pine for the creature that he was? Did he imagine, having touched my bare breasts and clasped my naked hips, that I would now forgo all life's other adventures for his company and pleasure? Perhaps. But if so, he had a lot to learn. Not only about me but also about the diversity of seed-stock and growing conditions which are the key to life and farm alike. In his arms he had found me teeming, in full spate, but so he would also find me beyond his reach, in thrall to the stars and the sounds they make, in the same way I was in thrall to the joy the two of us were capable of sharing amidst the throng of that sound. Whatever the case, Joe managed to disguise his disappointment sufficiently well. He agreed to stay back alone to look after the house and to help the Morgans with the work around the farm.

The night before we were due to leave Joe was keen for Uncle Ferny to describe to him what it was that was so important about the book we were picking up from Jones of Moolap. Sitting by the fire after dinner he began to interrogate Ferny on its contents. As Ferny explained, it was not only the contents of the book that gave it its claim and especial traction. The book had been published some seven years previous, and in that time it had travelled with Ferny through Greece and Egypt, and deep into the Russian interior. It had lived with him on the Via di Panico in Rome, in Fiesole on the hill above Firenze, and in Holland Park in London. It had been to Linnaeus' garden in Uppsala, to Tolstoy's village school at Yasnaya Polyana, and had even ventured across the Atlantic where it kept Ferny company during a brace of lovelorn days in New York City and then during a week of obligatory tedium with some relatives of his mother's in Baltimore. It had been read aloud in glamorous company in Hong Kong, had survived the sinking of an Islamic fishing junk in the South China Sea and, of course, had travelled many many miles on the great diagonal journeys of Australia: from Darwin to Melbourne, from Adelaide to Sydney, from Albury to Broken Hill and from Albany to Kalgoorlie. In that time Ferny had performed as a gold prospector, a stockbroker, a trader in archaeological treasures, a painter, a racing motor car driver, and, always, a gregarious benefactor of the progressive arts. And what had prevented him from going mad amidst the chaos of all these escapades was the eloquent wit of this very Australian yet international book. In a Bedouin tent in the Sahara he could ignore the sexual overtones of his Irish companion, one Jerry O'Rourke from Clontarf, by burying himself in the pages of his literary long paddock. And when love reached its heights for Ferny via Morris Frondeau, an Anglo-Gallic impressionist who had settled in Fiesole, it was once again the rebarbative and absurdist pomposity of the book's narrator, Tom Collins, that kept his tongue in his cheek and his own wits about him, even during the most terrible days of Frondeau's opiated demise. With the flickering light of our hearth-fire scoring mountain peaks of glaring fervour across his features, Ferny explained to Joe how he had come to believe that he could only travel, indeed he could only *fly*, if he had the ballast of the book on his person. 'That way,' he said, 'I am never at home and never away, I am in fact always in midair, with a generous and witful purview, knowing all the while that however or whenever I fall, I will only descend to the *most* interesting, *most* colourful and *most* companionable ground that there is: that of the itinerant worker of our common land.

'I have a taste for flight,' he explained further to an increasingly captivated Joe Sullivan. 'And I live for the beauty inherent in things, but I also know that the wealth and freedom I have inherited is not that of a bird of the air. No, it is we, the human race, and not the lowing bullocks, that are the beasts of burden. The men and women of this book know that, as does its fictional author, who is himself a ruse, a faithful preacher, a poet, a pompous charlatan and a most ingenious engenderer of images from life. It is, more than anything, these *images*, cacophonous as they are with the book's voices, that I value the most. When the sleet of life is coming sideways across my farmer's flesh I can have a chuckle or a think and as long as I have the book I can see an image in my mind of a glimmering illusory scrub in which all men are equal in the secret passion of their desires, equal too with the bullocks who carry the real human load, the load of things: silage, furniture, granite, grain, cotton reels, farm implements, timber, wool, blue metal, tanned hides, hats, water, ice, china, broad beans, medicines, poultry, coal, turnips, corsets, you name it. They carry it all across a parsimonious but seasonally well grassed land. This is the freight that reduces us, and lifts us up.

And it is the carrying of this very freight, the *things* of life, that is the book's mise en scène. For me then it is both a vade mecum and a taskmaster. In short, a reminder of the future. A future I would not be without.'

I was watching Joe Sullivan's face closely as Uncle Ferny made this speech, careful to note any confusion at the pitch of his account. But I saw none. As my uncle spoke of his unusual reliance on the book, a reliance we all tend to have upon something after all, I got to simply watching the dance of the fire's reflections on Joe's sweet features. For there is no better screen than innocence on which to project life's fiery dance. The logs crackled on, hissed and collapsed, even as the words began to dwindle on my uncle's lips, so that with the bullocking of his book in mind, and as he began to describe them individually and in more detail, I began to watch yet another lantern show, this time on Joe's face. He was, right then, as if a blank receiver, a white page. I wanted to take him then after all, to be myself the fire dancing upon his flesh just as he had become a new narrative in my soul. But I did not take him, and I could not, with his other love Ferny talking there of the Riverina and of Republican politics. Instead I rose from my orchid chair and went to the piano, whose case for once was closed and unprepared due to our departure the following morning. I played not something from my own imagination, not something from my own book of sound and glen; rather I played Schubert. Étude No. 6. To accompany my uncle's account, to sway with the flames, to calm my own passion, and so that I might have it to linger on during our journey along the cliffs and through the swamps the following day, just as Red Whiskered Joe might have its wistful residue to keep him company while he was alone in the owl-appointed house.

It is important for me to note however that I don't typically like to talk of owls as omens, as my mother used to do. In the house at East Melbourne she was always hearing boobooks that were not there, and likewise a girl I boarded with in England, Dulcie Evanshire, was as terrified of the poor feathered things as she was of the parsonage. It was Dulcie in fact who was tampered with in that very brick building, and when she came back to the dormitory, visibly distressed, she would only confide in me by rate of an allegory of owls. They had, she whispered through her sobs, unrelenting eyes and a terrible 'foresty' smell. I held Dulcie in my arms the whole night but, truly, she was inconsolable. I wanted to tell her that the life of wicked men is actually destitute of owls, being arid and mean in a way that no owl could comprehend. But I didn't. For poor Dulcie the owls became a way of describing the unspeakable, and I've no doubt that my own mother fell into that category as well. What had happened to her to fill her sky with owls? Something like what happened to Dulcie perhaps? Whatever it was, she was always clapping her hands to her ears against it happening again, or alternatively cupping her hand behind her ear in anxious disbelief at any peace and quiet she attained.

The point is though that I did know what would happen to the house and Joe Sullivan in our absence, for any vision I have of events along the line – incidents and phenomena occurring, as it were, outside of Time – does occasionally foreshorten so. What I see of future lives, awoken as they may be by emptying animalian inventories in the chemical weather that will seem a Rorschach test of the childish spirit of Man, is a simultaneous hurt. But nevertheless in the days and weeks of my own mortal span a brief window sometimes seems to open, by dint of nothing more mysterious than clear observation, on events just up ahead. And this was the case as we readied ourselves to leave. I knew Joe would be challenged while we were away, the glen would be violated in our absence, and thus my mother's and Dulcie Evanshire's owls were indeed *appointed*. They 'manned' the high boughs at all corners of the homestead, like messengers at the pass of Thermopylae, their two-note step-down song resounding between the valley ridges as if conjuring up what was to come out of the moonless night. But of this, for now at least, I've said enough.

X

THE DAY BROKE bright, with kangaroos and Jersey cows alike enjoying the sun on the pasture, and a sea-eagle gliding high over the squelchy green. We strained some water for the journey through the dried-out banksia cobs of late winter, lashed our cases to the spring cart, and breakfasted on porridge, eggs, and the excellent bacon of 1909. All good fare for a strong journey.

Unlike last time we found the track across the ocean cliffs not so much gluey and clay-caked but wet and slushy. The blaze of the horse – whose name was Ray – was bespattered, and we made slow going as we went around the bends, though the camber being sheened thus by the rains and pollen-winds allowed for a smoother, more sibilant, less jerky ride.

At the bridge over Swampy Creek, when we'd been travelling for less than an hour, we encountered a hawker's wagon, resplendent with painted decorations and brightly hanging pots, coming the other way. We pulled the reins and stopped to converse. Telling us he was bound for Lorne the hawker also announced, as much by the blueness of his eyes as anything else, that he was from the Lebanon. He held blankets, he told us, copper pots and pans, chicory, oranges and baklava. Ferny was immediately in his element, hardly believing his luck and getting down from the box seat to shake the hawker's hand and converse, as if high among the cedars. Eventually they wandered together down off the bridge towards a bathing box on its landward side, where they made a discreet exchange of which it was clear I was not to be privy. The hawker's name was Pascal, as in the philosopher. The name was, Ferny explained to me afterwards, an example of the French colonial influence in that part of the eastern Mediterranean.

Coming back up onto the bridge, Ferny said to Pascal, 'I have enjoyed baklava in Paris as well as in Tripoli. But I was not expecting to chance upon it here on the Swampy Creek bridge this morning!'

Giving Pascal the directions to the glen, Ferny implored him to stop a while there and sell his wares among the lighthouse families and nearby farmers before he travelled further into the west. 'You'd be most welcome to stop by on your return journey too,' Ferny enthused. 'We'll be back in situ by then, and I'd be more than happy to smoke a hookah with you and hear about your travels. We've some beautiful apples in our orchard too. They'd go well in the pipe.'

By the end of their encounter the hawker seemed even a little taken aback, such was Ferny's enthusiasm; but nevertheless, before we said our farewells he agreed to take up the offer of stopping at Ngangahook, which pleased Uncle Ferny no end. 'Our Joe is in for a nice surprise,' he said with relish, as he climbed back up into the box, and gee-d the horse.

We crossed the bridge. And as we climbed the hill out of the Swampy Creek settlement, Ferny talked nine to the dozen and nonstop all the way to Bells Brae. He spoke at great length of his time in the Levant and his fondness for the region, and by the time, some hours later, we'd reached the swanned soaks of the backlands behind Geelong, he had returned to the subject and was reciting what he knew of Arabic poetry. The poor dear. He positively reeked of nostalgia for his travels as he spoke of the magic of the oud and the saraband, and the distinctive and ancient tendencies of the Levantine poets towards extemporisation. 'You would appreciate Lebanon, Sarah, you most certainly would!' he cried, all the while tickling Ray with the reins, as we achieved our careful and slippery progress towards Moolap.

~

What is sunshine after winter? What is being but an ear? Gone was April, gone was May, June had plenished the reeds and glasswort, but July had worried the roofing. In the reflected gleam of the sun-sheet of the bay waters around the Bookbinder's land it was clear that August had positively harangued his panes and sills, and his sheep, that small but stubborn coterie who stood now in the sun as if in the presence of a god.

The world is a bell that sometimes only rings after long intervals: indeed it is often in the intervals where the suffering, and therefore the wisdom, lies. Hurled as I'd been as a girl from pillar to post, with my parents expelled by life from the trance of each other – my father off to breed his cattle by Christchurch, my mother breeding her own succubi in an aftermath of Gordon's gin – my own intervals had been prolonged. I thought of this now as the sun rang out on our arrival in Moolap, the way I'd been ejected as their marriage prolapsed, thrown out to the edge of the planetary sphere, as it were, with no shelter left in the domestic fold. There I had stood alone at the circumference, with dark space multiplying in front of me. That was the future back then, unpeopled and without delineation. It was all I had to fall into. Yet it is only on that edge, with a proud earth tapering away above and below, and with distant stars on every horizon, that we can most properly comprehend the majesty of the scale. It is terror too that holds us fast in our perception of that vast immensity populating our permeable skull, our self its landscape, airscape and soundscape, so that when the interval is defined by its node, in this case the September sun ringing out over the marshes of Moolap, we come to understand that such joy of light is not divisible from us, that we in fact consist of it, as does the swan, the spoonbill, and the snub-nosed coot.

Presently Ferny stopped the spring cart, for no other reason but to take in the moment. The train line arced by, and the season had changed. He said not a word but passed me one of the hawker's oranges and began himself to prepare his pipe. Though language emerges from us in order to match the world, to share it in an agreed-upon currency, there is in fact a deeper wealth that is shared before this. In silence. Or, if I may make the distinction, for it is distinctions like these that render language more than just noise, in *quietude*. Truth is, for as long as the blood of perception beats through our veins the world is never silent, though in calmer times it is often *quiet*. Yes, for as long as the blood of perception beats through our veins.

I peeled the orange, which had its own juicy music, of pith and flesh and fluid as highly structured as Jupiter itself. And therein too lay its seeds, ready as ever to perpetuate its miraculous colour amongst all the others in the field. Ferny lit up, and his blue smoke wafted across with the luffings from the bay, as I divided the fruit's segments. The orange was in itself as if an experimental earth, all shot through with one strong colour, and perfectly realised in its way. As Ferny puffed happily on whatever Pascal had given him, and I enjoyed the orange with swans and sheep surrounding, also the house and train line, and of course the worted marsh as well, it was never more clear how alike all things must be. Man and bird. Earth and orange too.

A curlew was in fact our companion there amongst the other birds, probing the mud of the marsh for her fare. Time gave her the tool, the experiment took place at evolution's slow pace, the prong with which she procures her sustenance and therefore perpetuates her flight. And now as I watched her I saw that even she could falter, as she prodded a little too hard into a collapsing pocket of nutrient mud and found herself face down into the squelch. Her head came up, all muddied with the Moolap ground, and I laughed. She was such a darling sight. But more than that she was like myself: aloof to strangers, averse to interruptions, and undivided, necessarily so, in devotion to her instrument and its art. Even with such an expertly evolved and long beak as she had, she'd *made a blue*, as they say in these parts, and was quick to remedy it. She stepped on reedlike legs across to a wetter wash of water where she immediately splashed her face and cleaned her beak as well. Her brindled features shone, her long prong reminding me of the kitchen. Yes, it was the curlew cutlery. She had washed up, and having done so, continued to set her faith in the world. She would perhaps, I thought, make the same mistake again, but never in the same place. So whatever it was that she was feeding on better beware!

From where we paused with orange and smoke, the Bookbinder's house in the mid-distance was glinting and gleaming, its stolid stone contrasted by glary panes and the whitewash of its trim and Georgian eave. It was still a good half mile from us, and I was surprised Uncle Ferny was not keener to hasten. But no, for the time being he seemed content to puff his pipe and let the winter thaw from his bones.

By the time he did loop the leather of the reins through his fingers again we had still yet to see a train go past. There, I thought, there is the beauty of the interval again, the space between events. This space was indeed an event in itself, a level procession of time in the lee of drama, and any proper salt marsh is proof of that. As Ray the horse finally went stepping squelchily on, I thought that I would like one day to make something so horizontal as a marsh, where nothing vertical obscures the realities of continuous time, no tree but a reed, no building but a nest, no tragedy but the closing of the day and life, as it reaches its allotted end.

*

Unlike on our first visit the Bookbinder was not quick to respond as we pulled the spring cart up to the front of the house. There was plenty of activity amongst the seaberry saltbush creeping along his boundary fence, with insects abuzz, but no movement whatsoever from the building itself. I waited in the box seat, continuing my reflections still on the rhythm of bell and interval. Ferny meanwhile knocked first on the front door and then, receiving no response, went around the back. There was no doubt that Jones was expecting us, so he could not be far. Yet when Ferny returned to view the house with his empty hands outstretched, it seemed possible that somehow our wires had got crossed.

'Lo, there are tanning sheds behind there,' Ferny said, 'and leathers drying everywhere. What a reek!' He paused. 'But there is also a cup on the garden bench. And the tea in the cup is warm.'

The prospect of a cup of tea in the September sunlight distracted me from my meditations. I watched on as Uncle Ferny, with hands on hips, took in the scene: the coterie of steadfast sheep, the gleamy expanse of marsh, the camber of the steel rails going past, the dark blue stones of the house cut from the volcanic plain. He turned then and, jovially parroting a ransacker, went to peer through the front window as if to find a way in. He turned quickly away though, too honest in his lovely nature to prolong even an imitation of a sleuth or thief. He shook his head as if to clear his mind.

Walking over to the dray, he placed his palm on the blaze of Ray and said, 'I don't know if it's the hashish the hawker gave me or what, but I think I'm seeing double, Sarah.'

'How do you mean?'

'Well, just now looking in through the window to the front room – it's where he received us last time, you know, with the skull of old Gellibrand dangling there.'

'Yes,' I said.

'Yair well by the look of it he's got the book out and ready to present to us. It's there on the table as promised.'

'Yes.'

'Yes. But if I'm not mistaken, it sits twice as high as it used to. It's twice as thick.'

'A different edition?'

'Well perhaps, but it looks exactly the same. Just thicker. With double the pages. Twice as high as I say. Unless I'm seeing double.'

He was perturbed, and made a questioning grimace as he looked at me, as if for an answer. I stood up immediately in the cart and began to step down. 'I will see for myself,' I declared imperiously, but also ironically.

Ferny grinned, and kissed the blaze. 'There's nothing like a Levantine pipe,' he said, as if to the horse. And then: 'Yes, take a look, Sarah, and confirm for me that I'm stoned.'

It was as my boot touched the Moolap ground however, that we heard the treadle of the Bookbinder's handcart coming around from the bayside of the house. And only seconds later it was Jones himself who appeared, pushing the handcart by its timber handle and dressed in an ankle-length oilskin coat, with a pale blue handkerchief tied around the lower half of his face. His coat was fairly smattered in marshgrit and ordure.

'Begod!' he cried through the mask on seeing us. 'Is that the time? Mr Hutchinson, Miss Hutchinson, my apologies please.'

He made quite the sight as he repented there, the contents of the handcart veritably steaming in front of him, and leaving us in no doubt by its vapour of why he wore the mask. In short it seemed the cart was full of shit. Hence the coat on such a warming day, and the kerchief.

'You see I don't like to take my timepiece when I'm doing such work as this. Could get ruined, by wet in its workings. But please, will you give me a moment to clean myself up before I welcome you in? I'd be most grateful. And yes, Mr Hutchinson, it's a most wonderful book!'

He set the handles of the handcart down. For a brief moment I thought he was going to bow, as if in supplication to Ferny's superior literary taste, but I was mistaken. Nevertheless he did seem instantaneously moved by his very mention of the book, which, of course, was rather odd given the sight of him, streaked in the manure of swans and other shorebirds as he was, yet on the verge of an aesthetic effusion.

'Of course, Mr Jones,' said Uncle Ferny. 'It's no trouble for us to wait here in your yard in this weather.'

Jones the Bookbinder of Moolap regripped the handle of his cart, bade us a brief farewell, and disappeared back the way he had come.

Ferny returned his palm to Ray's blaze and explained. 'The swan-shit, Sarah – excuse my French – is all for the books. It seems that Jones is his own pure-finder and is just back from collecting the bird masterings. He'll soak his hides in those tubs of liquid reek around the back, to prepare the leather and get the hair off for the bindings. He's got a canny location at that, here in the marsh with the beautiful birds defecating all about him. Who knows, it may even be why he chose the spot. We'll have to ask.'

I must have frowned quizzically I'm sure. The thought of every book in Ferny's library at the glen being drenched in the ordure of animals was disconcerting. All that eloquence, all that poetry, even the Bible itself, coming all bound up in a slurry of dung. 'Talk about feet of clay!' I remarked. 'Though it gives our literature a certain *authenticity* I suppose.'

Ferny saw the joke, and perhaps Ray did too, commenting as he did with his own fibrillating contribution to the 'pure' culture of the thereabouts. His heavy equine plops prefaced Ferny's justificatory reply.

'Yes, but the pages themselves, all the inked words upon them, don't have to survive such stuff. It's only the leathers that bind them, and they're all washed clean, needless to say.'

'Yes, of course, uncle, but the thought of it, the *history* of what you are holding in your hands.'

'Or wearing on your hands, in the case of kid gloves,' was his reply. 'Or on your feet.'

Indeed we were both wearing leather boots.

He had a point, but what struck me was the metaphor. The pale and soft-skinned scholars, all seemingly inoculated against the mess of life in their booklined studies, yet all of them, and all their chosen topics, having pedigrees of *shit*.

'It is perfect, don't you see, uncle,' I said. 'The *integration*. The impurity of a pure life cannot be escaped, and vice versa, the purity of the impure, despite what Plato says.'

Ferny nodded rather sagely. He was serious now, as we waited in the sun for our host. 'Yes, all is integrated,' he said. 'Wisdom and entertainment housed in a dung-pured cladding is actually quite an edifying idea. And dare I say it's rather like a she-oak nut being affixed to the strings of a piano.'

'Touché,' I cried. 'So right you are.'

Uncle Ferny giggled. And, at the risk of reminding you of old Chaucer himself, I must also report that Ray duly farted in a prolonged and once again fibrillating manner. Was he not somehow harping on our theme? And who said animals were dumb and could not improvise?

We settled then, falling silent in the airiness surrounding the Bookbinder's lair and workshop. In the distance I heard a ship's loud horn. Not far from where we stood, English and American vessels off-loaded their freight. What with the birds all about, the latency of the train tracks, and Jones' own industry, Moolap was a veritable hive of activity.

Presently, the Bookbinder appeared at his front door. 'My apologies again,' he called. 'Please do come in.' He had cleaned himself up. Gone was the oilskin and the gumboots and the handkerchief-mask. Instead he wore a clean tweed suit and looked every bit the bookman. As opposed to the nightman.

As on our previous visit we were ushered in to sit at his large binding table, with the human skull 'Gellibrand' hanging nearby. Dangling motionless there, but somehow full of potency, the skull seemed as poised to me as a kite above the quail.

To break the mood engendered by the skull, as we took our seats I ventured to tell Jones that since our last visit it had come to my notice that not one, not two, but three separate farmhouses within a twenty-mile radius of our own also featured dangling skulls and at least one of them went by the name of Gellibrand. 'This particular colonist,' I remarked, 'seems to have multiplied posthumously!'

The Bookbinder lowered his stout frame into his seat opposite us and raised his eyebrows. He gave me a confusing stare, surprised perhaps as he was that a young woman would speak up so.

'Yes, well he did in fact draw up the colony's founding document, so in that respect also he has proven to be quite *creative*.'

With his emphasis of this word he simultaneously patted the inordinately tall book that sat between us on the table. The book upon which Uncle Ferny's eyes were fixed. For now it seemed the skull called 'Gellibrand', no matter how iconic, was nothing compared to it.

It was clear to me then that we were in a territory of copies. No one skull of Gellibrand was the same as the other but was somehow purported to be. And now it seemed the book so dear to Ferny had also been replicated, and with a notable difference, before our eyes. For just as the four Gellibrands differed in profile, also in the protuberance of the forehead, the declivity of the chin and the number of teeth, so too in the book that lay before us the difference was *marked*. Though I didn't know the half of it yet.

For this was not simply the case of a craftsman rebinding a printed book. As Jones of Moolap began to explain:

'If it was just any old book, Mr Hutchinson, there would not have been such a delay. T'was a simple enough job after all. Clean the thing up, replace an endpaper, reaffix the tapes and adjust the spine accordingly; but no, this is not what I found. Not what I found at all. And I quote:

"Mrs Beaudesart possessed a vast store of Debrett-information touching those early gentleman-colonists whose enterprise is hymned by loftier harps than mine, but whose sordid greed and unspeakable arrogance has yet to be said or sung."

'Or this:

"No young fellow in that great rendezvous dared to embellish his narrative in the slightest degree, on pain of being posted as a double-adjective blatherskite; for his audience was sure to include a couple of critical, cynical, iron-grey cyclopedias of everything Australian — everything, at least, untainted by the spurious and blue-moulded civilisation of the littoral."

'Which brings me,' Jones said then, patting the tall book again, 'to what I've done.'

Well, I for one had no right idea what was going on. He had sieved our reintroductory moment through a very fine meshed colander indeed.

Beside me however, Uncle Ferny was beaming. 'So you read the book!'

The smallest of sly grins tweaked at the side of the Bookbinder's mouth. 'Yes,' he said. 'I was indeed thus waylaid.'

'But not only that,' replied Ferny, 'you've memorised whole passages!'

THE BELL OF THE WORLD

The Bookbinder's smile grew broader. 'It's true,' he said. 'And it came as a whole surprise. Typically I deal with the physical condition of a book, rather than with the content of the text itself. The house rather than the characters who reside in it, as it were. But just occasionally, a sentence, a turn of phrase, catches my attention. In this case, what began like that quickly developed into the most unforeseen concordance.'

He picked up the altered book from where it had been sitting patiently at his elbow. Grasping its extra dimensions in his hands, he momentarily brandished it in the air.

Behind him the marshy window winked. In front of him old 'Gellibrand' said not a word. He looked gaunter than he'd ever been.

'As you can see,' Jones said, 'it's all fixed up. Tight and snug it is now, the fascicles restrained, the boards repaired. I even went so far as to source a match so as to replace some thread of the stitchings. And look, it lies flatter now, as a Bible should.'

He laid the book out in front of us, and yes, it sat open there with no pushback from the pages. Uncle Ferny was impressed. And yet…

'I know you've made the journey up the deckle-edged coast from your Run,' the Bookbinder went on. 'And now I understand why you've gone to the bother. The book is… well… it is a rolling expansive creation tied on to a good age-old backbone of a tale. What isn't in it of life I do not know. The bullock bells, the log and chock fences, the lost chords, the eerie absences, the eternal quest of man and beast for free grass, the nettles of love and the lignum of belonging, the lingo of the goldfields, the luck of the emu. Blind creeks and easy profanities, august slang, and all the back country, scented with the peculiar eloquence, indeed the inadvertent loquacity, of the narrator.

A man's belly is his equator, the night sky is the source of dreams of wisdom…'

'And how about the laughs,' Ferny butted in. 'It keeps me afloat, Jones, like a sound boat upon your Corio Bay out there. My god, the *laughs*.'

'Yes, yes,' concurred our host enthusiastically. 'Enough mirth to swing my friend "Gellibrand" here right back into animated action. Or to lay him down dead. Once and for all. As if in "swino-philosophic contentment".'

Uncle Ferny hurrahed. 'I know the quotation! By god, man, no wonder you've taken the whole winter. You've memorised the lot!'

'Well almost, perhaps, but as you can see, that's not all I've done. Here, inspect the job. See if it's been worth the journey.' He pushed the open book across the table towards Ferny, who promptly took it up.

He could not help but be concerned by its newly thick dimensions, its irregular paginations, but, ever polite, he merely said, 'Ooh yes,' as he handled it this way and that. 'There's no more waggle. No more side-to-side. It's firm and supple as a good saddle. Here, Sarah, take a look.'

The 'repaired' book was passed to me. From the point of view of the craftsmanship of the object it was indeed firm and supple as a saddle. I flicked through its pages, but never having inspected the original item at all closely in the first place I was not quite sure how what I was holding actually compared. It did seem though to contain some rather irregular qualities, but who was I to judge? Knowing that neither man would object to hearing more from the leaves of their devotion, and with the skull of the Hobart lawyer reading over my shoulder, I read aloud:

'There seems something touching and beautiful in the thought that respectability, at best, is merely poised – never hard home.'

And then, a few tightly bound pages further on:

'Is there any rich man who cannot imagine a combination of circumstances that would have given him lodgings under the bridge? – that may still do, say, within twelve months?'

And then:

'the interminable "r-r-r-r-r" of yabbies'.

And:

'After supper we adjourned to the open plain. The night was delicious; and for half an hour the congress was governed by that dignified silence which back-country men appreciate so highly, yet unconsciously.'

And then finally:

'Nothing is more astonishing than the distances lost children have been known to traverse.'

I closed the book. On the other side of the Bookbinder's stone walls a sheep let out a *baaa*. Until then I had presumed that Jones' Polwarth precursors, which guarded the establishment as if waiting for the train – or the boat back to Tasmania – had no voice. But I was wrong. Even 'Gellibrand' seemed to raise an eyebrow as just then, in the further distance, we heard the train.

Jones of Moolap closed his eyes immediately, and kept them shut, either in reverie or frustration, until the train had passed. But what an *interval of noise* we experienced, between the announcement of the sheep and the reopening of the Bookbinder's heron-grey eye. It only compounded the strange illusion that somehow or another, on that day, the slushy marsh of Moolap was a central intersection of the world.

Once the train had sheared past, on its way to Queenscliff, the Bookbinder took up the volume himself. Like the original book that Ferny had delivered him it boasted a dull green cloth over the boards and spine, onto which had been printed a raggedy plant of the inland, with three pale red flowers blooming open upon its black stems and leaves. On the facing boards the title and author's name had been printed in the same black ink as the scraggly leaves and stems, but on the spine the title and author were in the same hue of red as the flowers, one of which was positioned, along with its creeping stems and leaves, in the centre of the spine, between the essential information of the title and the author's name. The plant then continued on around the spine and onto the rear board where it terminated in the top right-hand corner with three leaves and a single flower blossoming backwards in the direction of the title and the spine. When closely studied it was as if the book was double bound there so, first by the stitching of the pages and the fixing of the boards and spine, and secondly because of the creeping clutch of the tendrils of the back-country plant of its cover design.

Briefly then I wondered what on earth this plant had to do with the wit and eloquence within. It looked, after all, not so much like an ornament but a weed. And indeed it was precisely to what the cover lacked that Jones first referred as he commenced to hold forth on this strange and unforeseen creation.

'It is due to my indolence, or perhaps to the increase in my schedule since I've taken it upon myself to procure my own shorebird masterings, that I haven't as yet augmented the cover to match the smoother interventions I've made in the pages inside. The image of a whale spouting amongst the hardy creeping plant has long been in my mind, with seabirds wheeling above the title, and both a ship and a dray upon the spine. The original title *Such Is Life* is itself so Euclidian, so simply philosophic, so phlegmatic and encompassing, that I can make a case for it to remain, but I do nevertheless have my own pet name for the project, and I'll get to that in due course.'

Now I had so little idea of what he was talking about that I looked to Uncle Ferny for guidance. But Ferny didn't seem to notice my enquiry, such was his fixation on what Jones of Moolap had to say. Despite the delay in the mending of the book, and the events of conflict that were pressuring Ferny in the book's absence from the glen, the fact that the Bookbinder had fallen, positively *fallen*, for its pages, made Ferny's own longstanding obsession with the volume seem now lighter, saner, and also objectively verifiable, as if Jones had countersunk any idea that Ferny's predilection was folly. Thus, with the Bookbinder's few choice recitations from memory, and the strange new object his enthusiasm had generated, he had confused, but on balance won, my young uncle's affections and exonerated himself from being in any way to blame for the troubles at home. No, there was no distracting Uncle Ferny now from what Jones of Moolap was beginning to explain.

Jones proceeded then to open his new version of the book. Of course we could already see that the reason for its double thickness had nothing to do with any increase in the size of the typeface. No, the frontispiece was identical (except for the embossed stamp of the bookseller from which it had originally been purchased):

W. HAMPTON BOOKSELLER and STATIONER
of BENDIGO

as was the opening page with its, by now, notorious first sentence:

'UNEMPLOYED at last!'

With the book open before us we could see a certain unevenness among its sections, a sawtoothed rather than deckle-edged effect at the outer limits of the page stack. The paper stock too seemed of alternating hue, first lamb-white then foxed, and of different thickness also. Presently Jones of Moolap flicked through these undulations randomly, positioning a finger upon a page somewhat near the middle of the tome. He began thus to quote from his own creation:

'They were nearly all whalemen; chief mates and second mates, and third mates, and sea-carpenters, and sea-coopers, and sea blacksmiths, and harpooners, and ship-keepers; a brown and brawny company, with bosky beards; an unshorn shaggy set, all wearing monkey jackets for morning gowns.'

He flicked the pages on, and didn't stop there:

'All deep, earnest thinking is but the intrepid effort of the soul to keep the open independence of the sea.'

And then he continued:

'In times of strong emotion mankind disdains all base considerations; but such times are evanescent. The permanent constitutional condition of the manufactured man, thought Ahab, is sordidness.'

And on:

'The sperm whale blows as a clock ticks.'

He turned the pages again and then launched into a long passage wherein a man is lowered into the open head of a vast sperm whale in order to procure a most valuable substance which could only be found therein. And all this at wild sea and in extreme blue water conditions.

But in the middle of this most viscerally terrifying description, Uncle Ferny stood up abruptly in his seat.

'But, Jones,' he cried, 'what is all this? It's not the book I know!

Even if it is bound into the right covers. What have you done there, mate? What is this concoction?'

Jones of Moolap looked up from what he was reading and smiled a vindicated smile, like a fisherman who has just hooked a boisterous but instinctive trout. He looked down with satisfaction to the doubled book, flicked again through still more pages, said, 'Bear with me', and proceeded to read some more:

'The folklore of the Riverina is rich in variations of a mythos pointing to the David and Goliath combat between a quiet wage-slave and a domineering squatter, in the brave days of old. With one solitary exception, each station from the Murray to the Darling claims and holds this legend as its own.'

The sound of the pages continued to riffle as Uncle Ferny resumed his seat. I'd never seen him look so baffled.

Jones the Bookbinder of Moolap read on:

'Take my advice, and while you're at the station, give Montgomery notice. Let some more capable boundary man take your place. You're not worth your damper at this work; for no man's ability is comprehensive enough to cover musical proficiency such as yours and leave the narrowest flap available for anything else. I can see through you like glass. I could write your biography. And, believe me, you're no more fitted for this life than you are to preside over a school of Stoic Philosophy. You're a reed, shaken by the wind. Be a man, Alf. Turn your face eastward and southward, and challenge Fortune with your violin and your voice.'

I found it a rousing passage, no matter what book it was from. 'Oh I love that scene,' Ferny said. 'I know it well. And I love that advice. "Challenge Fortune with your violin and your Voice." But please, Mr Jones. Please explain!'

'I shall, I shall,' Jones said, raising an oathtaking palm. 'And more than happily, for I am proud of what I have done, and hope that you are a sympathetic audience. But first – it's been a momentous winter here on the marsh – I must, if you don't mind, make us all a hot brew of tea.'

He rose from his chair, and, gesturing with said palm for us to continue inspecting the doubled book, left the workshop for the kitchen.

Uncle Ferny and I shifted the book onto the table between us and began to properly pore over its contents. We had already almost completely forgotten about the very book we had come to take possession of, such was the oddness and the mystery of this newly augmented version.

From what we could ascertain (all the while with the dangling skull of 'Gellibrand' poised just above us) the inland scrubs and long bullocky paddock of Ferny's book had been interstitched with a positively sonorous account of life on a whaling boat at sea. Despite the distinctly inverted environments involved, there seemed, at even first and second glance, to be an oddly energetic fermentation bubbling up between these interleaving texts, and thus among the pages of the widely bound edition. My ear could sense immediately the harmonic logic of the Bookbinder's eccentric undertaking, just as Ferny pored over the joins and the differing typefaces with a look of disbelieving fascination.

For you up ahead, dear reader, a single mention of 'Ahab' tells you more than either I or Ferny could possibly have known as we'd listened to the Bookbinder's recitation, the famous whaling book of Herman Melville's being as rarely known in Australia at that time as due remorse over the violence enacted against the Aboriginals. Even more rarely known in fact, as having written his virtuosic Bible of the Whale & Man poor Melville found it almost entirely ignored. To be precise, this literary Creator, this human *antenna* of ultimate realities, died a good four decades later with the printed copies of his *Moby Dick*, originally numbering some 3000, still not having sold. The sadder truth however is that of those original 3000 printed editions of the book, approximately half were lost in a warehouse fire not long after publication, meaning that fewer than 1500 copies were sold during the author's lifetime of what we may all now look back upon as a Great American Book. In Australia therefore, where what books there are typically sail from England, the Book of the Whale was even more unknown, as I say, than the ancient languages of this land.

But there it was, and in our hands, expertly re-filleted and spliced by our bibliophile host, whose racket amongst the kitchen things went on even as we inspected his creation.

Ferny acquainted himself with the blended passages of American ocean-prose on the one hand and the astringent Australian music of his own landbook of bullockies and brown rivers on the other. All the while his lips were moving like a child's. It does not of course take much time to arrange a pot of tea with its china, and biscuits, but by the time Jones of Moolap had re-entered with the tray Ferny was already well on his way to being charmed by the compounded epic.

Perhaps because he was already being accustomed to, indeed disposed towards, the alteration of sacred cultural objects for the purpose of, and in the spirit of, aesthetic creation, ie: my preparations of the Mühlbach grand in the glen; or perhaps because of the effects of what Pascal the hawker had given him to smoke, Ferny displayed little initial resistance to this revisioning of his talismanic book. But even so Jones, distributing the Spode from the tray, and pouring the steaming tea into our cups, wasted no time in beginning his explanation of the hybrid that lay in front of us.

So yes, although he could not possibly have known it, Jones the Bookbinder of Moolap had chosen his guinea pig well.

'It was as I began to work on your book,' he began, 'some days after your previous visit, that bells began to go off in my mind. As I journeyed in the pages, out past the Murray, beyond Hay on the Murrumbidgee, and through the quartzy mirages of the Riverina scrub-horizons, and as the picture of the miscellaneous camaraderie of the long paddock, its vicissitudes and entirely specific bachelordom, was conveyed to me with such excoriating wit and such divine access to both irony and wisdom, a certain similarity began to dawn on me with this other special book in my possession, which is equally as elemental in both quality and mise en scène yet somehow as perfectly and symmetrically adjacent to your own book as night is to day, indeed as land is to the ocean. On the waterfront here in Geelong some two years ago, among the many seafarers one encounters taking their pause at shore before their ship sails off again, I got to talking one day to an interesting American sailor, perhaps quite young in years but with much experience of the ocean life, who when he found I was in the book trade regaled me with stories of a volume that had amused him endlessly during his previous two years at sea. It was a publication by a fellow countryman, one Herman Melville of New England, he told me, and a Great Book he opined, but one entirely unheard of by any other reader he'd met in the changings of crew on his own Yankee tub or in any other port he'd visited during his travels across the wide world. His own descriptions of the book were compelling, such that I expressed a desire to learn more about it. Promptly then he produced the book from his sailor's sack and kindly lent it to me to read for the duration of his docking in Geelong, that being a fortnight. Well, at the end of the fortnight, after many evenings reading by lamplight until well into the early hours of the morning, I grew to concur with the young American sailor in his view of Melville's work. Indeed I felt sure this Moby Dick was among the giants, indeed the true *leviathans* of world literature, and that I had therefore chanced upon something of a secret masterpiece. Consequently, when the fortnight was up and I reconvened with the young sailor in the Bunyip Arms Hotel, I offered him a sizeable amount for it, which he gladly accepted. And now, you see, Mr Hutchinson, Miss Hutchinson, there it all was again in the volume you brought to me for repair: the tricks of the light, the glim and the gloaming, and the beasts! There too were the working men and their voices, and yes there was the vast field of their mortal enterprise. One book intoned on the profound depths of the swirling blue paddock, the other on the vast interior of this dry continent, which it occurred to me, was a natural terraqueous counterpoint. Indeed with this initial realisation such convergences seemed to multiply with each sentence that I read, the bullock with the whale, the parsimonious ground with the treacherous sea, and me here, residing between them, in the bound margin of the Moolap marsh.

'For many days, even weeks then, I did not lift a finger at the restorer's task with which you'd charged me. Instead I read my working days away and into the long evening, twice from the beginning to the end of your book, then from the beginning to the end again of the book of whales, and finally, as my idea dawned, interleaving between the two. There is such a harmony, you see, in the two great volumes, one of the driest most inscrutable type of land, the other of the most rousing, emotional and changeable ocean. And everywhere, in the digressions and the main action of both books, and most particularly in their cadences, there lies the inflection and wisdom of the two grandest precedents: the Bible and the works of William Shakespeare. They are masked by circumstance, of course, by the apparent and obvious differences between bullocks and whales, also between the interminable, sharp and enigmatic bush and an endlessly wet sea, and yet it is only a *mask*. I believe the books are kin in both scope and vision, in provenance and inspiration, in their penchant for the fabled nature of their respective environments, and their authors' first-hand experience of them, and therefore in the very blood, or *ink*, of their creation.

'Thus I was propelled then by my own grand idea, of a single book uniting the ocean with the land, and both the skies above them. A portmanteau, a book of the world no less, or should I say, of the whole earth. Needless to say this vision gripped me like a knot, my stomach clutched, my heart rose unbidden into my mind, and, yes, I was away.

'Firstly, I had to unbind both books, to unstitch them and to trial the new sequences in which they might be joined as one. My luck, and I saw it early, was that the dimensions of the pages were at least almost compatible; not exact, as you can see here by the irregularities of the page stack, but similar enough for the dream to become a reality. To remove the binder's linen thread though, and then to re-sew the pages through the already extant needle holes, was a task so fraught as to significantly challenge my craft. And yet I remained undaunted. In fact, to be honest, I relished this new mountain, this ultimate mountain, that I had chosen to climb. I would not be thwarted, nor even interrupted, in this long wet winter that we've just had here in the marsh. The other tasks I had agreed to piled up, even as I knew, as I read and re-read, unstitched and stitched again, that your Australian book was not even mine to alter. No, it was yours, Mr Hutchinson, and it remains yours – and yet I pressed on. Like Milton's demon

I suppose. Inspired. Until the thing was done, the joins all set, in narrative, line, chapter, and in the physical object.

'The American book, the book of whales, had already been rare enough. My young friend had captivated me with his tale of the book, of its unacknowledged legend, and of how his own sea-father, also a sailor, had actually known the author Melville in his youth. I paid a handsome sum to add the volume to my collection, but now, I knew, I would go one better. I would make an even rarer book, a unique volume in fact, from your own book and it, from bullock and whale. And when the job was finally done, when I had sewn and taped my whole fantasy together – a most delicate surgical operation – when I had extended the spine's width, reglued the endpapers, and secured, without cocking, the tension and give of the new wonder, I sat down and commenced to read; knowing of course that the day would come when you would return and take your half of the whole concoction, your Book of the Earth, away. Or so I presumed, given that at least half of it was, and is, your own possession.

'It was only when I had read the whole book through that I sent the telegram to Angahook. Belated it must have seemed, and yet to me it could only be too soon. For I do believe the book is a marvel, a strangeling, like the world itself; and after spending over four decades as a bookman in the service of both author and reader alike I feel at last as if I have, in myself, united my two capacities. Yes, I have read and I have made. I have re-read and I have created. I should describe to you how, not being able in my youth to attain my dream of authorship, I resorted to the binder's trade. But now, with this (he once again patted the book) I have finally transcended my functionary station. I have authored, indeed *invented*, from the extra-ordinary ingredients put at my disposal – one by the young American sailor, the other by yourself – a book whose accumulated genius I believe cannot be surpassed.'

Jones the Bookbinder of Moolap fell silent, but only after emitting a most autumnal sigh.

For a few moments neither I nor Uncle Ferny spoke. I for one was thinking strong thoughts. So here it is, I was thinking, the axis upon which the world turns. A man lives alone in a southern marsh, alone but for his bindings, his sheep, his memento mori and the wildlife around him, but he, and they, are never quite alone at all. There is another spirit all along, living here always, the spirit of the universal maker, the creator, who yearns for a correspondence via craft with the immense scale and harmony of the world. It is this spirit, I thought, that has bound these two books together. In this case it seemed, at least as far as Jones was concerned, that one plus one did not, in the spirit of a transcendent universe, equal two, but a whole lot more! The book as he described it was not merely a medley, nor an eccentricity, nor was it a piece of bric-a-brac. Rather it was a unity, a new perpetuity as it were, seeded by the love which remains forever embedded in the energy of the imagination.

Despite thinking these things I did not say a word. It was with respect, rather, that I waited to see how Uncle Ferny would respond. For it was *his* beloved charm, *his* local bible of yarn that had been altered by Jones the Bookbinder of Moolap.

And so we simply sipped our tea. As people do in moments of crisis. The Bookbinder's face was blank. I fancied I could detect a hint of exhaustion around his eyes, rather than anticipation or hope. The book had been made. It was all he could do.

When finally Ferny gestured that he might like to inspect the book a little further, Jones gestured for him to do so, but without a hint of expression.

And so the book lay again in Uncle Ferny's hands like the very strangeling Jones had described it as. He saw how the green cloth with the straggly plant of black leaves and red flowers had been moved from left to right, how therefore a strip of matching cloth had been inserted as a slightly contrasting column down the rear board. A circular brand, presumably the publisher's mark, with a tall eucalypt set into a red background, had thereby moved from the bottom left-hand corner of the rear board to its centre. The vegetation which had formerly wrapped around the spine and onto the top corner of the rear board had likewise moved onto the widened spine, with only the tips of the black leaves showing on the back where previously a whole red flower had bloomed. I watched without a sound as Ferny once more acquainted himself with the altered object, and I waited as quietly as old 'Gellibrand' for him to deepen his engagement with what was inside.

I watched on as Uncle Ferny observed how, despite what Jones had described as their compatibility, the pages were obviously quite mismatched in size, the leaves of his original Australian book being nearly an inch wider from gutter to fore-edge than the American. But even so they had proved somehow workable in the skilled and ardent hands of Jones, and were bound thus so that the aforesaid fore-edge had become decidedly sawtoothed. Gone was the formerly concave edge created by the mirrored edge of the round-back book; in its place Ferny inspected the up-and-down edge of the Bookbinder's inspiration.

Immediately too Ferny saw, placed adjacent to each other on the verso and recto, the dedications of the two authors still extant but now sitting side by side:

> *Contrary to usage, these memoirs are published, not 'in compliance with the entreaties of friends,' but in direct opposition thereto.*

It has been pointed out to me that the prizes of civilisation – Municipal dignity, Churchwardenship, the Honorary Bench, and so forth – do not wait upon avowed comradeship with people who can by no management of hyperbole be called respectable. But there is a grim, fakeer-like pleasure in any renunciation of desirable things, when the line of least resistance leads in a contrary direction: and in my own case the impulse of reminiscence, fatally governed by an inveterate truthfulness, is wayward enough to overbear all hope of local pre-eminence, as well as all sense of literary propriety. Hence these pages.

❧

IN TOKEN
OF MY ADMIRATION FOR HIS GENIUS
This Book is Inscribed
TO
NATHANIEL HAWTHORNE

He stopped, in fact, to read them there, smiling at the familiar wit of the verso and obviously impressed by the mention of Nathaniel Hawthorne on the recto. He glanced up from the page and, looking at Jones of Moolap, he remarked, 'Your Melville keeps good company.'

Jones nodded almost imperceptibly, demurred, and Uncle Ferny read on.

He read for some time, for so long in fact that Jones returned to the kitchen to make a fresh pot of tea. Stealthily he had left the room, so as not to disturb Uncle Ferny's meditation, and in that span of quiet, with the *shhff* and *thsk* of the turning pages the only sound in the room, I heard outside the curlew's cry, the swan's honk, and the liquid song of the magpie. Whatever it is that Ferny is encountering in the pages, I thought, could hardly be so true and compelling as the music of the birds.

Yet it seemed I was wrong, for Ferny did not look up again for what must have been half an hour. Jones of Moolap returned with the fresh pot of tea, with fresh milk and vinegar cake, which he arranged in slices upon the table. He left the room again, without explanation, and, not long after, I heard a back door close. Perhaps he had chores to attend to, eggs to collect, washing to bring in, I was not sure. I understood though that the want of an explanation was entirely due to his unwillingness to intrude on the reading.

So there I sat, with my uncle poring over this minotaur of bullock and whale, the skull of the notorious colonist hanging like a suspended metronome beside me. If in my time in the cottage beyond the Big Cutting Hill I had doubted the capacity of the world to cope with my own mental superabundance, it was clear to me now as I sat there that I need doubt it no more. This continent is strange, even stranger again to visitors, but thankfully what was no longer strange in my wondrous life with Uncle Ferny was experiment, spontaneity, and creation. Was it any stranger after all, to find the land and ocean entwined in a book, the bullock and the whale as they are experienced and imagined by an Australian and an American, than it was for Ferny to commune in both body and soul with the masculine attraction of Martin of Mendips? Or with young Joe Sullivan for that matter? Indeed, of course not. The only strangeness in this world lies in the denial of variation, the uniquely human obsession with purity, when, after all, the world is as teeming and as cacophonous and as shit-smeared as the Bookbinder's pure-finding marsh.

I fell, in the silence, to interrogating the skull on such matters; at least, that is, in my imagination:

Did you always want your virgins pure, I asked old 'Gellibrand', your poetry rhyming, and your narrations straightforward?

Of course you did, despite all life's evidence. Yes, the evidence of mortal experience tells you one thing: life teems and continues, it recombines and regenerates, and all is endless interval.

Yet did you only seek the hammerblow? The rap of the gavel? Was that, after all, your preferred music, and is that why you are hanging so in countless backwater houses?

Yes, you are indeed a memento mori, of how <u>not</u> to be in this land; and before you judge this new book-of-the-world beside you, before you deem it too irregular or unlikely, consider your own fate and how you too have had your folly replicated even in the decades since your flesh has fallen.

Eventually this cross-examination – in which, admittedly, the old Hobart lawyer did not stand a chance – was broken by a movement from Ferny. He raised his head, stared as if out the window, seeing nothing but the images in his mind.

He turned to me then, with a stupefied look, and said, 'My dear, it is uncanny.'

'It is?'

'It is. The way they go together, the bullock and the whale, the ocean and the land. It is odd, as oddly natural, and palpable, as *sin*.'

※

That night, in our upstairs room at the Velar Nasal Inn, Uncle Ferny and I licked our wounds and soothed our limbs after what had been a long eventful day of travel and surprises. I took a bath in the facilities provided down the hallway, running the taps and listening as I did so to the whole building becoming an instrument of its water through the pipes. The little tiled room filled with steam as one pipe offered a clear A-sharp before it stepped up an octave as it reached the upper floor and began to resemble a piccolo trumpet. Another pipe rumbled like a timpani drum before arising into a clear middle C, a note which it held as it coursed through the hotel until climbing to a C-sharp before descending again a whole tone to a deeper bass B as it arrived on our level. As the tub filled I played with alternating the flow of each tap to hear the effect. Eventually, I shut both taps off and the building seemed then to resonate like a great silence in a concert hall, momentarily at least. Thus I enjoyed yet another magic interval. I slipped off my robe and stepped, a little gingerly, into the warm water.

    I luxuriated, soaped, and lay back in the pleasing after-sound of the hotel's piped instruments and the momentous day we'd had. After all, it is not only images that seek our souls via the emulsion of memory but whole atmospheres too. The marsh at Moolap, its watery air and reedy purview, the solid austerity of the Bookbinder's house, were now as if printed upon me. I was thus attached, through combinations of atmosphere and incident, to a new place. It is in my nature too that as I grow attached to such demesnes I also begin to worry over their potential demise. What then, I asked, as I lay submerged in the rainwatered hotel bath, will be done to that small sluicy nook in the world's topography? Will it be drained dry, rendered barren, the curlew exiled, the clubrush, the glasswort, the frog and the swan? Will their blessed soul-shapes have to roam further then across the world, in search of a place where they will feel half welcome? Will the train be decommissioned, the former haunts built upon, the marsh laced with a circuitry of bitumen that seals the soil? And what about the Bookbinder then – a long forgotten dream, his tanning tubs, his masterings cart, his purefinder's prong and his *art* – will his ghost remain?

And so I came there in the bath to ponder again on Ferny's reaction to the book. After much discussion over an eventual luncheon of silverside he had agreed to receive it intact as a new portmanteau, without demanding yet that the whole thing be cleaved apart – but with the provision of a trial. He would take it back to Ngangahook and live with it, he told Jones. He would see how he and this minotaur of a book got on.

To be honest I felt for both men. For Ferny because of the shock of having his touchstone and talisman altered so. (Don't forget that he had travelled with his original book through the Italian alps on foot, it had soothed his injuries after he fell from his horse at Gibraltar, and he had even read it aloud, with a mildly nationalist iconoclasm, in the columnar forecourt of St Peter's Basilica in Rome). And I sympathised with Jones of Moolap because of the long, studious but frustrated arc of life that had led to this ingenious creation. Undoubtedly the man was quite *touched* to have proceeded so, and the inconstancy of madness was perhaps best evident in that up-and-down sawtoothed fore-edge of his rebound creation. But who of us who pursue the life of spectres, who of us that give an ear to soul and its invisibilities in order not just to describe the seen but also the unseen – the heart, the mind, the spirit, their closeknittedness, the way these territories govern all that could, like our bodies, otherwise be called mere material – who of us could not suffer the same insane charge? Jones had been thus *captured* well beyond his commercial duties, and in allowing himself to fall that way he had the profound good sense to know that he therefore had to fall properly. To fall thoroughly. To fall into Art. This he had done, and painstakingly so: the complexities and convolutions, the permutations and metaphoric significances involved in sewing ocean and land together like that, the challenge to his affinity for paper, needle and narrative, not to mention sound and scansion, were, in themselves, leviathan sized. It was a whale of a task, as epic and heaving and cumbersome as a bullock-train. And yet, despite what he knew to be the miracle of his triumph, he knew always how it would come as a rude shock to his client.

And yet he could not unstitch it. Not as he had unstitched the two books that made it up. It was ungainly, uneven, its joins and seams had to be sought by the reader as much as delivered by his assembling, but still, no, he could not help himself. For, in fact, he had, through the obsessional workings of his imagination, helped himself to the whole world.

I soaped my body clean and through, and worried for them both. If nothing else I knew the doubled book, whose spine now was virtually as wide as a hand, would be too great for Ferny to lug across the farm. And he had always liked so much to have his book with him as he worked. It was, yes, a vade mecum and a friend, someone to chat to as the billy boiled at lunchtime, something to refer to when he felt cheated or chastened, or betrayed by the boredom or just the weather of life. It was not the Book of Job, nor was it *Smith's Weekly*. No, it was free grass to Ferny, the grass that grows between the heavy paving stones of a merely upright moral mind. But just as Jones had undoubtedly enlarged its vision he had also doubled its weight and thickness. There was no way that object would fit in amongst Uncle Ferny's preferred working clothes, unless we sewed a special bespoke pocket into his coat. Well, I supposed anything was possible with the right needle and the right thread, as Jones the Bookbinder of Moolap had shown!

I don't know for how long I lay reflecting there but soon I began to grow cold. I turned on the hot water tap. The hotel's music issued forth again with the water and the steam. I grew sensuous then, under the plashing and piping sounds. I felt a beat of desire in my nipples. I clenched my inner thigh and squirmed a little. I thought of young Joe's talons at my door, his health, and his desperateness. I christened the soap 'my Joe' and said it over with every press and stroke. The bath filled but my eyes were closed, and I only woke when it all spilled over.

❧

After further discussion of the Bookbinder's seams and joins over dinner that night, and after a delicious steamed Southport pudding for dessert, served with a glass of muscat by a fit-looking young waiter who worked with his shirt untucked as if he'd just come inside from a game of football on the street, Uncle Ferny retired upstairs to continue what was a growing fascination with Jones' unforeseen creation. I lingered by the dining-room fire, and began inspecting the collection of books assembled for patrons on the shelves of the sideboard. I got to reading a book I'd never seen, which I lifted free from all the *Bulletins*, the Boldrewoods and Scotts. It was a narrative account of the expedition of a school inspector on horseback from Geelong West to Mount Gambier some half a century previous. And what with the discussions we'd been having with our meal about Jones' hybrid literary creation, I fell to imagining how other books might be fodder for such new manifestations. I began in fact to experiment with inserting phrases of my own amongst this school inspector's prose. Sitting down then with the book by the open fire, I started to thoroughly enjoy myself, and I daresay if I had had a pair of scissors handy I may have even begun to cut and rearrange the prose, such was my absorption in the new possibilities and active atmosphere that Jones' inspiration had put me into.

It was, I suspect, in those moments there among the fire-dogs of the Velar Nasal Inn that I first thought of the events of my own span of existence, my own era and life, as experiences that could be placed not side by side, or end on end, but *interleaved* with yours. It was the quiet too that fostered this 'fakeer-like' state, and I bowed to consider as well the moss-like fact that a writerly person in your time may well find themselves activating precisely this kind of renewing energy via my very own poetry and prose; and that I may then begin to situate things so as to conjoin with this writerly person in a comparable collaborative triangle to that of the bullock, the whale, and the Bookbinder Jones of Moolap. It would be she, the writer in your time, myself, her conduit poet, and you, dear reader, yes you would be the binder.

Now though, as I think it through, I wonder if this was not some default colonial spirit coursing through me, an uneasiness with anything intact and vibrant that had lived before me and that I could love but not control. An unwillingness to leave other's things alone. We had not discussed that, Ferny and I, in relationship to Jones. Was his a case of *appropriation*? Should not Jones of Moolap have accepted his lot as a humble binder of other people's words, rather than a promulgating genius himself, and consented to listen? To listen to the marsh. To read his books, enjoy the sounds, and then pass on into the same nothingness that would greet the curlew and the swan. *Sic Transit Gloria*.

But what then of that pure but innocent glee with which the ideas came to me as I experimented in my own way with the school inspector's prose? And as he rode through Camperdown and expounded on the qualities of the volcanic plain with great geological and anthropological fluency – the Pompeian tufa and the proliferation of infant-shepherds, carbines and watchboxes all about – what of the liberating desire sparked in me by such scenes to sing of my own molten wedding dress, to sing of the way we all inevitably progress to become the place we are in, and how we thus are sacramentally married there? Would such inventions on my behalf not have fitted together in dovetail fashion with the school inspector's work? Would they not have both juxtaposed, exposed, and bound us all, and therefore the school inspector's writing, in an eternal behaviourism outside of ordinary time? Could this possibly be barred, and should it, as if all such naturally spirited motions of the triggered imagination are mere thefts and reductions?

No, and I claim it thus so stridently, which is against my preferred subscription to quietness. No. *Sic Transit Gloria*. And shall all glory forever continue to be born anew.

So I give my own writings up to be taken. In the spirit of *gifts*. To be imagined, and reimagined, in supple hands and listening ears. It was not to claim the school inspector's ride for my own that I grew so excited there by the dining-room fire. It was *his* ride, *his* sore limbs of an evening, *his* eyes which danced with the Wannon Valley moonlight west of the Grampians. All of this was eternally *his*. But what was mine was what he chose to give me, by writing it down. What was mine was what I pictured because of his inspiration. With his words he brought me to life, and thus we were in an immortal collaboration as I imagined the ways my words would fit with his, not as erasure, not even as an inundation, but as a shoreline of a kind, or yes a marsh, a meeting of the fresh and salt, which must, after all, in this life on Planet Earth, be in itself the most sacred of our metaphors.

Perhaps then, after all, Jones of Moolap had simply *become his place*. Just as a desert bookbinder would include the far horizon, the horizontal stillness and the teeming in whatever he made. Jones of Moolap had made a littoral zone, a marsh, in sympathy, and was a finder. A pure-finder yes, of his place among the landscapes of the earth.

Because I had no pot of glue or scissors I did not mark the school inspector's narrative let alone cut its pages. It was the hotel's copy after all. Eventually then I fell to watching meteors spark from the fire, and small glowing communities of timber being eaten by the flame, with aprons of ash spreading like grey polluted prairies over the baking hearth. The crimson and orange networks of life hissed and popped, spat and crackled, in their own unpredictable meter. I watched and listened until all creative intention emptied from me. I too became as instinctive as the fire, and soon I fell asleep there in the hotel armchair, with my left shoe half kicked off.

When I woke the fire had shifted down to a low volcanic outcrop with its once scalding heat now diminished, not unlike the You Yangs. I rose from the chair, put the screen in its place between the fire-dogs, and made my way upstairs to sleep more soundly.

❧

By midday the following day, which was a Thursday I recall, we were well pointed towards home, having breakfasted and left Geelong by 10 a.m. Uncle Ferny had come down the stairs in a firm frame of mind and declared over our eggs and soldiers of toast that he had made a decision. There would be no need of any trial period with the new edition. He had accepted that his attachment to his prior Furphy was a matter of sentiment as much as anything and that he could not bear to part with Jones' creation. Such were its fascinations.

'And what, after all,' Ferny said to me in his only words of justification, 'would Jones do with the damn thing — excuse my French — if we returned it to him out there in the marsh? Linger admiringly over his own handiwork? Read aloud from it to the skull? Display it to bewildered and uninterested customers? No, Sarah, I will send a telegram from the post office along Ryrie Street as soon as we have finished eating. I will wire him a handy sum, *double* the amount we agreed on yesterday. I will declare my recognition of his genius, but confirm my receipt of the book. I should also inform him that I will write again in due course as my investigation of the pages continues. And that I will endeavour too to present its peculiar magic to any visitors of a literary or artistic bent who grace the glen and to any whom I may meet on my international travels. Not to mention any bullockies or whalers who travel down our way, as they indeed do occasionally.'

He finished his speech and took a gulp of his tea. 'There,' he said. 'There you have it. And I have gladly packed the book into my luggage. So that's that.'

He did not ask me my opinion for — and I could sense this, despite the firmness of his tone, or perhaps because of it — he could not endure any more debate. Of course he needn't have worried on my account, for I felt that the Bookbinder's Book of the World was predestined to go out beyond the Moolap marsh that made it. And who knows, I thought to myself, as I too sprang clear of any ambiguity or doubt, perhaps Jones himself will be relieved to see it go out, as his own talented progeny, into the world.

So it was that we bumped along the cherty track through Waurn Ponds that morning, out over the Freshwater and Merrijig creeks, and on towards the cliffs and ocean. Our horse Ray would have heard us say very little as we went as both of us were still quite preoccupied with the marvel of the pure-finding binder of Moolap, how he would push his handcart out to fetch his daily masterings, returning home alone to his stubborn sheep and to 'Gellibrand's' dangling eye-socket stare. And also now to the widest of all possible gaps on the shelves of his library.

XI

It was the bell-less-ness that I noticed first, even before I noticed the half-burnt hawker's cart. Was every petal horn and bauble of the spring, every tea-tree icing bloom and trackside hazel cloud listening out to it? This was how indeed it seemed to me as our spring cart trundled in – and how I gave thanks for the music. Life often comes like the tide, oftentimes hurling against the cliff of sense, hence our call for a peace, a truce, a silence which, even when Death winks at us from the stars, will never be. For transformation itself is in the nature of sound.

The hawker knows this, as he is always on the move. That motion-cry, the sound of the world's wheels, and all its wares bumping and knocking about against gravity, the sound of life, he knows that, and plies his trade like the Bee, or if he doesn't he must perish. You cannot return to the same district with the identical pots and pans, and yet there must always be the staples upon which our nourishment relies. And so it goes. Perpetually.

Uncle Ferny had not requested that Pascal chock his wheels at our homestead, only to call in, say hello to Red Whiskered Joe, and drop off what we had bought. The blown-glass funnel, the calico and cochineal. But stay it seems he had, even amidst the local chagrin at the lack of bells. Where a bullock dray's wheels are stone-like spheres of iron-rimmed hardwood creaking in iron axles, the hawker's wheels are spoked and full of air, as spritely, by comparison, as a spring lamb to a woolbound hogget. And now, from all we saw as we rippled over the old Coach Road bridge and passed through our gate, this lamb had had its throat cut. Or half cut, as it lay there charred, indeed half cooked, under the large mimosa tree by the house dam.

So even the sweet bell of the world is often marred by human pain. For this was a commercial chariot half dead, and nothing else was burnt around. The pasture was not ash but green and lush, the coins of the leaves of the trees all shone, these trees that name the Ngangahook Run, and thus, I thought, as I alighted from the box seat, they need their bloody bell to cancel all the evidence of Man's catastrophe, in this case to redeem the violence that had befallen Pascal's cart. Ring that bell to outsound the violence, to out-peal stupidity, to out-ring what the locals here call the *blues*. The blues we make. Mistakes, mishaps, our errors, wrong steps. To retint these blues with the gold of an Ideal. When all along such gold lies all around.

Red Whiskered Joe came down the steps, a brown cotton kerchief around his neck for the sweat, which also pearled on his rufus chest-hair where the top buttons of his shirt were undone. He'd been ploughing the furrows, forking hay, chopping wood, butchering a Wiltshire lamb, all under the guidance of our manager, Jem Morgan, and only now had he been carrying the cuts inside to prepare their roasting for our homecoming meal.

And so Joe hailed us, enthusiastically, right there beside the half-burnt cart. The situation was one of those wherein the facts present themselves, the critical and most dramatic Facts, be they drowning islands or winter wildfires, and yet things continue as if it's business as usual. Joe hailed us, remarked on the weather, enquired as to our journey, regaled us with the tasks he and Jem had been engaged in, and all right there with a smile on his face, before we'd even got inside the house. But his body betrayed him. Blithe as he would have liked to have appeared, it was clear that, despite the fact his physical work was done, those pearls of sweat were now beading on his facial whiskers as well as on his chest, the brown kerchief was staining darker with his every word, and in his jaw was set up a constant involuntary quiver, like an eddy going around a snag. Ferny, being kind, kinder than I to be sure, waited patiently for his young lover to unwind his tale, hoping I'm sure that he would not tangle and bind himself back up into it as he went, as we always do when we lie, or at least when we ignore the truth. But Joe Sullivan blasted through, talking fourteen to the dozen, his jaw-flesh a-quiver, until eventually, inevitably, he had to stop to draw breath.

'And Pascal, Joe,' Ferny then simply said. 'I see he arrived with our gear. And never left by the look of it.'

'Aaah... yes,' Joe said, after an interminably long blink of his eyes. Clicking his gums ruefully he cupped his hand to his jaw to still the quiver. 'The hawker yes, and the cart. He's been... well, a bit of a handful, and what with everything else that's been going on...'

Ferny and I both could see that there was a dark and precipitous catchment behind the torrent of words that had been issuing from his mouth. Quite apart from all the work, and the sweat it had raised, the going had been steep, and time had not so much passed since we'd been away, but fallen in on him.

'Well, let's go up into the house,' Ferny said then with a pulse of clear energy. 'I'd kill for a cup of tea, and even a sandwich before dinner. And then you can tell us all about it.'

'Right,' Joe said, quite obviously abashed. 'Yes, as I say, there's been a bit going on.'

※

To re-enter one's room after an unusual absence is to insert a new syllable into a well-known word. This was my room. My life had known so many rooms but here it was, the glenny one I loved, the one I had become and was, and the one I write in now. And here was I again, with silt of the Moolap marsh still under my nails, yes come back the same but different as each morning's East – yes, like a new syllable in the word.

Was it Sasarah, was it Sosarah, was it Saraneah, Saparah, or nothing so explicable as that? As we sat for tea Joe Sullivan had in fact removed rather than acknowledged this sidereal Me. He called me 'Hutch' then, using Joe Badger's nickname for the first time, as he arranged some biscuits on the table.

O boy, had he had a time of it. To make of me such a 'mate' as that, by rendering me as common as a 'Hutch', was understandable on two counts. First, because that's how things are done around here, the long name shortened, the short name lengthened, in order to redeploy *yon borrowed English* and make it our own tongue in the place, or at least something tending towards it. But secondly, he called me Hutch to deflower me, to remove all lace and lingerie, to make me as raw real ground in a real raw world. We will rut, this Hutch and I, he thought, just as I and Ferny will. All of us born from the same God, we who must eat, and defecate, and devour each other.

Such were the basics of Joe's mood, after what he'd endured while we were away.

'So the book,' he began, a little more cheerily now, having made the tea and helped with bringing our things into the house. 'Did he fix it right? Do a good job?'

Ferny tilted back his head and laughed. 'You've no idea,' he said. 'But we'll get to that. In the meantime, where's our hawker?'

Red Whiskered Joe threw his own head in the direction of the second hallway. 'Try your study,' he said, and darkly.

Ferny raised his eyebrows. 'My study? He's a reader?'

'I suppose,' said Joe. 'Either that or he's asleep on your divan.'

What followed then was a description of what had taken place with Pascal's cart, how it had come to resemble a charry vehicular version of Eden's bitten apple. Pascal had, it seemed, been given the run of the place by Joe, and perhaps a little carried away at not being treated like a spiv but instead like a citizen of the new Nation, had in a hashish swoon accidentally set his livelihood on fire when boiling a billy on a tripod. Joe had come up from the plough for lunch to find the chariot alone and ablaze, and it was the best he could do to save the half of it. From there the hawker's high had been perceived, and as a consequence he descended low, and holed himself up in Ferny's study, where he'd been ever since. His celebration of dignity and freedom and the way he was welcomed on the Ngangahook Run had ended bitterly. He would not listen to reason, only to the shorebreak of the moon. By day he'd been sleeping and, yes, by night wandering the beaches. Joe only knew this by the trail of sand he would find from the front door to the second hallway in the mornings. When he'd knocked on the study door Pascal had told him to 'fuck off'. When an hour or so later he'd knocked again he was called a 'racist' and, once again, told to 'fuck off'.

Joe was concerned, he said, embarrassed in fact, and at his tether end, but that was not all. For along with the enigma of Pascal, who himself, unlike me in my room, was akin to a *very old* syllable inserted into a very *new* word, there had been some unforeseen events upon the roof of the homestead, amongst the quiet stalls within the stables, and also to do with the sign by our entrance gate which announced us to all passing riders as the *Ngangahook Run*.

But firstly, before I narrate the sly harassments, allow me to return to my room to speak, not of events as nodes in a passage of Time, but of the extreme stillness there which has so fostered the uncanny access I have to the simultaneity of all Life. Suffice to say it is not as uncanny as it would at first appear that I have your ear. For you too have mine as I sit here, with my wooden and single bookshelf of writers who have known like I how the light breaks upon the mind and spills its darkness everywhere so that it does not concentrate in one single place or person. So too it is with Time, which remember, is only our moniker for the wheeling of the stars and moon, the ticking of our hearts, whose similarities in kinship dissolve such fabrications and abstractions. A word does not suffice unless one inserts oneself into it, and returns it thus to sound, as I have done or rather, as the world has done to me. Such stillness then as that in my room is only ever witnessed and not explained, but it is a condition of its being a sanctified environment that all can be heard there even if not expressed.

And so as a renewed Syllable, the other side of sound, the heart of Time, I sat receding there – *Here* – like the cave in the cliff, and heard you asking, 'Tell us of what came before the colours of the climate ran, when the Great Wheel was still in true? Describe the seedlings if not the seeds, so we are not merely enmeshed in blossoming dark effects. Sing us the true note, not merely the note's transcription.'

So it is that I have placed the gumnut in the piano's strings, the honeycomb upon the hammers, to create a sound of which you might be touched by an echo. For an instrument without the world around it, as the house without the glen, or this room without the wallaby browsing on the other side of the window there, is what you fear you're stricken with. But nothing is pristine, airless, not even the world before the word for Time. You are with me here, and I with you, my reader and perceiver. We are faulty, and thus we like to pretend perfection.

Alas, as Joe Sullivan found when we were away for the book, such perfection is all with the butterflies. There was an empty she-oak fruit bowl on the table as he told us first of the roof-sounds, then of the doctoring of the Ngangahook sign. The orchard's apples shone in my mind with grist and mote and blemish, so too the golden pear. They were but flowers at that point in the spring but I sat imagining them regardless, in the bowl, as poor Joe continued to speak. See then how what is destined to come, the ripening of the fruit, its blush and blemish, can be our solace in difficulty, indeed in each present moment.

It was the first night that we were away, he told us, when hail came suddenly out of a clear and star-filled sky above the glen. 'The sound,' he said, 'was shocking, and the rhythm was irregular, as if some windless local storm was coming and going. But there was no storm, just from time to time an awful bloody racket and clattering on the roof.

'Eventually, after this had occurred three or four times over the span of ten or fifteen minutes, I decided to go outside to take a look. As I stepped onto the verandah and began to descend the front steps I heard a quick rustler's whistle from the trees back by the road and then a soft *cooee*. I stopped still and listened out. And after a few minutes I went back up the steps and opened and closed the front door, as if I had gone back inside. Instead I waited in the shadows of the verandah, listening for whoever it was out there to betray themselves.

'Sure enough they soon did. In only a few minutes the sound of a harness tinkling, the neighing and snorting of a horse, the flicker of a lantern in the trees came to me out of the night, and then hooves galloping off in the direction of the town. And the next day, when I climbed up onto the roof to investigate, I found quite a lot of blue metal, and an orange-looking gravel too, lying in the spouts.'

'Gherang gravel,' Ferny said, looking over to me with concern.

'Is that what it's called?' Joe said. 'Well anyway, some buggers had taken it upon themselves to shower it on the roof. And that was the hailstorm. An orange one. Orange as my hair. I would have thought it was just a bit of a lark on behalf of local larrikins but for what I noticed about the sign the next day.'

'The sign?' Ferny said.

'Yes, at the gate,' said Joe. 'When I went out to the trees by the road to see if I could see anything of them having been there, I was gobsmacked. At first I didn't notice what was different. It took me nearly a minute to figure it out. But I did in the end. You obviously didn't notice as you arrived.'

'Notice what?' Ferny asked, a little incredulous now.

'Well, they've sawed off the left-hand edge of the sign. Pretty roughly too. So you've lost a couple of letters.'

'How do you mean, Joe?'

'Well, as I say, the left edge of the timber's been sawn, so the word now starts with A rather than N; as in: ANGAHOOK. Of course I'm familiar with the untampered word, as much from your letterhead as the gate, when you were initially communicating with us Field Nats. So I couldn't figure it at first. It was disorienting. But then in my mind I saw the letters on your paper stationery. That odd spelling – the NG before the A. Ngangahook. That's right isn't it, Ferny?'

'Too right,' my uncle said.

Suddenly then, I noticed, the fruit had vanished from the bowl. And all in a thrice commensurate with the time it takes to utter that sawn-off sound. Indeed a spook came over the room, such a spook as I'd never felt before. It was like an east wind but with a frost in it. A death of the rising sun.

I looked hard at my uncle. I must have watched him like an eagle, to see if he would unsettle. Instead, he got up firmly, his chair scraping on the floor behind him. 'This,' he declared, 'I have to see for myself. ANGAHOOK my eye!'

❧

NGNGNGNGNGNGNGNGNGNGNNGNGNGNGNGNNGNG
NGNGNGNGNGNGNG
    NGNGNGNGNGNNGNGNGNGNGNG
   NGNGNGNGNGNGNGNGNGNGNGNGNGNNG
  NG
       NGNGNGNG
        NGNGNGNG
NGNGNGNGNGNGNGNGNGNNGNGNGNGNGNNGNG
NGNGNGNGNGNGNGNGNGNGNGNGNNGNGNGNNG
NGNGNG
   NGNGNGNGNGNNGNGNGNGNGNG
     NGNG
NGNGNGNGNNGNGNGNGNG
NGNGNGNGNGNGNGNGNGNNGNGNGNGNGNNGNGNG

The wind blew as if from all four directions as we followed Uncle Ferny out to inspect the sign. The blue smoke from the still smouldering hawker's cart shifted this way and that. The treetops all tossed about. Where was this wind earlier, when we had come in rather blithely? Never mind, it was there now, and from all points.

Uncle Ferny and Joe went in close to inspect the damage, and fell immediately to discussing what tool had done it. The bowsaw, the handsaw, or the longer two-man saw with the deeper teeth? They both favoured the simplicity of the handsaw, as did our manager Jem Morgan when he showed up only a few minutes later. Meanwhile, I crossed over the coach road and stayed at a distance of twenty or so yards, leaning on the bridge, getting a good look at the sawn-off word.

What Ferny and Jem and Joe were discussing now was *who*, and *when*, and *why*? Such was the cut in the sign that it was difficult to judge whether it was a carefully thought out act or something involving a little more happenstance. But the answering of *who* would go a long way to resolving that quandary. And finding out who it was would most likely also help us answer the question of *why*. But I could well see that the three of them were entirely baffled by the whole affair. It was a strangely innocuous and yet upsetting thing for someone to have done. I could see in Ferny's face that, yes, it had unsettled him greatly.

I stood with my back against the railing of the little bridge, half listening in to what the men had to say. On the south side of the track, among the trees on the slope rising to the sea, the deeper orange tint of the petal-tongues of the parrot peas had all opened their lips and were in flower. They had taken the passing kiss from the gold of the wattle. The sun now had some genuine warmth, even falling filtered as it did through the brocade of eucalypt leaves. The puddles on the clay were drying with every moment, as if in response to the birdsong, and from time to time a new season skink, its grey-brown skin shining with the fresh solar luxury, would dart out from the roadside to enjoy the temperature of the ground.

Even so, at that moment there was no warmth in our hearts. We had been *got-at*, as they say around these parts, and try as we might to think of the disfigurement as a spontaneous, eccentric, meaningless and random act, we knew in our bones that that wasn't the case.

❦

Back in the house Jem Morgan wanted to talk in low tones about Pascal. About the coincidence of him being on the Run at the same time as the disturbances occurred. But Uncle Ferny was having none of it. He refused to go and dig the hawker out of his study for a chat.

Instead Uncle Ferny wanted to talk about how the Run had got its name.

'According to the old people, who'd come in here to camp by the river even when my father was a boy, if you come from the west, which is often the way their people did come in the early days, before Melbourne or Geelong or whatnot, you'd taper out of the Otways on the coast, or you'd come on via the plains up over that saddle. It was here, pretty much right here, in our little rain-shadow, that you'd strike the ironbarks for the first time. In such beautiful stands I mean, stately and tall, and in such fine abundance. So when my grandparents took all this on from the sea-captain who'd first grabbed it from the black clans, my grandmother went back over the saddle to see her Cornish cousin, to talk about a name. And she gave us the spelling. It's written down everywhere on shire and government documents as ANGAHOOK, starting with the A, without the NG, or what our friend Mr Jones, the Bookbinder in Moolap, has informed us is called the "velar nasal". But that's not how my grandmother was taught it. Now I've seen it as ANGLOHAWK too, but that just shows you it's a can of worms. My grandmother's cousin was, as far as I can tell, one of the few who tried her best to listen. Not just to hear what she wanted to hear. You all know there's different sounds out here to England. No nightingales for a start, and likewise if you were going to embark on putting together a truly Australian alphabet it most likely wouldn't start with the Roman A. Our NGANGAHOOK's as a case in point, I've always thought. And I've liked it for that.'

Now there passed a minute or so where each of them practised the pronunciation of the word *Ngangahook*. The sounds clicked, droned, and sprang out of the back of their throats and their nostrils by dint of the pressure created by the *ng*. The word in fact sprang to life with its addition. And it was true, they realised for the first time, the two spellings made for two very different words.

✤

    NGANG   NGANG   NGANG
    NGANGNGANGNGANGNGANG
    NG   NG   NG   NG   NG

Later that night in my room, after writing out at my desk some different permutations of the sound, and a list of things the cutting away of the *Ng* reminded me of, I slumped on my bed exhausted. It had been a long day, and one with a curious end.

        An apple without its skin
        A day without a dawn
        A room without a door
        A billy without its handle
        A rose without a thorn
        The cart without its horse
        A tree without the bark
        A pen without its cap
        An open wound
        The sap pouring out

AAAAAAAAAAAAAAAAAAAAAAAAAAA
AAAAAAAAAAAAAAAAA
AAAAAAAAAAAAAAAA
VVVVVVVVVVVVVVVVVVVVVVVVV
AAAAAAAAAAAAAAAAAAAAAAAAAAA
        A
           A
               AAAAAAAAA
            A
             A
              A
       A
A   A
          A

I would, for instance, never have imagined as we left Geelong that by the end of the day we would be out by the gate inspecting such an anomaly as the sawn-off sign. Nor that the homestead spouts would be full of orange gravel. These were disconcerting events, to be sure, but I fell asleep regardless, from the weariness of the road.

I woke with a start at 3 a.m., as if by an echo from the future – perhaps too from some foreign place, Harbin perhaps, or Donegal – and as if I were being asked a series of questions.

Should we disassemble the piano then, note by note, string by string, pedal and hammer, frame by case?

What after all, can a piano say to us of here?

Octaves? What are octaves in a continent of subnote, drone, polywarble and pitchbend?

How can the heart sing true in this mess?

I lay for a while, with the wind in the trees. I noticed my pillow was damp with sweat.

I mouthed the words: *subnote, drone, polywarble, pitchbend.*

I said them over and over, as if fingering them.

There is a dam at a junction we pass when heading inland to Wensleydale. The junction is called Pinchgut. The yabbies there, when Ferny stops to put in his 'square hook', are the pale green of young gumleaves. Pitch-bend brought Pinchgut to my mind. And then, drifting back to sleep, I began mouthing other words in my hypnogogic delirium:

squarehook   angahook   pinchbend   pitchgut   squarehook angahook   angerhook   pobblebonk squarehoof bonkgut angerhoof –

and I thought of the frogs…

                              and as the echoing questions faded from my mind I was thinking of the way we call them banjos

                                      banjo frogs

and how that was close

                    BUT NOT QUITE RIGHT.

We grab for things the sounds remind us of... rather than letting them be the sounds they are.

❦

Pascal. It was as if he had inserted himself into the house like I might insert an object into the piano. All through that long first night after our return he stayed deep down in Uncle Ferny's study. He did not come out at any point, not to eat or drink, or to greet us. Whether or not he was at all to blame for either the Gherang gravel on the roof or the alteration of the sign, with his smoking cart in the house paddock out the front and his own silent presence at the back of the house, we all, I think, had a sense of somehow being surrounded.

It took Ferny then, the very next morn, to broach the situation. One kind knock on his own study door, a hot cup of chicory in hand, the weighty new edition from Moolap wedged under his arm, and yes, he disappeared for hours.

By the middle of the morning, with both Red Whiskered Joe and Jem Morgan off spraying the orchard with copper for leaf-curl, Ferny and Pascal had still not emerged. I went out into the vegetable garden, ostensibly to inspect the progress of the broad beans, the carrots, the lettuces, herbs and silverbeet, but in truth I was hoping to catch a look through the window at what was transpiring in the study. The first thing I noticed however, was the sprinkling of bright orange gravel here and there amongst the green paths between the beds. So this was where the gravel had been flung from, though no plants had been trampled and there was no other indication of any disturbance. From the vegetables to the road was only a short distance through the stand of trees growing on either side of the creek. Whoever it was could have climbed the fence, jumped across the creek at its narrowest, and avoided coming along through the gate and up the drive. But how did they carry the gravel, I wondered. From the look of what had spilt out on the grass they must've needed barrel-loads. It was certainly not just a handful of loose stones. For Joe to have mistaken it for a hailstorm there had to be more than could be carried in via coat pockets.

I picked up a few loose pieces of the gravel and put them in the pocket of my dress. As I took my hand out of the pocket I noticed how the colour stained, not only my hand but my dress as well. I'll be keeping an eye out, I thought, for telltale signs on the clothes of people in the town.

Standing by the broad beans now, I had a good view of the study window. I stood there considering the ratios of flower to fruit, sampling the produce all the while by carefully prising the early beans out of their plush and furry sheaths, while surreptitiously stealing glances at the scene behind the wavy glass of the window.

Where once Selwyn Atchison had stood rather doggedly outlining his campaign for the campanile and bell, mistaking Joseph Furphy for a slightly notorious haberdasher in the process, now Ferny and Pascal sat seemingly ensconced and side by side at the desk, poring over the pages of a volume or other that was captivating them.

How many moods one room does see! I bent down into the beanstalks, to camouflage my interest, and to wonder at what the pages might be that my uncle and the hawker had so in common. Pascal was a man of the bush roads; no doubt he'd peddled his wares far and wide on tracks that would have intersected with the bullockies. And surely too – no, certainly – his family had crossed the whaley seas from Lebanon. Perhaps, I conjectured, he was in fact the ideal reader of Ferny's new wide and worldly edition. That's, of course, if he could read!

With my view framed by the flowery stalks and fronds I could see, by their demeanour at least, that all was well. They were both happily pointing and commenting there, and occasionally laughing. Dear, dear Uncle Ferny. A man who could put the loneliest, the angriest, even the saddest soul at ease. He had a gift for amelioration, for defining common ground. For the generous perspective. It was as if whoever he met along the path of life had already known him some time before, and thus knew him well again, and without introduction. In this way what was a wonder to my uncle would be made a wonder to anyone along the track. That was the cast of mind that saw him present my prepared poems quite unabashed to the town. And now, rather than admonishing the hawker for holding his own booklined sanctuary as his hostage, he preferred instead to seek the pleasure they could share in it, the interest that would unite them, in all their human moods. One idea by the next, each question via its answer, they had found their way to the pages on the desk in front of them, as if the gravel in the spouts, the sawn-off sign, not to mention the smouldering hawker's cart, had never existed.

So it was that at lunchtime, some two hours later, Pascal joined us at the kitchen table for ham sandwiches and a bowl of soup. Nothing was mentioned of his poor treatment of Joe Sullivan, and Joe himself, after his morning with Jem in the orchard, didn't seem to worry. From what I could tell Joe preferred to concentrate on the sandwiches and soup. If Pascal spoke, Jem raised his face and listened pleasantly, and when a discussion began about preparations for the repair of the sign, the clearing of the spouts, and the fixing of the hawker's cart, Joe seemed more than happy to collaborate on any of the three.

Such humility is an effect of the glen, I've always thought. So it nagged at me, over the following days, how the gravel in the spouts and the sawn-off sign were so at odds with the place. And when, with the repair of Pascal's chariot underway in the horse paddock, I said as much to Ferny, I saw in response that a troubled look had got into his eye.

'I've an idea though, Sarah,' he said, 'which might help. With Pascal here, and Joe, I think it's high time we gave another of your Sunday shows. And at this one perhaps we could present something — a reading, a performance maybe — from Jones of Moolap's masterwork. I think it would be of interest to many. It could lift everyone's spirits too — well, it would certainly lift mine to have the chance to discuss it all with everyone.'

That Uncle Ferny had concocted this soiree as a means of taking his own reading of the temperature of the town I now, in hindsight, have no doubt. But such was my dismay at what happened next that I feel he should hardly have bothered.

Three days passed in assiduous industry, days in which I mostly kept to my room. By the third day, after consultations with the blacksmith and wheelwright, Pascal's cart was all but fixed. I too had re-created my own kind of wheel. This was to be the content of the performance Ferny had suggested, a little cycle of things borne both from, and from beyond, the Book of the Bullock and Whale.

It would start with a steady pattern of notes, prepared with timbers and iron shards cut off from the charred hawker's cart. From there it would run quite wild in a volley of atonalities, until an onset of words would calm it down.

Music, it would seem, was as much in the language as in the music. Language, too, was as much in the music as in itself.

But who would care to listen? One might well ask.

Well anyway, these were some of the words as I composed them for the evening:
>
> Become my place
> each time we kiss
> a world respires
> as the granulating ant
> excavates
> wings fibrillate water
> a honk among whispering reeds
> a ridge of gumclad stone
> notating codes in clayey echoes
> pianola of a small bird's beak
> chirping past
> using wind
> breeze, luff
> bell of life.

I imagined not applause but mystification. Anything but silence.

For silence, as life has already taught me, does not exist.

XII

Houghing. HOUGHING. At this point I should explain the word. For it is not I'm sure one that you come across often in your day.

Firstly then, the pronunciation. Linguistically there are a couple of possible alternatives here. Houghing with the *ff* sound, as in *coughing*. Or with the transient soft *w* sound, which turns the 'ou' into an 'oh', as in *soughing*. But neither of these could properly convey the violence of what we were dealing with here. Indeed, the only possible pronunciation was the one I first heard uttered, right here on the glen, in declamation of the crime. It was the older, harder sound, the Scots delivery of the word, which more properly *sounds like its source*. Specifically it refers to that part of a leg we might call, in butcher's parlance, the hock. And when the cleaver comes down on the bloodied bench, or in this case slashes across the stalls of Life in the otherwise starry demesne of the sugar glider and the powerful owl, the verb *houghing* is pronounced in all its percussive acoustic truth as *hocking*.

The hawker's cart was ready to go, its charred right fender and wheel had been replaced and freshly painted. Pascal had sorted his damaged from his undamaged goods and declared, with an optimistic smile, that he had a future. He would head west on the inland road, traversing the various towns and farms of the Stony Rises, his destination being Warrnambool. There he could replenish his stock and conduct a proper audit and assessment on a relative's property at Port Campbell. He figured that, if all went to plan, he might pass back along our way sometime in the new year. He would be forever indebted to our hospitality, he told us, and over dinner on that final night, he apologised to Joe Sullivan about his nasty behaviour before we had arrived back at the glen from Moolap. He explained in front of us all that the various sleights and insults of his unconventional migratory path from a home village in the cedar-clad mountains of the Lebanon did sometimes wear him 'back to the nub'. That's the phrase he used. He said he felt as if his skin was as thin as paper as a result. As long as he was being treated well and everything was going to plan – or, to use his phrasing again, as long as things were proceeding as 'Mary, mother of Jesus wanted them to' – he was a personable well-met fellow in the country. But as soon as something went awry he tended to lose all composure and to descend as if into his own personal version of Hades. Thus, when his cart caught alight on account of his billy and fire, he was at the mercy of this tendency. It was to his great regret, he said, that the darkness should encompass him so. But thankfully, due to Red Whiskered Joe's mild temperament (he'd obviously never laid down in bed with him!), everything had worked out well. Pascal apologised to me personally that he would not be able to stay for the concert I had prepared for the coming Sunday, but said he hoped that I understood it was the nature of his profession to always be moving on and along the road.

We all retired to our rooms at nine o'clock. Pascal intended to get away before light, and would not hear of either myself or Ferny fixing him breakfast, which nevertheless we still intended to do. Sometime around midnight the rain began to fall, and to such an extent that it woke me in my bed. I lay listening out to it as I would normally do, imagining it beading on the feathers of all the sleeping birds a-roost, the magpies on the eucalypt spars, the cormorants on the moonah of the dune hummocks, the white egret huddling in the town willow. Inserting my attention into the seam between the constant far-off roar of the ocean and the onpour of the rain I worked happily at denoting the difference between the two sounds. It was like listening to the most closely scored chamber piece, where the separate instruments work together in such sympathetic timbre as to become all part of the one sound. To try to distinguish between them is an exquisite process, precisely because it is futile. Is that the viola or the cello that is moving me so? And how can either be unbraided from the diapason and sub-bass of the organ? This is the pleasure of experiencing the perfect chord, and since coming to the glen I've often thought that the lost chord of which the Bible speaks is not to be heard upon dying but rather in mixtures like that of the ocean and the rain.

As I inhabited the realm where these two great sonic energies faced each other I thought too of how the ocean must inspire the rain and vice versa, the ocean being akin to the perennial constancy of the existence of the self under all the circuits and turnings of the mind and body. There it is, always, *consciousness*, always there with its low subliminal roar. And when the rain comes, at least rain so strong as that which fell on that fateful night, and went on falling, it is as if that self has surfaced and become a discernible presence, a *player*, in the sky, as it were, to sing from that moon-space which gives it its own life force. It is a circulation of sorts, a consummation you might say, by which the lost chord, the secret chord, the perfect chord, can be heard in the everyday. As such I firmly believe that these heavenly things do not rely on death for their materialisation.

Thus I lay listening, as if embalmed between two cliff-faces of sound. But the mind turns away, it always does; it turns on and runs on with the river of life. I shifted in the bed; my nightgown had ridden high onto my right hip and so I arched my back and lifted the fabric back down to my calves. And in this new position – so subtle a shift it was, it always is – I heard the sound anew; or rather, I *saw* the sound, the rain, to be specific, as a deluge of such fox-coloured gravel as had been thrown in handfuls onto the homestead roof while we were away. But these were no mere handfuls. Instead, in my mind, the dark sky had become tinged with orange hail as it poured out of the vault towards the earth. The image unsettled me; the world had undergone a great scouring, a great upheaval, as if earth had become sky and sky earth, in a stinging way. This was now no longer a chord but a disruption of life's concert. On and on came the stinging fox-hued shale, with even spread across our roof iron, as if attempting to pummel the homestead underground, to send us below, to a place where we might never hear the sound of the ocean again.

I could not sleep now, and the strangely visual rain did not relent. I got out of my bed, pulled a shawl across my shoulders, and stood looking out the window at the rain. It was a gauze of grey against an obsidian screen; I could not even make out the vegetable forms of the ironbarks along the creek. But the rain was not orange – that was only in my mind until I'd stood there long enough with my eyes fixed on reality's colours that they forced the fox hue out. My breathing stilled, even as the downpour raged, shielding the horse's tragic cry from my ears. I went back to my cot, with my shawl still on, and fell asleep in the midst of it.

When Pascal rose in the hour before dawn the sky was pouring still. He must have wondered, as he opened his eyes, and as his ears returned from the listening of his dreams, as to how he would get going in such a torrent. But go about his business he did: dressing, cleaning, and making sure the canopy of his chariot was all firm and fixed down taut. All of this he achieved in the roaring dark with his oilskin on and the cowl pulled up over his hat to protect him. This I know for it was I who was in the kitchen, in the quilted dressing-gown Ferny had bought me on his last trip up to Sydney, and fixing the hawker some porridge and hot chicory by the light of the morning candles. I stood at the range, poking the fire in the box and stirring the oats on top. I could still hardly hear myself think for the din. On and on the rain poured, barely alternating in its velocity and with no wind to distract it from the vertical. It was well sufficient, and out the window, as I looked around from the stove, I could see the hawker's cart truly tamped and slick in the wet. I could see too the puddles already forming in the drive from gate to house, and thought how well it was that due to the gravel being thrown on the roof we had cleaned the spouts so recently. Otherwise I felt sure that I'd be looking out the windows onto water-curtains spilling all about the house.

Even still it was difficult to see outside, such was the screen the rain interposed in the first glimmers of daylight. But yes, I could see the cart in its hood and thought that Pascal was either under there, arranging and fixing his wares for the sloshy ride ahead, or in the stable readying and reassuring his horse that the rain would only fall for a limited amount of time and could not do otherwise. I was expecting him back in the house any minute and was very much looking forward to surprising him with the hot porridge and drink. But really, I thought, as I looked out onto a dawn that seemed in the torrent to be struggling to ascend, really, how could he get going in such weather? He should stay put, I said to myself, keep his horse dry in the stable hay, and bide his time until tomorrow.

If only there'd been a wind that morning, a driving wind, I keep thinking, as well as rain, an assuaging wind such as that which blew when God remembered poor Noah, a wind to blow away the grief I witnessed next. As the rain and new light both were pooling in the grass of the house paddock I saw Pascal emerge from the stable door. He had his cowl thrown off, his face bare and exposed to the silver needles drumming down. His face was fixed, in an anguished cry, his mouth open wide in a voiceless scream, his features torn as if from opposite poles, as the sight of his horse, bled to death in the hay with his hamstrings cut, went searing through him.

Of course I did not know at that stage what I was looking at: a man, sodden and drenched before the sun even came up over the eastern ridge, his face torn open as if by the inexorability of the dawning light, his cowl thrown back, a carapace no longer needed, his open mouth a dark and endless universe unable to articulate itself.

He ran forth, stumbled in the multiplying mud, then kept

coming, I thought, up towards the steps and the shelter of the covered verandah. Concerned, I moved the pots off the heat and made towards the door to welcome him in, but at the last moment, as he neared the steps he veered away and down the grass, out deep into the horse paddock, where I watched him stumble, in obvious distress. He climbed the rails of the fence and went on, the rain in dashes and dots all around him, and over him, as he descended out and down onto the half-lit pasture of the glen and away, away, amongst the black huddling cattle and towards the lower creek and trees.

What did I just see? I wondered. A man, throwing off a light his grief could not countenance? A man with nothing now between him and the weather? A man with boots full of rain? A man beyond the shelter of a homestead, beyond the warmth of hearth and recounting? So what has he seen? I asked myself. Something in the stables. He has come out of the stable door with that look, his cowl back over his head, and is gone from us.

Something then, I realised, something terrible was in the stable.

※

For hours that day Uncle Ferny, Red Whiskered Joe and Jem Morgan searched for Pascal in the pastures and bush. The rain did not cease. By the afternoon it fell like stone and by nightfall our overflowing tanks only added to the sound. There was no pitter-pat but a continuous *thump*, and the three men sat at the kitchen table exhausted. I drew a bath for Uncle Ferny and Joe while Jem declared, before re-emptying his mug, that he'd be heading back to his cottage even despite the rain. Did I hear him mutter something into his shirt as he padded across the hardwood boards to place his mug by the sink? I could swear I did, but what it was I could not say, nor did I worry sufficiently at the time to ask him.

He left through the laundry door after a dejected farewell. We all knew the poor horse still lay among its congealed blood and hay in its stable stall. It had been most cruelly slain and would have to be attended to. Apart from anything else the presence of the corpse would be disturbing the other two horses. But its burial would have to wait until the morning when hopefully the rain would have ceased.

At the next day's dawn however, after a long and barraging night, the torrent was still onpouring. All night long I had lain in the sound, the world a-din, as if the sky was a working muscle, pummelling the Run. When I rose, Ferny and Joe were already at the stove, boiling six plover eggs and making toast and tea with sausages, to ready themselves for the immediate burial of the hawker's horse. Anyone who has ever buried such a beast will know the work involved, the weight of the thing, the depth in the earth that needs to be achieved to ward off its exhumation by others hungry in the thereabouts. To our advantage would be the stiffness of the carcass after it had lain there all day and night. A halter and rope would do to drag the mighty leftover husk of a soul to its pit.

The disadvantage though was the rain which, as the eggs boiled and the sausages hissed and spat in their fat, continued to put the proverbial dampener on all of us. Indeed we could barely hear the cooking for the thrumming on the roof, which, once again, fell straight. One could be forgiven for imagining that something high overhead had got us in their sights, and would not let up. So much that was adverse had now happened since our return trip to Moolap. The thought of the Bookbinder going quietly about his craft amongst the curlews and swans seemed as far away as another country entirely.

With breakfast eaten, Uncle Ferny and Joe adopted a resolute mood, donning their oilskins and hats and even passing jokes between them about the unsuitability of the conditions for a horse burial.

'The beast's burden is thoroughly ours now,' quipped Ferny.

'Yairs, and the track's rather heavy,' replied his mate.

Privately though I could see that my young uncle was perturbed, worried about Pascal no doubt, who was still out there somewhere in the tempest, and also worried now about the potential swelling of the creek and all its creeklets and tributaries. These fingerling waterways are ephemeral in their run but nevertheless crisscross the Ngangahook pastures in something of a maze. When such October rains as this did come they could therefore surround the cattle, or so Ferny had once told me. In the flood of '97 so much stock had been lost this way, and I well recalled his descriptions of how when those floods subsided, the piles of strewn and bloated carcasses were wedged into the doglegs and fallen tree traps of the courses. Such horrors had impressed themselves upon his mind with a mortal stamp. I knew they would be returning to his thinking now.

Joe Sullivan however, though conscientious by nature, and a feeling soul, was no doubt more in the mood for a dramatic rural adventure. To be sure, this kind of violent inclemency was a long way from his naturalist guilds in Ivanhoe. I detected a relish in his step, as if our whole situation at the glen was to him but a fiction, and I could see in the lightness of that mood he'd fallen to that he not only loved but also revered Ferny, especially by the way he followed him eagerly out into the rain. That they'd shared a bath and then a bed overnight you wouldn't have thought, and not only because you may be conventional in your thinking. No, as they stepped off the verandah and out into the deluge in search of shovels and a burial site, they looked indeed more like a patriarch and his dutiful son than Romantic lovers or *amours*.

Of course the ground they began to dig for the grave had been softened by the rain but nevertheless its slurries ran and slopped about, making things difficult. At twenty-seven hands the horse was no island pony; it had hauled its cart and wares for thousands of miles along the tracks of the Western Victorian world and consequently had the girth of a brewery nag. But dig and dig the two men did, eventually covering themselves in the Ngangahook mud and becoming almost indistinguishable in the rain. By the end of the morning they were both deep in the pit and up to their own human houghs in water.

They wouldn't hear of a pause for lunch, preferring to get the nightmare over with. Eventually they fixed the ropes to the beast's rear ankles and dragged him out of the blood-caked stall and over the fifty yards or so of grass to the hole between the stables and the horse paddock's south-eastern corner. I watched from under the verandah, through a continuing curtain of water tumbling now from the spouts, fearing that the poor horse's rear legs, which were of course the victim of the crime, might simply come away from the torso. Such was the strain on the rope as Ferny and Joe hauled it.

But no, we were at least spared that calamity, though all the while as they hauled, our own horses were sounding their alarms from within the stables, no doubt terrified by what they'd witnessed and were witnessing still. I saw our Ray standing at the open stable door, not daring to venture out, but from time to time tossing his head back and letting out the most otherworldly shrieks.

The hawker's big horse was eventually dragged to the hole, buckling into the cavity where, if it had not already died, it would have drowned as in a well. Such was the pooling. Uncle Ferny and Joe conceded to merely cut the rope away from the carcass, so spent as they were by the unrelentingly rainsoaked task. They bundled the rope, set to filling the hole from the high sodden mound, and at last came away, their faces black with mud, the whites of their eyes like the sea periwinkles of the dark reef under the lighthouse cliffs. On they came, up to the verandah where I stood waiting. They mounted the steps and stood for a brief time dripping, and looking out onto the scene, as if in shock. For a moment their gaze seemed lost in the trees. The horse was buried but Pascal was still out there, somewhere beyond the pasture, if he wasn't already floating spiritless among the foaming Otway creek.

The two men stripped naked there on the verandah, without modesty, Ferny declaring that they had to change and then go out again to bring the stock up to the high ground of the house. At this point Joe Sullivan's rural fantasia was surely receding. I could see his disbelief, and then a bowed acceptance of farming logic, as Ferny announced what needed to be done. There were no quips this time, from either of them, and they disappeared inside with the towels I had provided, to briefly stand by the kitchen range and muster up their blood.

All morning there had been no sign of Georgina Morgan, who came each second day to attend to various of the household needs. Her non-appearance was understandable in the weather. So it was left to me to bring in the earth-caked clothes, to take them to the laundry and begin their soak. But I was tired, perhaps just from watching that last ordeal. Also though, I suspect, I was weary from the stupid wickedness and the fact that by now I felt I knew where it was coming from.

Was it possible, you might enquire, for Pascal, the poor and innocent immigrant hawker, to be exiled into the forest of a trillion dripping leaves just because of a dispute over a bell? For this is surely the only plausible reason you have detected in the annals I have furnished you with so far for anyone in the district to have reason to sabotage us. But could a bell, or even what it signifies, really be that important to burghers such as the inordinately pious personality that was Selwyn Atchison? Could Ferny's reluctance – or more accurately, his prevarication about financing the bell – incite such violence and conniving?

To understand this better I believe you have to think for a good length of time about wildness. The wildness not of Uncle Ferny and Red Whiskered Joe's dripping clothes as they stood in a post-burial stupor on the verandah of the homestead, but of their naked bodies once they'd peeled those clothes away from them and before I'd handed them the Christy towels. If they had walked then, down the steps and away across the house paddock with nothing but their moon-white skins and grave-blackened faces and hands, away and across the post & rails and the pool-portalled pasture and into the trees, *that* is the kind of wildness of which I speak.

You must ask yourself in this life, what are you afraid of? Is it madness, is it death, or is it the fact you are an animal? Do the bells that ring, in Melbourne, in Boston, in London, Dublin, Palermo and Rio de Janeiro, do they announce that: 'We are not from this earth, we are not the soil's creatures; we have come from, and shall return to, somewhere else entirely'? Yet when the light broke its way into my mind during my time with Maisie in the cottage above the Big Cutting Hill, it spoke of how we are both, *both*: both, both and *Both* again. We are both from Here and There, from Earth *and* the Sun the Source of Light, from Reality *and* the Imagination. Anything that grows in this light, this faraway light that reaches us here, is a child of that light. And anything that grows in this ground, and partakes closely of this ground in leaf and fruit and meat, is of that as well. We are both perceiver and perceived, without beginning and end, Ourself and the Other; we are hybrids and One, here in the breathable atmosphere, the zone of life.

To ring the bell for that is not a wicked thing. But to ring the bell in *denial* of that, as if we are somehow superior guests on a Planet of Shame, who will soon return to our rightful Palace in the Sky, is another matter. That is a consecration of *dis*unity, of poor adhesion. On the contrary, the light that broke into my mind beyond the Big Cutting Hill was a unifying light, like the nectar of the grass-tree flower, the sweet nectar of the plant that also contains the world's fastest glue, and can bind all things.

Though the little cottage above Big Cutting Hill had only been there since the boom times of the 1880s it nevertheless had some large planted trees all around it. But initially it was the surrounding bush that was the terror for me, the crackling stands out beyond the figs, quinces and plums. These were the personages that worried me: Mr Endlessness, Mrs Eeriness and their unfamiliar Children. In those first days, when wallabies came at dawn and dusk to feast on the fallen figs, I was captivated but also alarmed. Maisie laughed at my nervousness around the Beasts, and also at the nightmares I told her about which, in part, I felt were caused by the harsh night sounds of the brushtail possum. When Maisie told me the story of how once, when deep in the forest and sound asleep with her family, she had a leech go behind her left eyeball and emerge out the other side only to then slide over her nose, enter her right eye and slip behind that as well, I would not sleep for days. At least that's how I felt. Maisie smiled, as if I was raw and stupid. She declared that when she woke with the leech traversing the bridge of her nose, she felt only curiosity. What would it do next? She wondered. And when it entered behind her right eye she felt only a slight tickling. 'Well, you think,' she said, 'there must be good blood back there at the back of the eye, good sucking, what with everything our eyes can see.'

I liked Maisie but this kind of thing was all too much. Until it wasn't. One day she killed a snake at the front step with one deft cut of a shovel and said she would cook it for us as long as I promised not to tell anybody. As if I *wanted* to eat snake!

I credit Maisie in part for showing me what the animals know, and therefore what we can also know of ourselves. What a leech can learn by slipping behind the human eye is no different to what we too can learn by slipping behind the house and into the forest. A vision site. The darkness that breeds understanding.

One night after I'd been at the cottage for some weeks Maisie asked me to come out into the garden to see. I'd been alone in my room, despite the lovely air of the late evening. Even so, I could feel it through my dress, its subtle massage, its sense of freedom – and needed not much cajoling to come outside.

From between the flowerbeds where we stood Maisie pointed out into the sloping wall of stars in the sky to our west. Astronomy had been included in my schoolwork in England, but she wanted to show me something else about the stars, something that belonged, she said, specifically to us girls.

Focusing and pointing, talking and directing my eyes to the wee spray of glitter that is the constellation of the Pleiades, she described how, in the stories she'd been told, these stars were beautiful sisters who had escaped a mad hunter after he'd found them braiding each other's hair by the river. They were safe now, away from his clutches, their beauty and freedom protected by their aloof position in the sky. 'This is Heaven for girls,' Maisie told me, and made me look at their beauty. 'These sisters are different from the other stars,' she said. 'They are prettier for a start, and a little bit further away. My Bobble told me (Bobble was what she called her grandmother) that before the modern magazines we get these days, with the pictures of princesses and other pretty girls, and before all the storybooks were printed, it was the sisters in the summer sky that young girls looked up to. That's how it was, Bobble said, when she was a girl. That was the kind of beauty she wanted to be. These were the princesses and the pretty ones.'

I stood there with Maisie in that small cultivated clearing cut into the forest and I saw what she meant. That tiny far-off constellation of stars, the way they glittered there, and how they were arranged beside each other, was unmistakable. They had a lustrousness and glamour, they were sky jewellery, and it was both old and new, and had never gone away. As I had been taught to preen in the mirrors of my life, and arranged my hair and dress, this was what I had always been reaching for. This was the interior Vision, of how I wanted to be seen in the world. It was these stars, these fizzy, fresh and elusive Sisters, that I had wanted to be.

And the truth there, in the garden of Maisie's cottage, did not escape me. I had had to go outside to see it. To see it and understand. Here was the correspondence to my soul, my counterweight in the Heavens, already there in the night sky. Yes, it was already there all along.

I cannot fully, or precisely, describe the effect of my sighting of the Seven Sisters that night. I cannot adequately express the faith it gave me, the way it *lodged* that faith into my very self, knowing as I now did that everything I wanted, everything I had always wanted and everything I'd feared as well, had all along already been in existence in our world. I understood for the first time the correspondence between the beneficence of faith and the ease with which the stars wheel through their course; and that human trouble in this world most often arises from not seeing what is already here. What is here is all, and all of us, *already here*. There I was, up in the night sky, in my perfect state, and down here too, with the dew between the flowerbeds, at one and the same time. I was, we all are, *Everywhere!*

The following day Maisie and I sat in the planted garden after breakfast and brushed and braided each other's hair. First I hers and then she mine. From the bush the wattlebirds and cockatoos delivered their raucous music and the wagtail sang its 'three cheers' song in the garden fringes. We talked of incidental things, with no need to mention what she'd shown me the night before. In the light of day it felt like both an ordinary, and an extra-ordinary, thing. But Maisie did, for the first time, ask me a question about my life before I'd come here. Until then she had shown no interest, not even to make conversation when I had asked her about herself. Of course this suited me well, such was the jaggedness of my mood whenever I was forced to reflect on how fragmented and confusing the run of my life had been. But now, as I brushed out her long black and grey hair, she asked me if in England I'd ever met the King and Queen. Immediately the sight of the Pleiades came into my mind. And then Maisie burst out laughing.

As soon as Uncle Ferny and Joe Sullivan had changed into dry clothes, they headed out into the paddocks to bring the cattle up to the higher ground around the house. And still the rain poured down. It had been falling for many hours now, for sufficiently long at least to wonder if it had ever been otherwise. In Georgina's absence I was immured among the dirty dishes in the sink. I would eye the piano jealously as I went to-and-fro, conceiving of long sustained chords across wide octaves, chords that I would prolong with the pedal in order to harmonise with the dense constancy of the rain on the roof iron. Would it ever let up?

Someone, somewhere, most definitely had the sustain pedal of the rain pressed most firmly down. Thus it would double-up on itself, as such pedalled chords do. The natural decay of the sound after the rain had met the roof merged with the newly arrived, the ensuing, and that which kept coming, unrelentingly, after. T'was as if the rain were the hammers and the homestead the strings, every corrugation and indentation of the roof providing an ever so slight tangent and inflection in the chord. I went about the housework humming with it, or attempting to, as very occasionally the pressure of the playing would increase, causing a shift in effect akin to a key change. At length I began to hear this instrument of rain & house as performing some sacerdotal chant, something Ferny might have heard on Mount Athos or in some other Eastern Orthodox sanctuary. But there, as I ran the gravediggers' clothes through the mangle before soaking them, so as to squeeze out a good percentage of the mud before sullying the heated water in the deep sink, I heard my imagined rain-monks dissolve, and the house, the house of weather, become itself again. This was a forested apron on the shore of the Bass Strait declivity, and this was its classical October rain, thrumming in an ancient catchment, nothing more, nothing less. It would not, in the end, stand any comparison I'd make, perhaps least of all with bearded celibates of the East. Thus I contented myself with hearing things as they are. I let the roar encapsulate me until, in time, my imagining was triggered again by the feeling of being like a whale in its pod.

See there how I cannot resist comparisons, the like with the likeness, a whole suite of likenesses of the world, such as the Bookbinder of Moolap would understand. See also the power of his talismanic book that seemed now to have brought the watery world to the world of the land. Hear too, as I caught sight of the black cattle through the streaming windows, arriving on the high grass from the increasingly squelching mire below, hear the way their *moos* and *yorls* insert themselves into the texture. Words came to my mind, along with the notes the cows made, words about the whale but also about the wet-buried horse, the sawn-off sign, the hawker in his exile, and how the orange hail had presaged the tempest. I sang to myself over the mangle and the steaming sink, of colours and darkness, of a near-forgotten rainbow, and how I would remain loyal to the prospect of its return.

But this, I sang, is not rainbow season; this is the season we are in:

No this is no Rainbow Season this is the Dark Season we are in.
The rainbow goes through the mangle, and all the colours run.

And still the steady rain poured on.

❦

The lunch hour passed with the cattle still coming, one by one, in lines and straggly groups, under Uncle Ferny's imploring switch. One had become bogged; another had already been swept away by the increase of the waters. But, eventually, all the others were high if not dry, safe, for the time being at least, and sound. With still no sign of Georgina, nor Jem, I had made silverside sandwiches, which now, at 3 p.m., Joe and Ferny ate, standing drenched on the verandah. They had made plans while working, that Joe should go out in search of Pascal before the deluge made all gullies impassable, while Uncle Ferny would ride into town to broadcast the news of the houghing, and to try to find the culprit.

For not even gossip can travel through rain such as we had. The Run was suddenly like a fastnet. In its obscured green majesty I was left alone.

❧

The hours passed. Hours which I spent in eustatic reflection on how ground that has been dormant all summer, and all heath in winter, and wattle then parrot peas and orchids in spring, will always return to the depths of salt. Dolphins will cruise over the garden, crabs and crayfish will click and tick along in the space of the bygone treetops, backwards and sideways, past the house. Seaweed will festoon the clouds. Roads will become pure archaeology. This will be the life of the valleys, valleys no longer of soil but of sand.

It is the pay-off for knowing such glittering beauty Maisie showed me that I must also know the darkness which surrounds it. The atmosphere by which all things are set in train. But I reach, even as the roof iron drums, I reach not to change the course of the stars but to improve our human alignment. I reach for us, for you, to catch the most pleasant ride. To not be isolated in your 'paradise', not static, not aloof from it, but to be in it.

To be more than just one book, not just a star but its story too, to be *prepared*.

That our naked eye only sees six of the Seven Sisters is true. She, the Lost Sister, the most beautiful of them all, as Maisie described it, is these days running late. She is making her way to heaven on earth, being the last to leave the deceitful wiles of the hunter. But she is free now, and she is coming. She *is* coming, always climbing the sky. She is fleet of foot too, so don't make her swim. She is you now, just as once she was me.

Combine dear angels, openly *combine*. Combine your spirit with your body, mix your body as if in a pestle with the stars. Combine the stars with the land and the body of another. Till your stories and water your tunes. Let the outside be inside, the inside be out. And for its own sake, as well as yours, nourish your glen.

༄

Uncle Ferny rode out across the bridge, only hours before it went under, hunched over his mare with the cowl of his oilskin pulled up and over his sportsman's cap. He looked a dark rider. A dark rider, riding into driving rain.

His intention was first to drop by the manager's house and talk to the Morgans. He had strategies to discuss, he had to tell Jem about the moving of the cattle, and to make sure there was nothing that they knew that he should know too. After that he would ride on into town, call at the Store, at the Hotel, at the lighthouse homesteads, even at Selwyn Atchison's house. There was a fruit fly in the orchard of his mind, and he planned to secure our immediate return to the crispness and nourishment of a good unsullied pear. The fruitful produce and temperament of the Ngangahook Run.

But that was almost the last I saw of him, in the ordinary run of things. And he didn't take his book. Not in that rain, not in that weather. It sat still on the dining table, where he had left it, even as the floods rose. The book remained still and impermeable, unless of course it was opened up, in which case its blue paddocks and long paddocks would all spring forth into the very air.

Eventually, with the housework done, I couldn't resist. I sat at the table and thumbed the sawtoothed edge of the forepages. Then I began reading. And in that seamy zone, the unlikely but adjunctive ditch where a naked and compassless man lost in the Murray River can take a headlong dive into the opened cranium of the sperm whale, where quartzy shimmer of the scrubby horizons greets the warping glim of the bent ocean, where the hirsute inland wilga meets the salted forecastle beam, I escaped from the unceasing rain.

Until it did cease, or rather pause, in the gloaming of the dusk. Swept up in the egalitarian pursuit of free grass and the maniacal obsession with a white whale as I was, I had hardly noticed that the sky-roar was tapering. It was not until I registered Georgina's step on the verandah and then heard her voice that I bothered to take stock at all. And it was true. The torrent had abated.

So let me lay down my high pitch in this lowercased pause, consenting to impart the information flow between two women over a pot of tea. Not that the flow of information did not deal in matters legendary, moral and mythic, and hence of *profound importance*, but so that you can feel the afterbreath of the rain as it nuzzled the contours of our conversation, so that you may hear the auditorium of the glen as if at the finish of a symphony, and so that you may also sight the sympathetic rising steam from the teacups of your inner eye with due clarity and sensual understanding. These long poems that I narrate to you in prose, they would be nothing if they were not amongst this, for that, in truth, is their philosophy. In my experience the world is an ambience in which I am told even as I tell, and in which the ordered sequences and durations of time are collapsed. This is what I deign to regale you with here. The world as I descry it.

And so, let us listen to the Spode as much as to the stirring of the tea within its cups:

'My apologies, Sarah, I could not get here any earlier. The children were scared by the strength of the rain, and there was no let-up.'

'No, I've only just noticed it lessening now.'

'Yes. Thank god it's stopped. The creeks have all risen.'

'As have the stakes. The kettle's on, George, would you like a cup of tea?'

'Oh yes, that would be *just* what I'd like. Everything under control here in the house? It looks as though it is.'

'Ha! Do you think so? But look at those muddy prints all over the floor. Well, at least I got them to eat outside.'

'Where are they? Ferny and Joe?'

'Well, Uncle Ferny's gone to town. I thought you might have passed him? He was going to drop in on you and Jem on the way but went round to your house via the road rather than wading across the fields.'

'No, I saw no sign of him. But Jem's there if he calls. He's doing inside work, boxing beans in the shed for Hastie's coach, if it ever makes its way down off the Saddle in this rain.'

'Well anyway, here's the tea. I'll let you turn the pot. I'll get some milk from the chest.'

'And Joe?'

'He's gone out to look for the hawker. Pascal. Oh dear. George, do you have any idea what has been going on?'

Silence reigned. The silence-of-no-rain, the silence of the turning pot, and the unanswered question.

'Now let me pour.'

'Thank you, Sarah. Ooh, this is lovely shortbread isn't it. Even if I do say so myself.'

'He might well have drowned, the poor man.'

'Oh no, he's a strong swimmer, Joe. Remember he and Ferny going all the way to the mouth?'

'I mean Pascal.'

Silence once more, silence so-called, yet replete with dripping, and the distant waves, and suddenly a pensive mood.

'What does Jem say? What does he suspect is going on?'

Does pensive make a sound? Is a prelude part of a piece?

'Oh, listen. Here it comes again.'

'Dear me. Let's hope it doesn't get any heavier.'

'You haven't asked me about the children, Sarah.'

'You said they were frightened by the rain?'

'Yes, they have been. It's the loudness I think. And having Jem stuck inside. It does nothing for his mood.'

'Ferny and Joe were out in it. They buried the hawker's horse and brought the stock up to the house.'

'It's not what he suspects, you know, it's what he knows. And what I suspect of him.'

'I beg your pardon?'

Suspense, and waiting. Both carry a tone. The tone preceding tone.

'Everyone's been biting their tongues.'

'How so?'

The rain, increasing steadily again now, grows louder.

'How will I get home?'

'Yes, it's coming on hard. Yes, here it comes again. Belting down. Did you ride?'

'I did. Just to see if you were alright.'

'Of course. That's kind of you.'

'But the children. I suppose I best get going. While the track's still clear.'

'Yes. But, Georgina. Biting their tongues about what?'

The pushing back of a wooden chair on a wooden floor is most certainly a sound. As is a cup settling back into its saucer.

'Oh I don't know. Everything I suspect. All the strange things.'

The words did resonate with the rain.

'My concerts?'

'Yes, well…'

With that admission another tone now, almost stronger than the rain. No, certainly.

'You better be going. For the children.'

'Yes.'

'Yes.'

'But not only you. Ferny's ways as well. Thanks for the tea and biscuit.'

'Yes. I see. *Anathema*. Goodbye.'

The door opened, the volume of the world, its wet relentless airs, its recommenced crescendos rushing in, as Georgina Morgan rushed out, adjusting her oilskin as she did, and arranging its cowl to cover her face while still allowing her to see.

So now I was Alone. As you may well be, with all connections riven by the rising waters. There were no more meals to cook, nor clothes to wash. The cattle were mudsocked and soon would be knee-deep in water.

XIII

It was not the *Pequod* that the swollen waters buoyed up out of the steep and grassy-banked winding creek; it was the small ribbed and blunt-bowed rowboat in which Ferny used to essay as a child. Slung on the slope of the bank a mile upstream of the Coach Road bridge, it floated itself in the waters that carried it and came eddying, and *butt-butt-butting,* against the western side of the verandah that wrapped around the house. It was a dark blue but motley painted thing, and pilotless, its oars being in the back laundry.

Because the house perched on a rising mound of ground, both above the glen pastures and above the creek running with the road behind, I looked down now as if from the vantage of a tall waterbird. Moving from room to room, from one hallway to the next, I saw the extent to which the rain had filled the valley and then, from Ferny's study window, I saw the boat. And heard it through the roaring scrim. The way it tapped against the foundations in the rain. Almost as if knocking to come in.

I went back out of the study, and returned to the big living room and kitchen facing the pastures of the Run. The cattle that had been brought up from the creek had disappeared in the night, along with the house paddock fences. There was one beast I could see, a snagged lump barely breaching the liquid surface of what used to be a farm. But I couldn't be sure. And still the rain belted down.

Walking across the floor I came to stand beside the piano. Itself a black lump, and still glossy in a way the Jersey cows no longer were. Blue-black satin. Ferny's darlings.

I touched this gloss with my fingers, while sighting Ferny's book where it sat in its unlikely dimension on the dining table. I felt a doubt rinse through my body, a flush through my features, of exactly what this strange book was capable of. It had been all dry land, all arid shimmer, with only the brown Murray and the occasional soak, dam and billabong, until it was altered in or by the Moolap swamp. Now it was as much a watery world as a soily one, as much a creature of giant squid and lost ships as of bunyips and hard squatters' stations. Had *it* brought the rain? I shuddered. There was a correspondence I could not deny, any more than I could deny the thundering roof over my head. So I asked myself crudely about the power of an object, the possibilities of the written word.

Was this a magic book?

Oftentimes it was a single word, or one single phrase, that opened the gate of a new poem to me. So I sat down at the stool and lifted the lid on the keys.

The sound of the rain was like having a band behind me. Or above me, or all around me. A band as much a picture as a sound. I pressed the notes all at once and with my whole forearm, in an attempt to match the sound of the world. I needed such broad ground so that, after a time, I could begin to sing.

THE BELL OF THE WORLD

A magic book
It's come to be
It's come to be
It's come to be

Behind that simple single phrase was always a process, a sequence of illumined nodes, phosphorescence on the shore. And so a song, a song–poem, became prepared in this way, like a glowing beach, full now of the tide that had preceded it, what had come before.

A whale has swollen the river
A whale of a sky
Don't tell me why
Don't tell me why
It was always thus
In glen and league
We wrote the world
We always will

I could feel the picture of the sound, of the rain, its mineral qualities, in my hair now. I took it out, unfastening the clip above my nape and letting it drip towards the keys.

The settler's hat
Fills to the brim
Unsettling him
Unsettling
It overspills
The hammers down
The fields once brown
The sea in me.

It was the binding I was singing about. The bullock and the whale. One originating in the other. The salt in my blood. *The sea in me.*

I played and played then, without need for any further words. I pushed the piano, and heard my interventions fall: the gumnuts, the honeycomb, the peg and spoon. All the things I'd fixed to the hammers and the strings. I heard them land like beats in the chord of the rain.

Time became truer then. No one came to fetch me, not the Morgans, not Red Whiskered Joe or Pascal the hawker or Ferny. No one came fording out from the town. So I played and played, until the light grew low.

It was then that I lit a candle. And moved from the piano to the book. As I sat down to open it, my heart swelled. I began to miss Ferny. To yearn for him. I felt the pain of it, across my lower back, and in my chest.

I opened the covers and read: the seams, the fields and swells, the voice in between. So many voices. And mine nowhere in that mix.

So I began to read aloud:

'Between one thing and another, it might have been about three in the afternoon, when, with Pup reposing at my side, I finally settled down to an after-dinner smoke from the sage meerschaum often deservedly noticed in these annals.

The two greatest supra-physical pleasures of life are antithetical in operation. One is to have something to do, and to know that you are doing it deftly and honestly. The other is to have nothing to do, and to know that you are carrying out your blank programme like a good and faithful menial. On this afternoon, the latter line of inaction seemed to be my path of duty even to the extent of unharnessing my mind, so that when any difficulty did arise, I might be prepared to meet it as a bridegroom is supposed to meet his bride. Therefore whenever my reasoning faculties obtruded themselves, I knapp'd 'em o' the coxcombs with a stick, and cry'd 'Down, wantons, down.' Briefly, I kept my ratiocinative gear strictly quiescent, with only the perceptive apparatus unrestrained, thus observing all things through the hallowed haze of a mental sabbath. There is a positive felicity in this attitude of soul, comparing most favourably with the negative happiness of Nirvana.

And then:

If the Sperm Whale be physiognomically a Sphinx, to the phrenologist his brain seems that geometrical circle which it is impossible to square.

In the full-grown creature the skull will measure at least twenty feet in length. Unhinge the lower jaw, and the side view of this skull is as the side view of a moderately inclined plane resting throughout on a level base. But in life – as we have elsewhere seen – this inclined plane, is angularly filled up, and almost squared by the enormous superincumbent mass of the junk and sperm. At the high end the skull forms a crater to bed that part of the mass; while under the long floor of this crater – in another cavity seldom exceeding ten inches in length and as many in depth – reposes the mere handful of this monster's brain. The brain is at least twenty feet from his apparent forehead in life; it is hidden away beyond its vast outworks, like the innermost citadel within the amplified fortifications of Quebec. So like a choice casket is it secreted in him, that I have known some whalemen who peremptorily deny that the Sperm Whale has any other brain than that palpable semblance of one formed by the cubic yards of his sperm magazine. Lying in strange folds, courses, and convolutions, to their apprehensions, it seems more in keeping with the idea of his general might to regard that mystic part of him as the seat of his intelligence.

It is plain, then, that phrenologically the head of this Leviathan, in the creature's living intact state, is an entire delusion. As for his true brain, you can then see no indications of it, nor feel any. The whale, like all things that are mighty, wears a false brow to the common world.

On one page it was a blank programme, the mind put into idle, to properly rest, so that it would be fit to greet what would inevitably come to it.

On the other page a brain was in recess under a grand delusion, hiding as if in some innermost citadel, and giving off the illusion of a mind just full of mush.

An 'innermost citadel' was now the homestead to me, as I looked up from the page. The window was a darkened eye looking out into far-off things. Things as they stand. Things as they are. The house my sole habitat now, my citadel against a world of sperm and junk.

That world still swirled, the chords of rain still droned; I was a brain within a brain, reading a breathing book.

I got up then, with the single candle, and stood at the window. If the homestead felt suspended, as if in a mental Sabbath, then Ferny was a line of thought that had gone out beforehand in enquiry through the obfusc of the rain. And Joe Sullivan too had contributed to this emptying of mind; he too was a thought gone out in search, a sympathetic thought, and one of duty.

But I was a thought standing still, far from unharnessed, and filling the emptiness. I began to think of all that was etched into Ferny's mind, and how he maintained it. His faith in my poetic experiments was as natural as his encyclopaedic interest in bovine genetics or funghi. He saw no juxtaposition where others saw *only* juxtaposition. Was it because he was attracted to men, or was it that something inside him, perhaps, in his own citadel, was simply free enough, and secure enough, to allow such an attraction?

Whatever the case I saw that he saw things clearly, without motes, or masks. He saw harm only where there was some, not in gentle and interesting activities such as altering pianos or smoking hashish. But others, I knew, I knew it *of my own mother*, others could breed harm where there was none; others could seed a crop of tightly packed fear that otherwise would have had no place in the land.

Poor Ferny. Who would be misconstruing him now, in the Hotel perhaps, in the lighthouse homestead, or perhaps at Selwyn Atchison's? What truth would he be talking as he went in pursuit of the culprits? Would he be explaining his ambivalence about the bell? Would he be explaining *Me*?

I could see no stars out there through the storm of sperm and junk, but nevertheless I felt a sudden desire to leave and go out into it. I would explain Myself by being out there. Or would I?

Alas, not all things are possible. Instead I turned from the glass and, sitting back down at the open book, I blew out the candle and waited. In the darkness.

Listening to the rain.

When the dawn came I woke in the tailings of a dream, imagining the townsfolk had erected a guillotine, had cut off Ferny's head and were using it as the clapper of the bell. As the bell rang I listened intently to how the timbre changed as the skull was progressively crushed. Then I came to, reuniting with my daylit senses.

I heard a kookaburra ladder-song climbing through the glen, and a repeating magpie motif.

'*Who's going to save me now?*' I whispered. '*And who's going to save our glen?*'

It had been a long and luminous descent from the cottage beyond the Big Cutting Hill, where now I imagined Pascal sleeping off his grief, with Maisie's help. A long luminous descent that was not quite complete.

And then I heard it.

The absence of the rain.

*

All around the house the world was swimming. Or at least floating: chickens swilled out of their enclosure, harrows and rollers, barn graips and tarpaulins were sailing past, ballooning and sticking up in my vision. There was a new sound now, a sound not of pause but of movement and neediness. It sought out every weakness in every structure, filling any hole or depression, finding every flaw. Needless to say it was not still but dynamic, this silvering hydraulic world which bound me mythically as a moat binds a maiden or a witch, or a maiden-witch, in her castle.

And as the dawn tunes finished I did indeed feel awfully imprisoned in this newly submerged league of the Run. How do you speak underwater? How do you sing?

Seeking my gumboots from the laundry along with the oars, I let myself out onto the side verandah where Ferny's boat still butted, wedged as it was as if in a divot of the house where the stairs came down. I heard a scurry though, as I stepped out onto the verandah, and to my left saw a drenched wallaby, crouched low and wizened in fear behind the wicker chairs. Its dark beery brown had gone damp-black, and there was grey frosting around its snout and brows. I figured it must have been there since at least the day before, having missed the coach to higher ground, so to speak. Immediately I pictured its subtle tracks in my mind, the faint traces it made amongst wiregrass and weeping grass and bracken, all buried now with the rest of the understorey.

I turned back to the kitchen and took any vegetable matter I could find – soft turnips, browning cabbage, stale bread, holey leaves of silverbeet – and brought it all out to the verandah. I left it where I was standing, so as not to panic the poor soul any further, and, without any further ado, stepped off the timbers into Ferny's childhood vessel.

In no time I judged my way out and over the old course of the creek, over too the submerged course of the Coach Road, through a riddle of hazel and ironbarks, and out into the buoyed-up riverflat immediately to the south of the glen. In front of me I could see the wide watersheet, all canopies gone behind; I could see all the way to the dune hummock off in the distance, and the lighthouse on the headland to its east. Between the hummock and the headland was the rivermouth. I would be heading for it as if to a plughole. Even the lower slopes of the ridge immediately to the east were underwater, rushing this way and that. The whole catchment and contour of the land, from Big Cutting Hill down to sea level, was whooshing south for the ocean.

Soon then I stopped bothering with rowing. There was no point. The current that had seemed to be confusedly pushing north around the homestead was here freed to run with the old memory of the riverbed, to run south for the salt and the pole. So I sat on the rear bench, the bench where Ferny had once counted his bream, and steadied one oar as a rudder in a rowlock over the stern, the other as a pole for pushing off obstructions. I went clipping along thus, with the velocity of the drowned world, at about five knots, and in no time was in vicinity of the town.

So now I became a true scanner, looking for signs, scanning for truth, combing each colouration and each vertical form, watching for where I could disembark against the eastern ridge and headland. Looking for Uncle Ferny most of all, as I sighted the Hotel building high and dry on the ridge, away and above me. I knew that could well be where everyone had gathered. I was more part of the flood than the gathering however, and I watched as in the western sky new clouds of blue-black massed over the ranges. Soon enough then my own trajectory would be drenched. But I sat still, looked out, my eyes still bright with queries.

What is it that a cloud knows and a girl does not?

How can a bank of power-water stay so smooth yet be so strong? Its beauty will sweep away the resistance.

The fish have a new sky, higher ceilings, another storey, a deeper heaven. But what have I? A vision of the future? A tiny boat, and a tiny human body caught in an instrument of energy, a pierless bridge in my heart upon which I want to ferry my faithful voice to you.

I have trees, all around me, breathing trees and sunken trees, a teeming world alive and dead, an oar to guide, and another to clear the way; I am travelling neither back nor forward, but I am on my way. Am I?

I see back into the peopleless house, along the hallway to my room. I imagine the open door. A page glows on my writing table, glows white but with sepia ink answers among the dark wood and even darker weather.

A cloud knows, in its very centre, what it will express onto the world. The weather it holds is future weather.

That which is both smooth and strong is a sum of parts. The coalescence of rain drops, each melody finding its face, and its strength, as much by intervals as by notes.

But what of the wallaby, when all the turnips, the cabbage, the bread and silverbeet is gone? Will it risk such terrifying currents? And for what?

And what also of Uncle Ferny's books on the shelves of his study, his natural history magazines, his quarterlies and journals, so still there, so patient and unread?

A wilder book waits, a binding of worlds, with all the vigour of the flood.

And then I am watching the shapes in the water beside me, all the curlings, the serifs, the tiny cliffs and even tinier avalanches of stream. So wet. All so *wet*. There are cords of water, lips of water, an endless procession of alphabets moving past and alongside. Swift. So swiftly.

So I scan the water as well as the land, where now I can see figures in the distance, moving about on the Hotel slope. I peer for Uncle Ferny's springy gait but I see only slower things, ploddy, in daubs as if from the detail of a painting. But right beside me runs the energy I seek, the Ferny in the flood, and the *ng ng ng ng ng*. That's what I recognise, the flowing wet-grammar alongside, the shapes in the water. The letters are eels, migrating like me; their bones are made from ngangahook shadow and coral fields beyond the hummock, and they flip about as they go: *ng ljfdalkjdflkjaldkjfalkjdflj.*

They straighten out too, reaching noseward: = = = = ========
then flip in the charcoal flow of the wide wet streaming wet, flip and flipping out of writing and being: *ng ng aj;djfalkdjfakjd*====== *kdkjfal*

I know I've known this all along, in East Melbourne, even in England; it was what Maisie knew too. The wallaby comes lightly down the stairs. And now I know I know and read the world. And looking up I see Ferny waving his arms on the Hotel slope, waving and waving. He has sighted me, in the distance, me: his only niece, his poor girl, his family his genius, I am up on the flood as if perched on the tongue of the place which is *speaking* he has known this too the steep chute of valley of glen and inlet once upon a time shaped by strong water like this so I ride up high in the coach of things and he decided, decided to listen to listen to me and to have the others listen to my piano-poems to the *excitement* to the world O Sarah he'd say and there she Is! and he is waving his arms knowing I know he knows the world and all its farms are made of sound the wallaby leaps off the house was never going to stay stuck in one book the wallaby mind the bell the boat hops south on an *aeternity* of retroflexing life untied

The Natural History of Eternity

I

Dear Editors,

I note in last year's October issue that Mr Ralph Evans from East Nassau talked of foraging morels as a break from a busy working life. While this is surely the case is it not in some respects sad that this is so? I note the non-partisan nature of fungi when I declare that we should all endeavour to bring our working lives into a better harmony with such undoubtedly pleasant activities. I for one am a hardworking composer of music, often thought of as an indoors activity, and yet I find you can remain in the music while you're hunting mushrooms. I wonder too why this shouldn't also be the case for other professions, for the accountant, the salesman or, indeed, the astronaut. I can myself see a case for viewing mushrooms numerically, or as a comestible in need of marketing, or indeed as analogous with the clusters and circuitries of the galaxies. In my own mycological field notes I have drawn up ledgers, strategies for selling (I do often sustain myself by selling mushrooms of the edible variety to the Four Seasons Restaurant in NYC), as well as metaphors for the constellations. So I would encourage all mushroom enthusiasts to become a little more mycelial themselves and to make the connections.

Your Stony Point Correspondent

※

In the inner sanctuary of her room, within the more capacious sanctum of the homestead, sheaves of her writing lay neatly on blackwood shelves. This was what you could privately print when you could not publicly speak. The story of the bell, the story of the flood, all arranged in silence. Only the gods for whom no bell need ring had ever read them. Not Ferny, not Geoff or Emma Hamilton. There was no one else.

So that when it eventually occurred to her, after she'd begun to read Ferny's subscription copies of *Natural History*, a journal from New York, that she could write a letter in response to the very interesting letters of a certain 'Stony Point Correspondent', the words came as naturally as the autumn sunshine. She burst the surface of a long deep soil, and easily, dashing the letter off just as she had written, written all down the long years, and with just a cursory hint of her long travail at the end.

※

We are fixed, as what we
Fix: the haunt, the melody
Every dawn an anniversary

Just as she had written. Down the long years. Sewing lichen onto bark.

One night, revisited by more than just the autumn, she dreamt of one hundred Gellibrand skulls, all sitting on the paddocks like mushrooms. There was a knock on the front door that morning too, a timid knock she'd never heard before. And opening the door she rested her eyes on a young chap who offered his hand awkwardly and introduced himself as Joe.

Joe Busch. He had lingered at the Ngangahook gate, wondering what he could ask to do. Then, feeling too nervous, he had retreated, hiding his bicycle in the bushes and climbing the high slope opposite the gate, where he sat down to watch the homestead, the river and the glen from above.

She didn't feel comfortable to shake his outstretched hand but she felt perfectly comfortable to welcome him in. For a start he had a kind young face, and she could see he was nervous, a little introverted by nature.

'Please, take a seat,' she said, pointing to the large dining table which sat between the piano and the kitchen. 'Would you like a cup of tea, or a glass of water?'

Joe Busch was looking around the room, a little bewildered. The windows onto the pasture were unusually large for a homestead of this vintage, and the grand piano had all manner of strange objects piled upon it (were they dead cockatoos lying there?). The straight-backed chairs of the dining table at which he was now sitting down were carved with the forms of the most delicate flowers, the very flowers he'd observed as he'd worked with the other track-cutters in the bush just beyond the Ngangahook north boundary.

On the green internal wall opposite the wall of windows looking onto the glen, a large painting in bright colours depicted nothing from the world that Joe could recognise. It might well have been just pure colour painted there. And over in the kitchen, where Sarah had now gone to put the kettle on the stove, two willie wagtails flew about happily, perching here and there on the bench and cupboard-tops, wagging their tails, and occasionally sounding their three-part song. Joe had seen swallows caught up in the inside of houses before, and he'd seen cockatoos in cages of course, but never willie wagtails with the run of a kitchen, or a pyramid of cockatoos lying dead on a piano.

Such was his fascination with these effects as he sat down that he forgot entirely to answer Miss Hutchinson's question. Until she brought two teacups over to the table and said, 'I recognise you from when you were cutting the tracks through the bush with the others. Sarah's my name.'

She put out her hand now, to complete the greeting Joe had attempted at the door. He shook her hand, lightly, a bit confused by the fact that she'd recognised him.

'Yes. Thank you,' he managed. 'Tea'd be good.'

Sarah returned to the kitchen and began to ready a blue teapot for the hot water, the two wagtails perched on the bench to either side of her, and, yes, wagging their tails. Joe didn't quite know where to look, so he turned away to stare out the big pasture windows. He could see right across the paddocks to the ridge where he and the others had cut the tracks through the bush on the other side.

With his eyes resting on the familiarity of the view he collected himself somewhat. It was all so sudden. He'd never have imagined she'd invite him straight in for a cup of tea.

'Sorry for disturbing you like this,' he said then, looking back to where the two wagtails were still swivelling at the bench.

'*You wouldn't read about it,*' he muttered quietly to himself under his breath.

'That's quite alright,' said Sarah. 'I see you're taken with the birds.'

'They're so tame,' Joe got out.

'Not really,' Sarah said.

'Yair well I seen 'em sitting on the back of horses, but never waggin' away in a kitchen like that.'

Sarah smiled. 'They must have known you were coming.'

She was still pretty, Joe thought, even despite her age, and with the grey streaks in her hair. There was hardly a line on her face, and even though she was quite thin she didn't have that pinched look that a lot of the old Biddys did.

The kettle began to steam on the stove. Sarah and the birds were on the move at once. She turned quickly from the bench to the stove, and the wagtails flew straight out the open window above the broad kitchen sink.

'What a pity,' she said. 'The kettle scared them I think. I've never had wagtails in the kitchen before.'

She poured the hot water into the pot and brought it to the table. 'Milk?' she said.

'No,' said Joe.

'Me neither,' she said, sitting down beside him.

'So how can I help you?' she asked, as they waited for the tea to brew. 'I imagine you're possibly out of work now the track cutting's over.'

Joe smiled, a little sheepishly. 'Yair well I don't exactly live around here,' he said, obliquely. 'I mean I do, well, I live in Winch, with my mother and my brother. Though he's just got his own digs.'

'I see. So it's not work you're after.'

'No, well yair, actually…'

'It's a long way to travel every day. Do you have a car?'

'No, Miss. My brother does. But I can ride my bike.'

'You come down over the Big Cutting Hill?'

'Nah, the road's a bit rough up there for my wheels. Nah, I come down through the gumflats and Kuarka Dorla. Takes me about an hour and a half. Not too bad.'

'You don't have a horse?'

'Well yair, Miss, I do, but she's a real old nag. She'd get bogged. Wouldn't be worth the bother.'

'I see. She'd most likely hate it too, I suppose.'

'Yes, Miss.'

'You can call me Sarah, Joe. I'd prefer that.'

'Righto.'

She began to pour the tea. It was peculiar to have a visitor in the house, especially because it didn't feel even the least bit strange. Ferny had had his own people visit through the years, but she'd stayed well out of it even so. They'd found a way, Ferny and her, a way to be, and people were always directed to the manager's house anyway. But here she was, with the teapot and cups at the dining table, hosting this new young man called Joe who'd come out of the blue.

At that moment an enormous brown spider with jet-black feet, a huntsman, appeared marching across the table towards them. Both Sarah and Joe saw it at the same time. As their eyes trained on the spider it stopped moving, midway between the blue teapot in the centre of the table and their two cups.

'You scared of spiders, Joe?' Sarah asked, amused.

'Well nah, not the old huntsman. Though he's a biggy, eh.'

'He is. I'll let him have a little ponder before I go pouring the tea.'

'Sounds fair enough.'

They sat in silence then for a few moments, watching the spider, whose black feet seemed to clutch at the table as he considered the options. If Joe was at home his brother Ger would have whacked the spider with whatever was close to hand.

'Which way do you think he'll go?' Sarah said eventually.

Joe Busch pursed his lips in thought. 'Well he's not gonna come our way. That's for sure. And I don't reckon they like to venture.'

'Yes, and the teapot's blocking the path to his right,' Sarah said.

Joe nodded. 'Which means he's most likely gonna head off towards the piano.'

Sarah smiled. 'I wouldn't be surprised if that's where he came from,' she said.

They both looked now towards the piano. The keyboard lid was down and the broad top was piled high with, yes, dead cockatoos, and other strange objects. Joe didn't want to ask.

'Well, in case you're wondering, Joe, I didn't shoot that pyramid of cockatoos,' Sarah said.

He nodded, politely, thinking about the day Ger shot a few cockatoos. 'They been stuffed?' he asked.

'They have. My uncle had them done years ago. We had a manager then who didn't work out. Well, he had a few problems. One of them was cockatoos.'

'Fair dinkum?'

'Yes. He went quite mad one day. The cockies fly over in the late afternoons heading back to their roosts upstream. They like to sing about it of course. And they love to hear themselves echoing back off the stone of the ridge. You know how loud they can get. Anyway, late one day we heard him shouting down there at the manager's house, and next thing he's firing shots.

We don't shoot anything here on Ngangahook, so Ferny, my uncle, ran out, but by the time he got across the paddocks he'd killed nearly forty. They were lying on the grass down there under the ironbarks, bleeding and crying and twisting about. They have the brightest blood. Ferny had to wring the necks of a few that weren't stone dead. And the ones he didn't shoot kept circling about. They were keening. It was awful.'

'Sounds it. What a crazy bloke.'

'They mourn you know, Joe. The cockatoos. I watched them over the next few hours that day. They were in distress for the ones they'd lost. Of course they were. So after a couple of days, when the mourning seemed to have run its course, and after making sure the manager had cleared his belongings out of the house, Ferny and I went and gathered up the bodies. He thought it would be an idea to take them to the taxidermist's. Gouldings, in Ballarat. We had them on the mantelpiece for years, and also on the sideboard in the second hallway. Never stuck away in a box. But recently I've been rearranging things a bit. I've also been reading about Egypt and how they worshipped birds. So I had the thought to make a pyramid.'

The cockatoos looked a little grey and tired but the pyramid structure that Sarah had built was exact. And the more Joe looked at it the less peculiar it became. She had carefully folded the wings and feathers of each bird so it interlocked with the one above and below it, and to either side.

'How long ago was this?' he asked.

Sarah thought for a moment. 'To be honest, I'm not exactly sure. But many many years ago now. We've had a couple more managers since that man. And Geoff's been here for years now himself.'

'That's Geoff Hamilton?' Joe asked.

'That's right. And his wife, Emma. Geoff runs the farm. Even more so now that my Uncle Ferny's gone.'

At the mention of Uncle Ferny's passing their gaze shifted back to the huntsman. It had gone, and neither of them could say in which direction.

Their eyes met, and they laughed. What years there were between them had disappeared. Sarah took up the pot and began to pour the tea.

II

Dear Editors,

What, we might ask, can elude all our current scientific classifications, indeed the whole entrapment of our human language, and thus represent something of the enigma of our spirit, and the mystery of what comes before? And possibly after? As a case in point, I don't necessarily believe in the notion of the Bible that 'in the beginning was the word.'

Nor is this topic to be treated as a mere riddle, for we devotees of cap and frill, of spore and mycelium, know the score. And I use the word 'score' in its musical sense, rather than as a tally of events.

Your Stony Point Correspondent

❧

After Sarah discussed things with Geoff Hamilton, who had spoken to young Joe for over an hour on a walk through the property, he agreed. Geoff said the young fella from Winchelsea was observant and good with his hands, and had a willingness about him. His strength was with wood, which would mean he'd be of great assistance with cutting and building the new boundary fence. He could also do some overdue mending around the homestead and the manager's house. He seemed decent. 'Thoroughly decent' was the exact phrase Geoff used.

When Joe Busch bumped into Don Atchison at the General Store a month after starting at Ngangahook, Don told him he was tinny. 'No one's been able to get in there for years,' Don said. 'How'd you manage it?'

'Dunno really. I just had the thought in my head that they might need a hand. So I got up the gumption and knocked on the door.'

'Fair dinkum? That easy? You didn't get mauled by the Alsatians or anything?'

Joe looked confused. 'What are you on about? There are no Alsatians. Geoff Hamilton's got a border collie but that's it. Sarah's got no dog. Or cat.'

Don Atchison looked annoyed. 'I bloody well knew those Alsatians were bullshit,' he said. 'I'd never heard 'em but people kept sayin' they were there. My old man included. And Geoff Hamilton never denied it.'

Joe shook his head. 'Nup, no Alsatians, Don.'

꙳

All through the autumn Joe Busch and Geoff Hamilton got to work on the boundary fence while Sarah continued to adjust to life without Ferny. At his funeral strong whispers had gone around. Whispers as to the fate of the future. It was like a congregation of she-oaks. But with no direct heirs Ferny had bequeathed his entire estate, not as a cleared amenity and adjunct to the park he envisioned through his dying days, not to 'the Abos' as some had said, but to Sarah. The level green dells, the homestead, stables and barn, manager's house, stock, and capital. This was all so many skeins of bark weeping from a manna gum, even as she understood how such lower cladding was critical in allowing the tree to reach majestic heights. When the course of the creek that was her youth had seemed barred, Ferny had given her the new dawn of physical and spiritual shelter, but now it felt as if she had been bequeathed a dusk. So she thought of going up, of climbing into the clouds, into the blue-grey gap between the white bunches, away from the whispering congregation, where she could lie back cushioned, not to pray or make petitions but to cry.

Instead though, she went out into the earth, walking.

What then is the rhythm of weeping bark
Which minds the verses dwelling in the topmost
Of the tree. Hear it in the branch's song
In the echoes of birds you know you'd rather be

❧

As Ferny lay dying on the divan in his study, the track-cutters he'd had Geoff Hamilton employ had sat around a small fire of cut logs some half a mile higher than the falls. They were camped there for the night, which saved them having to lug equipment to-and-fro and allowed them to work the longer days required to complete the rather epic task that had been assigned them: to cut walking tracks through the gorges and along the watercourses of the bush immediately north of Ngangahook, in order to demonstrate to an uninspired government the merits of establishing this part of the country as a natural haven, a sanctuary, a park. Don Atchison was the only one of them who lived around Ngangahook, but he had chosen to camp with the others rather than head back to his home of an evening.

After they had encountered her walking through the bush on more than one occasion, Don told the other track-cutters how she was a poet and how when he was a kid she had told stories annually around a bonfire amongst the bearded heath below the school. 'I remember once,' he said, 'she actually came into our class and read a poem. It was about a flood that started up above the Big Cutting Hill and swept everything, everyone, away. She was a real beauty and the poem was amazing. I was taken with her, even as a little chap. My dad reckoned she was up to no good, but she's always seemed alright to me.'

Later, after sausages were cooked and they were smoking and sipping tea, Joe Busch had asked Don, apropos of nothing in particular, why his father didn't like this Miss Hutchinson.

'Well,' Don said, 'my old man didn't like anyone much who didn't agree with his views. He and Mum were always takin' everyone's measure. Had little time for her Uncle Ferny either, but everyone knows he was a top bloke.'

Joe was interested. After all, there are few better situations for a story to be told than around a campfire. Perhaps it was no accident then that he asked Don Atchison if he remembered any of the stories this old lady-poet told around the bonfires all those years ago.

Don considered the question, squinting as a billow of smoke came his way. The wind was up from the south and suddenly blew more smoke around them. Momentarily, as he leaned towards the fire, Don became enwreathed. Closing his eyes, he disappeared into the blue-grey envelope.

The others waited, patient, dragging on their cigarettes. When the wind settled a bit and Don appeared again he opened his eyes into a squint.

'I remember,' he said, and paused.

A log of old messmate, contorted in its growth, full of knots and runnels and burrs, gave a loud pop under the compression of the hot fire. The other logs shifted like mates. Don put in a steadying boot, expertly calming the arrangement. Then remained silent.

'Well,' Joe piped up eventually. 'What do you remember, Donny?'

Don Atchison raised his chin and began to scratch his neck. Eventually his lips spread out into the thinnest of smiles.

'Some were good, some were bad,' he said. 'I remember that much. What I mean to say is, some were scary, really scary stories which they reckon little tackers love best, but I didn't. They terrified me. A bloke who bundled his kids into a covered spring cart and drove them into a dam. I had the ghosts of those kids spookin' me for days. Couldn't sleep. To think an old man would do that to his kids.'

'But why did he?' Joe asked. 'What did she say in the story?'

'That I don't remember,' Don said. 'I don't remember the whys. But I remember that covered cart and how it had a big oil stain on the canvas. And I remember the nightmare of those little tackers goin' under. And the others who had to dive into the dam.' He chuckled. 'She had a way of tellin' it, that's for sure. I reckon the whole town might have been sleepless for days after that.'

Three nights later they were camped under an outcrop of rock another half a mile again above the falls. As they were almost out of food by this stage, none of them having had any luck shooting bronzewings during smoko, and no one wanting to stomach a boiled echidna. They were eating porridge for tea. And quite enjoying it.

Settling back on full stomachs in their makeshift limestone couches, the track-cutters joked and jibed with each other around the fire. Then Don Atchison had told them he remembered another one. Another of Miss Hutchinson's bonfire stories.

The campfire burnt steadily with an apricot-coloured flame. 'Yair, it came to me today,' he said. 'When we were tamping that sedgy stretch level. But it's not a spook this one, no drownin' kids or nothin'. I've been havin' a pleasant think about it all arvo.

'So there was this bloke from Geelong who used to work for the Railway on the old Saddle Line that ran across the ridge out back here. He was a big roomy kind of bloke, tall, and with the funny name of Rabbits. Cedric Rabbits. That made all of us little ones laugh.

'Anyway, there was a half-Abo woman who lived on her own in a little house in the bush not far from the line's end. She lived pretty much like a hermit, with a garden and a coupla books for entertainment, but was often seen hangin' around the bush siding at Wensleydale, where she'd pick up her flour, oats, flower seeds and that, you know, the basics. Anyway, one day old Rabbits had a load of ironbark topple onto him when it was being brought in off a dray, and it was this Maisie who tended to his wounds. She had a wattle splint and torn shirt bandage on his leg in no time, and Rabbits was grateful for chancing upon such kindness in the middle of the bush. It was all blokes back then out there, as Miss Hutchinson described it. When Rabbits' broken leg had mended after a lay-up at his home in Geelong he got back to work, and first trip out to the Saddle Line he took the time it takes to load the return train to ride the station bicycle down off the saddle to where Maisie lived alone at the Big Cutting Hill. He had a box of jam for her – not just a jar, a whole box – and a cosy for her teapot, as a way of showing his appreciation.

'Well that was the beginning, and many times after that Rabbits' tea-cosy was put around Maisie's tin teapot and poured out for him on his visits with damper and scones and the like. The two found they could have a great laugh together, and Rabbits would tell Maisie stories from his life on the gravel and firewood train and she would tell him about the tough way she grew up around Birre and Colac, and how she'd decided to cut out on her own and prop up there on the saddle rather than put up with the bulldust of the towns. A lot of her people had died, though she had one brother who was on the German mission out in the Wimmera, and cousins and kin dotted around the place. When she'd been offered the chance to be a caretaker of a rich man's bush cottage, she had decided to take it on.

'Rabbits meanwhile lived with his ailing mother near the Breakwater in Geelong, and he had a sister too, who was a nurse. She'd knitted the cosy. He had been married, Rabbits, as a very young fella. Miss Hutchinson had us completely when she told how his wife had been shot dead in Moorabool Street in Geelong after getting tangled up with some bushrangers who'd come into town on a spree. Bushrangers in Geelong! I'd never heard anything quite like it. Certainly not in the bedtime stories my parents used to peddle out.

'Anyways, one day it was announced that the Saddle Line was to be shut down. Rabbits was transferred to work out of

South Geelong station. On his days off he'd put himself and his treadly on the Warrnambool train, get off at Moriac and cycle right alongside the ol' Saddle Line embankment and all the way out to Maisie in the cottage. They'd tend to the garden, watch the light go down over the western ranges, drink cups of tea from the cosied pot, and make each other feel better, all day and night. Miss Hutchinson told us how the cottage beyond the Big Cutting Hill was an absolute basic of love in the lonely bush. And by the time the story had finished, by god had she painted a picture. Right here in our neck of the woods too. There was a glow on everyone's dials that night and it wasn't only comin' from the bonfire.'

With the coming of the track-cutters came the sound of new mornings. Ferny lay on his study divan listening out for Doug Chivers' brown Wolseley ute and the red Dodge truck that the Busch brothers from Winchelsea drove to the edge of the bush beyond the Ngangahook boundary. When Europeans had first come into the area, Ferny's grandparents among them, so too had the percussion of horse-traffic. Also the jonking wood and metal music of the bullock drays and spring carts. The first time one of Ferny's managers, Jim Dovey, heard a car in the place, coming down as it was along the old coach route from the Big Cutting Hill, he thought it was a swarm of bees. He cried a warning. Of course they'd all gotten used to such things, even to the extent that a Cessna was now parked in the old stables, but as Ferny lay in his dressing-gown on the divan in his study, listening every morning to the arrival of the Dodge and the Wolseley, he couldn't help but think of Jim Dovey's misapprehension. 'So here are the bees,' he would mumble to himself. 'Ferocious and swarming.' A smile would creep into the dying man's dry lips, but like any good modernist, he was only half joking.

It made him feel good though, to know that the work was being done. He'd written letters to shire officers, to the Premier himself; he'd even set up a meeting with the Minister, to try to convince them of his idea. Ferny could see how things were going and wanted to take the bull by the horns. They were respectful enough, due to the old connections, but they wouldn't listen. So he'd taken matters into his own hands. Before it was all too late. One problem was that the glen itself actually looked much more like a 'park' than the bush to its north. But still, Ferny hoped the bush, with its gorges and waterfalls, would gather the name despite the fact that everywhere the wattle, tea-tree, *Pomaderris* and dusty miller choked the sightlines. It had become clear to him that he had to show the way. Spell the vision out for them. It would be a park with walking tracks – often called 'trails' in the American literature he'd been reading – and he imagined it to be for the use of everyone. But there would be no walking through this 'park' unless tracks were cut for the purpose – hence the coming that spring of the little group of track-cutters with their Dodge and Wolseley engines.

At the very least the sound of the engines in the mornings helped him picture some activity around the place. Soon, he thought, the pressure to cash in on the trees would be too great for the government to bear. The saws would be sharpened and the rude mysterium of the old logging coupes revived. On his own property he would do what he could, but when it came to Crown Land, well, he had to break a few rules. And providing work for young local boys was fine by him.

When Ferny finally succumbed though, wheezing away there in his study until Geoff Hamilton and Sarah had to drive him to hospital, Sarah came to see how his demise and his campaign for the 'park' and its clandestine 'trails' were dovetailed. Her uncle would tell anyone who wanted to know that when the government officials walked the tracks he'd had cut, the merit of the vision would be unavoidable. Opening his coffers for such a result was a last flourish for him, but still, what was unavoidable to Sarah was how the gouged-out tracks and the regularity of the engines had coincided with his demise.

So it was that in Sarah's mind what was affecting the clear flow of air in Ferny's life in his last fading days seemed also to be affecting the lungs of the trees. A few trails, running like new threads among the densely quilted hills, were not on the face of things any cause for regret. But timing is everything, and feelings of loss can be all pervasive. On a scenic route to the falls she would find herself suddenly bereft. The track-cutters had here and there cut hairpin bends amongst this rock, instructed as they were to blend access with the spectacular. But as she stepped along these newly levelled bush thoroughfares, she caught from the corner of her eye new glimpses of Ferny's shade, standing as another fern among the glades, or crouched down like a stunted banksia among the sagey Spyridium, watching her go by.

III

Dear Editors,

Recently I was walking in the woods with a group of students interested in mycology. We stopped by a fallen trunk, a large old thing, upon which whole congregations of fungi were thriving. Such was the fecund rot of their life's situation that I felt I could almost hear their choir sing. As I was about to direct the attention of the group to the various species of the community I could identify – and also to those that I could not – one of the students, a Russian man, Mr Romanoff, who always arrived at our meetings in a gleaming blue Cadillac, raised his hand in the manner of a child to speak. 'Life,' said Mr Romanoff, 'is the sum total of all the little things that happen.'

His was not, strictly speaking, a science-minded observation, yet in the moment I felt our day had been properly illuminated. No one spoke but most of us smiled. Mr Romanoff had put his finger on the way in which life combines, aggregates, accumulates, and often in the places in which death has pretended to leave its void. I say 'pretended' for it is so often in the rotting zones of death where life thrives most. That of course must be a key lesson of any mycological study, if not its whole point, or should I say, its holy fundament and font. 'Nothing ends,' say the woods, 'if you only cock your ear.' 'There is no beginning,' sing the choirs of that big old fallen fir.

The letter went on to discuss an issue of classification around what the Stony Point correspondent called 'the winter mushroom', officially known as *Flammulina velutipes*. But, naturally enough, this preamble captured Sarah's attention for other reasons. She was much taken with the correspondent's tone, which she found relaxing. And she was not so much consoled by the idea of death's illusion as she was by the reality conveyed by the character of Mr Romanoff. She pictured a far-off place, an America she'd never been to, and felt as if she could almost touch it. So that the winter mushroom – *Flammulina velutipes* – was made somehow all the realer by Mr Romanoff raising his hand. This in itself had the effect on her of a charming unplanned encounter, so that she barely blinked an eye at the sympathetic notion that the community living on the fallen-down tree could constitute a choir.

With the sound of the track-cutters working in the distance, she had sat on the front verandah of the homestead. Ferny had been a subscriber to the magazine for many years and had often recommended its various articles and items of interest to her. But she had never felt the need. It had all seemed too tight and scientific. Like something those old Field Nats would have read. But now she flicked through the pages of the rest of the magazine with interest. Through the agency of this Mr Romanoff the

February issue had sprung to life and for a good hour or so it was almost as if Ferny had never died at all.

> *We are made as the things*
> *We make. Teacup, sea sponge*
> *The tiny kindling glow*
> *Our whole perimeter on fire*

IV

She was bound by ridges, by cows, grass and the walls of rooms. Why then, Joe Busch asked himself, as he was making his way one day back out of town to the track-cutters' camp after a trip to the Store, why would someone, a great beauty no less, want to spend whole decades in exile from other people? It wasn't, from what Don said, as if she had nothing to say.

She had emerged from the Post Office, crossed the gravel outside the Store, and headed off alone along the empty ocean road. She'd been wearing work trousers. She had an open round face. She wore no hat or veil against the flies, and her hair was long, and not tied back. Joe sighted her first from twenty feet away; with a large brown envelope in her hand, she was staring straight ahead and speaking to no one. Then, as she went off, he found himself following her down the road. When she dissolved into the pine trees of the Hotel carpark, Joe stopped. He left her to navigate the short cut to Ngangahook along the east ridge of the riverflat, alone.

The heart so deep
It cannot be swum.
Instead we swim
Through depth's descriptions.

That very night, at the campfire, Joe and his brother Ger were playing chess. As Ger considered his moves Joe idly blew a tune on his mouth harp. When it came Joe's turn to make a move he would hand the instrument to Ger, who would do the same. Joe played the tune of the Italian song 'Santa Lucia', while Ger played the Winchelsea Football Club theme song. From time to time, when he wasn't reading the paper Joe had brought back from the Store, Don Atchison would pluck along on his brown ukulele.

When the game had ended, Joe piped up. 'Saw Miss Hutchinson at the PO today.'

There was no response, only the flicker and pop of the campfire, until Doug Chivers said, 'That so.'

Ger giggled. 'D'ya have a chat?'

'No,' Joe said. 'But I'd like to.'

'Yair?' queried Doug. 'And what the bloody hell would you two have to talk about? Anyway, I don't think she talks does she, Donny? Isn't she mute?'

'A mute?' Don replied. 'What are you talking about? You obviously haven't been listening.'

Doug Chivers nodded slowly with the realisation. 'Aw yair, that's right. The stories she told and that.'

'Yair,' said Don, rather grimly. 'A mute doesn't tell stories.'

'Could be a mime artist,' Ger chirped. 'Like that bloke who's at the Colac Show every year.'

'Yair, could be,' said Joe, annoyed. 'But she's not.'

'What is it anyway with you and her?' Ger asked his brother, aggressively now. 'You're always askin' about her and wanting more of Donny's stories.'

Joe muttered something, as if to the fire.

'Yair, well she's a bit old for ya don't you think?' Ger went on. 'She'd be well past it I would've thought.'

'Aw fuck off,' Joe said then. He got up and went out of the arc of firelight to his swag.

※

If you didn't talk to people, she'd figured, you could always write about it. Words on the pages, as quiet as a butterfly's wings. *Invisible as music*, she reminded herself, *but positive as sound*. Letters, she thought, are sounds we see. Like the wind in the tree.

To live in the weave of time's garment became the only thing. The silence of the words on the page could at least be heard by the gods.

The Gods: the fox, the sky, the sum of you.

Without an audience she could always exhibit to the Gods.

The Gods: the wallaby, the moon, the mirror.

V

It was rather unexpectedly, after only seven months of work, three of them while Ferny was alive, four after he was dead, that the cutting of the tracks was called to a halt. When Geoff Hamilton had taken an unexpected call from the solicitor John Cash he had presumed it would be about financial belt-tightening. And so it played out. The money being spent on the wages of Don Atchison, Doug Chivers and the Busch twins from Winchelsea, and on the cost of their materials, would be better spent elsewhere. However, what Geoff had not foreseen was that the shire had been in touch and was now demanding an official drawing of the boundaries of the Run along with the construction of perimeter fences. At the cost of the Hutchinsons. The track-cutting had 'frightened the horses'. It was John Cash's advice to comply in full. Geoff Hamilton was inclined to agree with him.

So, no more new tracks, no more morning Dodge, no more Wolseley? The decision would ultimately be Sarah's, Geoff Hamilton knew that. If it was Ferny's wish that the tracks be cut – and it was – then surely she would insist, despite everything, on that wish being carried through, on the subversion being continued. But no, much to Geoff's surprise, she did not object at all. She even seemed to welcome the decision.

'That men have to do something with land,' she told the farm manager, 'is a habit that not even Ferny could quite escape. And anyway, the cutters have done enough work to establish the idea of the park and the walking trails, without having to finish it all to the letter. I think Ferny's case has been stated well enough. You only have to go for a wander amongst the trees they've sawn and slashed to know that.'

Her voice was firm, collected. Geoff Hamilton, an open-minded man and a well organised one, was both pleased and taken aback. Pleased that her strength seemed to be returning, pleased too that she was amenable to the solicitor's advice, but taken aback at the lack of sentimentality she showed towards Ferny's project. And yet, the finances didn't lie.

For Sarah it all signalled a return to the welcome parsimony of the bush. As Geoff went through the details she was thinking how desire is one thing, premeditated desire quite another. The wallaby does not premeditate its own desire, and this truth alone secures the subtlety of its track, its lightness, its rumpled weave among the wiregrass. Unless you look you miss it, for it is barely even there. What was it that Mr Romanoff had said to the mycology group?

Life is the sum total of all the little things that happen.

So it is, she thought, and so much for grand ideas.

❦

In the following days, and with Ferny's wishes now overruled, she began to feel like a body without its blood, a heart without its impulse, the glen without its river. Life flowed on around her, and she observed herself going through the motions: brushing her teeth in the bathroom mirror, washing her clothes in the new machine, and now catching the Trans Otway bus into Geelong for her own appointment with John Cash to discuss the general state of the Ngangahook affairs. Outside his office, in the town they called 'the little smoke', as opposed to 'the big smoke' of Melbourne, she felt briefly as if she might faint. It was the first thing she had felt all day.

John Cash had never met Sarah before, shielded as she had been by Ferny from all such administrations. The solicitor was immediately aware however that this woman, whom Ferny had mentioned so often, was in no condition to apprehend the detailed nuances of her uncle's estate. Accordingly Cash, a rather statuesque man with a thick crop of salt-and-pepper hair and a well-organised yet kindly smile, assured Sarah that she had made the right decision with respect to the halting of the track-cutting on Crown Land, and that, for the time being at least, he could act as the administrator of the estate. He would oversee all of Ferny's rather extensive investments, and work when necessary with Geoff Hamilton, Ferny's trusted farm manager, to assure that the operations at Ngangahook, and Sarah's own livelihood, would be well looked after.

Cash's Geelong office looked straight onto that part of Gheringhap Street where the slope runs gently down towards Ryrie Street and the bay. A magnolia in the small yard between the office window and the carriageway was in flower, and as Cash reassured Sarah that she would have to do precisely nothing in the immediate future except sign documents of probate and the calendared cheques of the estate as they were issued, her relief manifested not so much in a sigh or a look of gratitude but in her noticing of the creaminess of the magnolia's flowers. As Cash rose to consult his cedar filing cabinets, his tall form blocked the view of the tree. Sarah leaned sideways instinctively to gain the sightline. The solicitor noticed and, following her gaze, commented not on the beauty but on the durability of the tree. Apparently it had been flowering for eighteen straight months.

When their meeting was over the solicitor showed Sarah out of his office into the hallway and to the front door. They shook hands, John Cash with empathy, and Sarah weakly, wristily. The heavy Victorian door clicked gently, with tact, behind her. She looked to the wide empty street beyond the solicitor's picket fence and gate. The bus depot was only a hundred yards or so further up the hill. But she had time, too much time. More time than she would ever need or want.

Looking to her right at the magnolia she examined it again, this time without the barrier of the office window. In clear air she imagined the fleshy white leaves of the flowers as peelings, fallings, of some prior being. Hanging there, the scented flesh of the dead. At the ends of the knotty branches she saw creamy hands, creamy palms, cradling secrets like water. Secrets she wanted to know, of where they'd come from, directions perhaps to the labyrinthine passages in which all souls transmute. The passages of the dead back to the living.

The tree seemed alive to her, alive with possibilities. Was Ferny in the tree? With a compensatory rush of hope, after all the hours on her own, she thought yes, this is how it would have to be. I would have thought a mountain ash, or at least the big blackwoods by our gate, but there you have it. I wouldn't know. The spirit cannot be predicted, only experienced. Right here in a solicitor's garden.

Some green nub, some moist tendril, began to prod inside her. This life was a trial. She looked to where some of the flowers had fallen. Lying there on dark nutty ground. Browning at the edges. There was a little forest too, a cluster of tiny salmon-pink mushrooms sprouting among the petals. They had long slender stipes and narrow caps and were all leaning the same way, in a tight bunch, as if they were pointing to something. Her eyes followed where they were pointing, but all she saw was the painted concrete slab under the solicitor's front awning. The tap in the corner, fixed to the brick wall.

On the Trans Otway bus on the way home that afternoon, Sarah fell asleep to the rhythmic burr of the engine before waking with a start as the bus descended noisily into Kuarka Dorla. By this stage of the journey she was now the sole passenger, the others having alighted at Belmont and at Bellbrae. As she woke to the engine's high descending gear she momentarily wondered where on earth she was. Through the window the tangle of coarse boughs and branches seemed utterly foreign. Her breath caught in her throat and she coughed, at which point she noticed the driver watching her in his rear-vision mirror.

On the other side of the valley, once they had crossed the new bridge over the Swampy Creek, she felt a sharp pain in her side. Through the front window of the bus the lighthouse came into view. At the simple sight of this she almost burst into tears, but the welling-up subsided like some preternatural tide, disappearing as quickly as it had come on. She adjusted herself to ease the pain in her side, gripping the steel frame of the bench seat ahead of her for balance. Now the pain disappeared with the tears, but still the driver was keeping a close eye.

Eventually, when they came down the hill past the Store and then the Hotel, she rose from her seat. Thanking the driver, she placed her foot back on the solid earth of the roadside opposite the bottom shop.

'Good day to you, Miss Hutchinson,' the driver had said in a friendly way as she stepped down from the bus. How did he know her name? It was only later on that night, as she was filling a hot water bottle in readiness for bed, that she realised her name – *Sarah Hutchinson* – was on the return bus ticket she had bought earlier in the day. And with that simple and seemingly innocuous realisation she did indeed, finally, burst into tears.

VI

Dear Editors,

I write in reply to your correspondent of Stony Point. I thought it might be of interest for him, and your other readers, to know that here on the southern coast of the continent of Australia, where snow is an uncommon occurrence and winters are relatively mild, the notion of a winter mushroom being rare is as strange as a squirrel. Our winters are in fact full of so many blooms (as I like to think of mushrooms) that local science has barely begun to record the variety.

It was with interest therefore that I read of *Flammulina velutipes*, the 'winter mushroom', and with pleasure of the philosophical wisdom which Mr Romanoff derived from his observance of fungi on the correspondent's mycological tour. Suffice to say that even here in Victoria 'the little things that happen' continue without respite.

Yours, *in situ*,
Miss Sarah Hutchinson

In the days after Joe Busch began working at Ngangahook, Sarah felt confirmed in her feeling that Ferny would have approved of the young man, of his good nature, his farm skills, and also his habit of playing the mouth harp in front of the stables in the evening. There were no horses in the stables anymore. The tractor was parked in the far bay, Geoff and Emma's Triumph sedan occupied what was formerly the bellows and blacksmithery, and the main stalls area had been cleared out and enlarged long ago to accommodate an airplane. The makeshift hangar now housed Ferny's last plane, the Cessna 120. A new wall had been put in on the house side of the Cessna bay, and hay, sacks of feed and other miscellaneous gear were stored in this end of the old building. There was still a large enough area for Geoff to suggest to Sarah that they could fix Joe Busch up some reasonable digs in there, to save him cycling through the dark in the winter working week. He could always go home for Sundays to see his Mum. Joe seemed happy with the arrangement; in fact, he was excited. After the day's work was over he would eat in the manager's house with Geoff and Emma, after which he would retire to the stables, where he liked to play the mouth harp by the firepit while watching the light go down over the bush beyond the glen.

Sarah would walk in the mornings and at dusk, as was her long habit, and now, with the appearance of her name in the American *Natural History* magazine, her walking took on another dimension. As well as taking her usual routes, where the ground had not been disturbed, she began also to use the tracks that Joe and the gang had cut. She walked with the American correspondent in her thoughts, and, because of that, with a burgeoning interest in funghi. With one spontaneous letter she had leapt out of the glen, beyond the newly measured boundaries of Ngangahook. And if Ferny had taken his talisman book with him on his overseas adventures in order to never be without the distinctive qualities of where he'd come from, likewise the slopes, gullies and gorges, teeming with what must have been a thousand types of mushroom, could be her international calling card. When in the following issue the Stony Point correspondent replied to her letter, she very much liked the way he called it 'mushroomy, in the way it just popped up' – particularly because the whole experience of writing the letter had just 'popped up' for her as well, albeit out of the deep loam of her mourning.

Dear Editors,

Gone are the days when I walked looking straight ahead. Or even in straight lines. My interest in fungi keeps teaching me the errors of my ways. But to hear from Miss Sarah Hutchinson in faraway Australia (Issue no LXI) was as unplanned an encounter as I could imagine. In short, her letter felt very mushroomy, in the way it just popped up like that.

It occurred to me over the following days how friendships often appear in our lives like fungi. And that millions of productive spores spring out from these friendships every day. This is how I prefer to think of the rather worn adage that 'love makes the world go around'. In actual fact, and at the risk of straying from the topic, I'd like to ask the question: what is 'love' after all? I figure it's a far more normal phenomenon than is generally supposed. Yet no less wondrous. Close observation of nature can teach us that. But not too close. Otherwise we might ruin the effect.

Your Stony Point Correspondent

So now, as the days and weeks progressed and the days grew shorter, Ferny's library began to turn into something of a seedbank for her. It had always been her habit to keep to her own room of an evening, but now, when she wasn't walking, she was often sitting on Ferny's armchair. She read, first this and then that, first the *Natural History* journal, then the surrealist novels, then 'Mr Ruskin', as Ferny had always called him, then Cavafy, Philip Oyler, Christina Stead, even Shakespeare. And again, the issues of the *Natural History* journal from New York. And so, at the beginning and end of each day, armed not so much with new eyes as new focal points, she walked in a welter of anticipation and discovery.

Dear Editors,

Keeping to the tracks immediately in the vicinity of my family's farm I ponder over the right conditions for each new (or new to me) species of fungi I see. We have one type here which, from my research, I can approximate as resembling the 'earthstar' or *Geastrum triplex*. It grows on our ocean cliffs, and in form rather than color it resembles a five-pointed star, and is thus aptly named. And if it has indeed fallen from heaven to earth then it goes on falling. One drop of rain on the proud center of an earthstar is enough to send out by pneumatic reflex the mist of a thousand spores, which arc and fall.

Thus the cycle goes on, the heavens rotate. We often think in large and general ways, but it is via the small that our thinking can become properly vast. And I agree with Mr Romanoff, the acquaintance of our Stony Point correspondent, that with such thinking we foster our own right conditions into perpetuity. For, like the earthstars, we are long evolved *in situ*. And it is *in situ*, so far away and yet with mycelial friendship, that I remain yours,

    Miss Sarah Hutchinson

❧

The ocean cliffs in autumn were a living maze of bristlebirds darting to-and-fro. Slowly over the years, on once overgrazed promontories, the native vegetation had returned, followed by the native birds. The cool sea-mists of the early mornings threaded through moonah trees laden with blossom turning bronze. The mists salted the clifftops, moistening the leafy mould under the moonah and bearded heath. It was nothing for Sarah to walk the league or more from Ngangahook to these cliffs, and then for miles to the east along the high tops. When she read in *Natural History* Issue LXX about Cree Indians in Canada measuring the depth of their grief by how far they walked in the days after death, she well understood. She thought too of the local aboriginals, who Ferny said had once come in a group onto the glen to camp by the river and to play football. They must be walking still, Sarah thought, on a walk that never ends. Enmeshed in her sorrow she then spoke aloud on the cliffs to Maisie of the Big Cutting Hill cottage, telling her of Ferny's leaving, and that she should be expecting him anytime now.

And yet, Sarah thought, looking down near her feet, there were also the earthstars. Keeping watch from below, living closer to hand. The shining lights not only lived on high but down low on the ground as well. It was all so close you could smell it. She breathed deeply from the earth, and exhaled tears. There, right there at her feet as she walked on, were the ancient reefs for a drowning spirit. *Geastrum triplex*, in the old Roman name, and inkcaps, field mushrooms, slippery jacks. Focal points that she couldn't predict, and that had already begun to take her, like a needle and thread, both into and out of the fabric of her sorrow. The stillness of these earthen blooms, along with the idea that they were the visible stars of an underland constellation, were all she needed to look up again and notice the light on the sea.

❧

Damp from her walking she returned one day to find Joe Busch replacing the hardwood bars of the cattle grid at the Ngangahook gate with metal tubes. She saw him from a long way off, coming as she was from the town side where the coach road crossed the old brown stream. Joe was wearing a checked workshirt, shorts and high leather boots. He'd set up two sawhorses under the trees and was measuring the span of each clean-barked beam and plank as they came out. As she watched him move a beam onto the sawhorses she admired the intensity of his physical strength, his muscular brown skin, under which his sinews moved like fish in clear water. This place is full of ghosts, she thought to herself. And then, as she stood watching him, her own spirit stirred for a moment. It was gone again just as quickly. Still, something was coming back to life in Ferny's absence. Who was this young man who'd just appeared on her doorstep one day as some kind of reincarnation of red-headed Joe Sullivan?

She greeted young Joe warmly, said she was a little sad the grid was finally being renewed – it had been needing attention for many years – and would he like it if she brought him out a cup of tea to have his smoko in the dappling light?

The dappling light. Joe was immediately affected by the phrase. Ngangahook was a place where such phrases could not only be said but felt right too, and such an idea came to him as a great relief. *The dappled light.*

He said, 'Yes, thank you, that would be good.' It was all he could manage, all he could bring out of himself, just basics, basic words, but maybe in time he would find a way. For the moment he felt a little embarrassed, not by his clumsy language but by the intensity of his feeling, which amounted to a peculiarly local variety of joy.

Sarah smiled, said, 'Righto', and jumped the gap of the half-dismantled grid like a much younger woman.

She went on up the driveway to where Geoff's dog Reg was resting. He got up to greet her. Bending down on one knee, she hugged the dog. 'You're keeping Joe company this morning, Reg? Good dog. Go now and help him finish the grid. Yes, you're a beautiful boy. I'll bring you out a bone with the tea.'

Standing up she watched as Reg did exactly as she'd suggested. Then she turned for the house. Is this some second chance? she wondered, stepping up the verandah stairs. Some new clearing Ferny has left in his wake? Am I perhaps meant to sing again?

VII

AT THE PUB Joe Busch found himself feeling uncomfortable from time to time due to the way Don Atchison talked about him getting the job. Not that Don implied anything underhand but just that he was so openly envious. It was Don after all who had told Joe and the others about the poet in the first place. Joe knew how much Don thought of Sarah – or Miss Hutchinson, as he still called her at the Hotel – and also that Don had become embarrassed as an adult about the role his own parents had played in the Hutchinsons' ostracisation. Joe thought how it would be some sort of full circle if Don started working at Ngangahook too. But that wasn't likely, and there was nothing Joe could do to help. So when Don kept going on about it, Joe felt annoyed. He was a blow-in after all, from a good thirty miles away, while Don went right back to the time of Miss Hutchinson's yearly stories by the bonfire. He knew Don was always scratching around for work – partly of course because he wouldn't have a bar of anything his parents might offer him – whereas he himself could probably have picked up something on a farm around Winchelsea anytime he liked. He'd felt the impetus to walk away from all that however, to do otherwise, and sometimes, as he fell asleep in the stables after a long day's work with Geoff, he marvelled at how it had all come to pass. He had gone from just a knockabout labourer from a town block in Winch to a plum job on what he considered a paradise station. They gave him food and lodging with no dock off his pay; he could go fishing and crabbing in the coves before or after work. Most importantly, he was treated differently than he ever had been. Both Sarah and the Hamiltons said nice things about his mouth harp, and Emma Hamilton often plied him with questions over dinner, asking him his opinion on the farm and on other issues as broad as politics or history. He'd taken an interest and always read the newspaper when it was near to hand, so he genuinely loved these chats. But he knew Don would too. What could he do? Nothing really, just enjoy it, he told himself. Poor old Don would have to look out for himself. Meanwhile he would answer Don's questions about Sarah as best he could.

'What's it like inside the homestead? I remember my parents talking about an enormous room.'

'Yair, the first room you strike, if you walk in from the front, or from the stables side, is bloody big. And the kitchen's in it too, behind a long hardwood bench. So yair, you've got the dining table, the big piano, the comfy sofas, and the kitchen, all in together. And everything's looking out through these big windows, almost floor to ceiling, across the farm and the river and over to the bush in the north where we cut the tracks. When you're sitting at the dining table the floor seems to go on forever. There's a couple of rugs, one or two, nice rugs, posh I suppose, with the grand piano and that, but not many rugs, no. It's all floor and windows that enormous room. There's even a glass door off the kitchen. And a built-in cupboard next to that which opens to the outside for putting the firewood in. Yair, that's where the wood's brought in, through that little cupboard, rather than from the stables side. It's always kept topped up from the stack. There's no wood kept in the stables, not even now there's no horses. She sorts the wood out herself a lot of the time. Doesn't ask the Hamiltons for much. Still swings the axe. Once we bring it up to her stack and that. Sometimes I see her sharpening the axe on the front verandah when I'm workin' in the paddocks.'

'Do you ever see her writing?'

'Yair well nah, she sits out on the verandah a lot, where I see her sharpening the axe. I've seen her reading out there, and I remember the book coz it had a strange name: *The No Plays*. Go figure. But writin', no. But she could be writing out there some days. She sits at a little round table and I've seen paper lying about. Her light's often on late in her uncle's old study. I can see it if I'm sittin' out front of the stables of an evening. So who knows what she's doin' to all hours.'

'Does she still play the piano?'

'Nah, well I've never heard it. But at the moment it's piled high anyway, with all kinds of stuff. Be a job to clear it all to open that big top. She uses it as a bit of a table I suppose. Displays stuff on it and that. Though I don't know who for. Coz no one's looking.'

'So she stays up late. Does she get up early?'

'Oh yair. You remember, when we were cuttin' the tracks, we'd see her in the bush not so long after sun-up. Yair, she's an early bird I'd say. Sometimes in the garden, or choppin' wood, or catching that verandah sun. "She'd make a good farmer," Geoff jokes. But nah, he's got a lot of time for her. Thinks the absolute world of her. Follows any instructions she gives to the letter.'

'Do you speak to her much? Does she ever tell you stories?'

'Aw, she's got a nice way of speakin'. It's proper and that, but I like her voice, if you know what I mean. Plus what she says with it. The way she describes things I suppose, being a poet and that. But nah, she doesn't really tell stories. We have a yarn, mostly 'bout nothin' much. She sometimes gives me a book to read. So does Mrs Hamilton – Emma. Oh but yair, one day Miss Hutchinson had a little joke with me about what she called her "changing stick". That was a bit of a story I suppose. So she reckons when she's walkin' she has a whole story in her head about the stick she uses. It's a bit of hazel, kinda light – Pomaderris, you know, we cut quite a lot of that stuff out o' there didn't we. Yair, well anyway, I was askin' her about it one day, coz it's real light ya know and usually old people walk with a bit of oak or somethin', or blackwood or whatever, but, anyway she reckons she changes it as she goes. I didn't cotton on at first; I thought she just meant she puts one down and picks another one up, given all the Pomaderris there is out there, but nah, she meant that she kind of *imagines* it changed. That she changes it in her mind I s'pose. "So," she said, "sometimes I imagine I'm walkin' with an old orange branch, or an olive switch. It amuses me," she said, "and the bush seems different as I touch it with every new stick I choose. And sometimes, Joe," she says, looking me straight in the eye, "I even imagine the stick's not wood at all." "How do you mean?" I say, and she looks past me and then she says, "Well, some gossamer stick, or a kelp stick, or a stick made out of a cloud." "Gossamer?" I say, and she says, "Yes gossamer, you know, spiderwebs, Joe. A stick made of spiderwebs. And on I go," she says, "with my gossamer stick." So that's a bit of a story I reckon.'

'A story, yair. Like a dream really.'

'Yair, like a dream.'

'What does she eat?'

'Dunno. She seems to like soup. She often offers me some. And occasionally, so Geoff tells me, she snares a duck. Occasionally she'll use other words for things too. Did I tell you that? *Tulum*, she calls the ducks. Or Latin. Or other words, which I got a feelin' might be the old Greek. And yair, she's been into the mushies a bit of late. Since they've been springin' up. She gave a bagful to me to cook on my brekkie pit out front of the stables the other day. They weren't fieldies though. Looked a bit dodgy to me, purple and orange they were, but she said, "If you die you can blame me, Joe." But nah, she's kind, and she's been here forever so she should know. So I ate 'em. Tasted a bit like crabs. Yum.'

'What's it like upstream there in the paddocks?'

'Bloody good. Yair real good, real lush, even when everythin' else is a bit dry. Well, everything's flowin' into it eh. From all points. Can only imagine the store of groundwater. The whole glen's full of seep, and there's these little round pools everywhere about, right in the middle of the pasture. Then, right up at the tip of the nor'-western end she widens out doesn't she, into the swamp. God, you should hear it at night. The frogs! Keeps me awake if the wind's from the north.'

'Does she ever talk about the old days?'

'The old days? Depends on how old you're talkin'. Every now and then she asks me about the footy, how we went on Saturday and that. She likes the footy. Loves it. Reckon she has a soft spot for Winch now, coz of me. And one day we were talkin' about the VFL and how exciting it would be to get to a game, and she told me about how they apparently used to play blackfella footy at Ngangahook. Before her time, she reckons. But back in her Uncle Ferny's grandparents' day. As I say, that was before her time. Even before Ferny's, who all in all sounds like a champion bloke. Seems a real shame everythin' went the way it did.'

VIII

Dear Editors,

I note with interest the trend at NASA to name new stars drily. X2X680 was a recent discovery announced in Paige Berenson's press conference only last month, and before that, in this decade alone, we've had 0X2660, PYX2X304, and even an asteroid with a hyphen. I thought of this with interest when reading Miss Sarah Hutchinson's letter from Australia regarding the *Geastrum triplex*, or earthstar, perhaps because of the debates here in America over 'true' and 'false' earthstars. The similarities between *Geastrum triplex* and *Astraeus hygrometricus*, or the Barometer Earthstar, revolve around the hygroscopic qualities of *Astraeus hygrometricus*, which sees its star cluster opening and closing depending on the weather. Hence it being referred to as the Barometer Earthstar. This barometric feature of course protects the spore sac until such time as the rain droplets arrive to express the spores by hitting the sac. The *Geastrum triplex*, on the other hand, never wraps up its rays, leaving the spore sac to cope with all weathers, which of course it does <u>proudly</u>.

The fact that the human community has taken, at times, to

designating the Barometer Earthstar as a 'false earthstar' and the *Geastrum triplex*, or 'saucered earthstar', as a 'true earthstar' seems at first to provide justification for NASA's dry approach. Could there, for instance, ever be a true X2X680 and a false X2X680? When one stops to consider (obviously having no other immediate and pressing concerns!) that indeed there could in fact be such value-laden denominations of acronymic names, then the case seems irrefutable that we should return to the increased descriptive charisma of words. 'What's wrong with Pluto?' I hear you cry. 'And where would our poets be without such precise adjectives as "Saturnalian"?'

In short, I enjoyed the way Miss Hutchinson drew poetic sustenance from the 'earthstar' name. I have looked at these mushrooms with delight wherever I have happened upon them and now am at liberty to view them as a philosophical aid as well.

Your Stony Point Correspondent

This letter in the *Natural History* journal, which had arrived at the Post Office as per Ferny's ongoing and now posthumous subscription, became a turning point of sorts. It was the policy of the magazine, and specifically of its Letters Editor, Martin Shaw, to keep the correspondence in the journal refreshed and diverse, and thus, only two days after this edition arrived, Sarah received another piece of mail from Manhattan, this time in a small envelope with the Natural History Museum letterhead printed next to the stamp and postmark.

Dear Miss Hutchinson,

I write to you as the Editor of the Letters page of *Natural History*, to thank you for your recent contributions to the said pages.

THE BELL OF THE WORLD

Growing up as I did in New Leipzig, North Dakota, a tiny outpost almost entirely reliant for its existence on the Northern Pacific Railroad, and having developed an early love of reading, writing, and knowledge of all kinds, I grew quickly to understand some of the various protocols involved in the management of the Letters page of the various magazines and journals which I wrote in to. I learned for instance, and quite painfully, the entirely common practice of terminating the most interesting dialogues among the written correspondents. As a young teenager on a cropping farm subscribing to the *Readers Digest* I was very upset to have my sixth response to Myrtle Jones of Freeport, Texas (with whom I shared an interest in the Cornish novels of Daphne du Maurier) go unprinted and unacknowledged in the magazine. I wrote again, in case the letter had got lost, but with the same result. Of course I never had any further contact with Myrtle Jones and occasionally wonder what became of her, even to this day.

Likewise, when I was a subscriber to a Minor League Baseball periodical called *Stitch*, I was rudely cut off (or so I considered) from making a third reply to one Jack Heffingham of Rapid City, South Dakota, with whom I was enjoying a discussion about the groundbreaking talents of Ted 'Double Duty' Radcliffe.

In my remote circumstances I had grown to live somewhat vicariously through the interest I took in lively topics covered by such magazines, which, needless to say, in some way explains the nature of my current employment! As of last January I have been with *Natural History* for 14 years.

This is all by way of informing you that despite the value of your recent exchanges on the topic of fungi with the subscriber-correspondent from Stony Point, Rockland County, I must request, in the interest of maintaining the diversity of our Letters page, that this dialogue continue among yourselves. To that end I am writing to help facilitate such a continuance. With your permission I would be delighted to pass on your postal details to Stony Point, and the two of you could take it from there.

I hope you'll understand how what happens to us when we are young is often so formative. In my case it has meant that I have an allergy to corn husks, treeless rural landscapes, and cutting off productive correspondence in-print without due reparations.

     Yours, Martin Shaw
     Ass. Editor, *Natural History*

❧

She began to ponder the possibility, which she felt was gently implied in the Stony Point correspondent's last letter, that she may have mis-identified the earthstars she'd discovered on the ocean clifftops. After a period of time in which she had been beginning to feel recollected, if not entirely redeemed by the way her grief was moving beyond the stasis of local pain towards a more universal connection, the ground of the glen, the bush slopes and the ocean cliffs began to swallow her up all over again. Why she should care about naming mushrooms, or about more general issues of categorisation, classification and scientific nomenclature, was beyond her. Where was that younger self who'd disdained, indeed floated above, the Field Nats on their visit to the glen all those years ago? Here she was now, giving a damn about appearing incorrect to men of their stamp and field, and men so far away!

She sat out on the verandah, with drying pasture, violet sky, and a warm northerly wind coming through the gum trees opposite. Back then only Joe Sullivan had seemed human, could feel and touch beyond cold pedantry, but where was he now? And these two Americans, first the correspondent from Stony Point and then the editor, this Martin Shaw, how did they think of her? As some princess of misnomers from the far south, virtually Antarctica? As a hick who could not quite kick her national habit of strangling language? She had written her letters on a wave of buoyancy and could not retract them, could not erase them, any more than she could bring Ferny back.

For a whole week then, after receiving Martin Shaw's letter, she stopped walking and took to her room. Eating soup, and bread which grew increasingly stale with each passing day. She felt humiliated by her sensitivity. It was a problem compounded by itself, and when, on the Saturday, she moved once again to Ferny's divan, she could have sworn the end was as near as his gun. It hung behind his cupboard door. She focused only on it, and forgot all the erudite books and journals.

On the Monday, having suddenly decided at 4 a.m. to shower and to shave her armpits with Ferny's razor, the thought emerged that grief itself, like madness, could be treated as coolly as a science. What category was this then? An episodic relapse? A gravitational impulse towards the lowlands of emotional loyalty? Ferny may have left – Ferny who gave her everything – but she would not leave him. But was this even her? She would have to find out.

IX

Dear Mr Shaw,

Thank you for taking the trouble to write. My father told me once, during my own unhappy childhood, that politeness was a strategy used by people of no feeling to disguise their utter lack. 'Sincerity is messy,' he said. 'Messy like life. But politeness is a cleaning agent that spoils things in the end.'

Well, I could tell the difference when I read your letter. It was a <u>messy</u> thing to have to do, and I appreciate it.

Please forward my address to our friend in Stony Point.

      Yours sincerely,
      Sarah Hutchinson.

❦

Her father had also told her that getting back on the horse after a fall was a stupid thing to do. This in a letter from Christchurch when she was at school in England. It suited her at the time to follow his lead and flout generally accepted conventions, but now it suited her to flout her father's own conventions even more. So she asked that separate part of herself, the part that saw the future and heard the timbre of the gods in the eternity of natural sound – she asked for the free restoration of her senses, to hear the wagtail's three-rung song, the liquid song of the magpie in the background, and the thick bed of ocean sound beyond that. For this was a journey of emotion and loss, and it had always been such a journey, from the days long ago when she lost her mother to the drink of her own despair, and her father to the insouciance of post-married life. She'd been put on a boat in a white dress, her parents' own wrack sewn into it. So that purity for her had always been stitched with something beyond language, or before language, something like sea lettuce, or Neptune's necklace, but yes, before the names that pinned things down. She needed to take the pins out again now, painfully, with the strong and nimble fingers of that other self, who had never, could never, be changed by anything but what was necessary, and by beauty. She disassembled, one by one, the facets of the vitrine that was enclosing her. The air rushed back in like the ocean does when the entire bush catchment above the glen descends to break through the rivermouth sandbar. Gone then was *Geastrum triplex* or *Astraeus hygrometricus*, gone and washed away into the stream, like so many agreed-upon notes of the piano. Only the chanciness of mushrooms remained.

A phrase came to her: *the whole world is fabricated by design.* This was an idea that brought her great relief. We are part of it, so we make things up. Gone then too, in time, like so many thin filaments of pollen through the air, would be the posts and rails of the very fence being built along the glen's northern boundary. Gone too would be Ngangahook, not only the whole sign at the gate but the whole word itself as well. Ngangahook. Angahook. Ironbark. Gone. All that would be left would be the tree.

And what would it say? Yes. *Ngangahook*, or some other collaboration with human-produced sound. All over again.

It was true, the spores of the earthstar were expressions of the land, the letters of its language, the alphabet of the ongoing. All anyone ever really needed to make a song was rain, and the rain's eternal dance partner, the sun.

※

It had only been a week but Joe noticed she was out and about again, as did Geoff Hamilton, and Emma. It was Emma she sought out though, as she did from time to time. She needed the company now and needed to wander lightly, without project or pin, common names or Latin, and without the businesslike or pastoralist's view. Geoff would likely want to talk about the long plan, Joe would hardly talk at all, but Emma would describe the recipes she'd recently cooked, a novel she'd read, some issue she was having with the bias of a hem. They'd lived on the same property for many years, and the lightness of their friendship had made its own contribution to the balance of things. With Ferny, Sarah would be her full self, like the black bream dwelling in the deeper holes of the river, and Emma, when she was with Geoff, would be sensitively poised, like the egret who glowed in the reeds downstream of the salt-fresh line. But together they were otherwise, just a pair of scanner insects skipping about on the surface of the stream.

And this was where a new network played its hand, as they meandered slowly along the winding riverbank, and Emma began to talk of what she'd been reading during her recent cold. High cliffs, rising winds, the bracing conditions that her cold wouldn't allow. And an old, old mystery, in Cornwall.

Old romance too. 'Just the tonic,' said Emma. 'And wonderfully strange. I want to read some more of Du Maurier now. Do you think there'd be any in Ferny's library? *Rebecca* perhaps?'

'I think not,' said Sarah, amazed, and wondering if perhaps she should put Emma in touch with Mr Martin Shaw! She'd never read Du Maurier, and it wasn't Ferny's type of thing at all. Martin Shaw on the other hand, at least as a child...

'You know, Sarah, there's a strange albino vicar in the one I read. *Jamaica Inn*. Gives me a shiver just thinking about him. And the albino vicar is only the half of it. It's very *dramatic*.'

They talked of other things, even of some gossip in the town concerning stolen craypots from around the road in Lorne. An Angahook fisherman had stolen the pots off the water under moonlight, saying the Lorne fisherman had cut the tea-tree for the pots from his land. It was a complicated issue, and Sarah grew interested. Who owned those pots then, after all? Without the tea-tree they wouldn't exist yet you couldn't catch crays with raw tea-tree; you had to know how to go to the trouble to bend and warp and bind them into pots.

As interesting as this was, it was thoughts of *Jamaica Inn* that Sarah was left with when she said goodbye to Emma and made her way back to the homestead. In Ferny's library she scanned the shelves to be sure. But it was the coincidence that struck her, rather than what Emma had told her of the book. Albino vicars and shipwreckers were one thing, but real conversations with editors from New York were quite another. What, for instance, would Martin Shaw, or the correspondent from Stony Point for that matter, make of the local conundrum of the craypots? And what a strange turn of events it was after all these years of habitude and currawong calls that these two men were now among the most important figures in her life.

As she strung the beans at the back kitchen bench by the glass side door, she considered how this was precisely the way Ferny had coped with the isolation down through the years. When he wasn't overseas he kept up an almost daily correspondence with all manner of interesting people far beyond Bass Strait shores, and he did this almost until the day he died. But Sarah, no, she had been truly on her own, even if this was not how she considered it. Aside from Maisie Cruik, none of the girls from Miss Hunt's had ever been in touch, and old Roiseaux was of course long gone. And yet now, in the absence left by her great companion and uncle passing on, new connections were being made.

X

THE MONTHLY ISSUES of *Natural History* kept arriving, but of course they were not what she was now waiting on. She would thumb straight through to the Letters page, which, with her new knowledge of its editor's background, she read with a slightly different slant. She checked the location of the correspondents against Ferny's atlas and found that, yes, from British Columbia to Kuching, the letters selected for print often came from isolated posts like hers. It was as if Mr Shaw was working hard in New York to put a fragmented world back in touch with itself, and not only by furthering discussions on the details of the threat modern life was bringing to nature.

On the second of May a light rain slanting from the southeast required Sarah to wear her slicker to the Post Office. The border collie Reg accompanied her on the trip, as he often chose to do. She looked down at the ground, far out to sea, and up into the perfumed scrim of bush as she went. If she passed anyone she raised her eyes to the sky and only ever spoke when she arrived at the Post Office. Yet her walking presence was a signature tune of local days, and just about everyone would have noticed if she'd ceased to appear. It would have been as if the lighthouse had forgotten to flash.

As soon as she was handed the pale blue envelope she knew it was the one. And there on the back was the sender's name and address. Reg was positioned dutifully on the mat outside the Post Office entrance, and as she walked towards him she ran her fingers affectionately through his coat. He picked up her excitement straightaway and began madly wagging his tail against the doorjamb.

Instead of going home her usual way via the short cuts past the Hotel, she headed south towards the cliffs. She walked out of the wind's buffet into the tea-tree colonnades with keen anticipation, before stopping above the Nyooroo cove where there was a six-yard length of rusted steel-pipe railing she could lean against as she read.

Dear Miss Sarah Hutchinson,
Gone are the days when I could walk through the forest thinking of other things. Now I know that there are <u>no other things</u>, that all and everywhere is richly connected. So I write as if along a hypha thread to you, especially so given that we have been forced to take our connection underground! How dark and empty they all think it is down here below the light, but how clearly we know and understand it to be otherwise.

The fact that we can predict the weather with the aid of an earthstar seems hardly an occasion to call that earthstar 'false'. On the contrary it would seem to be our <u>true</u> friend. Of course this is not from any <u>intention</u> on the earthstar's behalf, but neither do I believe that we intend half the things we do in life, and more than half of the best things we do. It is in the reductive and frankly anxious nature of science then to attribute judgements of relativity upon life forms which merely betray an inevitable diversity of qualities. Anyway, what makes a star so unique among the trillions, and who's to say which earthstar is the original, the most moral, or the best? Human language is noisy and so hampered by good, or powerful, intentions that I do believe we have an opportunity to become wonderfully porous to experience if we circumvent intention and give ourselves over to <u>what is already happening</u>.

So yes, here at Stony Point (and elsewhere) I wander about in a state largely of good humor, chancing upon what I see. We have a fine array of fungi in these parts, but of course hunting is always to start from zero, or, to put it in another way that I prefer: <u>Hunting is not looking for</u>.

However, I should admit that once I have found what I am not looking for I do like to ponder on, and even to <u>describe</u> its nature. Thus my vocabulary has expanded and I do know a lamella from a squamule, a stem from a stipe. But these kinds of descriptions come after the main event for me, which is about the moment of chance when I find a mushroom in fine condition. I also like to eat them. But we do have to be careful. As a wise old sage once said: Every mushroom expert dies of mushroom poisoning.

Really a lovely cautionary phrase.

Unfortunately, or perhaps fortunately, we don't have many earthstars in these immediate parts, so any tales you have of them would interest me greatly. It is in the descriptive phase, post the thrill of discovery, that I always become absorbed in further research, which opens up its own worlds. Thus here we are.

I remain yours, John (the Stony Point Correspondent)

XI

Despite ferny's championing of her talents she never called herself a musician, or a poet, or an artist, just as now she wouldn't call herself a farmer, or even a landowner. How about Grazier, Inheritor, Cocky, or L U C K Y B I T C H ? That's how some would arrange the letters and sounds available to them when they thought of her. When many years ago she had dared to contribute three pictures to the local art show, and had added some pencil strokes and shading during the evening when they first were on display at Mr Hastie's Guest House, the locals called her a 'nutter'. The implication was that she was insane – no one *scribbled* on pictures already hung on the walls of an art exhibition! And yet she had seen Roiseaux do exactly that in Rome. The pictures were her own creations after all, just as they were Roiseaux's. And nothing's ever finished is it? Surely there should always be a possibility of further evolution?

When she made her retreat from society the names they could invent for her grew in direct and inverse proportion to her absence. It was the type of absence that ushers in the ideal growing conditions for mythology. For Don Atchison the absence meant she had developed into a capital P Poet with something of the strange ruthlessness and enigma of the greats. And for everyone else she was amplified into every stereotype of witch and madwoman under the sun.

But she called herself nothing all along, and now, in response to the correspondent from Stony Point, she faced a dilemma. How would she go about it? If she talked of *Coprinopsis atramentaria*, or the common inkcap, would that then be her name? Or *Coprinus comatus*, likewise? Could she then be not Miss Sarah Hutchinson, but a shaggy mane or a lawyer's wig? She knew in fact that indeed she was the places she walked, the uplands from the glen, and, of course, the glen itself. She had let it be so; she had let the ground come slowly up through her body. And Ferny and her had had a myriad of nicknames for each other over the years: Lichen, Lichenheart, Mossy, Mossy Missal, Ken, and yes even Saf, for Sappho. He knew even better than her that most of the things around them that mattered *simply were* and had no names. Hence his obsessions with science, with natural histories, nomenclatures and orders. But for Sarah one question remained. Standing by his grave on the slope at the end of the westernmost pasture, she would wonder about decomposition. At what point, for instance, as he deliquesced from the body she knew into the ground of the glen, at what point would he cease to become Ferny? She longed to be able not to think of this but, even so, she also longed to be like one of the many mushrooms growing all about her that had as yet no name. Not shaggy mane or lawyer's wig, not graceful parasol, Scotch bonnet or *Marasmius oreades*.

So that's what she decided to do in the end. Write about this lack of names.

Dear John,

    When my uncle's grandparents initially came to this country it was for farming, though certainly not for mushrooms! However, by all accounts they had been religious people, and funghi grows through all religions, and will, of course, outlast them all. As soon as they began to get to know some of the native peoples here, on a Mission some forty miles from where I write, such details about what I might call *The Natural History of Eternity* became clear. These people were most heavily invested in the perpetual motion of the stars. But would the Mission listen? <u>Could</u> the Mission listen? After all, the motion of the stars makes a particular music, and takes a quality of hearing bound up with the spongey complexity of the ground.

    The knowledge of the Aboriginal people of the Mission fell largely on ears deaf to such music, and thus the civilising project was a disaster. But before it was officially terminated there was a cross-pollination of sorts in the rare moments of concord which did indeed rely on us interlopers listening with full attention. These were the faintest beginnings of an understanding, of how to be here, how to be here together.

    Apparently one minister on the Mission, with the help of the people he knew, and even despite his limited hearing, translated one or two passages of the Bible into the local language, and some friendships were made among the tragedy. I am describing here a bequest of fragmentation, but to some extent it has guided me nevertheless.

    When I arrived here at Ngangahook I came from Rome. There were stories of harmony as well as disharmony. Our glen seemed, to me at least, to be a place attuned to the journey of the stars. A place that, from time to time, those selfsame stars might feel comfortable to fall into. And when I walk now I am all too aware of the absence, not only of any Christianising bell in these parts (my uncle and I had a hand in ensuring this), but also of the lack of names for the things I see. And that includes a myriad of mushrooms.

Thus, from a natural history point of view it is probably fortunate that our correspondence has been sent underground. I have not that much to offer in terms of names, nomenclature, and organisation. I think it might – in fact I believe it most probably did – take a thousand years to even begin to construct any simulating order for the natural profusion. I've noted here how even when it comes to birds and birdsongs we Australians have been somewhat lazy imitators. For instance, if a bird was black and white, and common, we simply called it a magpie. Even when its song was frankly incomparable to that European head-bird. See, that deafness again. You do know that in Ancient Greece – which I never really think of being that 'ancient' at all – there was a story that hinged both on the perils of delusory self-love and also on how rudimentarily ugly the European magpie's song is. Nine sisters, the Pierides, challenged the Muses to a singing contest and lost. Calliope, mother of Orpheus and the Muse of Ecstatic Harmony, punished the sisters by turning them into magpies so that forever after they would be condemned to singing a song no one wanted to hear.

And yet here the bird we call magpie is not the equivalent of the daughters of Pierus but of Calliope herself! She sings not the ugliest but the most beautiful song. Here the story goes, or so it went on a long-ago visit in the Ngangahook glen, that the beauty of the magpie's song was present at the birth of sunlight in the world. Long ago, when there was darkness upon the earth, the magpies got together and pushed the darkness up off the land with sticks. Light came in for the first time, and when it did the birds tilted back their heads and sang. As they still do every morning. Thus every new day is akin to the beginning of everything. Every dawn an anniversary.

And so you see how names can be here. I've seen the local Aboriginal word for the bird spelt as <u>barroworn</u>. And even the Latin is likewise misused by the deaf. A football club, perhaps the most famous in the land, which uses the 'barroworn' as their mascot and calls themselves 'The Magpies', employs the Latin name of the European magpie – <u>Floreat *Pica*</u> – on their crest, rather than that of the Australian magpie.

So it is that I walk in a forest either misnamed or nominally absent, and wonder how I can describe to you the species that I see. Perhaps one solution will be for us to notify each other of particular differences. And to rejoice in them. I might even use my dead uncle's Voigtländer camera. Thus the funghi in my thereabouts may become my self-portrait, my soul having a convex or bell-shaped skirt, and my letter going out to you as a spore of enthusiastic friendship.

Yours, *in situ*,
Sarah

❧

She liked very much the way he left the door open through metaphor. It was clear that their correspondence would not be a litany of identifications such as a Field Naturalist of yore might have produced. She walked therefore not only with an eye for the undescribed but also for what could not ever be named. She took delight in this even if at times it left her feeling disorientated. This was perhaps partly what the Stony Point correspondent meant by that odd phrase: *hunting is not looking for*. But still the quandary remained about how to respond to the thrill of finding. Could the thrill be enough unto itself, or was there something in its very nature that required it to be shared, to be *expressed*, like spores from a spore sac?

She began to lay certain funghi out on the verandah rail to dry, and Joe Busch noticed. He even cautioned her about the perils of poisoning, but she reassured him that she did not view the mushrooms as food alone. There was something else. She could not quite bring herself to explain that not only were they helping her to communicate across the seas but also to put her in touch with Ferny and the other spirits of the so-called dead. We are all rotting in the ground, she wanted to say to Joe, and we are all growing with the trees.

Instead she called him up the front steps and pointed out the different types. She told him to watch over the next few days for which of the specimens would start eating the wood of the rail. 'Some of them can be like Labradors,' she said to him, laughing. 'They'll eat anything, but they especially like wood. Look,' she said, 'they call this one turkeytail, but I think of it as The Labrador because it eats sticks.'

In fact, The Labrador was attached to a piece of already rotting wood that she'd brought along with it from the bush. It was growing in pretty white and russet loops out of the wood, like the scallops of a dress. She very much liked the way the rotting wood was dressing up, even as it decayed.

As Joe looked at The Labrador he realised he'd seen it many times before, but that he'd never noticed it. 'I know this one,' he said excitedly to Sarah. 'But I've never…'

She cut him off. 'We know lots of things, Joe, without ever realising we know them.'

XII

Dear Sarah,

    I like to stop, look, listen. I have a penchant for intense concentration which might explain my desire to find but not to search for what I find. It also may explain the way I avail myself of the classifications once I have found a mushroom that fascinates me. Perhaps this is one of the differences between us, the differences of which you speak. I admit to quite liking to <u>know</u>, once I've made my discovery through <u>not knowing</u>. As you can tell, I'm still rather immature.

    The other day I chanced upon a small community of mushrooms that we call 'The Old Man of the Woods'. These are quite broad convex mushrooms with what the 'professionals' call floccose-fibrillose dark scales on the pale background of the sporophore. These 'Old Men' are hard to see at first so you really do have to chance upon them. <u>Strobilomyces floccopus</u>. After this discovery, and in my usual way, I went into a period of close observation, followed by some thorough research. The word 'floccose' dominated my investigations, perhaps because of its percussive music. It also provided me with another layer of discovery when I realised that it was used to describe the scales, which are taken to resemble 'woolly tufts', the feature which the word describes. But what gave me my thrill was that the word – Latin of course – is the origin of our English word <u>flock</u>, which comes from the Latin noun 'floccus'. What made me happy was that these Old Men of The Woods did indeed grow in little <u>flocks</u>, even though that was not the reason for the coining of the name. So I considered that there is some poetic synergy in the nomenclature which was originally used to describe the woolly scales but in fact describes something of the nature of the <u>community</u> as well as the <u>individual</u>.

I offer all this of course as a way of conveying to you the possible pleasures to be had in engaging with the scientific language of names. I had a double-thrill in this case which, once again, <u>I was not looking for</u>.

I should say too that I've grown quite fond of two words that I would, once upon a time, have considered quite amusical: <u>Ovoid</u> and <u>Adnate</u>. I am currently considering composing a sonata in three parts: Ovoid-Adnate-Floccose. It should be fun.

Adieu for now.

Yours, in language,

The Old Man of Stony Point

PS: Have you ever noticed how mosquitoes that bite us while we're looking for mushrooms don't bother us?

~

Dear Old Man of Stony Point,

For many decades, most of my life in fact, I lived in my own style of hermetic near-solitude here on Ngangahook. There were reasons for this, and specific episodes which resulted in my retreat, but I don't need to go into those here. What I would like to tell you though is how important <u>written</u>, as opposed to <u>spoken</u>, language became for me during those years. I have shelves here in our homestead as full of pages as the forest is of mushrooms. And every one of these pages is likewise full of letters, words, lines, sentences. So despite my notion that we should rejoice in our differences I wouldn't like you to think that I am not at all susceptible to the beauty of written language.

Despite my young uncle encouraging me not to shut myself off from conversation with the town – a community which, as he always said, contained coldhearted and fickle elements but nevertheless retained as much goodnatured realism as any other – I preferred not to test my lack of trust but to print my feelings in ink on paper which, facing skywards, would only ever be read by the inhabitants of such a sky, ie: <u>by the gods</u>. For me these reader-gods included Ariadne, Arethusa, St Francis of Assisi, the Bacchae, even Dante and Montaigne, as much as they included the Virgin Mary or the Christian Trinity. In my mind they also included those native ancestors seated around the local campfires of our sky, the spirits of the eagle and the crow, and other personalities of our thereabouts – wallabies, gliders, echidnas – who in their unobtrusive perpetuity I thought of, and still do, as eternal.

I had this notion in my thoughts only the other week after observing the extreme shyness of an ant-eater attempting to obscure its true identity in the roadside bank while I was walking past it on the way home to our Run. A young farmworker in our employ was replacing the hardwood bars of a cattle grid at the main gate. We had a friendly exchange but, once again, how could I transport the deep crosscurrents of such thoughts into the surface of our conversation? I concluded, just as I had after I first felt overwhelmed by the violence exhibited by the town in the years after my arrival, that I could not convey such immensity in everyday chat. It made me vulnerable and thus I fell back on the silence of writing in those early years, and for decades afterwards. I do so again as I write to you now. It is a comfort that you now at least, and for certain, can hear me. For I must admit there have been long periods over the years when I have doubted there were any readers in the dark sky at all.

You <u>can</u> hear me, can't you? When I try to untangle the implications of how the names we bestow serve both to distinguish and to entrap a free world? I feel you are listening when I say that nothing is one, no word or name, no man or woman, no mushroom. And when you say you like to 'stop, look, listen', I hope it's also to the… multiplicity of me.

I know you are a composer and you should know too that in the years before the events that led to my retreat I was an enthused performer. I took it upon my young self, in my first year here on Ngangahook, after returning from my time at school in England, to hold piano and poetry recitals right here in this room where I now write to you. In my first flush of love with the place, in the years before the Great War, and buoyed up by exposure to my uncle's coterie of Surrealist friends in Rome, I took to the somewhat unlikely practice of doctoring the innards of our grand piano. By placing elements of the bush on and between the strings – gumnuts, bark, sturdy leaves, riverflints, pieces of kangaroo and parrot bone, even blue shards from the bowerbird (I'm ashamed to say), as well as the odd teaspoon and clothes peg – and by affixing similar elements to the hammer felts, I was able to play a <u>new</u> instrument. My Uncle Ferny thought this an even grander piano than before and went about the town describing to everyone how much it improved Grieg, Debussy and Beethoven. He arranged soirees here in the homestead at which I unbound like the foam of the creek, with no thought of the audience on the dry banks. My uncle was, at this stage, my bridge, and he gave me confidence that all would be understood. But of course it wasn't, and poems which may have interested his friends Russolo, Roiseaux and Martin of Mendips in Rome met with only polite approval masking a deeper bemusement.

What I did not realise until later though, and nor did my uncle, was that my expressions had also come across to some as a threat. In hindsight I suppose that if you open up the senses enough to allow the sound of kangaroo bones and riverflints into the music of the great masters then it follows that, by that attitude, the precise nature of our antipodean <u>difference</u> will be revealed. And of course in such a newly federated nation as ours then was, there were not many, indeed very few, who would have found such an exposure of our difference welcome. So many of the citizens back then still spoke of England as 'home'.

I feel I can say to you, here on the page, what I haven't expressed into my local air, except of course to Uncle Ferny. For myself, <u>home</u> must necessarily be a synonym for <u>truth</u>. Ngangahook is a truth for me, even when from time to time I'd go up with my uncle in his little aeroplane and I espied it from the air. Thus have I preserved it through the years of my retreat. For though a home must feel deliciously familiar it must also offer us what we never rightfully expect. <u>Magic</u>.

With this key aspect of nature's truth in mind then, I am quite thrilled by your philosophy of hunting. You have given my walking new impetus. I'm covering perhaps more ground than I have for many years, and always with unforeseen funghi as my nodes. Do you know of the 'Stinkhorns' I wonder? Specifically of what one of my uncle's field guides call 'The Veiled Lady'? It casts the most unusual and synthetic-looking net from the underside of its sporophore, which looks like nothing as much as a string bag. All manner of flightless insects climb amongst it, centipedes and the like, which is presumably the manner in which it distributes its spores, for it seems as if they are not expressed in any other way. And you see, if I did not have this impetus you've given me I may not have ever discovered such a wonder. Indeed I think of this mushroom – <u>Phallus indusiatus</u> – as an emblem of an <u>Ancient Surrealism</u>, where things we can hardly imagine, or perhaps only dream, come bursting through into the ordinary. And names, yes, names can be fun. 'Indusiatus' being Latin for 'wearing an undergarment', the net of 'The Veiled Lady' also resembling the crinoline which my farm manager's wife Emma still wears to some formal occasions in Geelong to keep her full skirt belled out. From now on, thanks again to you, I'll always be keeping a lookout for insects crawling up her legs!

So rest assured that even from afar you are creating the right conditions for this backwatered lady to be finding things she has not gone looking for. 'The Veiled Lady', the 'Old Man of the Woods'. An unlikely couple, borne from an unexpected friendship.

Yours, from Bass Strait shores,
Sarah

XIII

Because of Sarah's description of how she had 'doctored' the piano at Ngangahook, the Stony Point correspondent did not write to her for quite some weeks. He had to collect himself. Even with his devotion to the randomness of chance encounters, this new information took some time to digest. At her prompting, the final lines of Euripides' drama *The Bacchae* came to his mind, and in his partner's apartment in Manhattan he dug out his copy to check exactly how it went.

> *What we look for does not happen;*
> *What we least expect is fashioned by the gods*
> *And that is what has happened here today.*

He told his partner what the letter from Australia said, and he too was amazed. He read Sarah's description out aloud. 'I took to doctoring the innards of our grand piano. By placing elements of the bush on and between the strings – gumnuts, bark, sturdy leaves, riverflints, pieces of kangaroo and parrot bone, even blue shards from the bowerbird (I'm ashamed to say), as well as the odd teaspoon and clothes peg – and by affixing similar elements to the hammer felts, I was able to play a <u>new</u> instrument. My Uncle Ferny thought this an even grander piano than before and went about the town describing to everyone how much it improved Grieg, Debussy and Beethoven. He arranged soirees here in the homestead at which I unbound like the foam of the creek…'

His partner said, 'Wow' and 'Have you told Duchamp?' but he said, 'No. Why would I?' His partner said, 'Come on, I think he would be interested. I mean "pieces of kangaroo and parrot bone".' And he said, 'Yeah, I guess. A fellow pioneer.' And his partner said, 'She's just so naturally surreal. Like Joe Cornell.'

In truth though the correspondent from Stony Point didn't feel like mentioning it to anyone. Australia was such an exotic figment, which was partly why he had begun the magazine correspondence with her in the first place. He'd been curious, and now he wondered what the hell else was going on down there.

He thought too of how when Debussy had first heard the Javanese gamelan at the Paris exhibition in 1889, it had had a powerful impact on him. The 'Pagodes' had been a beacon in his own work for years, and its crosscurrents and asymmetrical trills and runs came sounding back to him now. It was as if there was a third hand at play. He wondered if Miss Hutchinson had any recording equipment. She had a camera, and she'd mentioned they had an airplane on the ranch, so maybe. He would like to know. But not yet. First he had to settle this uneasy feeling the whole episode had given him.

He drove out of Manhattan back to the cabin at Stony Point, eating an apple at the wheel. He got there just on dark on a Monday, after narrowly missing a big buck deer on the road. He brewed some turkeytail tea and tried to read on the sofa.

But he was too fascinated by himself to concentrate. Over the years he had become so well known for this one 'gimmick', as it was so often described, that it had grown to frustrate him. Only the previous week, in an interview with *Contemporary Sounds* magazine, he had discussed how the novelty value of his 'prepared piano' pieces had turned him into something of a sideshow act. He had joked that the way in which he was treated had the whiff of the animal enclosure. Or the shooting gallery! What, he had asked mischievously in the interview, had his sonatas and interludes got to do with riding an elephant in a leotard?

But now he felt the double jeopardy possibility of him being also viewed as a fraud. The dubious lap of honour around the big top was not even his to make.

And why should he care? Theoretically, he didn't. He had worked assiduously over a number of years to renounce intentionality in the artistic act. And with that renunciation came the implication that any ownership of ideas by the artist was absurd. Surely that would apply then to the notoriety and acclaim he had accrued from devising the prepared piano. Absurd! Well, yes... he would say yes. And yet he lay on the sofa perturbed, both by what Sarah Hutchinson had told him in her letter, and that the letter was having the effect it was. The feeling of fraudulence lay also then on not one but two levels: one, by virtue of the fact someone had 'prepared' a piano years before him; and two, that he had presented himself and his work as emblems of creative non-attachment, while he felt he now had cause to doubt they were anything of the sort. So did he need to rethink his approach?

Recently he had occasionally taken on the role of driver of the VW minibus for his partner's dance company. He was actually more than just a driver; he was also a conceptual director of sorts, a troop leader, and a supplier of music as well as fresh mushrooms and plants, which he would stop the bus in order to pick from the roadsides. On Wednesday of the week he had received Sarah's latest letter they were due to embark on a month-long tour, and he would have liked to write back to her before they left.

On the Tuesday at Stony Point however, despite having slept more soundly than he had for months, he woke up to find his private crisis continuing. He went out into the woods to settle himself down, but picked no mushrooms. Instead he stared into the filtered light of the pines, looking up and out rather than down. He scrutinised the branchings above, the nodes and patternings that he knew were also mirrored beneath the coppery ground he walked upon. He breathed in the resins of the forest, wandering for hours, and in those hours thoughts of *The Bacchae* returned to him, those fecund Dionysian women of Greece who would tear limb from limb anyone too transfixed on their own power and ambition. He let the fresh air dance around his face as he walked. It was cooling, soothing. Euripides' line kept repeating in his mind, as if on a tape loop:

What we look for does not happen. What we look for does not happen. What we look for does not happen.

As the phrase came around and around, a new perspective arrived each time. That the sun was a path. That discovery is remembering. That a pine holds no revelation. And thus the bind came again to frighten him, that his intention to free his music from his own likes and dislikes was exactly that: a like or dislike. He had sometimes thought of the chance operations he used to compose his music – tossing coins for instance, in the manner of the I Ching – as being like a returning waft of crisp fresh air rinsing out the ego of the Western arts. But now, at a new depth, he felt the gulf between such a notion and the reality of fresh air itself. The fresh air that he could feel on his face as he walked. The fresh air that was beyond description.

He was part of a correction then. His method and manner of making were more similar than he had thought to traditions he was trying to shuck. Over a small lunch of pumpernickel and hummus back in the cabin, and with the cabin's glass wall wide open to the trees, he felt stripped bare and humourless. It promised to be a long month on tour.

※

As things developed so too did the most unlikely of opportunities. *What we look for does not happen.* When he finally wrote to Sarah in late May it was with some significant news. But first he had to express his genuine amazement at what she had written.

Dear Sarah,

It has been some weeks since I wrote, weeks in which the winter mushroom, *Flammulina velutipes*, has gradually been joined by its spring compatriots. The snow has now long melted and my own mind too has been going through something of a thaw, connected, I suppose, as it always must be, to the seasons. As I write however, an icy wind is whipping through the woods outside my cabin, reminding me how the transitions between seasons are never as definitive or simplistic as the calendar makes out.

I found your most recent letter remarkable, and for the following reason. Many years ago, in 1940 in fact, I myself conducted adjustments to the piano similar to the ones you describe in your letter. I had been composing music for percussion for some months, and had also been teaching some

THE BELL OF THE WORLD

experimental music courses at the Cornish School in Seattle, which was quite progressive. One of my former teachers, the composer Henry Cowell, had often plucked the strings of the piano, or strummed them. I remember him once even running darning needles over the strings in search of some new sounds, and with a new approach to sound. While in Seattle I began to experiment with placing objects on and between the strings in order to alter the sound of the notes while leaving my hands free to play the keyboard. I started somewhat extravagantly with a pie plate, which kept bouncing around on the strings. Then I tried a nail but that also moved. So then I tried a woodscrew, which I placed not on the strings but between them, and that was just right. After that I used nuts and bolts, pieces of rubber, weather stripping, and so on. It was all very interesting, and since then I have composed quite a few sonatas and interludes using this technique, which I have given the name of 'prepared piano'. What's more, it has caught on here in the States, and quite a few of the more interesting and adventurous composers, or <u>sound artists</u>, have taken to writing new music in this way.

Perhaps then you can imagine my surprise when reading your letter. To think that you were already preparing pianos so many years before the idea came to me is fascinating. To be truthful it has made me think again about the process by which official traditions gather and are cemented. How many other inquisitive and natural souls have been doing this, I wonder, in the far corners of the earth? In all likelihood there may well be prepared pianos in the furthest outposts of piano-loving Siberia, or far up the jungle rivers of Borneo, where I have heard of pianos being transported by junk. Though that of course is not to downplay your own most wonderful ingenuity. How I would have loved to have heard your 'grander piano' played, and to hear the effect of kangaroo bone and riverflint on the sound!

Which leads me to the further turn of remarkableness which has happened since I received your letter. I have been touring a lot this year with a dance company I am involved with. We have made a couple of overseas trips lately and have also been performing here on the east side of the States. While this has meant that I haven't had as much chance as I would like to be out in the woods with the fungi, it has opened up some interesting musical possibilities, one of which is the prospect of my playing a concert in Indonesia. This would be of great interest to me, as in many ways the gamelan music that comes from Java and Bali is more stimulating to me than most Western music. The gamelan involves a largely percussive orchestration and rhythmic structures which bear some resemblance to my own work. The chance to hear the music *in situ*, therefore, feels a little like Christmas to me.

As a result of my accepting this invitation to perform in Yogyakarta in Java (an offer which came about, I should add, while I was performing in Japan at an international symposium), it was suggested that I should take the opportunity while in the region to also perform in Australia. A possibility of a concert in Adelaide was proposed and subsequently cancelled (perhaps due to a lack of interest!), but now we have confirmed a concert date at the Melbourne Town Hall in September. From what I can gather it will be a night largely given over to the works of your countryman Percy Grainger – including some of his compositions for invented instruments – but also that of Henry Cowell, and with my own contribution forming the final third of the programme.

Given our recent correspondence and, in particular, your last letter, it feels rather uncanny that events have turned this way and that I should now be coming to your part of the world. Of course I do not know your exact circumstances, nor exactly how distant from Melbourne your ranch is, but I am hoping you would do me the honor of accepting my invitation of a ticket to the concert. It seems we have much in common, so much to discuss, and it would therefore be excellent to meet.

Please let me know if you like the idea. I for one find it entirely wonderful, but not at all random or coincidental, that our interest in mushrooms has connected us. If nothing else it confirms my long-held view that no matter where we live on earth a life spent in contemplation in the woods is more than compatible with an immersion in music and sound.

        Your Stony Point Correspondent
        (drawing near!)

XIV

Her first thought was that she would like to take the Cessna. It was either that or she might just take off and fly to the concert on pure adrenalin. She had in fact almost forgotten that she had mentioned her long-ago performances in her previous letter. But there it was, spelled out in purple ink and all the way from America. She had the unmistakable feeling that his letter had come to her from a future she had always been inhabiting.

But anyway, with Geoff Hamilton afraid of heights and Ferny no longer around to pilot the plane, a miracle would be required for her to bank above the trees like a swan and cross the forests and the cloud-phrased plain. With the letter in her hand she walked by the usual short cuts back to the glen.

When she got home from the Post Office she stood and stared at the piano for a long time. Still in pride of place in the large room but piled up now with the cockatoos. What would it have sounded like, she wondered, if the evolution that had taken place on the pages in her room had been expressed through this instrument, and to a willing audience? She gasped. Lord, it would have been something. Ungainly chords, sonorous songs, wild stories climbing the octaves, jokes smashing into one another. Everything that would be fun, and true, and prayerful, and that would please the children. She might even have set passages from Ferny's special book to music, both the bullock and the whale. Like Jones the Bookbinder of Moolap she would have both shown the joins and hidden them. She could have lain dense chords at the feet of Christ and used iron ploughshares as gongs. She would have cleared the air, then let it all come rushing back in fresh over the strings. Perhaps football could have been played again on the grass by the river, at first with Gellibrand's skull as the ball, until finally it was put to rest, the players nimble and enjoying the challenge of dodging the hammers as they fell. The sound would have been at one with a sounding glen, and the dancing would have been as common as eating.

She sat down on the stool at the keyboard. Lifted the lid. But did not play. Instead she listened.

'Unemployed at last,' she heard Ishmael singing, in a soft brown American burr, through the green ocean of blue trees.

Unemployed at last.

Later that day she was out in the stables looking at the Cessna when Joe Busch came in.

'Must be a beauty when she's up in the air,' he said, standing beside her.

In the old stable, with its high roof shingled in blackwood, and cobwebs catching the light in every corner, the aeroplane still looked impressive despite the fact it hadn't been flown for five years. One of Joe's jobs was to keep it in shine, to keep pressure in the tyres and the dash instruments wiped. Once every three months Geoff would grease the engine as best he could, fling the concertina of the barn doors open, fire up the engine and let it sit in the sun for an hour. The gleam of its silver fuselage with red stripes running up to the nose and down over the wheel pants would have tempted just about anyone to take it up. But not just anyone could. Once Ferny started ailing there was no one in the thereabouts who had a pilot's licence. For a couple of years Den Bentleigh, a mate of Ferny's from the Colac Aero Club, would travel over with his son Eric to take it for a spin. There had been talk of Eric taking the plane on once he got enough hours up, but when Den got sick that never happened; Eric never came back. Sarah had never got her licence, though in truth – given all the hours she'd spent in the air, with Ferny showing her how everything went – she could have flown the Cessna if she'd needed to. She had in fact flown it once, nearly all the way to Cressy, with Ferny instructing her. But she preferred the freedom to look that came with being a passenger and had never felt any desire to go up on her own.

'Ferny and I had some wonderful times in her,' she told Joe. 'And in total time she's done over a thousand hours. He was often flying off here and there on his own. He flew out to Wilcannia once, stopping for fuel at farms all the way, zigzagging about. I remember when he got back he said it was better than his trip along the Nile. And the Cessna didn't miss a beat. But no, she's grounded now.'

Sarah smiled and Joe couldn't help but notice how happy she seemed. He lingered beside her, forgetting he'd come back to the stables to fetch his tobacco. She turned from the Cessna and thought again how fit and attractive he was. He lowered his eyes, embarrassed by the openness and beauty of her gaze. He noticed the airmail envelope poking out from the pocket of her dress. He looked up at her again, and she noticed the blush creeping into his tanned cheeks. It was as if the low winter sun peeking into the wide opening of the barn had dissolved anything that might stand between them.

She reached out her hand and touched Joe's shoulder. Once again she felt the mildest hint, a familiar stirring of her body's joy. And then she took her hand away and closed her eyes. When she opened them again Joe was still looking at her in wonder. 'Can you roll me a smoke before you go?' she asked him, and, suddenly, he remembered why he came.

XV

That night the moon grew fat in her bedroom mirror, even as she stayed up late in Ferny's library to read. It was the midnight hour, when strange things were also natural things. She felt the homestead like a pouch of fur around her. In the distance the ocean roared and crashed, and the damp ground around the house was all in song too. Each window held at least one star, each star a voice in the throat of a frog.

She consulted the book, the book bound from their littoral circumstance. In both its key ingredients – the whales at sea and the bullocks of the long paddock – it was a creation built from wide experience. As she turned its pages she heard the ocean and frogs outside her windows, and the voice of the American, now so immediate in her ears.

I am hoping you would do me the honor of accepting my invitation of a ticket to the concert. It seems we have much in common, so much to discuss, and it would therefore be excellent to meet.

So it would! And yet she was scared. She had not been to Melbourne for so long. Not since she farewelled Ferny to war in 1914. Back then she had stood amongst the mothers, wives, grandmothers and little daughters in a purple rayon dress and flat shoes, with no hat. Like everyone else she held a handkerchief in the heel of her palm, but unlike everyone else she couldn't bring herself to wave. The ship's horn sounded, and the vessel slowly moved away. She could see Ferny, in uniform, all caught in sunlight and striking up animated conversation with another officer on deck. So would be his course, she told herself. He would talk his way through the war. And she would return to Ngangahook and wait with the ocean, the wallabies and birds. What they didn't know about war, no one knew.

But large sheets of time had spread out since then. She could hear the difference of the city, even on 3AR. The way people spoke, the softening of the vowels, the sirens in the background. She'd catch a train to the concert she supposed – another thing she hadn't done in a long time – and briefly she thought of the smashed cabin glass of the train on the old Saddle Line. That train didn't run anymore; it had stopped years ago, well before the Second War, not that long after the First in fact... but she couldn't really remember. What she did remember was the arch of trees above the line as she came in. The way the branches occasionally clipped the carriage. And the neck of the guard, she remembered that too, bunched up in tight wads under his railway shirt collar.

As the moon hovered silently in her bedroom mirror, she remained in Ferny's study. She would read a sentence or two from the book and then glance up, and try to talk herself around. Of course she could... *of course she couldn't*. Around and around her mind would go in this superficial quandary, for she knew that what had been laid down ahead of her was already so. It was simply mortal behaviour to consider it via circles.

When finally she put the book down and left the library, the moon had passed from the bedroom mirror and was instead gleaming on the leaves of the big gumtrees by the front gate beyond the garden. One effect of the letter was to make her look again, as if by contrast. To reimagine her world, in an American way. How close and tangy the eucalypts made it seem. How rough, and old too, and slow. Everything seemed to revolve around the heat. The lead-up to the heat, the heat itself, the heat's aftermath. She pulled up the window and let the cold hit her. It was thin and clean. She felt her shawl almost instantly dampen. Her nostrils filled with the astringency of home.

❧

Gone then were her years of isolation, gone as easily and as suddenly as slipping land. Forced by circumstance, uncanny events, these strange mycelial and planetary connections, she had now the burden of organising it, of coping. A few days after replying to the letter – a reply that was brief, and enthusiastically positive – she found herself in the Hamiltons' house, first in the bright newly laminated cream kitchen with Emma, and then in the unrenovated library with both Emma and Geoff. Sarah had come to sound them out, and even perhaps just to tell them. In Ferny's absence it was only Geoff who could understand, or rather that she needed to understand. She knew she would not get anything too enthusiastic from him, but something caring, and sensible. Geoff would consider the angles and how they might benefit or harm Sarah, while Emma might actually see it all as a bit of a thrill.

Geoff's library was not as well sealed as her Uncle Ferny's, and his books had that smell of sunlight and silt that Australian farm libraries often have. The Hamiltons had originally come to Ngangahook when, after a long run of difficulties with finding a manager he could trust, Ferny took up his old university friend Toby Hamilton's suggestion that he talk to his younger son Geoff. The books Geoff had inherited from his father's collection were in one well-turned red cedar case against the southern wall. Sarah knew that Geoff and Ferny had spent many evenings sitting at the table in the middle of the room, sorting through their strategies for stock and grass, with Ferny taking any opportunity to peruse the esoteric pages of what he liked to call 'Toby's impossible evidence'. This was a reference to two leather-bound books on the Eleusinian Mysteries of Greece that Toby Hamilton had picked up in Athens.

Geoff now poured the tea into the silence. The Hamiltons had been at Ngangahook for well over twenty years, and Sarah had never had 'news'. Until of course the day Ferny died, but then no words could say it. She simply answered the door when Emma knocked that morning and fell into her arms.

Now the tea fell into the cups with a river-sibling colour of brown to tannin gold. All three of them saw it and knew the sight of their own pale limbs in summer, swimming in the bush-born river pools that punctuated the glen.

'You know,' she started, when the cups were filled. 'I have not been to Melbourne since Ferny went to war, but I have a mind to go there in September.'

Geoff and Emma glanced at each other. Then Emma said, in a particularly bright way, 'Wow, Sarah. What's on the agenda?'

The agenda? For a moment Sarah was confused by the word. It was obviously now a turn of phrase.

'Well, it can't be nothing if you're going all the way to Melbourne,' Emma said. 'What's the occasion?'

Sarah recounted to the Hamiltons the series of events that had led to her being invited by an American composer to a concert he was performing at the Melbourne Town Hall. The composer's name was unfamiliar to them, but they had heard of Percy Grainger and knew also that only events of a certain stature were put on at the Town Hall.

As Sarah could have predicted, Geoff swung straight into practical mode, asking her which hotel she might stay at and offering to drive her to town in the Triumph. He and Emma had always spent a lot of time talking to each other about Sarah's situation. On a few occasions after Ferny's death they'd seen from their bedroom window the light of her torch through the trees, as she went wandering about at all hours. They had known, from the untouched food they'd delivered to her, that back then she wasn't eating. They'd refrained from intervening, but when the question of marking the northern boundary came up Geoff had thought it a good way to engage her. Things seemed gradually to have improved and Ferny's comment to Geoff in the weeks before he died that he'd 'never have to worry about Sarah' seemed to have been proven. But Geoff was still on the lookout, knowing how much Ferny thought of Sarah, almost to the point of being in thrall to her. And he did wonder at times about the effect of the privileges that both Sarah and Ferny had inherited. Although Ferny had proven to be a clever and progressive farmer, his impulsiveness in other matters – including his devotion to Sarah – had sometimes seemed unwise to Geoff.

He knew however that the Hutchinsons' history in the area was unusual. Ferny had proudly told him all the stories. Every generation going back to the 1840s had worked in ways that set them at odds with many in the local area. It was a family tradition which Geoff had respect for, but that he also thought of as being partly a product of a passionate, even reckless, family temperament. His own father Toby had filled him in before he came to Ngangahook, so he knew the score. As he looked at Sarah sitting across from him at the table, he thought of Toby's advice when the offer had come through for Geoff to manager Ngangahook. 'Ferny'll do things differently,' he told him, 'so get ready for a ride. But he's sharp. And I daresay he knows his land. You two'll work well I think. And you'll be a good steady hand.'

And so it had been. They had developed a working partnership, and their experiments with stock rotation, the mixing of crop and cattle, and light grazing were still raising eyebrows. Inevitably it fell to Geoff's stoic nature to worry about Sarah now Ferny was gone, even despite his declaration of her invulnerability. If she was to make a trip to Melbourne, then surely he should accompany her.

'I actually thought I might fly up in the Cessna,' she joked, before quietly confirming that she planned to take the train. 'Don't forget I grew up in Melbourne,' she told them, after they expressed their doubts. 'I won't get lost. My mother and I used to attend events at the Town Hall – when of course she was sober enough to get on the tram.'

Eventually they agreed on a compromise. Sarah would indeed take the train, but Geoff would drive her in the Triumph from Ngangahook to the station in Geelong, thereby saving her the trouble of catching the Trans Otway bus with her luggage. She would book a room in the Windsor Hotel for the night, and Geoff would meet her again at Geelong Station the next day. 'How exciting,' Emma said, when all this was agreed. And Sarah too nodded and smiled, thinking that, yes, if she had to go back to the city where she spent her first difficult years of life, this certainly felt like a good way to do it.

XVI

It was another month before confirmation of the concert came in a letter not from America but from the Conservatorium of Music at Melbourne University. The envelope contained a brief typed letter inviting Miss Sarah Hutchinson as a 'distinguished guest' of the Grainger Museum to the New World International Evening Concert at the Melbourne Town Hall, commencing at 7 p.m. on September 22. Two concert tickets were enclosed, along with an invitation to 'supper in the Hotel Australia dining room upon completion of the musical proceedings'.

Sarah took the roundabout way of the clifftop and riverbank home from the Post Office. Coming down from the cliff and pausing at the rivermouth she watched a flock of terns diving in the open flowing waters of the inlet. When the terns moved on, so did she. On the third bend of the river, as it wound down north from the mouth to the glen, she paused under a tangled copse of bursaria to look again at the letter and the two tickets in her hand. The tickets were printed on a green card and came in a heavy red sleeve, with the Grainger Museum letterhead printed on it. She began to wonder about the second ticket. Should she take Emma perhaps, or Geoff? But no, she decided she wouldn't breathe a word of the second ticket; she would much prefer the whole event, and the whole trip to town, on her own.

She did however drop by the Hamiltons to show them the letter, and the single ticket, when she arrived back at the glen. They were happy for her and Geoff made a joke about the concert only being three weeks away so he'd have to get to work on the Cessna if it was to be ready for her to fly.

Later that night she sat rugged up out on the homestead verandah, feeling highly conscious of how the arrival of the tickets had changed everything. Those green tickets in the red Grainger Museum sleeve felt like invitations to more than just a concert. They made her tense, anxious. Would anyone there in the Town Hall audience have any idea?

From where she sat she could see the flickering light from the fire young Joe often burnt in front of his lodgings in the stable. Inwardly she noted this sign of his presence, and she peered across to catch the wandering glow of his cigarette as he removed his cooking grate from the top of the firepit. She knew that with the lights off in the front of the homestead he couldn't see her. She forgot about the concert, left off wondering whether her Stony Point correspondent would write to her before September the twenty-second, and thought instead of how Joe Busch slept in there just as Joe Sullivan once had, though with the mute company of the Triumph and Cessna instead of the everbreathing horses and their hay. Something exploded then in her mind: the memory of Pascal the hawker's charred cart transformed into the car and the aeroplane catching alight. With eyes shut tight, her body trembling, she saw the whole wide stable on fire, a screen of red-orange, monstrously alive beside the ironbarks. She heard the loud contusions of heat explode like giant mallee roots from the engines. She smelt the petrol, continuing to shake until with the flames flowing high and fast and as easily as wild water she detected another more plangent sound amid the roar. She opened her eyes to see the dark shape of the big stable standing, perfect and complete, with young Joe sitting now at a lit angle to his firepit, playing his mouth harp.

She happened to know the tune from the radio. 'I Still Miss Someone' by Johnny Cash. They'd been playing it a lot, though Joe played it slower, drawing out the tune and letting the tremolo of his instrument resonate in the winter night air. What may have sounded forlorn calmed her in an instant. That life was full of sorrow was a truth worth acknowledging, and it was only through this acknowledgement that the sorrow could be transformed. After all these years the mouth harp sounded perfect in the glen.

XVII

Dear Sarah,

    I don't know whether this letter will reach you in time, as I am writing not from Stony Point but from Yogyakarta in Indonesia, where I am attending a symposium on the exchange of Javanese gamelan music with western styles. Last night I performed a concert of my sonatas and interludes for prepared piano to a rather bemused audience. But the <u>real</u> news I have to tell you is all in the image I include here. Walking out of my bedroom in the guesthouse this morning I glanced beyond the tiled colonnade which shelters my window to a lovely little garden of plants and gongs. And there, humbly situated under the bright purple fronds of a local plant, was your old friend, *Geastrum triplex*. The earthstar! I immediately thought of you of course and had my host, the esteemed gamelan musician Dr Ketut Panggarang, take a shot of it with his whizzbang Polaroid Land instant camera. And here it is.

    Taking this as a rather good omen for our lovely mycelial connection, I am very much looking forward to meeting you, and playing for you, in Melbourne. I trust all is in hand regarding the tickets. If not, I'm sure they will arrive in good time. And I hope I do too! It's very hot and sweaty here.

    Until Sept 22 then,

    Your Yogyakarta Correspondent

XVIII

THE TRIUMPH'S SEATS were of strong red leather and Sarah's Louis Vuitton overnight case was in red leather as well. The duco of the car was a Bermuda-green, actually not unlike a local magpie egg, and the dress and jacket Sarah wore happened to be a similar hue. It was a Saturday and they planned to meet the ten o'clock train. Sarah had dreamt all night of ringing railway bells, of water trucks such as she used to see in Melbourne as a girl, and of a lyrebird with a fan made out of bakelite. When Geoff knocked on the kitchen door at eight o'clock, she'd been awake since long before an egret went honking overhead at dawn. 'What would frighten a white giant?' she said to herself as she drifted in and out of wakefulness. And her answer was: 'The railway bells.' From there a dialogue had settled in on her pillow, the transition of darkness to light articulated by the inverted sense of true vision floating away. She'd never felt such nerves as a younger woman. It would only be a brief meeting after all, she told herself, but there would be no earthstars sprouting in the Town Hall, and she was sure her throat would be too tight for her to speak. Was there something she could take him, some tendril of glen that they could hold in their fingers to connect them? But then, in another envelope of sleepiness, she saw whole fields of drought and desiccation, with every moist moss shrivelling to a brittle chartreuse. She rose, and washed it all away in a nonetheless shallow bath. She could smell rich soil in the rainwater, which relaxed her. But with every stroke and pad of her drying towel, the anxious questions of her mind multiplied.

By seven she was eating breakfast standing up in the kitchen, seeing the whole vast room as if with outside eyes. A mullock heap of stuffed cockatoos on the piano, the two radios, the lurid Roiseaux canvas on the wall. Would it have been so bad after all, she wondered, if they'd let them have their bell? Could she have lived then more as the gods might intend, as just another plant among the many? She sighed at the thought, and spilt her tea in the process. So she swore and, wiping down her dressing-gown, remembered how it was, how it really was. The air, the sweetness of its trembling, the breeze in the cumbungi reeds up in the big Ngangahook soak, their papery rustling that always reminded Ferny of Lake Mareotis outside Cairo. So what would a bell remind anyone of? Not the cumbungis, that's for sure. And so it would go on, and on, ringing into eternity like the bell Edward Hutchinson had flung into the Moorabool. That ghost bell. But there's no need to drown a bell that has never rung – no need to drown anything in fact. All the more reason to remain buoyed up by the tide. All the more reason to let the world itself ring out.

At eight she let Geoff in at the glass door.

'All set?' he said, jovially.

She wanted to tell him that she was, and always had been, but she wasn't and she didn't. Nothing in fact, as sharp and as clear as it was to her, had ever been 'all set'.

'Joe's got his footy final in Queenscliff,' Geoff said. 'So we'll take him part of the way. He's pretty toey himself actually, and he's usually as laidback as anything.'

The mention of the football relaxed Sarah, just as Geoff had told Emma it would the night before. He'd figured that in the Triumph Sarah'd talk to Joe about the game and it would almost be as if that's where all of them were heading. And then, when Joe jumped out at Mount Duneed to get a lift with his brother Ger, Sarah and Geoff could go on talking about his prospects as they travelled on into Geelong. That's how he'd described his strategy to Emma, and, by the look on Sarah's face, so far so good.

'Anyway,' said Geoff, 'just came to tell you that. See you at the car at eight-thirty sharp.'

※

They drove out the front gate and along the town road through the riverflat. They turned left at the Ocean Road and went up past the Hotel and the General Store, with Geoff at the wheel, Sarah in the windscreen light of the passenger seat, and Joe Busch with his football kitbag in the back seat. It seemed almost impossible to any of them that they would know what to say. It was as if suddenly they were all living in Ferny's wake, all in their disparate ways, as Ferny was responsible for all three of them coming to Ngangahook: Sarah because he was the only family member who could understand, Geoff because of Ferny's connection with his father, and Joe because of Ferny's wish to have the walking tracks cut and the bush reserved. It was Ferny who had brought them together, but in those few moments as the Triumph exited the town it was his very absence that was keeping them apart. The world turned upon this alternation of Ferny's presence and absence just as it turns upon an axis producing darkness and light.

Out the window then the messmates sped by, then the heath, and the vast blue plate of the ocean to the south. Larger forms that were the daylit, and starlit, constants. By the time they were crossing the Swampy Creek bridge at Kuarka Dorla, their three solitudes had begun to mix again, and they were, as Geoff had foreseen, discussing Joe's footy final. Ferny could so easily then have been sitting on the back bench seat beside Joe, smoking his meerschaum and nodding in agreement that Queenscliff would provide stiff opposition. He might even have piped up himself, in order to draw Sarah's attention to the resemblance – quite obvious once you'd noticed it – between young Joe and old Maisie the caretaker of the Big Cutting Hill cottage. The cottage was long abandoned, its garden overgrown and left to blend back into bush after Ferny had decided to let it be so when the Saddle Line fell into disuse. But the blood of all the old situations still flowed on. And if Ferny's spirit had returned bent on reunion, for the time being all he needed to do was puff on his pipe in the blood-red back seat, lending the aromas of all lost connections to the otherwise salt-bright Saturday morning air.

Sarah had been amused all along by the idea that the young track-cutter was some reiteration of the long-ago Joe Sullivan. Her eyes had filled with their two young bodies' resemblance; her breath had caught in the recollection of how Joe used to come to her at night, when she was so much younger and such things were plausible. But now she perceived Joe Busch in a different light, looking not at his tanned body but straight through the windscreen as his voice said from behind her:

'Yair, their big ruckman's a bloke I wouldn't want to meet in a dark alley. Can play too.'

'What's his story, then?' asked Geoff, keeping his eye on the road.

'Dunno,' replied Joe. 'Coghlan's his name. Someone said he's a fisherman. Most of 'em are. But this fella's dangerous on land as well. I'll be stayin' out of his road, that's for sure.'

As Joe and Geoff laughed at this, Sarah began to fancy she could hear a familiar humour in the cadence. Her heart filled with the arrival of the unexpected thread. Maisie had drifted off into the Otways before Ferny had let the cottage go. But the way the boy had turned up, so alone and unexpected, just knocking on the homestead door like that when no one else had ever had the gumption, made the two things — the long absence, the sudden presence — feel suddenly related. *Related*. But what did young Joe know?

'Will your family come and watch you play today?' she asked, turning around in the passenger seat to look at him.

'Well, my brother's on the team. Maybe Mum'll come.'

'Your Dad?'

'Nah. Wouldn't reckon. Mum'll probably get a lift with the Wrights. Mr Wright's our coach. Mum's friends with his wife.'

'What about your grandparents, are they around?'

On asking this she caught again a faint whiff of smoke from Ferny's pipe. She looked away from Joe to the empty red leather on the other side of where the footballer's black kitbag sat in the middle of the back bench seat. The pipesmoke was rich in her nostrils, then it drifted away.

'Nah. They're not,' Joe said.

They drove on to the north-east, away from the sight and sound of the water, until they were approaching Mount Duneed. Once they'd turned out of Ghazeepore Road, Joe said, 'It's just this gate here on the right.'

Geoff turned the Triumph into a little farm lane that ran towards the house, all three of them in a jocular mood now. 'Well, I hope you get lots of kicks,' Sarah said, smiling back at Joe before training her eyes on the house and farm.

'Yair,' Geoff Hamilton agreed. 'A little leather poisoning never hurt anyone, Joe.'

As Joe got out and said his farewells, his brother emerged with overalls on from an open tractor shed. He was lighter haired than Joe, with the same blue-eyed look, but much taller and skinnier. Beside the tractor in the shed was the red Dodge ute they'd be driving to the game.

Joe went to greet his brother as Geoff turned the Triumph and drove out past them towards the grassy lane. The two brothers waved.

All the way from Mount Duneed to Geelong, Geoff listened in silence as Sarah regaled him with her memories of the brothers' grandmother Maisie.

XIX

The sound of the train was relentless, but the whole world was too. And always had been. It just kept going, and despite the illusion of schedules and timetables, nothing that ever began would ever end. It just wasn't possible. Which also meant that nothing ever really *began* but only *continued*. Beginnings were illusions created by a world picking up its layers along the way.

Sarah sat in the window seat of the 'doggybox' compartment, thinking about this all the way to Melbourne. Thinking about Maisie, thinking about Joe. Thinking too about how the resemblance between the two Joes had distracted her from a deeper connection. It would have come as no surprise to her then if she'd learnt about the way Joe Busch had grown fascinated by Don Atchison's stories over the track-cutters' fires. Nor even if she'd learnt how he had followed her that day when he spied her coming out of the Post Office. Such events were a set of concordances that had very little to do with the surface of time, and more to do with less straightforward connections. It was a case of like seeking like, across the divides of society's convention.

Not in order to be identical but to exist in concert. To be seen, heard, understood. To be together.

As the train rattled on and the You Yangs sped past, her mind began also to turn to what was ahead of her. The city for one, now so full of engines. Cars, trucks, buses. Geoff and Emma had warned her. She knew she only had to catch a taxi to the Windsor Hotel when she got off the train at Spencer Street. One ride up Bourke Street. Right to the top. She was returning after many years, half a century in fact, to a city that had once bogged her father's carriage axle but which was from all reports now clad in concrete and hard tar. 'Expect words up high,' Emma had told her, strangely. 'Giant words, on signs. Adverts everywhere. And noise. Car horns and tram bells, people shouting in the street, police bells ringing, ambulances with wailing sirens, sprinting couriers, paperboys calling, and motorbikes. You'll feel like blocking your ears after so long. You mightn't know where to look.'

But she did know where to look. Straight out the window as they passed through the western suburbs of the sprawling town. Emma was right: she wasn't yet in the centre and all over the buildings language was everywhere. HOADLEY'S and SAVE TIME! and SUNSHINE BISCUITS and RAIMONDO TAILORS and even SHEER HOSE FOR PRETTY GIRLS. DAVIS GELATINE, SAVE TIME! again, and KEEP LEFT and LOOK RIGHT! PET SHOP CARP FOR SALE, GIORNO SHOES and KEEP YOUR FAMILY SAFE. All rushing past, much faster now than the You Yangs ever could.

There was a couple with her in the doggybox now. They'd got on at Lara. A large woman with steel callipers, and a thin balding man with a birthmark over one eye. They'd said a polite hello when they'd sat down and since then had been silent. They too were simply staring out the big picture-frame window. It was all so entertaining, like watching a fire burn.

Slowly the stops grew more frequent, and one of the signs – APEX BELTING – was actually lit up in neon red and green. They were certainly getting closer now. Sarah's stomach began to flutter.

Finally, as the train moved into a broader expanse of multiplying tracks, the ten- and fifteen-storey city buildings came into view. The train came to a halt and passengers began immediately to file past the glass windows of the doggybox door. Sarah waited for the couple to get up from their seats, but they did not. She realised it would be necessary for the woman in callipers to avoid any rushing crowd.

With her red overnight case in hand Sarah stood up, said good day to the Lara couple, and stepped out, first into the corridor and then into the acrid air. From the bitumen platform she descended into a dank underground tunnel, which led to the main station lounge and then out onto the street. As she stepped into the large station lounge she understood that Melbourne was no longer the city she had left behind. The ceiling of the lounge soared overhead, it had a bright linoleum floor, and there were large walls of glass everywhere she looked. She longed for a cup of tea but dared not sit down. She kept moving, remembering what Geoff and Emma had said about the taxis being directly outside the door. She crossed the threshold automatically, carried along by the crowd leaving the station, and walked straight to where a taxi was duly waiting.

XX

In her Ngangahook world the only thing as copious as the people along Bourke Street were the leaves on the trees. There seemed to be millions of them! So that when she got to the hotel and was escorted up the stairs to her second-floor room (she chose not to take the elevator), the quiet and solitude after the door was closed came as a great relief.

The room was small but plushly furnished: a single bed with a shimmering damask bedspread, an armchair in matching pale gold, a writing desk and chair, a small coffee table with crystal ashtray, a marble mantel with a large mirror bordered in a baroque style. Opposite the bed and beside the writing desk was a window looking out onto Little Collins Street. If she pushed the heavy curtains aside and looked to the south-east through this window she could just spy the statue of the poet Adam Lindsay Gordon in the small park abutting Parliament House. She knew that statue from when she was small and she used to walk into town from East Melbourne with her mother. But oh how strange it felt now to be so far from Ngangahook. Her urban reference point now was Rome, not this city of her childhood.

THE BELL OF THE WORLD

Kicking off her shoes she lay down on the bed. And as she lay still, the initial quietness of the comfortable room began to fill up with the sounds of the city outside.

Before long, and without so much as a glass of water for refreshment, she began to doze. The roar and chugging rhythm of machines drifted through her. The things she'd seen as she came up from the station in the taxi: a stalled smallgoods truck with bluesmoke billowing out a vertical exhaust; the enormous front of Manton's drapery store; a double-decker bus; and cars, cars of so many colours: spearmint-green, wattle-yellow, cars with two tones: brown and white, blue and red, cars everywhere in a broad phalanx across the breadth of the road, and parked, one after the other after the other, along its sides. As she rested there in the low filtered light of the room, the machines continued outside, revving and whirring, interrupted by the occasional clanking caused by divots in the roadways, or by the tooting of a horn, or a shout from a footpath.

She had promised Geoff that she'd place a call through to him when she had arrived. She remembered this now as she lay there too leaden in her body to rise and make the call, instead playing out an imagined conversation in her mind. Geoff was shouting at her from the street. 'Are you there, Sarah? Are you there?' And she was answering in kind. 'Am I here? Am I here?' It all seemed so urgent until she turned onto her side, shifting the conversation, beginning to tell Geoff in a calmer voice how the age difference between herself and Roiseaux had actually made her uncomfortable. 'Well,' Geoff told her, 'Maisie and Mr Rabbits dropped by in their biscuit tin, and they just wanted to check. Maisie kept insisting you were hardly born and that old Roiseaux was barely alive.' 'Yes, that was what we had in common,' Sarah assured him. 'Tell Maisie that,' she said, 'when she gets out of her tin.' 'I will,' said Geoff. 'You were hardly born and he was barely alive.' 'And check the Vatican gardens while you're at it,' Sarah instructed him. 'The earthstars should be everywhere by now. Please take photos.'

Before long a delivery truck began to idle right under her window on Little Collins. The sound reverberated between the narrow brick walls of the street. She had been expecting a room facing east onto Spring Street and Parliament House, but now the sound of the idling engine in the small side street seemed to be augmenting a dark Platonic cave. And the afternoon light had lowered behind a tower of cumulous clouds coming in over the streets from the ocean and bay; perfect light for a restful afternoon nap and the projection of shadows.

The idling truck eventually moved on, and the space left behind was the relative quiet in which she slept free of imagery. When she woke it was late, darkling late, just past 5 p.m. Her breath caught as if on the chandelier, and she was stretched diagonally across the bed, as disorientation again overwhelmed her. She sat up in the hotel gloaming, with no chance of a heron overhead, feeling ragged and spent like the jetsam of her own half dream. Was someone knocking on her door? She dared not answer.

She held her breath until the knocking stopped, then felt around for the switch on the bedside lamp. She would have to ring Geoff. But to tell him what? That the wallaby census of Melbourne was low? That modernism was now drapery? That the activity of the city would gather vast shadows unto itself? That such enterprise would pass like a chuckle of honeyeaters in the bearded heath? That she therefore would be going naked to the ball?

Given light, and given wind
I could live forever

was what she sang to herself instead of making the call. Was that what the honeyeaters were chuckling about?

Gradually, minute by minute, the world of facts and temporal circumstance reasserted itself. Even in the privacy of her hotel room she became part of the scenery.

> 'Born and bred on Hotham Street East Melbourne and on the
> family property at Yea a woman late of the Western
> District has attended a Concert at the Town Hall tonight.'

So would go the social pages of *The Argus* – so she bloody well better get dressed! 'Come on, Sarah,' cried the other Maisie, the Maisie Cruik from Devon. 'Put your wig on straight. Otherwise we'll be late!'

XXI

By 6.45 p.m. the Town Hall had begun teeming with the musical cognoscenti of the town. The night had an international flavour, what with the American composer on the bill and in person, and the Australian Grainger who had been so successful in England and America, and who, apparently, had been a good friend of Sibelius. Geoff Hamilton however, after steering the Triumph headlights over the cattle grid and into the stables, knew none of it. And Joe Busch, as he got out of the passenger seat into the smell of hay, molasses and aircraft oil, would have thought, at this stage at least, that Sibelius was the name of a racehorse. But things can change; people can begin to care about what previously never interested them, and they do.

Geoff said bye to Joe, and 'well played', and took off across the paddock towards the kitchen light of the manager's house at the far end of the glen. Moonlight spangled the dew on the grass as he went, and off in the trees a Powerful Owl was low-noting. Earlier in the day Geoff had been touched by Sarah's departure. She was in her green dress and short jacket, with her long hair briefly gathered by a clasp before falling past her neck, and it struck him that her step up from the quiet platform onto the Melbourne train was a courageous one. Little did he know, even after all these years, that the thirst for freedom had never been a matter of courage to Sarah. If her father was insouciant and her mother ill-fated with a remnant narcissism, then Sarah was always, and had always been, alone. Whether in ferny glades or busy foyers.

But Geoff had taken what he wanted from the disappearing train: the creation of an interstice, the right conditions for Eleusinian divination such as his father had bequeathed to him, a day of grass-fed thinking, of world reading, out of schedule or sequence, a day out on his own.

Returning to the Triumph alongside Johnstone Park near the Geelong station, he had taken a left turn into Ryrie Street, then pointed the car's nose towards Queenscliff. Travelling along the city street, past the hospital and onto the open road, he could already sense the ocean air piling up beyond the windscreen at the Port Phillip Heads. Joe's game wouldn't begin until two o'clock, so suddenly, like Sarah, Geoff had all the time in the world. He would drift, he thought to himself, have a pie and a beer. Stand on a salty half forward flank to watch the Blues and the Coutas battle it out. He pictured the red telephone box, near the Queenscliff post office, where he would call Emma. To tell her where he was and to make sure Sarah had arrived alright. He tapped his money pocket to check for change. Plenty. 'And plenty of time,' he said aloud to himself, steering the Triumph past the Connewarre swamp. Yes, that was what he'd say to Emma when he rang. Plenty of time. We've all got plenty of time.

There was no catch, only a vacuum of joy that must be filled. A shaft of starlight that widened as it descended to encompass first one peninsula, then the next. As starlight slept through the afternoon, the sun shone on rufous sedge warblers and swans, and a Bermuda-green Triumph driving by. And as the sun set behind its goalposts, the starlight rose and picked its way out over an increasingly glary earth, seeking the eyes that seek the gaps through city streetlights that seem to multiply as if from a blow on the head.

Sarah peered skywards, as she got out of the taxi, but could not seem to penetrate the local glare. She tackled the big steps then, took the green ticket from the red sleeve, and offered it. She was shown to her seat by the usher, an orange-headed girl who seemed to Sarah to be dressed like a box of chocolates but whose manner was more that of an undercooked condiment. *En friche*, her mother might have said. Nevertheless, her seat when she was shown to it was good, central, with a close exit and high above the stalls. The hall was similar to how she remembered it, broad and musty, and dominated by a proud organ of many pipes which, despite its dimensions, seemed to speak of civic rectitude. Thankfully, according to the programme, it wouldn't be in operation tonight.

Days cease to be days, as music ceases to be sound. Life takes over, and settling in her seat after the utter whirlwind of her arrival, she noticed a chunk of gold ring on the finger of the man sitting next to her. He smelt of cologne – a scent she had not been exposed to for many a long year. She wondered if it always smelt that lonely. And yet he was with his wife, and it was she, Miss Sarah Hutchinson of the Ngangahook Run, who was on her own.

She was free, free to receive the music. Which when it came, came not in sweeps of vista-strings or overhanging woodwind fronds but in plainer harmonies. The music of Henry Cowell, the music that was composed for a woodwind quintet but had been arranged for a string quartet, perhaps due to a lack of local musicians. The piece was brief and so the large audience was still, and by the time the adagio cantabile arrived Sarah was seeing a paddock slowly turning back to heath. Remetamorphosis, with three sad pauses in the process, perhaps representing the violent thrones of Tyre, Venice and England. She found the experience lovely, and had no trouble at all being positively transported. Nor it seemed did the rest of the audience, for the scale of the applause at the end was shocking. Sarah found it shocking. It reminded her of those three violent powers even more than the sad pauses did.

The concert had been well advertised for the 'modern experimentalism' of its programme, and the next piece by Cowell left nobody in any doubt about that. In the days and nights ahead Sarah would read and re-read the programme notes on the background of the works performed. The second Cowell piece was for piano, but with a difference. The programme included the following explanation by the composer:

The Tides of Manaunaun was written as a prelude to an opera based on Irish mythology. In Irish mythology Manaunaun was the God of Motion and of the Waves of the Sea; according to the mythology, at the time when the Universe was being built Manaunaun swayed all of the materials, out of which the Universe was being built, with fine particles which were distributed everywhere through the Cosmos. He kept these moving in rhythmical tides so that they should remain fresh when the time came for their use in the building of the Universe.

The hall began applauding again as the pianist came onto the stage. She was a tall woman with black hair, dressed in a black evening dress. Turning to the audience she acknowledged the applause with a big smile and then sat down at the keyboard. For a time she was motionless and the hall remained perfectly rapt in a hushed anticipation. Finally she bent forward over the keys, but instead of using her fingers to produce the opening notes of *The Tides of Manaunaun* she leant her whole left forearm over the bass octave and, with her foot on the sustain pedal, began thumping down on the keys with her arm. Sarah sat up straight in her chair, realising immediately what was going on, even before the pianist began accompanying these outrageous thumps with a structural melody played in the middle octaves with the fingers of the right hand.

The structural melody had a slightly mechanical rhythm to it. As it progressed in even time it gradually took on the wistful quality of an Irish air, like something from the Thomas Moore songbook. But underneath this air the forearm thumping of the bass octaves continued, the resonance aggregating with each crashing thump so that indeed it was like listening to a piano and to the workings of a piano at the same time. Sound grew thick, woollen, dense, chaotic and unified, indeed as if the bass notes represented not only the workings of the piano but the hidden workings of the entire world, while the right-hand air represented the way life and the emotions might appear on the surface of things. This was certainly the effect when the right-hand air then moved into a soprano melody. Sarah understood that both creation and the process of creation were being expressed. The treble notes had a preternatural quality, modified as they were by the enlargement of the universal resonance, dark and thick, and almost dirty as it was, surrounding them.

Sarah's eyes were open wide, her ears even wider, her imagination wider still. She was transfixed by the performance.

The heath that had returned to the paddock had now been augmented by a vastness of reason, a mythological reason she had not anticipated. This, she thought, is music as a metaphor for how the world was made, and *is* made every day, breath by breath, note by note, from the epic and indeed the *monstrous* abyss out of which all things come. By halfway through *The Tides of Manaunaun*, she was thinking excitedly of how she might describe such music to Geoff and Emma upon her return. There was really only one word that would suffice, an overused word whose power had been winnowed by the false romantic poetry of historical convention. Even as she took in the music she was herself dwelling in all such layers: her senses a portal to her imagination, galaxial space on the one hand, the universe as a giant internal piano on the other. And yes, there were all the tiny flowers, all the everyday loves and conversations and cups of tea in the right hand's melody, the bass cluster an eternal night, the Irish air like the incidental life that goes on in the span we've been given. And yes, as that soprano melody climbed, merging then unmerging in rhythm with the tides, she resolved that the word was *sublime*, for all its awe and terror and beauty. There was only this one word that could describe the music that Henry Cowell had made, with its structural workings and the terrifying scale of its sources revealed; and yes, she thought, as the piece transitioned through the middle octaves into a sense of its own ebbing aftermath, the word she would use in Geoff and Emma's kitchen, that little farm kitchen with its bakelite bottles, among the trees and in the immensity and brightness of the rotating sky, the deep darkness of all the soil and rock that goes down, reaching down until it turns into space and stars, the word she would say over the little table with her little tongue that was also made from such music such tides would be: *sublime*.

This was the ocean crashing on the shore of individual life. When the music finished Sarah felt drenched in the sound. To hear the ocean was one thing. To hear the ocean being heard was quite another!

Leaning back in her seat, quite oblivious now to the surroundings of the hall, she sighed deeply. She could not have said if *The Tides of Manaunaun* was a long piano piece or a short one, if it was a sonata or a scherzo, an air or a rhapsody, or how many bars it might have run for. All she could have said of Time in this instance was that suddenly, unexpectedly, she had the sense that, finally, she had arrived in her own.

As the piece came to an end the applause in the Town Hall was muted, perhaps partly from confusion. No musician had ever played a piano in this hall with her *whole left forearm*! An air of alarm and suspicion had entered the auditorium, or was it merely the disorientation of novelty? Whatever the case, people fidgeted and whispered, readjusting themselves in their seats. But on the stage the tall woman in the black dress was not done yet. She stood up from her stool but stayed hovering over the keyboard, leaning forward, as if looking into the very workings of the open piano. Had she lost something? In fact it was the opposite. She sat down again, but the restlessness in the hall continued. Sarah became acutely aware of the crowd's reactions. She sensed the unease, firstly with disbelief, then immediately afterwards with a familiar recognition. Briefly her body quivered with horror and she thought she might be sick; she raised a closed fist to her mouth as a precaution. It was as if a life spent alone in her room had gone sundering down through the floor beneath her. She turned to look at the man to her left, but he also was turned to the left, whispering into the ear of his wife. Sarah saw that his right hand, with its fat gold ring, was beating agitated time on

THE BELL OF THE WORLD

the armrest of his seat. He was obviously unnerved by what he'd just witnessed, but it was early in the programme. Soon, Sarah thought, he would, like the rest of the audience, at least grow hopeful about what he would hear next.

Yet it was dark in the forest, and wet, and a thick layer of humus lay clustered and cloying underfoot. She had walked many times in starlight, moonlight and rain, feeling the resonances in the open wonder of the sound of waves, the forearm of the Universe thumping on the shores of earth. It was unmistakable what she had just heard. The architecture of nature. It was the sound that filled Joe Busch's ears every evening, Geoff and Emma's too, the whole of Angahook's in fact, whether they knew it or not. It was the very thing that had drawn Joe down that Old Coach Road on that day when he had knocked on her door. Now he dreamt each night, as she always had, as the tall pianist in the black dress did, as Henry Cowell obviously had, a dream that was part of something larger, wilder. Something that threatened to bring the whole Town Hall crashing down, like the very waves the music had described. What a sound that would make!

⁂

When Geoff walked away towards his manager's house, Joe was surprised at how happy those words made him. 'Well played,' Geoff had said. 'Well played.' When Joe had seen Geoff standing alone on the half forward flank at the beginning of the second quarter, he'd thought it was odd. Geoff was meant to be going back to Ngangahook. But then, when the ball broke free from congestion and spilt towards Joe, his spirit moved as if he suddenly had something extra to play for. To perform for. He let the ball find his left palm, then swung around to the right and took off. When a Queenscliff player began to charge out from the back pocket to meet him, he feigned a simple cunning step towards the boundary and then promptly changed direction and stepped inside. The ball as it spiralled through the goals brought first gasps then cheers from the crowd. And Geoff Hamilton said quietly to himself on the half forward flank: *I had no idea.*

Such wonders had continued all day. A single gaze and the whole thing felt even better than it always had. And now Joe stood in front of the stable, smiling broadly to no one in particular. Behind him the Triumph was quietly ticking, its engine cooling in its hay-bound berth. On the way home Geoff had asked him a few questions about the game. He'd made his joke again about the low risks of leather poisoning. Joe had simply laughed and said it was a bonus to get a lift all the way home. He hadn't expected that either.

He put his kitbag down on the cold night earth, took out his football, and passed it from hand to hand while looking up to the stars coming and going behind passing clouds. Replaying his goals in his mind. He was not even tired, not one bit. But he was hungry! He put the footy back on top of his bag and set about lighting a fire. A steak, a beer, and a blow of the harp over the glen – that was the best cure he could think of for leather poisoning.

XXII

THE PROGRAMME NOTES held the clue to what the pianist would play next. But for the time being she sat still on her stool, perhaps wanting to build further suspense, or perhaps waiting for less divided attention. Just as Joe's fire caught in the cold air in front of the stables, its orange flames flaring and darting, so too did Sarah's eyes as she tried to distance herself from the rest of the audience by reading Henry Cowell's explanation:

The Fairy Answer was composed after a visit to my grandfather's place in Kildare. An old gardener took me to a certain spot – a glen – and he said, 'I hear you're a musician now and I said, 'Yes,' and he said, 'If you play your music in one end of the glen the fairies will come out and answer you from the other end of the glen with their own.' And he looked at me rather quizzically and he said, 'Of course if you're very materialistic you might think it was an echo. But then in order that you should know that it was not an echo they always change the music about just a little bit, so that you will know it's they themselves.'

With the tips of her fingers, the pianist played four chords in close succession. Then, lifting her hands from the keys and leaning forward, she began to play four corresponding sounds by running the back of her right hand across a carefully selected section of the piano's strings. The effect was unexpected, like a ghosting of the four chords at the source. Once again she played four different and slightly descending chords, in the middle octave, followed by four more passes with her fingers across the corresponding set of strings. The fire struck. Sarah could hardly believe her ears. Any consciousness of the rest of the audience was again entirely displaced by her immersion. The music and the echo, the steak now searing on the flame, as the lightness of the pianist's fingers once again ran through the strings like the breeze through the leaves surrounding the stable.

Apart from the stage the hall was in total darkness, but everywhere she felt the light. The pianist had surely taken them all to Kildare – all except Sarah, who was too struck to shed a fond tear for any old Ireland, too alive in the likeness and resonance of her own life. What was ether to most was solid ground to her, as basic, natural and yet majestic as the sun rising rosy through the trees or the convivial smell of cooking meat. The conviviality Joe was enjoying was with his own self, the self that he often dreamed of and that had come to life that afternoon on Queenscliff's salty grass. The best self, fluent and full of grace, the unthinking self unwracked by the lack he did not yet understand, the good and sated self, not so much an echo as a unity of opposites, communing together there by the cooking fire, in the glen and in the mesmeric piano and its strings delicately sounding in the big city hall.

A hall of treed walls with sparks flying towards the sky-roof. Sarah was distracted now as if by a glint of those sparks, as the fat gold ring began again to move about beside her. The pianist remained in her Arcadia; *The Fairy Answer* was a story, and she was telling it. She played and she strummed and now, as the notes descended gradually towards the bass, she plucked, and in twos not fours. The consort had lessened; the piano was a great harp in a box, with the audience falling away. The fat gold ring spoke now, above a whisper. 'What *is* this?' Sarah heard. This is Everything, she wanted to say, and did say to herself, as her own fire turned from convivial to a scald. Joe slugged the beer from the bottle and wondered if he'd ever be able to do it again. To play like that. He doubted, as if his selves had been separated again and it hadn't been him after all who'd climbed so high, who had danced through the violence of the game with the ball as a mere prop he used to express himself, who was the talk of the ground, the recipient of cheers, whose exploits would fill the talk at smokos for miles around. Was it him? What was this?

He slugged the beer again and, sighing, slung the ready steak onto his tin plate and covered it with sauce. He sighed once more, this time less dejectedly, and chewed. He was starving. For all manner of things. Others might have wanted to hit the town after a game like that, and if Geoff hadn't have showed he might have. But right now he felt it good to be at Ngangahook. The day had been a kind of miracle, and he didn't quite understand it. But yes, he thought, cutting another nice slice of steak and sauce, that was me flying through the air.

When the final notes of *The Fairy Answer* sounded, there was much restlessness and giggling. There was talk of 'a childish art, if you could call it art', and relief that the three Henry Cowell compositions were over. Briefly the lights came on, and Sarah closed her eyes. She was torn, like a tree after a violent storm. She contemplated leaving, just standing up and walking out amongst the tittering, but she couldn't of course. Her correspondent from Stony Point was still to come. He was the international guest and she, yes she, was his guest in her own childhood town. Which seemed still to be full of hard children.

So she closed her eyes against the starkness of the first intermission, and waited for the Grainger.

XXIII

When the intermission lights finally switched off she felt it on her eyelids and also in the gradual diminuendo of the room. She'd been thinking of how she could not be a character in her own imagination, despite all that she had visioned long ago, the *access* she'd had and the words she'd spent so long writing down. Could she rise up and out of what she was always sure had been predestined? Could the world? Was there a new space to enter, some parallel avenue of concurrent times that could intervene to spread the magic of old rivers? O' how what she had just heard had flushed her with hope! But o' how the imperviousness of the audience around her was frightening. So frightening! Each moment of this book she found herself in, this ongoing and unwritten chapter, was it all to be wasted? That, she decided, as the first whimsical folk tune of Percy Grainger's began to relax the crowd, *that* was the question she would ask of her correspondent from Stony Point when she raised a glass with him at the Hotel Australia after the concert. They would raise a glass to *The Tides of Manaunaun*, to the ancient workings of the oceans, to the echoing of the grieving glen that had brought them together into this pocket of eternity where she knew she belonged. And they would toast the mushrooms. Those great emblems of the connectors. The scholars and the artists binding the world under our feet.

※

With his hunger satisfied, Joe Busch took up his mouth harp and began to play. The air was cold but the food and the fire, and now the music, warmed him. He played a ragtime tune with a jigging lilt, 'The Coney Island Trolley', enjoying the attack and decay of each pulse in the jaunty rhythm. Far down the glen the reedy strains rang out, spreading over the heavy dew, through the crisp sepia air, until they bounced back off the northern slopes where the tracks had been cut, and came towards Joe beside his tiny glow of gumcrack fire as he sent the next notes out on their way. Somewhere over the paddocks then, perhaps over the flat ground where the Cessna used to take off, Joe's harp notes and their echoes met like a seam of currents in the sea. The question meeting the answer, and the stars shining when there was a gap in the clouds, glistening for the way a man and his fairies could embrace.

He took the mouth harp away from his lips and listened. Reaching down then to the bottle beside him to take another slug of beer. He licked his lips, breathed through his nose. He saw the outline of the night homestead off to his left, and far away to the east the window lights of the manager's house, golden and diffuse in the transient night mist beginning to drift through the glen.

All these elements settled him now, the gentleness he drew from the Hutchinson house, the way Geoff taught him and

THE BELL OF THE WORLD

coaxed him, admired him for his inborn skills, and joked when it was just what was needed. There was something laid out for him here, he knew that, but he didn't understand how. The past was as mysterious, as hidden and strong, as the future. So he listened to the night, his limbs becoming pleasantly sore, and still with the comfort of mud on his knees, and mud dried in the hairs of his calves, the smell of it still in his clothes, and in his hair, the earth upon which he had played so well.

And now he played well all over again, with the pleasant soreness, the steak and the beer, and the fire, and more so, even more so in the perfect auditorium of this rivered farm. He played the Johnny Cash tune again, 'I Still Miss Someone', taking pleasure by slowing it right down, letting it sound into the right space, the lungs of air in his match-fit body, the lungs of air between contours of his land.

He knew it. Right there he knew it. And he began to understand that although they said he was only twenty-two years old, he had known it all along.

He played the song over and over, stopping only to stoke the fire and roll himself a smoke. It was the way he slowed down the music that made it feel so true, so beautiful, the sad truth in the song. He played another jaunty tune next, this time old Jelly Roll Morton, tapping his foot as the possums tuned in, and the bug-eyed gliders, the swans up in the swamp with their eel-necks under their wings, the mopokes, the quolls with their star-strewn hides, and Geoff Hamilton as he came out his back door to take a beery piss. Young Joe's harp brought a smile to his eyes, and he went back inside to tell Emma. She came too then, out to the back step, to hear the music drifting over the glen. 'That sounds so nice,' she said to Geoff. They watched the distant fire glow tapering into the night air across the pasture. 'Yeah,' Geoff agreed. 'The kid can play.'

In fact he played for the whole length of the four works of Percy Grainger at the Town Hall. The longer it went on the more the world seemed to enjoy it. The music was topping off the sporting success, the frogs twanging along, and he worked with that, the way Sarah once would have when she could see it all laid out before her. The Grainger pieces were oddly bright, even chintzy, but nowhere as strange to the crowd as what had come before, nor as exhilarating to Sarah. The music simply wound about in circles, and Grainger was 'one of us' she heard someone say, in the midst of relieved applause. It was horn music with a chamber ensemble, replete also with the inevitable colonial nostalgia. 'Ye Banks and Braes o' Bonnie Doon' brought the house down with its high piping melancholies and soft falls. And 'Sailor's Hornpipe' had them tapping their programmes on their knees. But Sarah's mind, her ears and heart, had begun to wander home, and she sat in the hall picturing her empty house, Ferny's house, Ferny's parents' house, Ferny's grandparents' house, old Edward and Mary, until the trilling of Grainger's 'Norwegian Folk Song No.14' receded behind these picturings. She walked both hallways, first to Ferny's room and then to her own, and lay down in the beds of both. It was a cold night indeed, and the fire being lit for her by Grainger was indeed her own.

It was strange then, in a different way, when the lights came on again. The audience applauded and she felt happy for them, that they'd got their money's worth. Happy too for her friend, who would be up next, and for whom she worried they might treat with a dissatisfied disdain.

XXIV

As any clouds cleared from the sky over Ngangahook, Geoff Hamilton was slowly undressing his Emma by the fire in the manager's house. What will his music be like? Sarah wondered, not for the first time. She watched as stagehands wheeled a table with objects onto the stage, and also a second piano, this time a baby grand. Emma Hamilton giggled and reached for her vegemite glass of claret. And as the moon lit up the space around his fire Joe Busch stood up straight and stretched out his back. He bent down and took up his football and began kicking it to himself, just as Geoff began to wonder again about his old man's Eleusinian Mysteries. Those two brown leather books in the red cedar case. Yet still his fingers moved across his wife's fire-warmed skin and her homemade lingerie, sewn from cotton she'd bought in Geelong and patterns she'd found in the Adamson catalogue. The night was full, replete, exactly like its possums, and Sarah sat forward on her seat as Mr Jonas Ridley, the Master of Ceremonies, came onto the stage to announce the Special Guest. And when he had done so, a wiry man appeared, dressed very informally in slacks and what looked like a factory worker's blue jacket, with his mouth wide open in a gleeful smiling expression, looking out into the audience and waving as if he was already, even before he'd played a note, having so much fun.

When the smiling composer had joined Mr Jonas Ridley in the middle of the stage, it was conveyed to the audience that there would be a brief explanation given about what they were about to hear. At which point the Master of Ceremonies handed over to Sarah's Stony Point correspondent, who nodded and, in a slow and gentle American voice, wished everyone 'a very fine evening'.

Sarah was peering across the serried seats, peering at the stage, slowly absorbing the inevitable shock of finally having a face and body, and a voice, put to the words. Whatever she had previously imagined, straightaway, as soon as she saw that open-mouthed grin, she completely forgot. Whatever had been in her mind was erased by the sight of this casual-looking, even nondescript man – nondescript that is except for that open-jawed smile. It reminded Sarah, in the broadness of the lower lip, of a frog. Yes, the genial Stony Point correspondent seemed nothing at all like a 'serious composer', not even like the flamboyant avant-gardists she'd known in Rome. He was more like some ordinary citizen from the street who'd somehow made his way onto the stage and couldn't believe his luck.

But he was *her* friend – well, a friend of sorts, a pen-friend, a friend who had *made sense* in the milieu of earthstars, a sense that was both far from ordinary and as commonplace as earth underfoot. So she felt immediately defensive of him, protective, as she felt first the confusion then the disapproval of the audience at his demeanour and appearance. But he was about to play wasn't he? He had walked over to the table of small objects that had been brought onstage and he would explain, no doubt persuasively, compellingly, *Americanly*, and this would settle the crowd.

Indeed he began to talk, but once again in a quiet voice, which Sarah could sense everyone was straining to hear, and which seemed to align with what had already been construed as his uncharismatic, even *unprofessional* appearance. Was he a composer of international repute, or the Town Hall cleaner? And what were these equally commonplace objects he was picking up from the table and talking about? They were tiny things; they looked like things you'd be more likely to find in a hardware store than at a musical concert.

But Sarah, although she too couldn't quite hear what he was saying, began to have a sense that she might actually know why these objects were being discussed. And with that realisation another extra layer of predestination pervaded her being. This was familiar ground, and even more so given how unforeseen it all appeared to be. As the Stony Point correspondent finished his largely inaudible preamble, the moon in the clearing enabled Joe to kick the ball and kick it even higher before catching it on the way down. He was standing just on the rim of the firelight, and each time the ball ascended it would briefly disappear from view as it merged with the darkness at the top of its flight, before reappearing in the reflected glow as it came back down. He started to enjoy the challenge of the ball vanishing and suddenly reappearing so. For the briefest of moments he would lose all bearings and a sudden onrush of disorientation would overcome him. But this would be mixed with the life-charge of intense anticipation as he waited with heightened alertness for the ball to reappear. This brief blank in time and motion became the real challenge, and so he kicked the ball even higher now towards the tree canopy and the stars beyond, in order to prolong the blank suspended feeling. As Sarah's Stony Point correspondent sat down at the baby grand and began to play, the night-ball, briefly transcendent, returned to the player's hands. Notes were struck, the audience shifted, but Sarah sat as if she herself was in suspension in her seat, in an equipoise of affirmation and recognition, as yes, a ball that she had long before propelled towards eternity had returned to the poetry of human time.

The piano didn't sound like a piano. Or rather, it sounded like more than a piano. All Sarah could hear was Uncle Ferny applauding from the wings. 'The world is so boring and brutal,' Ferny would often say after encountering something he enjoyed. 'Boring and brutal, brutal and boring. And yet this is not the world I know! For a start there is love, as there must be, and then Art.' As the eclectic array of notes and tones filled the stupefied hall she remembered his reaction when she'd first started bringing in objects from the bush and other ones from the kitchen, and inserting them into the strings of the homestead piano. 'You are a godsend!' he'd declared, before imploring her to play on.

As thuds and gongs, thsks and clangs and knocks of the altered piano rang round in patterned cycles, the audience reaction was at first surprise, a surprise which would have been in part ameliorated if they'd been able to hear the composer's explanation of how, and why, he placed common objects – bolts, screws, pieces of rubber – into the strings of the instrument, thus altering the sound of tradition with a technique he called 'prepared piano'. Then, after surprise, they felt confusion, as they wondered exactly how the sounds were being produced, until finally they began to quite enjoy what they were hearing, mutually agreeing that this was music – if you could call it that – that should be received in the manner of a gimmick, or sideshow act.

Sarah went through her own stages of reaction – surprise, confusion, enjoyment – but inevitably her surprise was more personal and profound, her confusion more critical (as she swiftly analysed the composer's choice of objects and the timbral quality of the sounds they produced), and her enjoyment had a quality of sincerity born not so much out of a sense of vindication as personal entanglement. It was now clear to her that what had appeared as merely a correspondence about funghi across the Pacific Ocean was exactly that and so much more.

So now the hall, and the music played in it, began to glow for her like the ghost funghi that lit the bases of the trees of Ngangahook with a bright green effervescence. The sounds sprang up first here then there, in a way that even the most musical person, even the one most attuned to the landscape, could not predict. Up the ball went, as Joe settled into an unthinking and meditative rhythm, a sporting compact with appearances and disappearances, knowing and unknowing, and Emma Hamilton began to flutter her husband-farmer's naked chest with kisses. This was the mystery and allure behind the mechanical spokes of the wheel of life come right to the domestic forefront. In a deep valley, on a cold late autumn evening by a warm fire in a house standing on a land of ancient import, the childless lovers at life's middle age raised themselves via love and its physical correlations to the heavens. No book on Geoff's shelves could hold this fast, and no notation could fill a whole Town Hall with such innocent, and experienced, pleasure. The ball travelled through the barrier of light and back again. Up to the level of the sugar glider and falling back into equally natural human hands. Until finally, stepping further out from the warmth of his firepit towards the sharp cold truth of the dark, Joe kicked the ball with all his might and it didn't come back.

He heard it flick, then brush, then the woody thud of the leather wedging itself and settling in a high branch of the trees. In his enthusiasm and extra effort he had skewed the straight line up, kicked it at an angle to the stars, and it was stuck. The three pieces for prepared piano – Sonata IV, V, and Interlude No. 2 – were over. The audience, Sarah Hutchinson included, applauded. And down there in the manager's cottage, as Geoff and Emma lay sated on their rug of Polwarth fleece, Ferny's applause also could be heard, ever so faintly, in the whisperwings of a tiny bat dancing its way by sound alone through the old and solemn trees.

For everything now, just as it appeared to have finally reached its point of exhaustion, was in true motion. And it was this that Sarah had been living for all along.

As her correspondent rose from his prepared piano, two stagehands appeared to wheel it from the stage. The table of objects – bolts, screws, pieces of rubber – were also removed. All that was left was the big black Steinway in the centre of the stage, standing there like a bullock in a field of rye grass, or a whale breaching a moonbeamed ocean.

XXV

This then would be the final piece of the evening. And if, as it is said, Joe's old people were all sitting around their campfires in the sky, they surely would have turned their heads now, in anticipation of marking the ball he had just kicked towards them.

In the world of true and natural music there are no mistakes, as the audience in the Town Hall were about to find out. What first appears as a wrong note, on second hearing has found its home. A home which, on the third hearing, is proven to include the heavens as well.

The ball hung suspended, the farmer's mind was emptied of its mysteries as the wonder of his wife lay breathing quietly on his chest, and the composer sat down at the piano to play.

The audience consulted the programme. The final piece was dedicated to Irwin Kremen and it was in three movements, each of which was called *Tacet*. The title of the piece was described as 'the total length in minutes and seconds of its performance'. Thus: '4′33″'.

Sarah watched as her correspondent-composer, dressed in his casual slacks and factory worker's jacket, readied himself to commence the piece. But instead of beginning to play the notes on the grand piano in front of him, he leant forward and closed the lid of the keyboard. And sat there. Making no sound at all.

This simple act of closing the keyboard lid was what struck Sarah at first. It came as another surprise to her, but a surprise which seemed also a reversal, as if the American had just done something backwards: instead of opening the lid, closing it. She cocked her head to one side in her Town Hall seat, like a bird assessing new movement under trees. She watched and, like the rest of the audience, waited. Seconds passed. Was this beginning actually an end? she wondered. Or was the end of the piece, the closing of the lid, in fact the real beginning?

There were only questions – any answers were impossible. All that was left for her to do was listen.

With his physical exertion ceased, the football suspended in the darkness above him, Joe also encountered silence. The night became vast and he was suddenly aware that there was not a breath of wind. The ball would not be coming down anytime soon. He walked back into the aureole of his fire's glow and held his hands up to the warmth. Soon he was listening to the crackle of the fire, its pops and wheezes, and further out to the world beyond. He watched too, with newly adjusted eyes, as the threequarter moon sailed high over the glen.

Lowering his eyes he saw again the hulking shape of Sarah's homestead just over the way. He looked east next, as if one house referenced the next, towards the Hamiltons' house where, he noticed, the lights were now out. He slipped his warmed hands into his pockets and waited. He could not have said what for. It was more a sense of waiting he felt, rather than the thing itself.

There was a cough, a clearing of a throat. Then another cough, not quite as loud. Next to Sarah the suit of the man with the fat gold ring rustled. As the seconds went by she felt the exasperation building inside the hall. Yet her Stony Point correspondent sat utterly still and, as the programme indicated, *Tacet*.

What Sarah now became aware of was sound coming from outside the auditorium, and even sounds from beyond the Town Hall building. The dull thrum of cars going by on Swanston and Collins streets, an occasional engine louder than the rest. The rattle and then the squeal of a tram. A long wailing siren that reminded her of a loping bird flying off into the north of the night. Then there was another cough, and tittering behind her, and intermittent whispers along the aisles, which sounded a bit like the way sheaves of summer corn sometimes rustled outside her bedroom window. And then, as her mind involuntarily and unexpectedly turned to thoughts of the atom bomb, the first movement ended. Or so it appeared, as her correspondent-composer lifted his hands from his lap to open the keyboard lid again. Very deliberately he turned the pages of the score in front of him. Down near the front a person began to laugh outright. Then another. Sarah too felt the amusement in her lips. Everyone exhaled; a sense of release filled the air. Everyone watched as the American leant forward, and with great poise and composure he once again closed the lid of the keyboard. The second movement had begun. *Tacet*.

There was compression at hand here, compression of the world. The way the sounds between movements, the curious sounds, the querulous sounds, the sounds of mirth and the bodies stretching and unwinding, the breaths uncoiling from where they had been held near the heart, were suddenly reset to modernity. For this was what it was, wasn't it? This piece of 'music' in three movements, the title of which was 'the total length in minutes and seconds of its performance'?

Indeed the hall was silent, a silence which, as the second movement progressed, the members of the audience – or at least some of them – realised was no such thing at all. Be it a pause, a prelude, or an aftermath, there were scratchings, minute shiftings in the creature of the building, the momentary groans of colonial timber, an insect seeking a deeper darkness in the darkness, another insect whirring for the light, a hand in a pocket of keys, another hand in a pocket of shillings, a shoe-creak, a hurrumph, another hurrumph, the small pneumatic expression of a smirk, a mutter of realisation, a describing word on a quiet vessel of breath, a cufflink clapped open and shut against the soft cloth of the cuff, the reversal of air that calibrates a gasp, a wandering phrase free now to inflect into air, the sound of the mind's workings, the pulleys and levers of the world, and breath, everyone in their own close and unclothed breathing.

The second movement – *Tacet* – stretched out, went high, down deep, and for many got stuck in the broad plain of a nowhereish middle. It went sideways, and askew, felt penumbral, and long. It went on; some consulted their wristwatches as if they were its conductors, as if what was contained in the acoustic frame could be synchronised. And on it went, with the Stony Point correspondent, the unplayer, *John*, sitting perfectly still before the instrument. Sarah restrained a giggle, thinking of how far he had come, via Java!, to do this! And as Joe considered the homestead even further it was as if it really was more than a sum of its parts, a creature breathing over there in the darkness, a living thing, now silent, now adjusting its close-clad timbers in response to the descending dew, which also made a sound, if we could only hear it. And he wanted to, Joe, he was in the mood to hear the dew, in the chilled ambience, and so he pulled his lumber jacket tight and stepped again outside the glow, out into the smokeless dew, and towards the creature-house.

So the dew felt his tread and climbed as if with affection up onto his boots as he went from the front of the stables, over the drive, and on up towards the verandah steps. And paper rustled as the listeners consulted their programmes, not for directions, nor intent, not even for conception, but for *duration*, so that they would have their bearings in this sea or desert or savannah, this world, so they would have horizon. And yet the cousinliness shared between one single second and the whole of eternity was now so proven, by modernity, by what some ancients knew as the cold truth of Styx, that, even as Joe set out, the stars were laughing above his head, laughing and laughing, and the dew was laughing too, laughing all over his boots and socks now and up his trouser leg, laughing on the tip of his footballer's nose and on the heavy fabric of his shoulders, starring the plaid, starring the lumber jacket with laughing dew. Even as they readied themselves to accept the message he sent, readied themselves to fly up around those campfires to take the highest mark of all, they were laughing at such a notion as *duration*, as if Time was just an elapsing thing, as if it didn't cycle like a song wheeling rusty as bursaria, time tumbling and rolling in larvae and milt, laughing at the rustling of the paper the checking of the length as if whatever it was, this composition, this 'music', this *prank*, didn't contain the whole world. Laughing and laughing, the world in delight above old country, the dew and the stars.

As Joe stepped up onto the verandah stairs, the boobook sounded such old wheeling time in the bush beyond the paddock – *boobook boo book* – notching up the night of Ngangahook the thousand and second night which is endless night even dreaming beneath the days and she heard his step on the stair, another note among the notations in the hall. The American sat; this was Melbourne being notched up, remembering how to listen. To what is always there. She had found her country her correspondent making kindred of her childish town, and just as she thought this Joe opened the door and stepped inside. The keyboard lid was raised. The second movement – *Tacet* – was over.

XXVI

THE LARGE ROOM was dark, yes, but lit through all that glass with moonlight. What had occurred there was a sum of her, a marsupial pouch, warmth and sustenance, the beginning of a new life a new world the buffered life, the love, but was it modernity? And so, to answer once again, to answer for all eternity, the stars began to spark up once more, taking on shapes in their mirth, animal shapes a brolga an emu a crayfish and then the pot to cook them in; they were laughing so hard, eating so well, partying so hard, shining so bright that Joe could feel them in the room as well as the moon. To think they'd just consider Ferny and Sarah Hutchinson posh, or posh-modern, or as commos. The audience, more familiar now with the logic of the pause between movements, between *nothings* really, began – almost – to relax. They loosened their shoulders, husbands turned to their wives to smile, musician-listeners shook their heads and laughed but not so hard as the old stars. This, Sarah thought, this is Maisie's song. 'The world's a nut,' she used to say to Sarah in her distress, 'the world's a nut until you open it. Then –' she winked at Mr Rabbits '– then it's everything you need.'

To think, Sarah thought then, and to think again. And not for the first time. To think, and think again, as a wallaby finds her truffle. To think, she thought, looking intently at her correspondent up on the stage, to think of all that can be unleashed. By doing nothing. By being. And that is how the nut is opened and all the fruits inside. To think of a mushroom coming through the surface of things. And all its woody smell. To think – as up on the stage the keyboard lid was closed to commence the third movement: *Tacet* – to think of how I needed that, she thought, to know that I don't know, don't know if Ferny can go on, will go on, don't know where the earthstars of the underground sky will appear. 'Oh god,' she exclaimed quietly to herself, as the audience entered its deepest listening darkest settling, and she realised what this was and what she'd done.

Amongst all the dead birds on the piano he could still see the lacquered lakey gleam. He was drawn to it like he'd been drawn to Sarah in the first place. Lying there on his elbow in the bush by the track-cutters' fire, listening to Don Atchison's accounts and knowing his balance started there. So now he ventured to sit on the stool and wait, taking in the moon's silence, the sound of its wallaby light as it spread and grew through the big windows. Large sections of the audience now began to dream, to loosen, and to see, and Sarah felt the balance too. She was a standing kangaroo. Then she dived, as if right through the centre of her neighbour's fat gold ring, this brand-new entrance into the glenny portal pool. Through the old boreen. 'All we had to do now was never ring the bell,' a happy voice said quietly down in the shaft of the pool. 'To listen to what was already there.' 'And that is what we did,' another, sadder, voice replied. And then: *Here, Sarah, dry yourself with the Christy towel.* She smiled, and as her hand reached out he opened the lid, having waited himself until he felt part of things, a sensitive member of the moonlight's coterie. And there was the ocean's piano all before him. And having known all along, and having company in her joy, she said simply, into the silence that never was and could never be: 'Go on, Joe, go on. Play.'

Author's note

The two novels that Jones the Bookbinder of Moolap binds together in his 'book of the world' are *Such Is Life* by Tom Collins (Joseph Furphy), first published in 1903 by the Bulletin Newspaper Company, and *Moby Dick* by Herman Melville, published by Harper & Brothers in 1851.

The italicised reflections of the local priest, Father Farrell, are direct quotes from the words of Fr Mark Freeman, as published in the *Flinders Island News* in 2019. Thanks to Fr Freeman for his permission to repurpose his words in this way.

Sarah's phrase, '*I felt a great scream go through nature*' is taken from the caption of Edvard Munch's lithograph print of his 1893 painting, *The Scream*.

Sarah's phrase, '*And then I found a great light was breaking in my mind*' is a variation on a comment made by Rachel Carson in a letter she wrote to Dr Morton Biskind. The letter is quoted in an article on Carson by Meehan Crist in Vol 41 of the *London Review of Books*.

The sentence '*The horse of the mind must submit to the harness of the word*' is from Roberto Calasso's essay 'Meters Are the Cattle of the Gods' from his collection, *Literature and the Gods*, translated from the Italian by Tim Parks and published by Vintage in 2001. *La letteratura e gli dei* by Roberto Calasso. Copyright © Roberto Calasso, 2001, Adelphi Edizioni S.p.A., used by permission of The Wylie Agency (UK) Limited.

'Invisible as music, she reminded herself. But positive as sound.' comes directly from Emily Dickinson's poem 'The World Is Not Conclusion'.

'What is being but an ear?' is a variation on a line from Emily Dickinson's poem, 'I felt a Funeral, in my Brain'.

'Letters, she thought, are sounds we see' is an excerpt from "These Flames and Generosities of the Heart" by Susan Howe, from *The Birth-mark*, copyright ©1993 by Susan Howe. Reprinted by permission of New Directions Publishing Corp.

The fictionalised John Cage in the novel was inspired both by John Cage's music and by his books, and two in particular: *Silence* (50th Anniversary Edition) published by Wesleyan University Press in 2011, and *A Mycological Foray*, published by Atelier Editions in 2020. I was also inspired by Kyle Gann's *No Such Thing As Silence: John Cage's 4'33"* published by Yale University Press in 2010.

The line *'…yet I find you can remain in the music while you're hunting mushrooms'* refers to a comment John Cage made on p. 67 of his *A Mycological Foray*.

The programme notes for Henry Cowell's 'The Tides of Manaunaun' and 'The Fairy Answer' are based on the recording, available on Youtube, of Cowell's own comments about his work.

Lastly, the town in which *The Bell of the World* is set, and the landscape which, along with Sarah, is the novel's main character, is a made-up world. The book is a work of fiction invented from a combination of imaginary, speculative, and real-life ingredients. It should not be read as history. It is perhaps worth mentioning too that not all of the ingredients that have gone into the novel can be described in words or even heard in the conscious mind.